Elaine Coffman

If My Love Could Hold You

WHEELER
PUBLISHING, INC.
ROCKLAND, MA

★ AN AMERICAN COMPANY ★

Published in Large Print by arrangement with Ballantine Books, a division of Random House, Inc. in the United States and Canada.

Wheeler Large Print Book Series.

Set in 16 pt Plantin.

Library of Congress Cataloging-in-Publication Data

Coffman, Elaine.
    If my love could hold you / Elaine Coffman.
        p. (large print) cm.(Wheeler large print book series)
    ISBN 1-56895-689-4 (softcover)
    1. Large type books. I. Title. II. Series
[PS3553.039I49   1998]
813'.54—dc21
                                     98-46752
                                         CIP

For my son Chuck

CHAPTER
❧ ONE ❧

West Texas, 1880

There were only two trees in Two Trees, Texas, and both were in Miss Charlotte Butterworth's front yard.

That was probably why a wild bunch of cowboys rode in a dust cloud into her yard and picked the larger of the two elm trees as the place to hang Walker Reed. When the dust settled, there were six men in all—five to administer justice, one to receive it.

And it was such a nice yard, too—fastidiously kept, just like the white frame house it surrounded. The respectable-looking one-story dwelling had a rather sleepy aura about it late that afternoon just as the sun was sinking behind the elms and dappling the shrubs and flowers that drooped in the heat.

Behind the house was a sparse little garden braving the intense heat. There, too, everything was neat and orderly: two rows of okra, two of black-eyed peas, one of yellow squash, and, farther over, along the fence, trailing vines of tomatoes.

Inside the neat clapboard house, Charlotte Butterworth, whom everyone in Two Trees affectionately called Miss Lottie, was in her kitchen, checking the progress of a vinegar pie baking in the oven of her brand-new Champion Monitor six-hole stove. The sudden pounding of hoofbeats mingling with the deep boom of voices coming from the road in front of her house startled her, and she slammed the door on her new Monitor harder than she had intended. She was immediately thankful that she had decided on the vinegar pie instead of the Robert E. Lee cake, which surely would have fallen flatter than a flitter when the oven door slammed.

The sound of shouting drew closer. It was probably those rowdy Mason boys chasing another scrawny coyote and trying to corner the terrified animal inside her fence, just as they had done last week. The week before that it had been a half-starved rabbit. A woman living alone had to maintain a constant vigil or find herself taken advantage of. That, and the need to protect her flowers from being trampled again, caused Charlotte to drop the two pot holders she was holding into the proper drawer and close it with her hip. Then she dusted the flour from the front of her white apron, overlooking the smudges on her nose, and headed for her parlor. Removing her spectacles, because she never let anyone see her in her spectacles, she marched with authority to her front windows and peeped discreetly—because she had been taught that a lady always peeped with discretion—through the only lace curtains in the whole county to see what all the ruckus was.

Her gaze crossed the planking of the wide front porch, going over the trailing coils of Carolina jasmine tangled in the porch rails and winding around gimcracks, to see five mounted cowboys from the Triple K Ranch. Just as she had feared, they were trampling her snapdragon bed. That brought a sputter of outrage to her lips, but before she could act on her sputtering outrage, she saw that wasn't all they were doing. They were securing a lariat to the sturdiest branch of her prized elm tree. That in itself was bad enough, but, to her horror, Charlotte Butterworth discovered—locking her eyes on the lariat looped over her tree and following it backward—that there was a most displeased, if not downright unhappy, stranger attached to the other end.

"Dear Lord," she whispered, "they're going to hang the poor man." It suddenly occurred to her just where they were going to hang him. "In my tree!" she said, as if not believing it herself.

Her mind teeming with thoughts about what was going to occur in her front yard, Charlotte stared, white-faced, at the man's dark hair. Even from her window she could see it was matted with what looked to be blood and caked with sand. His clothes—what was left of them—were torn, and his blood was seeping through a dozen rips. It looked as if he had been tied behind a horse and dragged for some distance. It was quite obvious he hadn't come willingly, but what was one man against five?

She saw that his hands were bleeding and raw and tied behind his back. With heart-quickening alarm, she watched as his fingers clenched and unclenched, the muscles in his arms straining until the blood vessels stood out prominently.

But it was the stranger's face that held her attention, and she watched him for a long moment, absorbing the masculine beauty of his bronzed face with its high cheekbones gleaming with sweat. From the side, his nose was straight, his chin strong and powerful. When his horse danced nervously at the rope hanging along its flank, the stranger turned, and Charlotte saw his eyes were a deep, dark blue, chilling in their intensity and hard with determination. In spite of his impassive and aloof expression, she had the feeling his pride was hurt. It struck her immediately that the man looked ruthless, defiant, and quite capable of violence. Yet, there was an aura of integrity about him. He might be many things, but surely a criminal was not one of them. Something in the proud carriage of his head, the straight line of his back, the clenching of his jaw, the way he did not grovel and beg or speak one word to save himself—all proclaimed his innocence.

Charlotte was reminded of another time and another place when she had watched in horror as someone innocent had been murdered. Only that time she had been a child, and unable to help.

Charlotte Augusta Butterworth stood watching from behind her lace curtains, her blue eyes fixed on the stranger. A pain thrummed in her head, and there was a thickening lump in her throat where her hand rested.

She had never seen a man hang.

And she wasn't about to see one hang

today, either—not if she had anything to say about it. After all, that was her tree they were using, and she had a right to decide if it was going to keep on being a shade tree or become a hanging tree.

Charlotte had easily recognized the cowboys as Triple K hands, led by old Clyde Kennedy's youngest son, Spooner. She also recognized quite easily that the cowhands were not accustomed to lynching a man. One of the men she knew only as Bridger was nervously chewing on a small sliver of wood that protruded from his mouth. Bridger was a quiet, shy cowhand, not prone to trouble-making. Two of the hands she had seen on occasion but could not recall their names. The Mexican she knew only as Chavez. It was to him that Spooner spoke.

"Chavez, you whip his horse when I give the signal."

Chavez nodded and pushed his sombrero back on his head, the string catching against his throat in a way that reminded Charlotte of what the stranger would be experiencing in a moment if she didn't do something. Chavez swung down and tied his blood bay to one of the pickets of Charlotte's fence. Then he moved to stand beside the rump of the stranger's horse, firmly holding a quirt in his right hand.

Spooner turned toward the stranger. "You got anything to say before we get on with this?"

The stranger, sitting on the horse, his weight resting in the stirrups with the tension

5

of a coiled spring, didn't say anything. Charlotte saw that his eyes were alert, shifting from one man to another.

His face red with anger, Spooner spurred his horse closer to the stranger, his hands reaching out to draw the noose tight around the taut cords of the man's neck. Neither man said a word, but the stranger's eyes were clear and searching as he looked at Spooner, who sheepishly turned away.

That made Charlotte's blood boil with righteous indignation, and whenever Charlotte Butterworth's blood was boiling with righteous indignation—well, there wasn't much in the way of what she wanted that she didn't get.

Mere seconds later Charlotte stood on her front porch, took careful aim with an M-1873 .44-caliber Winchester, and blew a hole through the star on Spooner Kennedy's Texas hat, sending it sailing off his head.

The lynching was postponed.

The steel-blue eyes of the stranger were the first to lock on Charlotte's small frame, hitting her and dismissing her with a look that sent a chill through her, but he said nothing.

Spooner Kennedy, however, wasn't so polite.

"Dad-durn-it, Miss Lottie, what are you doing out here?" he said. "This ain't no place for a lady. Now get yourself back inside." Dropping from his saddle and retrieving his beloved hat, Spooner poked his finger through the neatly placed hole. "Dad-dammit!" he shouted. "Look what you did to my hat."

6

"You better be glad it wasn't your fool head, Spooner Kennedy," Charlotte answered while taking another bead with her Winchester.

The words were uttered in a high voice that sounded as sweet as a chorus of heavenly hosts to the stranger. Her voice, he decided, was about as close to a heavenly host as he wanted to come—at least for several years. He released a long-held breath, thinking just how close to meeting his maker he had come. Feeling the noose tight around his neck, he realized he wasn't out of the woods yet.

"Miss Lottie, this is no concern of yours," Spooner went on. "We've got some business to settle with this killer."

Charlotte's intense blue eyes grew wider at the word *killer*, but her aim remained steady. "You'd best be taking your business up with the sheriff, then," she said. "That happens to be my tree, and hanging a man in my tree *is* my business."

"Now, Miss Lottie," Spooner said, "you know damn well there ain't another tree over five feet tall within twenty miles of here."

Charlotte was not swayed. "Jam!" she shouted. Then again, louder: *"Jam!"*

A few minutes later, a cotton-haired old black man came around the corner of the house, in no apparent hurry despite the urgency in the boss lady's voice. "Jam," Charlotte said firmly, "take my horse and hurry down to Sheriff Bradley's and tell him to get over here fast. And hurry up. Don't you dawdle none, you hear?"

7

"Yes'm."

Jam's hurrying gait was the same as his taking-my-own-sweet-time gait, so he ambled away, staying well away from the cluster of men until he was around the corner of the house. Minutes later he headed down the road on Charlotte Butterworth's old piebald mare, Butterbean.

The stranger shifted his position, his eyes hard on the hands of the cowhand who held the reins to his gelding. Those shaking hands were all that stood between him and hanging. He knew if the cowboy fumbled and dropped the reins, the gelding would bolt and he, Walker Reed, would be left swinging by his neck.

Walker's nose started itching. A hell of a position to be in, with his hands tied behind his back. He thought about raising his shoulder to rub against it, but any shift in his weight might make his horse more skittish, and the horse was skittish enough. The rigid line of his mouth quirked at the thought of him sitting there with a noose around his neck, concerned about something so insignificant as his nose itching.

"You have a strange sense of humor if you find hanging something to smile about," Charlotte said. "Especially when it's your own hanging."

Slowly, purposefully, Walker let his eyes sweep over the cluster of men to rest on the small-framed woman who was his salvation. "It was a smile of relief, ma'am."

Walker studied the woman's face as she

8

accepted his answer with a curt nod. In the shade of the porch her face seemed severe—all sharp angles. But then she took a few steps forward, out of the shade of the porch and into the amber glow of the late-afternoon sun, which brought out her magnificent coloring. Her face was anything but sharp angles, and as far as the rest of her—her leanness was deceptive. A woman like that was as unexpected in this flat, desolate part of Texas as her immaculate yard, whitewashed fence, and brilliant display of colorful flowers. She seemed to be a lot like her house—quiet, respectable, and fenced in. He was suddenly aware he was feeling a stir of something more than gratitude. She was a lovely thing—or would be if she'd release all that glorious ginger-colored hair from the ridiculous knot perched on her head.

Wearing a glossy blue calico dress, she stood there so slim and so stiffly starched that she looked fragile and delicate, but Walker knew that a woman who handled a Winchester the way she did was anything but fragile and delicate. The woman intrigued him, and he wondered how he could feel a stab of desire at a time when his every thought should be centered on self-preservation. Desire, he thought, could rear its ugly head at the most damnable times.

Charlotte caught the flare of interest in the stranger's eyes and felt a gush of discomfort that left a telltale stain on her cheeks. The sheer masculinity of the man was distracting. She neither wanted nor needed to be distracted. Not now. Not when she needed her wits about her like a pack of yelping pups to keep her on her toes.

Charlotte sighed, wondering if Jam had made it as far as the sheriff's office. He might be meandering aimlessly along the fencerows, wandering from one side of the road to the other, finding everywhere things to distract him and feeling quite happy to be the only idle bee in the swarm. She well knew Jam could be fascinated watching a caterpillar crawl up his sleeve.

Suddenly the evening stage came rumbling along the dry, dusty road that ran from Abilene to Two Trees. Hezekiah Freestone, the driver, was working the brake with his foot, the heavy leather of reins from six horses resting in his left hand and the long braided rawhide whip in his right. Just as he drew even with Charlotte Butterworth's porch, he replaced the whip and waved, just as he always did, as if he saw nothing out of the ordinary going on in her front yard.

"You could at least stop!" she yelled after him, wondering how any fool could pass a hanging with nothing but a smile and a wave.

The stage passed in a cloud of dust that settled over the six men and on Charlotte as well, then it sped on down the road, the wheels hitting an occasional pothole or rock that sent the stage bouncing into the air.

At that moment Sheriff Archer Bradley rode into the yard, while Jam, taking his own sweet time on Butterbean, was still some distance behind. Charlotte had never felt so relieved. Now that Archer was here, things would move right along and she could clear this mess of confusion out of her yard.

Archer drew rein and sat there for a spell taking in the situation. His hat of worn felt was pulled low over his eyes, and now and then a quid of tobacco could be seen moving inside his right cheek. Taking careful aim, Archer spit, scoring a direct hit on one of Miss Lottie's irises. Then he wiped his mouth with the back of his hand. He was a man who didn't like to be hurried, and just because a man was sitting before him with a rope around his neck—well, that was no reason to hurry. A jump to wrong conclusions is what happened when you hurried, and Archer never jumped to wrong conclusions.

"Now, just what's going on here?" he drawled, not missing the look Charlotte gave him—a look that said any fool in his right mind could see what was going on.

Deciding the look wasn't enough, Charlotte said sharply, "There's a hanging going on here, Archer...or there was until I stopped it."

"With that Winchester?"

"Of course," said Charlotte. "Have you ever known a lynching to be stopped with a few kind words—unless they're backed with lead?"

Archer's mirth wasn't hampered in the least by his scowl. His eyes shifted from Charlotte to the stranger to Spooner and back to the stranger, who by this time was looking mighty expectant and mighty relieved.

Once again, Archer took careful aim and let

fly with a wad of tobacco. Everyone seemed to be waiting on someone else to say something. But no one did.

While they waited in silence, a dust devil came out of nowhere, rattling the leaves on Miss Charlotte's two elm trees and nodding the heads on her drooping snapdragons before it tugged a few tendrils of fiery red hair out of her carefully coiled bun and whipped them across her face, one spiraling filament sticking to the corner of her mouth. Charlotte let it be, keeping the barrel of her Winchester pointed at the white disk on Spooner's tobacco pouch, which dangled from his shirt pocket. She was busy thinking how men could waste so much precious time standing around spitting and scratching.

"Miss Lottie," Archer said, "you can put your Winchester down. I'll handle things now."

"You took your time reaching that decision, Archer." She turned the full power of her magnificent eyes on him in what could only be called reproach. "Untie that man first."

Archer directed a visual command at Spooner, who passed it on to the man mounted next to him. "Okay, Jake," Spooner said uneasily. "Untie him."

Jake slid to the ground and nervously approached the stranger. "Just a minute!" Charlotte pointed her rifle at him. "You go around the other way," she said, "so his horse can see you coming. I'd sure hate to have you unintentionally spook his horse and hang him by accident."

Jake stopped. "Why's that?" he said with a cocky grin.

Charlotte did not respond to his grin. "Because then I'd have to shoot you."

Jake was careful to swing a wide arc as he approached from the front and, reaching the stranger, untied his hands. At that instant a shot whizzed past his ear, causing him to dive for the dirt at the same time as the lariat tied around the stranger's neck snapped in two.

His horse snorted and sidestepped nervously. When Walker had him under control, he turned toward Charlotte, feeling much like a banked fish that had just mercifully been tossed back into his natural element. "I'm much obliged for your intervention, ma'am," he said in an accent that was neither southern nor Texan.

At the sound of his low voice, strangely velvet smooth and husky, Charlotte looked at him, meeting his clear gaze for a moment, before she drew a deep breath, her eyes narrowing. Something about him frightened her. Perhaps it was the intensity of his look, unthinkably familiar, considering she had just saved him from death. A shiver of apprehension ran through her, and she was awkwardly aware that every eye was trained on her. She lifted a brow, sending him a look full of so much venomous dislike that he felt a constriction in his chest. The look was both direct and quiet—a reproof withdrawn as hurriedly as it was sent and patently meant for him alone. He dipped his head ever so slightly in recognition.

Charlotte's heart stirred nervously in her

chest. "Don't be thanking me," she said. "I just bought you a postponement, not a pardon. You may hang yet. That's none of my affair—as long as it isn't from my tree."

Walker inclined his head once more, this time in a curt gesture, his hard glance deep and penetrating as he caught the grating edge of spite in her words. The woman had just saved his life. Why did his gratitude chafe her so? He was not a vain man, yet he had been on the receiving end of enough sultry looks and honeyed kisses from beautiful women to know that women were attracted to him. That this woman would stick her neck out for him and then insult him when he expressed his gratitude both surprised and irritated him.

He studied her face, the mouth so sensitive that it was difficult to believe it had spoken so sharply to him. Her manner and words bespoke cool control, but he saw in her clear blue eyes a shadow of uncertainty and vulnerability. Something made his heart contract, the blood gushing through his veins. Whether she liked it or not, the woman had done him a tremendous service. He was thankful enough and gentleman enough not to provoke her further.

"Nevertheless," he said slowly, "I am in your debt." He continued to watch her, torn between anger and curiosity over her behavior, studying the aloof tilt to her chin, the stiff shoulders. There was something about the hint of panic he had seen in her eyes that told him she didn't find him repulsive.

Charlotte couldn't help but notice that the stranger was handsome—in a raw, ruthless way. The man's hair had at first appeared dark, but when his hands were freed and he moved out of the shade of the elm tree, it seemed to absorb the setting sun, glinting with golden highlights. His hair was longer than the men in these parts wore, yet his face—in contrast to the assortment of beards and mustaches that surrounded him—was clean shaven.

He was different. In fact, everything about him was just a shade different—his skin a little browner, his eyes a little bluer, his bearing just a little more regal than any man Charlotte had heretofore encountered. When the stranger looked her over with a stare that penetrated her white muslin pinafore and calico dress, then went right through her nainsook petticoat and linen drawers, she looked away, her gaze resting on Archer Bradley, who'd just repeated his question to Spooner.

"I said, what's been going on here?"

Spooner went on to relate how he had been tending herd when he heard a gunshot. Taking several of the Triple K hands with him, they'd ridden in the direction of the shot and found the stranger standing over the body of a dead man, his drawn Colt still in his hand. An envelope in the dead man's pocket contained several thousand dollars and a bill of sale for three brood mares out of Old King, a famous running horse. The dead man's name was Walker Reed. He was from California.

15

"I'm Walker Reed," the stranger said. "I'm from California. I came out here to buy horses. The man I shot robbed me last night and took the three mares. I'd been tracking him since dawn. When I finally located him and rode into his camp, he drew on me, and I had no choice but to shoot him in self-defense. I was just about to retrieve my horses and my money when these men rode up, jumping to conclusions."

"You have any proof of what you're saying?" Archer asked, fully understanding what the stranger said about jumping to conclusions. This part of Texas seemed to him the jumping-to-conclusionest place he'd ever seen.

"The only proof I had were those papers you heard about, but you could wire the sheriff in Santa Barbara. He's known my family for years. He could identify me."

And he could, of course. Walker's grandfather, Richard Warrington Reed, had come to California during the gold rush. A rich vein had provided the necessary capital to buy a large hacienda and ranch from a dwindling and impoverished family of Spanish descent. Three generations of Reeds had lived there. The sheriff in Santa Barbara had personally known two of those generations. It was the two youngest members of the latest generation of Reeds, Riley and Walker, who had, as youths, caused him more headaches than he cared to count. Riley had finally married last year, at thirty-six. Walker, a year behind his brother in age, seemed in no hurry.

Archer studied Walker for a moment. "You

16

understand I'll have to hold you in custody until the sheriff in Santa Barbara can verify what you say and positively identify you?"

Walker laughed. "Believe me, being detained in a jail is infinitely better than the last offer I had in your hospitable town."

There was something breathtaking about the man's smile, and while Charlotte was struggling to find just where her breath had been taken, the stranger dismounted with lazy ease and approached her. "I owe you my life," he said. "It may be nothing to you, but to me it means a great deal. I'll find some way to repay you. I won't forget."

The caress of his warm steel-blue eyes made Charlotte's pulse thump rapidly. Before she could snap back an angry reply, the man turned, and she watched as he crossed the yard and mounted his horse. Something about him stuck in her craw. Walker looked from Charlotte to Archer and smiled, a tight, knowing little smile that barely lifted the corners of his mouth. Then his gaze went back to Charlotte. He looked like a coyote that had cornered a polecat. The hair pricked along Charlotte's nape. What an arrogant man! His fancy saddle. Those Mexican spurs. The expensive shirt. He probably stole them from the last man he'd shot. She should've let the Triple K boys stretch his insolent neck. She was still staring as the men turned and quietly rode, single file, out of her front yard, leaving in a much more orderly fashion than they had arrived.

Charlotte looked sharply away and, with a

sigh of annoyance, surveyed her poor snap-dragon bed, then her trampled lawn where clumps of grass had been turned up by the bite of horses' hooves. Then she noticed the lariat dangling like a dead snake from her tree, and with a shudder of revulsion she turned and went into the house.

The gloomy silence was broken by the hall clock striking eight, reminding Charlotte that this afternoon's adventure had spoiled the habitual order of her life. The eggs hadn't been gathered. The cows hadn't been milked. The vegetables for tonight's supper were still on the vine instead of simmering in a pot on her stove, their fragrance filling her house as it always did when the hall clock struck eight.

But there was a smell of some kind coming from her kitchen. A strange smell. A smell that had never before penetrated the walls of her house. It took a few minutes for her to figure out just what it was. Suddenly she threw her hands up and, with a helpless shriek, flew down the hall.

Moments later she was in her kitchen. And there, after the day's intense heat, too many chores, abominable dust, a near lynching in her front yard, and a stranger with a look that made her feel a few shades worse than naked, she found and removed from her new Monitor stove a burned vinegar pie.

CHAPTER
❧ TWO ❧

The next week passed like a prairie fire, hot and blazing. The sky was a brilliant, deep blue, rising endlessly over the scorched land. No breezes stirred. No rain was in sight. Nothing could be counted on—nothing but more heat and more work.

That's what Charlotte found as she busied herself with her chores. Monday she spent in the henhouse, stirring up a cloud of feathers and chicken droppings, raking them into tidy piles, then carrying them outside and dumping them in the back of the wagon so that Jam could spend the next afternoon spreading them as fertilizer for the new field he was plowing.

On Tuesday, the flies were worse than Charlotte had ever seen, so she spent the day in the house, husking corn and throwing the worms she found inside the ears into a bucket so she could toss them to the chickens. As she listened to the rustle of dry husks, she thought how much the sound reminded her of what she was feeling. Dryness. Her life was full, if not rich, crammed with the business of eking out an existence in a land that was hostile and unforgiving. As her days passed in a smooth, orderly fashion, filled with too much attention to the mundane details of survival and too little attention to the yearnings she'd long ago smothered, she tried to repress the sweet stirring of something new.

Wednesday brought the ladies from the church filing into her house, their heels clicking against the gleaming waxed floor as fast as their busy tongues clacked in their mouths. When they finally filed out, leaving the polished floor liberally sprinkled with crumbs and one of her prized teacups shattered, Charlotte heard the first whimperings of the children she would never have. She tried to let the time-consuming task of washing her mother's china blot out the pain left by the group of unthinking women who could find nothing to talk about but their husbands and their children.

Thursday's work amounted to no more than stripping her bed, gathering the week's laundry, and hauling it to the back porch, where the washtubs waited, one filled with hot soapy water and borax, the other cool rinse water. By late afternoon the fruit stains had been removed with Labaraque solution and the rust stains with salts of lemon, and everything, clean and fresh smelling, had been hauled to the clothesline and hung in perfect order, with Miss Charlotte's unmentionables hanging on the middle line, out of sight.

On Friday, Charlotte sewed a new pair of yellow gingham curtains for her kitchen, made twelve jars of green-tomato preserves, and baked a butter sponge cake for the Stevenson family, whose youngest son had died late the night before from rabies.

When Saturday arrived, Charlotte read her proverb for the day—Waste not, want not—and decided she didn't need to spend her egg and butter money on something as frivolous as a length of green silk. Instead, she spent it on a pair of sturdy, serviceable black shoes that were as ugly as they were heavy.

The following Monday found her in town, her buggy tied across the street from the jail. When she went to untie her mare, she caught a glimpse of the jailhouse out of the corner of her eye. Before she could glance away, the front door opened, and walking out behind Sheriff Bradley was none other than the man who had come close to getting himself hanged from her elm tree. The man who claimed to be Walker Reed.

Walker Reed. How many times had that name wormed its way into her mind over the past week, and how many times had she chased it right back out? *And how much good did it do?* asked a little voice in her head, and without really answering, Charlotte knew it hadn't done a bit of good. Unwanted thoughts, like bad pennies, kept turning up.

Suddenly, Charlotte realized that she wasn't the only one who had noticed Walker Reed. The steady staccato of heels tapping along the wooden walks had suddenly diminished. Charlotte looked around, first one way and then the other. The women who had been wandering up and down the street in little groups had assembled near her while they directed their attention across the street and looked their fill.

Two Trees women were not known for being expressionless or incapable of frank speech, and apparently not one of them had been taught that it was rude to stare. Of course, Charlotte couldn't really condemn them for staring, since she herself was guilty of as much. Surveying the faces of the women, Charlotte decided that there wasn't so much wrong in staring as in the way one stared. Take Prissy Ledbetter for instance. The way her eyes bulged reminded Charlotte of a great horned owl. And the way Mary Alice Tiplett's mouth hung open was so much like a catfish gasping for breath that Charlotte had to cover her mouth with her gloved hand to stifle a laugh.

Charlotte listened to gasps and titters as the name of the stranger talking to Archer was passed around. According to Mary Alice, the man was waiting to be identified so he could claim a fortune that had been stolen from him.

"As you can see," explained Mary Alice, "he really isn't under arrest, since Archer takes him to the boardinghouse to eat twice a day, while the other prisoners get regular jail food."

Mary Alice went on, informing her enraptured audience that her papa had already spoken to Archer about having Mr. Reed to dinner on Sunday afternoon.

"To dinner? How utterly divine," said Prissy, wishing that her own papa had had the foresight to act as prudently.

"I've also taken the liberty of speaking to the reverend about a picnic social, possibly even a raffle of boxed lunches to raise money for the new parsonage. Of course, Archer and his guest would be invited, and once they were there, Mr. Reed would feel compelled to purchase a box lunch," said Mary Alice.

"I wonder whose lunch he would pick," Prissy asked, sighing, while also directing a smile at her second in command, May Cartwright.

May, taking her cue from Prissy, said, "Why, I'm sure he would pick yours, Prissy." Then, looking around, she said, "Have you heard about the magnificent hatbox decorated with lace and ropes of pearls that Prissy's mother brought all the way from Paris?"

Judging from the instant collapse of faces around her, Charlotte guessed they had not.

"Of course I'm not bragging," said Mary Alice, with more passion than Charlotte had thought she possessed, "but you know *my* box lunches have sold for the most money two years in a row."

As Mary Alice rattled on, laughing and positively glowing from all the envious attention she was receiving, she glanced at Charlotte standing primly beside her buggy, her eyes on the stranger across the street.

"It's too bad you don't ever decorate a box for the raffle, Charlotte," she said very sweetly. "If you change your mind, I would be glad to find someone to bid on your box so you would be sure it sold."

"Why don't you do that," said Charlotte, equally sweetly, "and in return, I'll cook the food to go in yours, because everyone in Two Trees knows you can't boil water."

Mary Alice's mouth fell open. Prissy's eyes bulged. A unified gasp went up from the other women.

Charlotte turned, taking her time to untie

Butterbean. Then she climbed into the buggy, taking even more time to settle her packages and smooth her gray poplin skirt before tying onto her old Tuscan straw bonnet the crepe lisse scarf she had just purchased. Taking the reins in her hand, she slapped Butterbean lightly on the rump, guiding her into a turn.

Across the street, Walker Reed stopped talking and turned to stare at her as she passed, then he raised his hand in a gesture that would've touched the brim of his hat had he been wearing one, and flashed her a smile. A delicious thrill of excitement ran through Charlotte's body, from her new serviceable black shoes up to the Tuscan straw bonnet, and lingered like a chill in the area of the thickly coiled bun at her nape. With impeccable politeness, she dipped her head in recognition, then lifted her chin to a regal height and made a clicking sound to encourage Butterbean to pick up the pace. The well-mannered old mare broke into a smart trot as Charlotte headed out of town.

Perched on her buggy seat, Charlotte tried to deal with the exquisite radiance that welled within her. The curious significance she attached to that brief salute and engaging smile soaked into her like rain into a parched desert. In fact, all the way home, Walker Reed was heavy in Charlotte's mind as little fragments of him kept popping up: his chestnut hair gleaming, the way he stood with Archer, one hand braced against the building and the other on his hip, his head bent, deep in conversation. Would he also be deep in conversation with the woman whose box lunch he would buy? Would his glossy head be bent toward her as he talked in a gentle, quiet voice, leaving her breathless and giddy? Or would he take her hand gently and lead her away from the crowd and, once they were alone, wrap her in those strong arms and take her mouth with that ruthless arrogance she had seen in him the day of the hanging? All at once Charlotte felt that she could not bear to give up her small part of him to another woman. With a sigh, she wondered what it would be like to be Walker Reed's lady... for just one glorious day.

But being above all things a very sensible woman, she knew those imaginings could never become a reality for her, so she urged the mare to a fast canter, as if by doing so she could leave her thoughts of Walker Reed in the dust behind. But before long she noticed that thoughts of him were still tagging along, covered in dust but more persistent than ever. It occurred to her that this vein of thought was absolutely absurd. Why would she, having lived twenty-odd years in peace without any man in her life, save her brother, suddenly find herself in turmoil over a man who had nothing better to do than run around the country like a wild outlaw, robbing and murdering one minute, grinning and tipping his hat like a fool the next, and more than likely ravaging every maiden who crossed his path.

Once she reached home, Charlotte headed straight for the kitchen, determined to work out her frustrations on a helpless lump of dough. Soon she was up to her elbows in flour as she cut the last sourdough biscuit and dipped it in bacon fat before placing it in her cast-iron skillet. But busy as she was, thoughts of that scoundrel still pestered her. That she would waste precious time thinking about a man—any man—just didn't sit well with Charlotte.

Right on schedule the following Wednesday, the ladies from the church came filing into her house, their heels clicking against her gleaming floors as they always did. But when they filed out again, Charlotte wasn't thinking about the floor, which was liberally dusted with crumbs. All her concentration was focused on a small piece of paper Mrs. Farnsworth had handed her, saying, "Oh, Charlotte, my dear, I almost forgot. Sheriff Bradley asked me to give you this. Bless me! I nearly let it slip my mind."

After shutting the front door with her hip, Charlotte unfolded the paper. It was a circular, the kind Archer tacked up for public notice around town, always having someone drop one off at her house. Her eyes skimmed the page. A week from Sunday there would be a box social. All the ladies in the county were invited to decorate a box lunch to be auctioned by the Reverend Thaddeus Tate, the proceeds going to rebuild the parsonage that had burned last winter.

Tucking the paper into her pocket, Charlotte busied herself with the lumpy cushions on her horsehair sofa until a gentle gust of wind billowed her lace curtains and rattled one of her mother's prized teacups. Charlotte crossed the room and was reaching to close the window when she heard voices coming from the vicinity of her honeysuckle bush.

"Don't you wonder why Archer went to all the trouble to have Martha bring a notice about the box social to Charlotte?" said a voice that Charlotte recognized instantly as May Cartwright's.

"Yes, and I almost wish Charlotte *would* donate a box. I'd love to see her face when the reverend held *her* box up and it received no bids," Mary Alice replied.

"You know Nemi would bid on it," said a third voice, which could only belong to Prissy. "He wouldn't let his sister suffer that kind of embarrassment."

"Yes, but you forget that Nemi isn't due back for a while from the cattle drive," said Mary Alice. "It would serve him right, too, Mr. High-and-Mighty. I don't know why he always acts so uppity. My mama said they were nothing but poor Confederate trash... coming to these parts after the war. Not third-generation Texans like we are."

"What about Archer?" asked Prissy. "I think he would bid on Charlotte's box. Everyone around knows he's been sweet on her for a long time."

"Yes," May said, "and look where it's gotten him. Nowhere. Besides, Archer can't bid on *any* box. He's always been on duty when we've had our box socials, so his deputies can have the afternoon off. He can't bid when he's on duty."

"And that's a relief to us all," Prissy put in. "Every woman in Two Trees knows Archer isn't a good catch. He's poor as a church mouse. That's why he has to settle for Charlotte. Why, I don't think I've ever seen her in a silk dress. She never wears anything but calico and gingham... or that ugly blue serge in the winter."

"Did you see those shoes she bought last week?" May added, and they all laughed.

"Clodhoppers, you mean," said Prissy.

"It doesn't make any difference anyway," Mary Alice said. "Charlotte would never in a million years bring a box to the social. Oh, I daresay she'd like to, but she wouldn't risk the humiliation. What could she do to decorate a box—paint it white and plant flowers on it?"

"I have a wonderful idea," said Prissy. "Why don't we invite Charlotte to come this year? She can cook the food, *we'll* decorate her box."

"She wouldn't come," Mary Alice said scornfully. "Not if we paid her. She'd rather hide out here, away from everyone, behind her white picket fence and her flowers, acting respectable."

Charlotte, clutching her stomach, tears running down her face, turned away and walked softly to her bedroom, where she flung herself across her bed, giving vent to her hurt and anger.

She felt bad, not so much for herself but because of the nasty things they had said about Nemi and Archer. How could they talk so scathingly about two kindhearted men? Nemi and Archer's many kindnesses weren't just for her; they extended to the whole community. There was never a need or an appeal that they didn't answer.

Tears had never occupied a very large place in Charlotte's life, usually going as quickly as they came, and today was no exception. In the kitchen she vigorously released her hurt at the pump, and when she had a full bucket of cool water, she dipped a cloth in it and placed it over her face. When the cloth was warm, she dipped it once more, letting it absorb the heat from her skin. Then she went to the barn and picked up an armful of hay.

Jam had penned the donkey, who let out a loud bray when he saw her. She piled the hay in the manger, watching the donkey eat and scratching the downy soft hair between his long, floppy ears. "Why would anyone call you an ass?" she asked, running her hand along the length of one ear and then the other. "I think donkeys are much nicer than people. It's people like Mary Alice and May and Prissy who are the real asses of the world. Don't you agree?" At that moment the donkey stretched his neck for another bite, then tossed his head up and down to dislodge it from the rest. It looked so much like he was agreeing with her that Charlotte couldn't help laughing as she threw her arms around his neck, giving him a big hug before leaving.

As she crossed the yard, Charlotte noticed that Jam was feeding the peacocks. The male was busy strutting, his long train spread in a beautiful fan. As she watched, the peacock paraded slowly and majestically, as if he knew just how beautiful he was. Charlotte looked for the smaller, less vividly colored peahen and finally locating her behind the brilliant plumage of the male. A smile tugged at the corners of her mouth. The drab little peahen was pecking away at the grain in the trough, apparently unaffected by either her own plainness or her mate's arrogant display. By the time the proud peacock folded his feathers back into a train and strutted to the feeding trough, all the grain was gone. People, it seemed, could learn a lot from animals. And so Charlotte took a lesson from the drab little peahen.

The Saturday before the box social, Charlotte decided to do something she had never done before. She was going to take a box to the social. She wasn't sure just what had prompted her to break her loyalty to the past by trying something new. But she suspected that the real cause was that she was tired. Tired of being predictable. Tired of being proper. Tired of being respectable. For once in her life she wanted to follow the promptings of her nature and throw caution to the wind. She wanted to do something just a little daring. Perhaps Mary Alice and her vapid friends had done her a service, for there had never been any doubt in Charlotte's mind that the conversation she'd heard outside her window had been intended for her ears. Just as there had been no doubt that the malicious girls had intended to provoke her to compete with them on their level. She might be simple, but she wasn't simple-minded. She would compete. But not on their level. Only a fool stood behind an ass.

No royal cook or famous chef had ever entered into the preparation of food with greater abandon or relish than Charlotte did the Saturday before the box social.

First came the assorted meat pies, with crusts so flaky they dissolved at the slightest touch. Fried sweet potatoes were next, succulent and with a sugary glaze. Then she made corn fritters and tomato salad. Next came a jar of her spiced peaches, then one of chow-chow, followed by a jar of plum conserve, and a half-gallon jug of her best cherry brandy. For dessert she made a lady cake with a dash of whiskey (and one more dash for good measure) and a fresh peach pie. When everything was ready, there was so much food that it covered the top of her kitchen table. How would she ever find a box small enough to carry yet large enough to hold it all? She decided to sleep on it. Something would come to her by morning, she was sure.

On Sunday afternoon, Charlotte hitched up Butterbean and drove herself to church, having delivered her box at ten o'clock that morning so that the picnic lunches could be assembled without anyone knowing which box belonged to which lady.

If she was thankful for one thing, it was that she had always attended the church socials and auctions, even if she had never participated by decorating a box. At least no one would suspect anything just because she was there. Spying Mabel Stratton and Pearlene Carter, Charlotte headed in the direction of the two older women seated with their children. Perhaps she could hold Pearlene's baby—anything to take her mind off the auction. By this time, she was feeling utterly stupid for ever considering that she would donate a box for the auction.

An hour later the auction was well under way, with seven of the fifteen boxes already sold. Prissy's box was the fourth to go, selling for five dollars to Spooner Kennedy. That was two dollars higher than May Cartwright's, but May didn't care, because her box was bought by Virgil Thompson, the banker's son. In passing, with Virgil in tow, May remarked to Charlotte, "I don't care if Prissy's box did sell for more money. Everyone knows Spooner doesn't have as much money as Virgil."

Moving Pearlene's baby, Custer, to her other shoulder, Charlotte said, "I thought the Kennedys were about the richest folks around."

"Well, Virgil is richer."

"He is?"

"Yes, he is. Honestly, Charlotte. Sometimes I think you are so dense. Virgil has a whole *bank* full of money."

"I would never have made that particular connection," Charlotte said. "At any rate, I wouldn't advise you to spend any of it. You could end up in jail."

Giving Charlotte an exasperated look, May said, "Come on, Virgil. Let's find us a nice spot."

Mary Alice's box was the tenth to go, and

although it brought a dollar more than Prissy's box, everyone could tell that Mary Alice was livid.

"Why is she looking so prune-faced? There isn't anything *wrong* with Chavez. His money is as good as the next man's. He's an honest, hardworking cowboy, just like most of our men are. He must've spent three weeks' wages on that box," Mabel remarked. "Mary Alice could do with reminding herself that the money is for a good cause."

"The only cause Mary Alice recognizes always involves men. I think she's in a huff because she had her heart set on that tall man standing with Archer," said Pearlene.

Charlotte had her mind on her own box as she turned her head to the two men standing together and was totally unprepared for what she saw.

Perfect surprise held her motionless, and for a long moment she did not breathe. He was leaning toward Archer, listening to something he said, engrossed in the conversation, unaware that so many female eyes were upon him. There was something quiet and peaceful about him, and Charlotte felt that she could almost reach out and touch the stillness that seemed to surround the moment. A cloud drifted across the sun, leaving him in shadow, then it moved over the flat prairie, taking the shadow with it, leaving him bathed in sunlight once again. And suddenly everything around her began to take on new meaning, as if the whole world had been washing clean.

She stared at him, her gaze moving over long

legs encased in tight pants, going across powerful shoulders straining against a faded blue shirt. There was brutal strength there, but overriding that was an incredible feeling of gentleness and peace. What was it about Walker Reed that eased her so, and sweetened the moment? Standing next to Archer, looking more like Archer's best friend than his prisoner, it was difficult to remember that the man was very possibly a killer. Why wasn't he in jail? Why was Archer being so carefree around him? Why was he here at the picnic? And most of all, why was she feeling as foolish as a calf in clover? As respectable and as inexperienced with men as she was, Charlotte knew nothing of the exhilarating sensation of being held in a man's arms and kissed, yet the unfamiliar sensation that swept through her made her feel as if that was precisely what was happening. But that was ridiculous. She knew nothing about kissing and such; she was beginning to think she knew even less about Charlotte Butterworth.

"Don't you agree, Charlotte?"

Pearlene had caught her off guard. "Don't I agree about what?" Charlotte asked.

"Don't you agree that Mary Alice is all prune faced because that man with Archer didn't buy her box?"

"Why would you say that?"

"Because she's been battin' her eyes at him the entire time," Pearlene replied.

"Evidently he didn't bat back," Mabel said, and the three of them laughed.

"Mary Alice *always* has her eye on some

man," Pearlene said, between gasps for breath.

To which Mabel added, "She'd like to put more than her eye on one, if she could find one who'd let her get close enough."

Charlotte looked at Reverend Tate, who was just handing Becky Lacy's box to Spooner Kennedy's brother Carl. With a gasp, she realized there were only two boxes left, and one of them was hers. Her gasp must have disturbed Custer, who began to fret, so Pearlene took him. Charlotte couldn't understand why she had been so foolish as to set herself up for ridicule like this. Sooner or later, everyone in Two Trees would know she had brought a box. What made matters worse was, they would know just which box she'd brought. There were fourteen boxes that were decorated, and painted, and curled, and tucked, and glittered, and gathered, and pleated, and festooned with every imaginable decoration known to man. And then there was one box that didn't have a single solitary decoration on it. Not one. Well, unless you counted the black letters stenciled on the sides and across the top. But those had been on the box when she got it and had not been written by her, so they couldn't be considered decorations.

Charlotte watched Reverend Tate reach for one of the two remaining boxes, praying that God would grant her just a little more time. But before she could finish that simple request, the preacher selected the next box and brought it up to the auction table. It was such a funny sight to see him carrying a wooden crate with WHISKEY stamped in big, bold, black letters on all four sides and the top, that a roar of laughter was imminent. Keeping in the spirit of things, Reverend Tate said, "If I was a woman and wanted to get a man's attention, this would be about it, I reckon." Everyone laughed.

"Maybe she just wanted to get into his blood a little faster," someone yelled from the back.

"Maybe her cookin's so bad you gotta get drunk before you can eat it," another voice called out.

"Or perhaps the hands that prepared this box don't give a fig about outward appearances. Maybe those hands put all their efforts toward preparing what's inside," the preacher said. And at that moment everyone knew.

A hush settled over the entire congregation. The only sound was that of bodies shifting in their chairs as every head turned to stare at Charlotte.

At that moment she looked away, only to feel her face grow even hotter when she encountered the slow, amused smile of Walker Reed as he inclined his head toward her in the merest suggestion of recognition. She would've liked to hit him over the head, for that arrogant smile of his, but all she could do was give him a haughty look before Reverend Tate boomed, "What am I bid for this... this cleverly packaged lunch?"

"Five cents, if it contains a bottle of whiskey."

Charlotte didn't recognize the voice, but she

was thankful for the laughter, which smothered any further comment.

"Come on now, folks. You don't expect me to go through another winter without a house."

"Twenty-five cents—if you keep the box."

Another guffaw.

On and on it went. A lot of laughter, but not much money. Charlotte was dying of shame to be the laughingstock of the whole community and to see her box going for less than seventy-five cents, the lowest bid of the day—by several dollars. Then Doc came to her rescue and bid five dollars. Charlotte could have kissed the dear man.

"Going... going..."

"Fifty dollars if the woman that made it will let me pick the place to eat."

Walker Reed.

Charlotte would have known the husky tones of that voice in her sleep. At first she was simply stunned. No one had ever purchased a box for any amount near that. Fifty dollars. It was a fortune. More than her egg and butter money for a year. And then she began to hear the whispers, to feel the eyes of speculation upon her. Puzzled, she stiffened her back, trying to hide her discomfort. It was bad enough to have everyone in Two Trees know that she had donated a box; she didn't want the entire citizenry to ruminate about the reason why, particularly when she didn't know the reason herself. What really rankled was that she, who had never done anything to draw the eyes of the entire population of

Two Trees upon herself, had done it up double on the first try—primarily by donating that fool box, and secondly by *his* buying it, and for a ridiculous sum.

But what could she do now? What could she say? That she'd been goaded into it by the comments of a few spiteful women? *Never in a million years.* Would it be honest to admit that for once in her life she wanted to do something unexpected? *Yes, it probably would.* But she wouldn't for the life of her admit anything to that throng of peering eyes. For what seemed longer than a wet week, she sat there, stiff backed and angry, feeling the blush of acute embarrassment creep over her. She stole one quick glance at Walker Reed, who was standing to one side, looking as lazy as a pet coon, and she felt her embarrassment replaced by stampeding outrage. He was the cause of all this, so why was he standing there looking as fine as two-dollar cotton? This was her town, and Walker Reed had no right to come riding in, bold as the devil, flaunting himself before God and creation, drawing everyone's attention and making a spectacle of her. If this was the way he showed his gratitude, she would hate to see what he did to someone he didn't like. It was bad enough that everyone in Two Trees would be wondering just *why* Walker Reed paid fifty dollars for her box, but they would be making all sorts of speculations about where Walker would choose to have lunch.

Just at that moment, when her discomfort was at its peak, she heard someone behind her whisper, "Why do you suppose he wanted to pick the place to eat?"

And the reply: "You don't think *Miss Lottie* would pick a cornhusk mattress, do you?"

Charlotte would have been humiliated at that comment if it hadn't brought her back to reality. She would be eating lunch with Walker Reed. Alone. At the place of his choosing.

How many times had she lain in bed at night and wondered what it would be like to have a man court her, take her to church and for buggy rides, and yes, even on a picnic. Suddenly she had been linked with a man who was handsome enough to set any woman's heart to thumping, and all she could feel was alarm. Where would he take her? How long would it take them to eat? Would it go faster if she didn't eat at all? Was food *all* he wanted?

Charlotte felt the weight of probing eyes leave her as Walker stepped forward to take her box from Reverend Tate.

"If all your money was stolen, where are you going to get the fifty dollars to buy that box?" Mrs. Carstairs asked.

"I'll loan it to him," Archer said, stepping forward.

"Humph!" Mrs. Carstairs said. "Where you gonna get it, Archer? Everyone knows you're as poor as Job's turkey."

Archer laughed. "Why, I'm gonna get it out of Virgil's bank."

More laughter. Reverend Tate pounded the table with his gavel. "Now, folks, let's get back to our rat killin'." He looked at Charlotte. "Miss Lottie, judging from the color of your face, I'd be willin' to bet this here crate contains some of your good cookin'. Is that right? Is this your box?"

Charlotte was too mortified to do anything but nod.

"Well then, would you be agreeing to Mr. Reed's terms?" When Charlotte hesitated, the preacher said, "Charlotte, will you agree to let Mr. Reed pick the place for your picnic?"

Once again all eyes were upon her... at least two hundred eyes—no, two hundred and one, counting old Heck Pipkin, who had only one eye. And that was just too many eyes staring at her. Charlotte would have agreed to eat with the devil in a boiling caldron to be released from those speculative looks. Her only thought was to get away from there the fastest way possible and to put as many miles between that place and herself as she could. She nodded in agreement, feeling a sinking sickness in her stomach when Reverend Tate handed the whiskey box to Walker Reed.

Mabel clutched her arm. "Oh, my goodness! Charlotte, do you realize *who* bought your box? You're the luckiest woman alive."

But Charlotte was feeling anything but lucky, and she wasn't feeling very alive either. As she stood up, she felt her knees go weak— as if a courtroom full of anxious faces had just witnessed a stone-faced judge order her execution.

She did not see the thumbs-up sign that Walker gave Archer or notice that Archer walked over to Reverend Tate and handed him something. In fact, she wasn't aware that Walker had come to stand beside her, her whiskey box tucked under one arm, his hand outstretched toward her. "Are you ready, Miss Butterworth?" he said, a devilish gleam lighting his blue eyes.

CHAPTER
❧ THREE ❧

Charlotte placed a doubtful hand in Walker Reed's warm, steady palm as she stared, bewildered, into his eyes. There was so much there, it surrounded her like perfume. Later, she would remember thinking that there was nothing as beautiful in a man as gentleness, and nothing as gentle in him as strength. Gentle encouragement, not force, enabled her to walk toward her buggy with him.

His quieting presence, and the way he tucked her arm through his, worked to free up her frozen joints. Seeing the spiteful looks of a few of Two Trees's finest young ladies, and recognizing them for what they were, he squeezed Charlotte's hand for encouragement and whispered in her ear, "It's only at the tree that's loaded with fruit that people throw stones."

At those words, Charlotte caught a glimpse of Mary Alice looking as pale as a gutted fish, and for the first time that afternoon she felt the urge to laugh. And that put a little bounce into her walk.

But once she was seated in her buggy, and Walker had taken his place beside her and picked up the reins, the old fear and dread returned. "Where are you taking us, Mr. Reed?"

"Down the road a piece."

"You know there isn't any shade to be found in the whole county, don't you?"

Walker turned toward her, a knowing look in his eyes, but his grin was teasing. "I've heard all about your infamous elm trees from Archer... as well as a few other things about you."

Her cheeks heated as she wondered just what "few other things" Archer had told him about her.

Charlotte kept her eyes on the countryside as they headed down the road and passed her house. Occasionally Walker would ask her something and she would make some exclamation about the scenery, or the weather, always careful to avoid talking about herself. Once, without really realizing it, she had allowed her eyes to rest on his long legs, noticing how the space between the dash and the seat was too small for him, making him spread his legs, his thigh pressing against her skirt. She tried scooting farther to the side, only to realize that she had already done that and her hip was rammed against the seat rail, making it impossible for her to move any farther. With each bump she felt his leg thump against hers, and each time his leg thumped against hers, he gave her that slow, lazy smile that left her dying with embarrassment. She adjusted her hat and folded her hands in her lap, reminding herself to keep her backbone straight, her conversation controlled and aloof.

A few miles down the road, Walker turned the buggy onto a narrow, rutted lane that was overgrown with grass and weeds. "Why are we going down this road? It doesn't go anywhere but to the old Spencer place."

"That's what I heard," he answered, stealing a look at her perched on the edge of her seat like a little brown wren, poised, alert, and ready to take flight at the slightest hint of danger.

"Why would you want to go there? The place is all run-down and overgrown. The well's gone dry. That wouldn't be a good spot to have a picnic."

But her words seemed to have little effect on Walker. He simply clucked the mare into a faster pace, and said, "Since we're almost there, we might as well have a look-see."

When the buggy stopped in front of an old barn that had seen better days, Charlotte looked at Walker. "Is this where you want to eat? Here? In this old run-down barn?"

"Do you have a problem with that?"

She stole a look at him, but she found the courage to go only as far as his chin.

There's something wrong when even a man's chin looks intimidating. Charlotte Augusta Butterworth, get yourself together. He's only a man.

I know, came another little voice in the back of her mind, *and that's the problem.*

"Well? Do you?"

"Yes, Mr. Reed, I do."

"I should have known."

"What is that supposed to mean?"

"Just what I said. I should have known. I daresay, Miss Lottie, that *any* place I picked would find disfavor with you. I'm beginning to feel you and I have gotten off on the wrong foot once again."

"It's not that."

"What is it, then?"

"I just prefer to eat somewhere else."

"Where? Would you rather go back to your house?"

"No!"

Her answer was so fast and high-pitched that Walker couldn't help smiling. "Why? Something wrong with your house?" The smile widened to a grin. "Why, Miss Lottie, don't tell me you didn't make your bed this morning?"

"Of course I did!"

"Leave your unmentionables scattered about?"

"Certainly not."

"Then why don't you want to eat at your house?"

"Because I don't know you well enough, and it isn't proper."

Walker turned and looked down at her, catching her looking up at him. He appeared to be enjoying the situation. "Excuse me, I thought we were talking about eating."

44

She cast him a puzzled glance. "I thought we were, too."

"Well, the kind of fuss you were making... I thought for a moment you misunderstood— that maybe you thought I meant share a bed instead of a meal."

She swallowed painfully and looked down at her hands, then took a bolstering gulp of air. "I never for a moment thought that, and I doubt you did either. You were just looking for some underhanded way to embarrass me. I know all about your kind, with your flashing smiles, good looks, and shifty eyes. Always making suggestive remarks. You're not to be trusted."

He started to speak, but she jumped the gun on him. "I am not accustomed to being talked to like this. If that's why you purchased my box—so you could ridicule and embarrass me— I feel I should return your money to you."

"That's not why I bought your box. I'm just trying to figure out if we have a problem here. Just *how* well do you have to know someone before you can eat with them?" Before she could answer, he sighed. "Never mind. That doesn't matter. We aren't going to eat at your house. We're going to eat right here, in this nice shady barn. You know me well enough to eat in a barn, don't you?"

"I don't know you at all," she snapped.

"You will by the time we've finished."

That, of course, was what Charlotte was worried about. She didn't want to know anything more about Walker Reed. She knew far too much already.

A moment later Walker came around to her side of the buggy, the whiskey box tucked under his arm, and helped her down. Charlotte tilted her head and studied the barn, or what remained of it. Only the main supports were left, all the walls and doors having been removed. The roof was still there, although it was missing large sections of shingles, leaving holes for the sunlight to stream through, touching the grassy floor of the barn in the pattern of a patchwork quilt. Walker, testing the thickness of the grass with his foot, selected a shady spot and spread out Charlotte's Lone Star quilt, placing the whiskey box to one side.

He turned his slow gaze to her as she settled herself and began to take things from the box. The barn was surprisingly cool and shady, the grass rustling as it bowed to the breeze that lifted the sunny white faces of buttercups blooming in scattered clusters where the sun touched. Walker leaned against a support beam and chewed on a long piece of bluestem as he watched her, silently observing the way she moved. He felt the soft stirring of desire when she stole a quick look at him, caught his eyes upon her, and turned away quickly. But not before he saw the faint blush that sprang to her cheeks. She wasn't indifferent to him.

It was true. Charlotte was anything but indifferent. She fought a constant battle to keep her eyes on what she was doing, to keep them from wandering to the strong thighs wrapped in tight twill pants. And while that

46

battle was going on in her head, strange things were happening to her heartbeat, and to her respiration, which was joined by a queer fluttering in her stomach. Then she began to drop things. First a knife, then the lid to the chowchow, and finally the lid to her butter crock, which, unfortunately, landed in her lap, then rolled across the quilt to stop with a soft thump against Walker's boot. Charlotte leaned forward and half-crawled toward the lid. Reaching to pick it up, her head was just inches from Walker's knee when his foot shifted, coming down on top of the lid, making it impossible for her to pick it up. Still on her knees before him, Charlotte glanced up, only to see that Walker had leaned forward and his face was now a scant inch or two from hers. Their eyes met, and Charlotte knew the immediate, unbearable yearning of a woman who finds herself drawn to a man. But then the conditioning of her past caught up to her, bringing back the old fear, and she turned her eyes away as if shamed to feel like a woman, terrified that he might treat her like one.

"Charlotte..." he said hesitantly, as if he weren't sure what he wanted to say. But she sprang to her feet and walked quickly away from the barn.

She walked down a narrow bluff, stopping when she reached a shallow creek. For a moment she just stood there, staring down at the water, as if it formed an impossible barrier. Behind her she heard the whisper of grass, then the soft tread of feet, and she froze. She was a fool to have come here with him. A man like him... he would expect certain things from a woman... things she was incapable of giving to him or to any other man. Then she heard him say her name, softly, gently, like the wind's soft caress, and she circled her waist with her arms and lowered her head as if suddenly gripped with pain.

Coming up behind her, Walker placed his hands on her shoulders. Surprised at their narrowness, and feeling the tension there, he lowered his lips to the porcelain skin of her neck. Nudging the downy fluff of curls at her nape, he nuzzled her there. He heard her gasp, then she stopped breathing altogether, her body stiff and unyielding before him. "Let's call a truce, Charlotte. Can't we at least be friends?"

She spun away from him, her eyes welling with tears, her eyes full of panic. "Oh, we can be friends all right. As long as you keep your groping hands off me. I'm warning you now. If you ever lay a hand on me... if you ever touch me like that again, you'll regret it. Do you understand?"

Walker looked at her strangely. "Perfectly," he said, and he turned away, walking back through the barn and out to the buggy.

Not understanding, Charlotte trailed after him, and as he untied Butterbean, she said, "Are you leaving? Don't you want to eat?"

He turned slowly, his eyes flicking over her, noticing the way her arms were still folded across her middle as if the sight of him sickened her. "No need to be so dramatic, sweet

Charlotte. Cold fish has never been a favorite of mine."

That cut her to the quick, and Walker knew it, but he held himself in check, wanting to see just how far she would go to get things back on an even keel. For he had learned one thing about Charlotte. She liked order in her life. Besides, he didn't think he could control himself around her much longer. As it was, he was torn between throwing her over his knee and blistering that cute little butt of hers and tossing her down and making love to her until she admitted that it was what she'd been wanting since the day they'd first set eyes on each other.

When Walker began to lead Butterbean away, she followed him, curious. "Are you going to take the buggy and leave me here?"

He didn't bother to look at her as he led the mare around the barn to the shadier side. "No, I'm not. You keep the buggy. I'll walk back to town. I'm just going to tie her here, in the shade."

Charlotte watched him tie Butterbean, then he turned toward her and nodded, "Good day, Charlotte." He wheeled and walked toward the quilt, stopping to lift his hat from the rusty nail where he'd hung it.

"Don't you want to take the box with you? You paid for it."

"No, Miss Butterworth, I don't. You keep it."

"But what will I do with all that food?"

"Take it to bed with you."

"Just what is that supposed to mean?"

49

"You figure it out, Miss Butterworth. You figure it out." With that, he walked around the side of the barn and out of sight.

A few minutes later he heard her coming up behind him, stomping through the grass, moving faster than a prairie fire.

"Now see here, Mr. Reed," she said, coming up on his left, her words coming in quick little gasps. "This is ridiculous. That is perfectly good food back there, which you paid *dearly* for, I might add, and it will go to waste if you don't eat some of it. Besides, it's a long way to town, and in this heat..." Her words trailed off when Walker stopped and turned to look at her.

He didn't look so frightening now, his shirt damp from sweat, burrs and last year's seedpods clinging to the legs of his pants, his boots covered with dust. Straightening her back and smoothing her skirts, she said, "And on top of everything else, I know you must be starving."

Walker looked at her, seeing the blush that began to climb from the fair skin of her throat to her cheeks. Observing her, he thought her at odds with herself, a study of contrasts. He knew that her asking him to eat was genuine, but he could see how difficult it was for her. Why? Suddenly, he knew the answer.

"Charlotte, you don't have to be afraid of me."

His voice was rough and seductive, bathing her with the soft fragrance of wildflowers. And down lower, other parts of her were doing their own responding to that voice. "I'm not afraid of you, Mr. Reed," she said coolly. "I just prefer to keep things in perspective, that's all."

"You mean at a distance, don't you?"

"Whatever you prefer to call it, but there isn't any reason why you can't enjoy the meal you paid so handsomely for."

"No," he said lightly, "I don't suppose there is."

She walked back to the quilt and began sorting through the food. She gave Walker a stiff half-smile when he dropped, easily and gracefully, to the quilt across from her, as if accepting his offer to sit well away from her.

She poured him a glass of cherry brandy, offering it to him, noticing the way his strong fingers curled around the stem, brushing against her unsure hand. She cleared her throat, her hand passing over the food she had assembled between them. "What would you like?" she said, offering him a plate.

"You fix it for me. I trust your judgment."

She put the plate in front of her and, reaching forward, took two meat pies and placed them on the plate. Her eyes went to the long, masculine legs stretched before her, crossed casually at the ankles, and without really thinking she reached for another pie and put it with the other two.

Walker's laugh was husky and short.

She turned her head to gaze across the flat prairie. Two scissortails flew overhead, dropping to land in a mesquite bush. She felt Walker Reed's eyes upon her, reading her expression, judging her reactions, like an engineer deciding how much weight a bridge would support. Swatting at a pesky fly that buzzed in her face, Charlotte looked back at the food, took a spoon to lift the sugary-sweet potatoes, and placed a mound next to the three meat pies. Around that she laid two corn fritters, three spoonfuls of tomato salad, two spiced peaches, and a heaping spoonful each of chowchow and plum conserve.

Offering the plate to him, then watching him take it from her, Charlotte fought the desire to reach out and rest her hand on the firm muscle of his forearm, bared below his rolled-up sleeve. It would be warm and hard, like those long legs. But of course she didn't. She simply stared at it while her mind betrayed her with imaginings that her body reacted to: tightness here, a gripping sensation there, and everywhere a strange new trembling.

She made her plate quickly, refilling Walker's glass between bites, wondering why everything she ate tasted the same. When he finished she offered him his choice of lady cake or fresh peach pie. He ate some of both.

Sipping the one glass of cherry brandy she allowed herself, she became self-conscious as he gazed at her, watching the movement of her throat with each swallow. Embarrassed, she put down the glass faster than she should have, spilling some on her skirt. Grabbing a tea towel, she began dabbing at the spot, her breath catching in her throat when Walker's hand came across the distance to push back her hand, taking the edge of her skirt with it.

Charlotte slapped his hand away and shoved

her skirt over her petticoat, but it was too late. His eyebrows went up and a wide grin split his face. "Well, I'll be damned," he said. "It's red."

So was Charlotte's face.

"You know, that surprises me, Miss Lottie... a woman of your standing in the community, a pillar of the church—wearing a *red* petticoat."

"What I wear, Mr. Reed, is none of your business. You may be free to discuss anything you like with women in California—if that's truly where you are from—but here in Texas, a man does not mention personal things like that in front of a lady."

He laughed. "That's the sort of propriety I expected. A woman who wears a red petticoat—a *ruffled* red petticoat, mind you—and then castigates a man for noticing it."

"You didn't just notice it, you reprobate. You *lifted* my skirts!"

"And enjoyed every minute of it, too."

"If you're finished—"

"I'm not. A man likes a little shut-eye after a meal like that."

Before Charlotte could reply, Walker leaned back, stretched out before her like a corpse, and placed his hat over his face... when she thought there was another part of his anatomy he should have covered instead.

"Mr. Reed—"

"Just a *short* nap, Miss Lottie. Just a short little nap."

Charlotte sat there looking at him for a few minutes, until she was sure he was asleep and wasn't going to get up. With a sigh, she eased the stiffness out of her back and began to repack the leftover food and dirty dishes into the whiskey box.

Then she went for a brief walk, but he was still asleep when she returned, so she sat there on the blanket, thrumming her fingers on her skirt, her chin resting in her other hand, wondering how she could wake him without touching him. *A fine kettle of fish you've made out of things, Charlotte.* She tried coughing, and finally a sneeze or two, but he slept on. Finally giving up, she began thinking about what Walker had said earlier about the food. For a long time she thought about that. And it still didn't make sense: *"Take it to bed with you."* Now, why on earth would he say something so stupid? *Because it probably wasn't stupid, nitwit. It probably has a perfectly logical meaning. You're just too stupid to figure it out. Honestly, Charlotte, you'd have to study hard to be a half-wit.*

Suddenly, Charlotte began to understand. *Take it to bed with you.... Take it to bed with you....* As clear as a wallflower's dance card, the meaning began to form in her mind. How low of him to imply that she would never have anything but a miserable picnic basket in her bed. And suddenly she began to give vent to her mounting outrage. "Of all the miserable, lowdown, spitefully mean..."

All that squawking brought Walker around. He had just pushed his hat back from his face and raised himself on his elbows when Charlotte sprang to her feet and grabbed the whiskey box. Before he could inquire what she was doing, she stood in front of him, and Walker, thinking that she wanted to talk, leaned his head back to look at her, just as she turned the whiskey box on its end and dumped the contents into his lap.

He looked down just in time to see the lady cake slide across his shirt, the peach cobbler topped with chowchow smeared from his hipbone to his knee, everything else scattered in between. "Just what in the name of hell do you think you're doing?" he said, just as he felt the contents of the broken jar of cherry brandy seeping into his pants.

"You figure it out, *Mister* Reed," she said, stomping around the barn and over to her buggy. A complete mess, Walker stared at her as she turned the buggy and drove right by him, shouting as she passed, "*Take it to bed with you* and figure it out."

Then Charlotte put Butterbean at a pace that would have made a Thoroughbred racer envious. She didn't slow down any, either. Not until she reached her house. And once inside she vowed that if she never saw Walker Reed again, it would be too soon.

Later that day, Charlotte was in the kitchen, still feeling a certain amount of satisfaction for getting Walker Reed's goat. As she closed the oven door she was suddenly aware of the distant thud of hoofbeats and the faint rumble of voices. The hoofbeats grew louder. A gruff voice boomed out, echoing through her house and seeming to bounce off the walls to echo again and again. Hard upon that came several more shouts, each one louder than the last, until she was sure that the commotion had moved into her front yard. Closer now, the scattered shouts were urgent and quickly spoken.

She paused to listen. Quiet suddenly pervaded her kitchen. Whatever the ruckus was, it had evidently passed, which was just as well. She didn't want her biscuits to burn.

Charlotte turned to the dishpan and had just put her hands in the water when she heard the front gate slam. Next came loud voices and the sound of someone crossing her porch in a hurry. Before she could dry her hands and get to the door, the person on the other side almost pounded the oval glass pane out of its casing.

"Hold your horses!" she said, wiping her hands on her apron and slipping her spectacles into the deep pocket. "I'm coming."

"Lottie, it's me, Nemi. Open up. Quick!"

Charlotte became excited instantly. It had been several months since she had seen her brother, although Nehemiah, whom almost everyone knew as Nemi, lived on a ranch only a few miles south of Two Trees. Her brother had been gone since last April, driving a herd of cattle to Kansas City. Nemi was a handsome man, four years older than Charlotte, and even though he had a wife and four children, he looked out for his sister, dropping by to see her once or twice a week when he wasn't on a trail drive. It was Nemi who had used the money from the sale of the family farm in Kansas to buy the small ranch for Charlotte, building the clapboard house for her himself, with the help of a few ranch hands. And it was Nemi and Nemi alone who knew the real reason why Charlotte preferred to live alone, going to town occasionally and attending church but otherwise burying herself in her chores, refusing the attentions of men and the companionship of a husband. But not even Nemi knew the horrors that Charlotte had seen that afternoon on their family farm. The afternoon the raiders came. The afternoon their mother was murdered.

Charlotte hadn't been the same after that. Day after day she had sat in a rocking chair, staring out the window, accepting food when it was offered to her, allowing Nemi to take her hand at night and lead her to her bed. She carried the memory and horror inside her, never talking about it to anyone. There was little change until their father returned from the war. When he saw his wife's grave, he went berserk, committing a sacrilege, a desecration, in a rage and anguish that left his daughter more damaged and withdrawn than ever.

After their father's death, Nemi brought Charlotte to Texas. While she lived in his house while hers was being built, he watched the friendship form between his sister and his wife, Hannah. A large and loving woman with a heart as big as her bosom, Hannah took Charlotte under her wing and, by the time her house was ready, had her smiling again.

Hearing Nemi pound the door again, Charlotte smiled at his impatience and quickened her step.

"Well, I declare," Charlotte said, opening the door, and then again, "Well, I declare." Before she gave him the hug she customarily greeted him with, she added, "Nehemiah, whatever is the matter with you, trying to knock down my front door?" She never called him by his full name unless she was just a little ruffled with him. Normally, when Nemi sensed that Lottie was out of snuff like this, he would go out of his way to ease her, but today he had more important things on his mind.

"We've got a man that's shot up pretty bad, Lottie. I've sent Snuffy into town to find Doc, but we need to get him stretched out. He's been slung over the back of a horse for a good five hours and he's bleeding like a stuck hog."

Charlotte stood back, nodding at the men she knew as they carried the bleeding man into her front bedroom. Watching the men, Charlotte saw the scarlet splatters of blood alternating with the prints of dusty boots on her glossy floors. She wasn't one to begrudge a bleeding man, but did he have to bleed all over her polished pine floor?

"He's all yours," Nemi said, and stepped back, waving the other men from the room with the order to send Doc in as soon as he arrived.

So, for the second time in a few short weeks, Miss Charlotte Butterworth came to the aid of a stranger, while earnestly praying that this wouldn't become a habit. All in all, she decided, she would rather be weeding her snapdragon beds.

The man lay on the bed on his back, and Charlotte began to unbutton his bloodstained shirt. She thought she was prepared to see the wound that caused so much bleeding, but she was wrong. Seeing the mass of torn and swollen flesh and the size of the hole, still open and bleeding, she had to hold her breath against the waves of sickness that threatened her.

Charlotte did what she could, washing the dried blood around the wound and placing a clean cloth over the bullet hole to absorb the seeping blood. Once that was done, she bathed the man's face, noticing that the beads of sweat returned almost immediately. His skin was pale and clammy, but the room was unbearably hot, almost to the point of suffocating. Whatever coolness had collected during the night had disappeared, leaving the temperature in the bedroom only a few degrees cooler than the broiling August sun.

"Open a window, will you?" she asked Nemi. "It's stifling in here."

"You don't think the dust might cause an infection, do you?" Nemi replied, but he was moving toward the window as he spoke.

"Judging from the dirt in the wound, he's probably already got a dandy of an infection," she answered.

When she had done what she could, she sat in the ladder-backed chair Nemi had placed beside the bed and waited for Doc.

Half an hour later, Dr. J. M. R. Tyree

arrived, breathless and mopping the sweat from his bald head. Charlotte, who had come near to dozing off in the intense heat, jumped to her feet, and Doc dropped his black bag into the chair she had just vacated.

"Afternoon, Miss Lottie," he said, rummaging around in his bag, not bothering to look up.

"Afternoon," Charlotte answered, watching Doc apply antiseptic to the wound. She watched each procedure he performed, but when he began to probe for the bullet, she turned her head away.

The man was big—much bigger than Walker Reed. Whereas Walker was of medium height and lean, this man was much taller and massively built, like a bull terrier. He literally filled the bed, his feet and outstretched arms dipping over the sides. And he was hairy. Terribly hairy. Everywhere. Well, everywhere she had seen, that is.

"This poor fool's lucky to be alive," Doc Tyree said after he finished the last stitch and bandaged the man's chest. "I don't think he's got enough blood to keep a mosquito alive, but he just keeps on breathing." He dropped his implements and supplies back into his bag, leaving a few bottles and bandages on the small bedside table.

"You'll have to keep a pretty close eye on him over the next few days, Miss Lottie. That's when his condition will be most critical," Doc said. "More'n likely there'll be a fever, and a dandy one at that, unless I miss my guess." He shook his head. "That wound couldn't have been much dirtier if he'd been wallowing in hog slops. What did Nehemiah do, drag the poor cuss in here by the heels?"

Doc picked up his bag. "I've done all I can do. You can do as much for him now as I can. Just give him the Dover's Powder when his temperature goes up. It will cause him to sweat a little, and there's opium in it for pain. If there is pain but no fever, use just the tincture of opium drops." He winked at her. "You can give it to him if he gets too restless for a little thing like you to handle." He looked at his pocket watch. "Seems I'm always a day late and a dollar short. Here it is five o'clock and I'm way overdue at the McCracken place. Old Joseph's got a carbuncle on his posterior that needs lancing." He paused when he saw the uneasy look in Charlotte's eyes. "Now don't you worry none, Miss Lottie. There ain't nobody in these parts that'll do the man up as properly as you. I'll check on him as often as possible, and of course if he takes a turn for the worse, you send Jam for me."

Charlotte made two attempts at speech before she finally sputtered, "But you aren't going to leave him *here*, are you?"

"Of course I am," Doc said, his tone of surprise holding a warning of what would be coming if she didn't shut up, but shutting up had never been one of her strong suits.

"Can't you move him somewhere?" she asked, looking not at Doc but at the wounded man.

Doc paused in the doorway and peered over

the top of his glasses. "Just where in tarnation do you think I should put him? You're the only person in the whole county with a couple of spare bedrooms. Sometimes, Miss Lottie, you act just like a woman." Charlotte wondered what other choice she had, but then Doc went on talking and she didn't think any more about it.

"The man wouldn't survive a move across the hall. If he's got any chance at all of making it, it's gonna be right from that there bed. Now, Miss Lottie, if you can, with a clear conscience, tell me to have him moved, I'll speak to Karl Himmler and see if we can set up a cot in that small shed behind his blacksmith shop."

Charlotte's face flushed from the verbal pelting. She glanced at Nemi, who was fighting for control over the laughter that threatened, and losing. When Doc left the room, he threw back his head and laughed. Charlotte's eyes flashed hotly. "Nehemiah Butterworth, you say one word, utter one sound, and I'll pin your oversized ears to the side of your head with my oak rolling pin."

Nemi's blue eyes sparkled with the tolerant affection he might have shown a frolicsome puppy. "You've put my mind at rest, Lottie. For a while there I was worried about leaving you here all alone with a wounded man, but since you possess such skills with the rolling pin, I'm sure you can hold your own."

Charlotte glared at him.

"Now, now, little sister, don't glower. It's not becoming. Pretty is as pretty does, remember?"

"Oh, go chew your own tobacco."

His eyebrows rose. "Do you want me to stay here with you?"

"Humph! That's just what I need—another man to take care of."

He smiled then. "Would you like me to send Hannah over to help you?"

She gave him her most irritated look. "And who, might I ask, would help *you* with the children?"

Nemi started to say something, but Charlotte cut him off with a wave of her hand. "Stop wasting your cajolery on me. You better save it for when you get home. Hannah was expecting you last week, and she's mad enough to chew splinters."

Nemi looked serious. "Lottie, you know I wouldn't have brought him here if there'd been any other place to take him."

"I know that, Nemi. I'm just letting off a little steam, I guess. You get on home and give Hannah some relief from those youngsters of yours. You're needed there."

He grinned. "Are you trying to tell me I'm not welcome here?"

"You're always welcome, Nemi, but you're not needed. Not right now. Now get out of here so I can get some work done."

"You'll send word if you need anything?"

"I'll send word."

"I'll be back soon to check on you. Just keep that fellow pumped full of opium. Keeping him asleep is the best thing for both of you."

"I can take care of things around here. I don't think he'll be giving anyone any trouble for quite a spell, judging from the looks of him." She followed Nemi out the door and closed it softly behind her. When they were in the front room, he picked up his hat from the horsehair sofa. Charlotte walked to the front porch with him.

"Well, I guess I'll be getting on home then... if you're sure I can't do anything around here."

"The only thing you can do is promise me you won't bring me any more strays."

Nemi laughed, hurrying down the front steps. Once he was mounted, he waved, then headed down the road.

And then Charlotte marched from the room. Catching a whiff of something burning, she hurried to the kitchen. To her horror, she recollected that she had left her sourdough biscuits baking in the oven. In her hurry to open the oven she burned her hand, uttered something very unladylike, then backed up and removed a pot holder from the drawer before going at it again. For the second time that month, Miss Lottie removed from her new Monitor stove the charred remains of what had been a promising attempt at baking. With a cry of despair, she looked down at the residue that lay, black and porous, in the bottom of her pan.

To round out an otherwise perfect day, she hurled the mess, pan and all, out the back door, then went to her desk and proceeded to write a list of the reasons why she never wanted a man in her life.

CHAPTER
❧ FOUR ❧

A happy little mockingbird in the oleander bush outside her window woke Charlotte the next morning. She turned over, refusing to open even one eye, but then the old red rooster crowed, and she groaned, wondering if it was possible to grow old in one night. She was exhausted from at least two hundred trips into her front bedroom during the night to check on the stranger and force opium-laced sips of water down his throat.

With a sigh, she crossed her arms behind her head and stretched, then looked around her room. Everything was in order and as neat as wax, from the ruffled dimity curtains on her window to the oilcloth squares in front of each piece of furniture. There, hidden in small boxes stacked in her wardrobe and tucked into out-of-the-way places in her sachet-fragrant drawers, were all of Charlotte Butterworth's treasures and collectibles—everything from her mother's golden locket to her grandmother's button box. Truly, everything was just the same as it had been yesterday, she thought, eyeing the stiffly starched doilies on each table and the pot of geraniums blooming profusely on the plant stand in front of her window. Yes, everything in her life appeared to be the same, yet everything was somehow different.

Charlotte began wondering if her life would ever return to normal. The past few days had been nothing but a series of things going wrong, from leaving the eggs out of the corn bread to putting her shoes on the wrong feet. When, she wanted to know, was her life going to return to the simple and calm existence it had been until a few weeks ago?

First there had been the near hanging in her front yard, and now a half-dead man of questionable background was occupying the bed in her front bedroom. It occurred to her that bad things come in threes, and she was suddenly curious as to just how long she was going to have to wait for the third installment.

Not long.

A short while later, Charlotte was in the chicken yard having a confrontation with a hen she had selected to simmer into a thick broth to feed her patient. She made two circles around the perimeter of the chicken yard and still wasn't any closer to snagging the squawking hen than she had been when she'd started. She stopped to take a deep breath, deciding that the hen had plans that did not include ending up in Charlotte Butterworth's cooking pot.

A change in technique was what Charlotte decided she needed. Rolling up her sleeves and then twisting her skirts and tucking them into the waist of her apron to give her more freedom and mobility, she eyed the hen, which was eyeing her, both of them standing there like they were wondering what the other was looking at. Then she pounced.

The hens ran clucking, half-flying, half-running all over the chicken yard. Feathers floated on the thick, choking dust, and still that one hen ran back and forth along the fence, darting and turning, trying to poke its head between the boards to gain its freedom. Three falls later, Charlotte had the hen in her hands and moved quickly out of the chicken yard. Once she'd locked the gate, she moved to the side of the barn, held the chicken by its head, and gave two circular swings with her arm.

Charlotte gutted the hen and headed toward a caldron of water boiling over a low fire that Jam had set. She had almost reached the caldron when she saw two riders approach, coming around the west side of the house, drawing rein a few feet in front of her. Raising her hand to shield her eyes from the sun, she recognized both of the riders immediately. One of them was Sheriff Archer Bradley. The other man's face was hidden under the low-riding brim of his hat, but she would have known that face blindfolded.

Walker Reed.

He leaned forward, crossing both arms over his saddle horn, and smiled. Seeing that smile, Charlotte realized that he wasn't holding any big grudge against her because of the picnic box she'd dumped in his lap. Catching the direction of his interested and amused stare, she looked down and, to her chagrin, saw that both men had a clear view of her drawers and petticoat. With a gasp and a quick tug she dropped her skirts, then handed the hen to Jam.

"You go ahead and start plucking this hen while I find out what Sheriff Bradley wants,"

Charlotte said to the old man, without taking her eyes off the two riders. Jam went over to the caldron and dunked the bird into the scalding water, then sat on a nearby stump and began plucking.

Archer swung down from his saddle. "Afternoon, Miss Lottie. Looks like you're having chicken for supper."

"I'm sure you didn't ride all the way out here just to tell me that, Archer," Charlotte said, wondering what Walker Reed, or whatever his real name was, found so amusing that he just sat there grinning.

Archer laughed. "No, I didn't. As a matter of fact, I've come bearing gifts. Judge Saunders has ordered Walker to be kept in custody until his brother comes from Santa Barbara to identify him."

"That's a long way to come. Couldn't they wire you a description?" Charlotte asked, noticing that even Archer was calling him Walker.

"They did, but the description could fit the dead man just as easy as Walker."

"Well," Charlotte said, looking at Walker, "I hope you enjoy your say in Two Trees."

In a voice rich with laughter, he said, "Oh, I'm sure I will, especially if you serve chicken every night, Miss Lottie."

Charlotte gave Archer a quick glance that said she smelled something and it wasn't a wet chicken. Archer was looking mighty sheepish. "Well... uh... you see, Miss Lottie..."

"No, Archer," she said, her tone showing just how put out with him she really was. "I don't see."

Archer stammered and stuttered some more, finally managing to say, "Judge Saunders said we had to keep Walker in custody—"

"You've already said that, Archer," Charlotte said with a hint of irritation to her voice. She was hot and tired and a mess and wanted a nice bath, not a sunburn from standing in 105-degree heat talking to a grown man who didn't appear to know come here from sic 'em.

"Well, I was just getting around to that, Miss Lottie," Archer said. "I ain't exactly got room in the jailhouse for Walker, since I'm holding the Stoner boys for trial, so Judge Saunders decided that since you were the one inconvenienced with a near lynching in your yard, you should be the one to benefit from a little free labor. He ordered me to bring Walker over here to your place so he can work for his keep until his brother shows up."

"Absolutely, positively not," Charlotte said, scowling.

"What?" said Archer.

"No. No. No," said Charlotte. "I'm playing nursemaid to one wounded man of questionable background, Archer. I adamantly refuse to open my doors to another one. I am not running a boardinghouse. Does this"— she waved her arm toward her house—"look like the Wayfarers Inn?"

"But, Miss Lottie—"

"*No!*" she shouted. "I don't care if it's a decree from the governor signed in blood. I just want to be left alone with my chickens and my garden and my snapdragons. Can you understand that, Archer?"

"Yes, Miss Lottie, I can understand that, but I don't think Judge Saunders would. This may not be an order from the governor signed in blood, but it is a court order signed by Judge Saunders in official ink—and it's got the state seal. See?" Archer produced a paper and handed it to her.

Charlotte snatched it away from him and read it, then handed it back. Her scowl quickly turned into a downright unpleasant snarl. "Well, just unorder it," she said.

She allowed her anger and hostility to show, even though she had a niggling feeling that slashing her wrists and begging on her knees in front of Archer Bradley would have little effect on changing the havoc that piece of paper had wrought.

"You'll have to appear before Judge Saunders before we can make any changes," Archer said.

"Very well," Charlotte said irritably. Then she whirled around. "I might as well go with you right now. Give me a minute to hitch Butterbean to the buggy."

"Who the hell is Butterbean?" Walker couldn't refrain from asking.

Charlotte stopped dead in her tracks and turned slowly. "Do you find something amusing about the name of my horse, Mr. Reed?" Placing her hands on her hips, she turned to face him more fully. "I suppose you have a much more appropriate name for your horse—something like Fan Dancer? Naked Nubian? Heavenly Delight?"

"Yes, I guess you could say I find the name of my horse appropriate."

"Well? What is it? Was I close?"

He grinned. "Not by a long shot."

He was in one of those grinning and teasing moods, but she wasn't in the frame of mind to put up with such nonsense. "What is the name of your horse, Mr. Reed?" By this time, Charlotte was determined to have the name of his horse, come hell or high water—if she had to choke the name out of him.

"Hired Hand, ma'am, by a stud called Traveling Man."

"Humph!" she said. "I expected something more like Assault, by Bandit."

Archer had the audacity to laugh, but Walker's grin was filled as much with surprise as with amusement.

Ignoring that, Charlotte said, "As I said, if you'll give me a minute I'll get Butterbean."

Walker had to fake a quick spasm of coughing to cover his laughter. Butterbean? Was she serious? Would someone really name a horse that? He decided that a woman who wanted to be left alone with her garden and chickens and snapdragons was probably loony enough to name a horse Butterbean. He allowed his attention to drift back to the conversation between Charlotte and Archer. It was showing promise of becoming very entertaining.

As Charlotte marched toward the barn, Archer called after her, "Judge Saunders ain't there right now, Miss Lottie. He's gone to a trial in Abilene. Won't be back for two or three weeks. You want to see him, you'll have to go to Abilene."

"Oh, never mind," she said in her most

put-out tone, making a sharp right turn and heading toward her back door. "Just put Mr. Reed in the barn, Archer. I've got things to do besides standing here baking my brains and jawing with the likes of you. *Some* people have to work for a living and can't spend all of their time gallivanting around the countryside imposing on people." She yanked open the door. "When you get settled in the barn, Mr. Reed, Jam will show you around." Leaving the two men staring after her, she squared her shoulders and stepped into the house.

When she stopped in front of the washbasin in her bedroom, Charlotte brought her hand up to her breast with a gasp. Her dress, besides being splattered with chicken blood, was streaked and stained with dirt and perspiration. Her face wasn't in much better shape. Her hair, too, was a sight, hanging as limp as last week's buttercups in old Miss Higginbotham's front window.

Staring into the mirror as she washed her face, Charlotte found herself comparing the two men who had come into her life so violently. The wounded man, she decided, had to be a gentleman. Although he was huge, burly, and hairy, she imagined him as gentle and docile as a kitten. Walker she wasn't so sure about. While everything about him—his manner, the way he dressed, his speech—bespoke wealth and education, there were some things that he said and did that no gentleman would ever be guilty of doing. She hoped that it was no more than a response to the fact that he might still be proved a thief and murderer. But she knew the truth. And all she could think was, *Why him? Why this man?* Why, indeed, when she neither wanted nor needed a man in her life. As a child she had learned the bitter truth about what men did to women in the physical sense. Any desire within her to be accepted as a woman by a man had long ago been snuffed out. She prayed that he was the thief and murderer he was suspected of being. She could deal with that. But if he wasn't, if he really was Walker Reed... she could only pray that he wouldn't choose to force himself on her as those men had done to her mother so long ago.

Finishing her bath and hurrying to the kitchen, Charlotte found the plucked chicken lying on the table. She snatched it up and stuffed it into a pot of water before clapping on the lid. While it simmered, she drank a dipper of water and focused on how she was going to handle having Walker Reed around. True, another hand at this time of year was a godsend, but a man like Walker was not just another hand. Like it or not, she reacted to him with feelings she had never felt toward another man.

She returned the dipper to the bucket, catching a glimpse of Walker crossing the yard with Jam, moving with the stealth of a cat stalking a bird. There they came again— goose bumps. It seemed she broke out with goose bumps every time she saw him. *Char-*

lotte Augusta, whatever in the world is the matter with you? The man caused more eruptions than poison ivy.

He also fascinated her. His sharp wit. The fluid movements of his body. His smile. His eyes. She would never have thought she could betray herself in such a wanton way, but she had. Perhaps it was a blessing to realize what was happening. Recognition of the problem would aid in its solving.

She would have to be very, very careful around Walker Reed. And she would be. She would be as businesslike and cautious as she was around a perfect stranger. She would take care to see that she was never alone with him for any longer than necessary. He could not be removed, but he could be avoided.

Charlotte changed her clothes, then hurried to the huge wardrobe in the spare bedroom, and, more to get her mind off things than from any concern for Walker's comfort, she began to search for a few necessities to take to the storeroom. She dropped a clean set of sheets and towels, a bar of soap, and one of her old but serviceable quilts into a basket and went to the barn.

When she entered the small storage room she had used from time to time in the past to lodge an extra hand, Charlotte saw that Walker had already been there and tossed his saddlebags and bedroll onto the small bed. A quick survey of the room told her she couldn't expect anyone to sleep here until it was cleaned up a little. She went back to the house for the broom, the mop, and a pail of warm soapy water.

The room was small and unbelievably dim, the only light coming from a small dirty window. There wasn't much in the way of furniture—a bed with a lumpy mattress, a chair, and a small table. Nevertheless, Charlotte went to work, and soon she had the place scrubbed and swept, the bed covered with clean sheets and a bright patchwork quilt. On the table she placed a kerosene lamp. She stood back to survey her work, wondering if she should light the lamp, and decided she should.

"Not exactly on the level with the St. Charles in New Orleans, but a marked improvement," said a deep voice.

Charlotte whirled around to see Walker standing with his arms braced in the doorway. He was deeply moved that in spite of her reluctance to have him stay with her, she had taken it upon herself to clean the cramped cubbyhole for him. His eyes moved from the neatly made bed with the embroidered pillowcase to the stack of clean towels folded over the back of the chair. That these things were from her house, there was no doubt. The question was, why? And why did this small consideration that she gave him touch him in such a special way?

Charlotte was trembling, her heart pounding in her chest. Her eyes were dark with fear as she stared across the small room at him. She felt cornered and trapped, and that put her at his mercy. For all she knew, he might not be Walker Reed at all, but the cold-blooded killer Spooner Kennedy said he was. But then she remembered that the times she had been around him, the worse thing she'd gotten was goose bumps.

She turned her head slightly to one side, a question in her vivid blue eyes. He met her gaze, his own honest and clear. The room was dark, but the kerosene lamp cast a dull golden glow over him, giving him the patina of polished teak. So perfect were his features—the eyes that held the light like precious stones, the arrogant splendor of his lean body—that he seemed more than human, a creature somewhere between man and God, a half-deity, an archangel made mortal.

He was still braced in the doorway, one leg bent slightly at the knee. He gave her a slow smile that she felt inside like an ache. Then his eyes were once again assessing the changes in the room. His voice smooth and even, he said, "Thank you, Charlotte. You went to a great deal of trouble for me. The question is, why?"

Charlotte met his steady gaze and gave him a cold one in return. "It was nothing, Mr. Reed. I would have done the same for anyone. Even my animals are well cared for."

The warmth went out of Walker's eyes, replaced by a hard blue glare. The woman was a study in confusion. One minute she was saving his life and going out of her way to make him comfortable, and the next she was insulting him without provocation. He was both surprised and displeased, and that made it practically impossible for him to maintain a pleasant attitude.

"Since you have placed me on the same level as the animals you care for, I will try not to disappoint you by allowing any of my more human instincts to sway me. If it's an animal you want, Charlotte, it's an animal you'll get." His voice was steady, without any change in tone, and yet that very lack of inflection was like having her attempt at kindness stomped under his feet.

Her thoughts were running ahead of her like dry leaves scattering before the wind. Without really meaning to, she had insulted him. But it was his own pigheaded fault for deliberately twisting her words and hurling them back at her.

With irritation pricking her, making her words crisp enough to crackle, she said, "I don't *want* anything from you, Mr. Reed, especially your presence. But you are here and I am doing my dead-level best to make the most of it, which includes making you as comfortable as possible during your stay. Now, is there anything else you will be needing, or would you rather stand here hurling insults and twisting everything I say?"

He did not answer right away, and when he finally did speak, she did not look at him, but kept her eyes on the hook on the wall that held his hat. "Your compassion overwhelms me."

"As your arrogance overwhelms me."

He chuckled. "Tit for tat... No one makes anything off of you, do they, Charlotte?"

Hearing the admiration in his voice, she smiled to herself. "I've been known to let a slight or two pass unnoticed."

"Ah, but where's the satisfaction in that?" he asked, his tone going soft and throaty.

His words sent a quiver through her. She moved to the chair, smoothing the creases on the folded towels. "I don't aim to find satisfaction in everything I do. Quite the contrary. Since most of my undertakings are to provide myself with the simple and basic needs for survival, and not easily confused with things that give me pleasure, you could say I find very little satisfaction in most of the things I do."

"And pleasure?"

"I have precious little time for that."

Ah, that's a pity, sweetheart, because if there's anything you were made for, it's pleasure.

"Tell me, what kind of things give you pleasure, Charlotte?"

"Well..." she said hesitantly, having no idea of the havoc she was wreaking upon him. "I love..." She let the words die, the agony of being caught about to reveal something of herself giving her a stricken look.

"What, Charlotte? What were you going to say? You love—"

"Springtime. Babies... actually, baby anythings... soft, fresh, innocent, with that wonderful smell that only babies have."

"And?"

"Old people."

"Old age?"

"No! Not old age. I hate those words. But I love old people."

"That's an interesting observation. Tell me, what do you love about old people?"

78

She looked toward the window and sighed. "Because being old is the best of both worlds... when you're both adult and child. When you're old, you can do anything that pleases you and get away with it. It's like magic. Nothing an old person does surprises anyone. You can snore in church, wear clothes that are eccentric and ridiculously out of fashion... and people are always giving you the best seat when you enter a room, or first choice when the chicken is passed. It's like having flowers in winter. You can show the world how much of the child still remains in you. And when you're so old you can't set bad examples anymore, you can give good advice. Youth is like sunlight, but old age is night, when the stars come out to play."

Behind her, she heard the click of the latch dropping into place as the door closed. She and Walker Reed were alone in the room... with the door closed. Her heart plummeted to her feet. She turned toward him in time to see that he had moved toward her and was standing only inches away.

She dared not breathe. "I must go now—"

"I think not." A wry smile tugged at Walker's mouth when he thought how close he was to dragging her into his arms and kissing away her discomfort. Lord, had he ever been that innocent? Had anyone? She was like the flower in winter she'd mentioned, and he despaired at the lack of conscience that allowed him to cultivate desire in her that would be better left alone. He couldn't go back now. He knew that much. It had already gone too far, become inevitable. *Look at me with those big blue eyes of yours. I want you to understand what's happening here. What's happening between us. I want to sleep with you, Charlotte. I want to do things a lot more wicked than seeing your ruffled red petticoat. Don't pretend you can't read what is in my eyes. Don't blush and turn away. It's called desire, sweetheart. It's that basic.*

She was staring at him, her mouth slightly open, a dewy sheen of moisture on her lips. But she looked frightened enough to bolt. With a will he didn't know he possessed, he restrained himself. He looked at her lovely face and wondered if he should bluntly tell her what he was thinking, which would send her scampering out of there. But he couldn't. He wanted her there, with him, for a little while longer.

And he couldn't stand her talking like this without tossing her onto the bed. His only choice was to guide them back to the bickering and sarcasm that happened so often between them it was becoming a natural pattern. "Tell me, Charlotte, what are you doing here, apart from the obvious excuse of preparing my room?"

"I told you—"

"And so you did. But your answer is like a circle where the ends don't meet. A deformed arc that will hold nothing. Just like your excuse. If you find me as offensive as you say, why would you go to this much trouble for me? Or have you come like the horde of false women that have passed before you? Are you

Salome, here to dance for my head, or Delilah, sent to weaken me?"

"Neither," she snapped. "I am Lot's wife, turned into a pillar of salt. So why don't you take your foxy eyes and your fleshly thoughts and use them on someone willing to put up with your nonsense. I am stone to you, Mr. Reed. Cold, hard stone, and destined to stay that way."

She went on sputtering, but by now he was so amused and enraptured with her that he forgot the reason for turning their conversation in this direction in the first place. He simply crossed his arms over his chest and enjoyed listening to and observing her. A few seconds later he noticed that she'd stopped talking.

He grinned. "How do you expect me to win a hand if you keep changing the game on me? One minute you give me a tongue lashing that would turn a convict straight, and before I can figure out a way to deal with that, you suddenly shut up."

"I can save you the trouble of having to deal with me at all, Mr. Reed. Kindly get out of my way and let me out of here. I have other things to do besides standing out here chewing the fat with you."

"Do you have any idea just how delicious you look right now... just like a little girl?" And she did look delicious. It was the only word he could find to describe the way her rosy curls tumbled along the delicate curve of her hairline, framing a face that an angel would envy.

Each new thing he discovered about Charlotte was both a delight and an assault on his senses. And his senses had had about all the assault they could stand right now. Before she knew what he was doing, Walker, with his silent way of moving, had swept her into his arms and carried her through the door.

"What do you think you're doing? Put me down! Have you gone daft?"

His laughter answered her. "Don't whine, little girl. It's not becoming. I'm doing this only to save your virtue and my shattered nerves. Besides, it's raining, in case you haven't noticed, and I'd hate for you to get your dainty little slippers wet."

Thinking about her serviceable black shoes that were heavier than a smithy's anvil, she began to thrash her legs, hoping he would stagger under the strain of it.

But Walker simply laughed. "I think you've got a wild gypsy spirit," he said softly, and gave her that wide smile that turned her bones to custard. "And it pleases me to discover it."

"I don't give a hoot what pleases you, but it would please me greatly if you would keep your baronic eloquence to yourself and put me down."

"Did you know you wear your respectability like a gossamer veil? When the light is at the right angle, I can see clean through it and get a glimpse of the real woman inside. You're no prude, sweetheart, in spite of what you'd like people to think. If a man could find the right key, he could unlock a door and discover a woman with more wild abandon than the most accomplished wanton."

"You always have to get back to this, don't you? You take extreme pleasure in insulting me."

He lowered her until her feet touched the steps, but he didn't release her. "I'm not insulting you, sweetheart. Impossible as it may seem, I'm doing my damnedest to meet you on even terms." Then he kissed her lightly on the mouth, seeing the anger flare in her eyes. "I didn't plan on doing that," he said, "but people who always do the expected lead dreary lives."

He looked at her for a moment, still holding her by the arms, surprised that she hadn't kicked him. "Charlotte, look at me." She refused. But he waited, knowing that she wouldn't be able to withstand the temptation for long. When she glanced at him, there was something in his eyes that held her. "I can match wits with you for only so long. I'm a man, Charlotte. When I feel desire for a woman, I want to make love to her. Since that doesn't seem to be an option at the moment, we'll have to select an alternate activity." He released her arms. "What time is dinner? Or do you intend to starve me to death like that poor fool in your front bedroom?"

Charlotte's hands flew up to her face. "Oh, my goodness gracious!" And with that she whirled and ran to the house, up the steps, and inside.

Walker turned and moved slowly to the barn. When he reached his room, he sat on the bed, intending to pull off his boots and change his clothes, but then he remembered something she'd said: "Foxy eyes and fleshy thoughts." With a hearty laugh, he fell back on the bed and crossed his arms behind his head. It would be quite a task to bring Miss Butterworth around to his way of thinking. He had his work cut out for him, he could see that.

Charlotte went immediately to work, whipping up a batch of dumplings to drop into the pot of broth while the chicken cooled enough to remove the bones. When the dumplings were ready, she put them aside and boned the hen. After placing the boneless meat back into the pot, she dropped the dumplings on top of the bubbling liquid and clapped on the lid. The secret to good dumplings, she well knew, was never to lift the lid while they were steaming. To do so would make them tough.

When the dumplings were ready, she removed the pot from the heat and lifted the lid. The hen, she had to admit, made a more impressive showing in the nest of dumplings than it ever had strutting around the chicken yard.

She set the dumplings aside and hurried to check on the injured man. As she walked to his room she was hoping to find him awake. When she reached the bedroom door, she hesitated. The man was sprawled on the bed. His eyes were closed and his body was restless. The sheet was damp and twisted across his lower extremities, covering, thankfully, the things that needed covering.

It was most unconventional to be in the presence of a man while he was in bed. It went far beyond convention to be in a man's presence when he was half-naked. But how, her practical side asked that side of her that was worried about propriety, could there by any harm in rendering aid to a wounded man, regardless of his state of dress?

While she wrestled with convention and propriety, the man moaned and thrust one long muscular leg out and away from the sheet. His skin was dark, looking even darker under the covering of black hair. Stepping farther into the room, Charlotte tiptoed to the bed and extended an unsteady hand to place on his brow. He was burning with fever.

She hurried to the kitchen for a dishpan of cool soda water and began bathing his body in an effort to bring down the fever. When she realized the futility of what she was doing, she opened the doors of the commode stand, pulled out several large towels, and began soaking them in soda water and placing them across his chest and arms.

As soon as she'd used all the towels, she removed the first towels, which had already grown warm, and dipped them again in the pan of water. All night she labored over the injured man, returning to the kitchen pump time and time again to refill the dishpan with cold water.

It was almost daylight, the streaked shadows of early morning filling the dim bedchamber, when Charlotte noticed the slight cooling of his skin, the steady, undisturbed rhythm of his breathing, and that his body no longer tossed and thrashed about but lay perfectly still in deep slumber. She removed the towels, which seemed to have grown unbelievably heavy, and tossed them into the dishpan, for what she hoped was the last time. Her body hurt in a dozen places and ached in a dozen more. She didn't have the strength to push herself away from the bed, much less walk to her room. Still on her knees beside the bed, Charlotte dropped the last towel into the dishpan and drew the sheet over the sleeping man. Then, without being fully aware of what she was doing, she left her hand, still clutching the corner of the sheet, resting on his chest, and lowered her head to the mattress beside his hip. Her eyes were closed before her head touched the damp sheets.

Walker was up early, the gnawing hunger in his stomach making sleep impossible. Taking a clean shirt and a bar of soap, he headed for the well. Once he had washed up, he walked toward the house, thinking it strange that he could detect no signs of activity, not even a light in the kitchen. He stopped a few feet from the back step. Maybe Charlotte didn't intend to feed him breakfast, either.

A few hundred yards away, Jam's long legs trailed down the sides of Rebekah, his mule, as he rode along the dusty road toward Charlotte's as he did every morning after he left the tar-paper shack he called home. Walker waved at him and pointed at the house while making an eating motion with his hands. Jam nodded and waved back, his white teeth gleaming brightly against the rich brown of his face, and kicked Rebekah into a faster gait toward the barn.

Walker knocked on the back door, but no one answered. His ribs were clanking together, and for good reason. He hadn't eaten since breakfast yesterday, and he was thinking that there was no way in hell he could put in a full day of hard labor on an empty stomach. After the third knock, he opened the back door and went inside to find Miss Charlotte Butterworth and demand his breakfast.

He found her, all right, but the way he found her—her face uncomfortably close to a man's bare hip, her hand tangled in the confusion of black curly chest hair and the sheet—was not in line with the chaste image he had painted of her earlier, nor in keeping with the prudish attitudes of a maiden lady. He was about to leave her to whatever pleasure she found in taking advantage of a wounded man in a defenseless naked state when he noticed the dishpan heaped with wet towels.

Stepping closer, Walker saw the lines of strain in the deep furrows on her brow, the faint gray smudges of fatigue beneath her closed eyes. He looked at her disheveled hair and the damp signs of toil and sweat that stained her dress. He knew then that it wasn't the sleep of a sexually relaxed woman he was observing, but the sheer exhaustion of a woman who had obviously been up all night battling what he could only guess had been a raging fever, only to find herself too exhausted to move once the ordeal had passed.

Placing a hand on the man's brow and finding it cool to the touch, Walker gathered Charlotte in his arms, remembering the near-weightless feel of her. She reminded him of a dog he'd had once—a dog covered with thick shaggy fur that gave the appearance of being quite large and hefty, but when dunked into a tub for a bath, he had come out a spindly beast that resembled a weasel. Charlotte was like that—covered with layers and layers of clothing coupled with her strong will, she gave the impression of being much stronger and larger than she was.

With a surging rush of tenderness he looked down at the lamblike creature asleep in his arms. He nuzzled his face against the softness of her cheek, then he turned to carry her to her room.

It was easy to tell which of the two other bedrooms was Charlotte's. It was dainty and ruffled and sweet-smelling with cleanliness and starch and rosewater, just like Charlotte herself. He carried her to her bed, where he loosened her clothing, removing her outer garments down to her chemise and petticoats, unable to keep himself from noticing that she didn't wear a corset. Through the old, thin fabric of her chemise he could see her breasts plainly. Walker had seen a good many breasts in his day, and had done more than look at most of them, but these were the most beautiful breasts he had ever seen. He stood there, his eyes lingering on her breasts, then traveling slowly down the rest of her body to her feet. He found it odd that instead of a stabbing jolt of desire, what he felt for this woman was aching tenderness.

He began searching for a button hook and, finding it, removed her shoes. He held one tiny, slim foot in his hand, stroking the pale softness of her instep, then he placed his outstretched palm against the sole of her foot. His hand was larger. His eyes traveled over her once again as he lowered her foot to the mattress. So many contrasts housed in one small body, and he had the feeling that he had just scratched the surface. For a moment he felt a pang of remorse that his stay with Charlotte would come to an end when his brother, Riley, arrived.

Walker's stomach rumbled again—louder this time—and he turned to the door, checked himself, and turned back to Charlotte. When he reached her side, his large hands began to probe the thick mass of hair piled rather haphazardly on top of her head until he located a few hairpins and removed them, allowing the richly colored coil of hair to tumble free, trailing across and down the side of the starched pillowcase like the spiraling tendrils of Virginia creeper that lined the back fence. Walker held a silky lock in his hand for a few minutes, rubbing it against his rough fingers, remembering the feel of a woman's hair, a woman's skin. With a softly mumbled oath he directed his thoughts into safer territory and let the soft strands of her hair sift through his fingers before he turned and left the room.

It was late afternoon when Charlotte began

to stir, instantly aware of the enticing aroma of food. Opening her eyes, she looked around the room, trying to decide where she was. Her room. But how had she gotten there? The last thing she could remember was the heavy weariness that had descended on her when the wounded man's fever broke. Her exhaustion must have been so great that she didn't remember coming to her room. She glanced down.

Neither did she remember removing her clothes. And she never slept in her chemise. Lost in thought, she touched a curl that lay across her breast, wrapping it around her finger. Nor did she remember taking down her hair or, for that matter, placing the pins on the nightstand. Then she noticed the tray of food beside the bed, highlighted by the glow of her kerosene lamp.

Someone had prepared her dinner and lit the lamp. But who? Then she noticed her clothes folded neatly on the chair. And why? Not only did she not remember folding them, but they were folded rather clumsily. As a man would fold them.

A man?

And not just any man. Charlotte looked at the tray of food again. Fried chicken. Jam couldn't find his way to the kitchen with a map—that much she knew—and unless the wounded man had undergone a miraculous transformation, he couldn't get out of bed, much less kill a chicken and prepare it. Curiosity made her pick up a leg and take a bite, tasting it tentatively. It was cooked to perfection. Whoever had prepared it knew a great deal about cooking. The only person who could've done it was Walker Reed, but he didn't look like he could boil water—blood maybe, but not water. No, his expertise, she was willing to bet, lay more in the direction of the bedroom than the kitchen.

The thought of Walker in her bedroom left her feeling weak. That he should take it upon himself to enter her house without her permission and take liberties with her person filled her with anger. But then she looked at the tray again and remembered that the arrogant man who had violated her home and her privacy was the one who'd prepared the mound of fried chicken.

A warm flush began at her throat and spread over her face. Walker, she decided, was a lot like the wind. She just never knew which direction he would be coming from. He could infuriate her with his words or thrill her with a simple look. He could tease her with cool proficiency one minute, then cause her cheeks to flame with embarrassment the next. The whole thing was so unsettling. Just how did one go about bringing order and eliminating chaos? Or, if the chaos wasn't the kind one wanted to do away with completely, how would one harness it a little? But she knew that bringing a man like Walker Reed to task was about as easy as subduing lightning.

She picked up another piece of chicken and took a bite, crossing her legs in front of her, and contemplated Walker Reed. When she finished her third piece of chicken, she had a full stomach but no more insight than she'd had when she started. But all wasn't lost, for she had reached two conclusions: Walker Reed wasn't all bad. And he could fry chicken. But those conclusions still didn't answer the question of what she was going to do about him.

She wondered if he'd fed the wounded man in the front bedroom. At the thought of the injured man, Charlotte leaped from the bed and grabbed her dressing gown, which hung on a hook behind her door. Tying the sash as she hurried down the hall, she rushed into his room, only to find the room much as she'd left it, except the lamp beside the bed was lit and turned low and the basin and wet towels had been removed.

What a complex man Walker was, she couldn't help thinking, as she placed her hand on the wounded man's brow and found it cool. She made herself busy, straightening the sheets, brushing his thick, unruly hair back from his forehead, and opening the windows so that the room would be cooler. But the entire time she was ministering to one man with the gentle touch of an angel, Charlotte Butterworth's thoughts were of another.

CHAPTER
🌿 FIVE 🌿

Walker stood at the window of his room. Even through the opalescent glass he could see the outline of Charlotte's house, dark against the faint pink blush of early-morning light. He was buttoning his shirt, with a look on his face that was somewhere between annoyed and pensive. Unable to remove the sight of her as she had been a few days ago, Walker was remembering, as he had every morning since, the image of what lay beneath Charlotte Butterworth's starched exterior. The perfectly formed breasts, the small, nipped-in waist, the shapely legs, the overall appearance of her as he undressed her with his mind—none of that meshed with the woman he saw with his eyes. Why was a woman like that unwed? And why did she intentionally play down all her glorious assets? He wasn't sure why. But he intended to find out.

Right on time, the red rooster flew to the top rail of the fence and flapped its wings, then crowed three times in succession. Walker's eyes went to the window in Charlotte's bedroom. A minute later a light came on and he smiled. As punctual as her rooster. Then he saw her shadow move in front of the window and the smile left his face. He stared at the place he had last seen her, his eyes dark with the knowledge that she was dressing. He had no business thinking about her like that, no business at all.

The sound of someone whistling reached Walker's ears and he stepped outside in time to see Jam coming around the house on Rebekah.

"Mornin', Walker," Jam said, sliding off Rebekah's bare back.

While Walker and Jam discussed the day's

93

chores, Charlotte walked stiffly back to her bed and fell across it. A few minutes later she was still there, wondering if she had what it took to stand up a second time.

She did. So for the second time that morning Charlotte rose to stand before her mirror and survey her face. It didn't look any better than it had the first time she'd looked at it. She stuck out her tongue, tested the tightness of the skin at her throat, and checked her hairline for gray hairs. Finding none, she still wasn't convinced that what she was feeling wasn't the rapid advancement of old age.

She remembered talking to Doc about it yesterday, when he'd dropped by to check on the wounded man. He'd said her patient looked better than she did. Maybe she should have taken him up on his offer to leave her a bottle of liver tonic. She sure wasn't feeling too good. Her head ached and her eyes felt like someone had played marbles with them. She had been up again most of the night with the wounded man. She reached for her hairbrush and felt an immediate stiffness in her right arm. So this was old age. She knew that had to be it, because the weather hadn't changed in days. She didn't think about the possibility of her arm being stiff from the fifteen buckets of water she'd had to haul from the well yesterday because the seal in the kitchen pump had picked that day, instead of one of the other 364, to wear out.

Sometime later, when she had a pan of biscuits in the oven and a skillet full of gravy and sausage keeping warm, she cooked a pan of oatmeal for the wounded man. The sound of steps on the back porch turned out to be those of Walker. She watched him enter the kitchen with a pail of milk.

Every time she saw him she couldn't help remembering that he had probably looked at her half-naked body at his leisure while removing her clothes the other morning. At first she had been too embarrassed even to look at him. Then she'd decided that the incident hadn't made much of an impression on him one way or the other, or, if it had, he wasn't letting on. How strange to think there had been a man who'd had her alone in her bedroom and removed her clothes and hadn't taken advantage of her. It made her feel all mixed up—pleased that he hadn't and yet unable to understand why. She didn't know how to act around a man who had seen her almost as naked as a sheared sheep. What was the best way to handle it? Express her displeasure? Make her obvious embarrassment known to him? Pretend it had never happened?

The last suggestion, she decided, was the wisest. She looked up and saw him still standing there with the pail of milk in his hand. He was doing nothing wrong. He was just watching her. Perhaps he was simply watching to see what she would do. But there was something unnerving, even disturbing, about the way she often had a sudden, prickling sensation that someone was looking at her, and when she lifted her head to see, she caught him watching her as if in deep concentration.

"Just put it on the table."

"Yes, ma'am," he said in a tone mocking enough to draw a haughty look from her.

"I can do without your sneering remarks."

"Judging from your nasty mood, I think you've been doing without a lot of things, my girl."

"Sleep being the primary one."

"That's not what I had in mind."

"I'm sure you're waiting for me to ask what you had in mind, but I'm onto your tricks. I'm not in the least interested in what you were thinking of. And I'm not in a nasty mood. I'm never in a nasty mood."

"Oh? And here I thought you were human."

She ignored that. "I was going to say I can sometimes get perturbed."

"Perturbed? Is that what you were when you dumped the picnic basket in my lap? Perturbed?"

"I'm not putting a dog in that fight, so if you're looking for an argument, you can just take yourself out of here." Charlotte opened the cabinet and reached for the sugar, which slipped through her fingers, and as she grabbed for it, she knocked over the basket of eggs she had just gathered. She looked at the mess of cracked eggs and sugar and felt like bursting into tears. "See what you made me do?"

Walker came to her and put a hand on her shoulder, from which she jerked free.

"What's the matter, Charlotte?"

"Just get out of here and leave me alone," she said angrily.

"I can't just walk out and leave you here so upset."

"Nothing is going right and I don't know what to do about it. I don't even know what the problem is. I don't know what's wrong."

"I do."

She turned to him. "You know?"

"You're confused."

She looked out of sorts again. "You don't need a medical diploma to tell that. Of course I'm confused. I'm confused about why everything in my life has suddenly turned upside down."

"You're confused about your feelings."

"Oh no I'm not. That's one thing I'm not confused about. I know what my feelings are. Exactly. Everything I'm feeling right now can be summed up in one little word: anger. I'm angry about a lot of things... more than I have time or patience to tell you about. But I'm angrier at you than anything."

"I know, and that's why you're confused—because you don't really have a reason to be angry with me, and yet you are."

"Hah!"

"You're angry with me because I haven't lived up to your expectations."

"The only expectation I have of you is I expect you to get out of my kitchen, out of my house, out of my life."

"You want nothing of the kind. What you really want, if you were honest with yourself, is to have me carry you into your bedroom and make love to you until your toes curl. You're not angry at me for anything I've done. You're angry for the things I haven't done."

"You're insane," Charlotte said with so

much rage that she almost lost control. She clenched her fists at her sides and concentrated on long, slow breaths. When she had restored some order to her emotions, she said calmly, "Get out of my kitchen and get out now."

"I'm going. I've got to wash up, but I'll be back in time for breakfast."

To his retreating back she shouted, "I wouldn't give you all the hay you could eat."

His laughter made her even more angry. All she could think of as she finished cooking breakfast was that she wished she had a poison mushroom or two to put into his gravy.

She gained some control as she cleaned up the broken eggs. She dipped out a bowl of oatmeal, then began straining the milk through cheesecloth. Once she had the cream separated, she poured some into the oatmeal, added a little sugar, and placed it on a tray.

When she entered the front bedroom, she saw that the man was lying much in the same position as he had the night before, but now his eyes were open and rather glassy. He was dead. The thought so frightened her that she almost dropped the tray, but then he blinked as if he were coming out of a trance.

"Where am I?" he said hoarsely.

Charlotte crossed the room, put the oatmeal on the table next to the bed, and pulled up the ladder-back chair. "You're in Two Trees." When that didn't draw a response, she added, "Texas."

"Who are you?"

"Charlotte Butterworth. My brother, Nehemiah, found you a few days ago and brought you here. The doctor thought it best not to move you. You've been a very sick man, Mr...."

"Granger," he croaked. "Jamie Granger." He looked around the room and obviously did not see what he was looking for. "Where are my clothes?"

Remembering that she was the one who'd removed them brought a flush of embarrassment to Charlotte's face. Turning quickly to hide it, she moved to the commode stand to pour a pitcher of water into the basin. She layered a clean cloth and towel on her forearm, then dropped a bar of soap into the water and carried the basin to the bed, placing it on the braided rug beside the bed.

"Your clothes?" she repeated, thinking back to the afternoon Nemi had brought him in. "Why, I had to throw them out, Mr. Granger. They were covered with blood and in quite a state of disrepair."

Taking his arm in her hand, she began to lather it. When she finished, she rinsed and dried it, then moved to the other side of the bed, doing the same with the other arm.

"I don't suppose anyone found a saddle-bag full of money?" he asked.

"No, I'm afraid not. There wasn't even a horse around. My brother figured you'd been robbed and left for dead. They did find a few personal belongings scattered about. I've put them in the wardrobe over there."

Before Jamie Granger was aware of what she was doing, Charlotte was washing his upper body, only a faint glow of embarrassment tinting her flawless cheeks. Then she moved to his face. That finished, she left the room for a minute. When she returned, she carried a nightshirt, a toothbrush, and a small glass.

"This nightshirt belongs to my brother. I'm sure he won't mind you using it, Mr. Granger." She placed it at the foot of the bed while she assisted him in brushing his teeth by holding a small saucer beneath his mouth. As she pulled the soft nightshirt over his head, being careful not to touch his bandaged chest with her hands, she said, "If you're feeling up to it, I'll shave you tomorrow, Mr. Granger."

"I'd like that." He paused, his face taking on an expression Charlotte could only call embarrassment. "Pardon me, ma'am, but would you be Miss Charlotte Butterworth, or Mrs.?"

"Miss Butterworth, Mr. Granger. I'm not married. You may call me Miss Lottie—everyone around these parts calls me that."

"Thank you, Miss Lottie."

"Now, it's time to get some solid food into you, Mr. Granger. We'll have time to talk later."

He opened his mouth to say something else, but Charlotte shoved a spoonful of oatmeal into it, so he had no choice but to eat it. She smiled when he finished the bite and immediately came at him with another spoonful. Jamie opened his mouth while thinking what a splendid-looking woman she was. Before she rammed home another bite, he began to think what a nice thing it was that her brother had found him and brought him here. It had been a long time since he'd had a white woman fussing over him—not since his mother had died, and that was fifteen or twenty years ago.

As he glanced around the room, it all began to come back to him—what it was like to live in a home like this. He had lived in that big ranch house down in the Rio Grande valley so long with nothing but Mexican women to run his household, he'd completely forgotten what it was like to have the touch of a woman of his own kind around.

When he showed signs of slowing down on the oatmeal, Charlotte said, "I know you're feeling full, Mr. Granger, but it is important to get your strength back, and eating is the only way to do that. You can't quit until all this is gone."

"Call me Jamie," he said. When he looked at her, she looked hastily away.

After a period of silence, Charlotte decided to find out more about Jamie Granger. "Where are you from, Jamie?"

"The valley, ma'am. I have a cattle ranch near Laredo." He watched the way her hand, so smooth and delicate, carefully measured a spoonful of oatmeal and scraped the spoon on the edge of the bowl before bringing it to his mouth. "Do you raise any cattle here, Miss Lottie?"

Charlotte went on to explain how Nemi was the cattleman in the family and how he had found Jamie on his way back to Two Trees after selling his herd in Kansas.

"If he made it back with his money, he did better than me."

Her eyes met his. "I'm sorry about your money."

He leaned back thoughtfully. "It was my own damn fault. I should've put the money in the bank instead of carrying it on me like I did."

"Yes, you should have," Charlotte agreed. "There are a lot of people out there who would rather relieve someone of his pocketbook than do an honest day's work. It was most unfortunate that you had to run across some of them." As soon as she said that, Charlotte couldn't help wondering if there could be any connection between Walker's killing the man who robbed him and the men who had robbed Jamie. If Walker Reed wasn't really Walker Reed, but was in fact a thief who had no qualms about killing for money, then it was very likely that he could be the very man who had shot Jamie. But Walker was still in jail when Jamie had been shot, and she remembered the way Walker had cared for Jamie the morning after his fever and decided she was being foolish. But still, the thought was there in the back of her mind.

By the time he'd eaten all the oatmeal, Jamie had learned quite a few things about Miss Lottie that pleased him—the musical lilt to her voice, the serious expression on her face as she scooped up each bite, the way her face colored when she caught him staring at her. Yes, Miss Lottie was a lady, but she wasn't stiff necked. He'd be willing to bet that lying underneath that stiffly starched bodice was a warm, affectionate heart that pumped blood as passionate as it came.

When Charlotte began replacing the dishes on the tray, Jamie asked her if she had any books.

"Books?" she said in a rather astonished way. "You mean, to read?"

He smiled. "Of course to read. You didn't think I wanted them to throw at you, did you? Believe me, you're much too pretty to throw books at."

Her voice sounded flustered by his compliment, but her self-esteem was soaring like an eagle on an updraft. "Well, of course I have books, Jamie. Would you like one to read now?"

He nodded.

"Do you care for Byron, or would you like Cooper or Dickens?"

"You pick, Miss Lottie," he said, glancing around the room. "Your taste seems to be perfectly in line with mine. Right offhand I'd say we were perfectly matched."

Of course he didn't mean it the way it sounded, but when she glanced at him, his eyes were twinkling with such devilment that she wasn't so sure. He was a tease, Jamie Granger was. A big old burly Scot with an eye for the ladies and a heart as big as Texas and the nature of a gentle old hound. She cleared her throat. "Let me get some books for you, then. I'll just pick some of my favorites. You're sure to find something you like among them." She paused. "I don't suppose you've read Eliot's *Middlemarch*, have you?"

"Why no, I haven't, but as you might guess, Eliot is a favorite of mine."

Charlotte floated light as a feather to the parlor and pulled her treasured copy of *Middlemarch* down from the shelf.

"I don't suppose I could talk you into reading to me," Jamie said as she came back into the room. "My eyes aren't functioning too well, and after hearing your lovely voice float in and out of my consciousness for days, I know hearing you read Eliot's words will add a whole new dimension to the story. Do sit down and read for me, just like a bird perched on my windowsill."

If Miss Charlotte Butterworth had been invited to England to visit the queen, she would never have expected to hear such eloquence. What was a gentleman like this doing in the wilds of west Texas—lying in her bed? A shiver of anticipation ran over her as she imagined him reading *Sonnets from the Portuguese* with that low, vibrating voice of his. Such a gentle giant, she thought, a huge man with a soft, tender nature. Nothing like Walker, with his smaller-framed slenderness that left her breathless and flushed. Suddenly she remembered that Walker was waiting for his breakfast in the kitchen. She really should hurry. But then Jamie turned those soft brown eyes on her, looking as trusting as old Bessie the cow, and Charlotte didn't have the heart to deny the first request he'd made. He was lucky to be making any requests, so near to dying he'd come.

Charlotte settled herself in the chair and

began reading, not stopping until she reached the end of chapter one. She would've gone on, but she began hearing noises from the kitchen that sounded like someone had just turned a herd of yearling heifers loose in there.

"Do try to get some rest, Mr. Granger," she said, knowing that that would be impossible until she stopped the loud clatter coming from the kitchen. Scooping the tray into her arms, she said, "Perhaps I can read to you again later."

"You've got the disposition of an angel, Miss Lottie," Jamie said. "I'll lie in agony until you return."

Charlotte's heart began pumping so much blood into her veins that she felt weighted down by it all and quite unable to move. When her feet responded to the command to move, she was afraid she might walk smack into the wall, so light-headed was she. Little Italian arias trilled through her mind, and her knees felt like cardboard, but buckled knees and all, she managed to make it to the door and, giving Jamie a shy smile, slipped from the room.

The little Italian arias vanished the moment she entered the kitchen—and so did her angelic disposition. That brute with the devil's own blue eyes was slamming the lid to her cast-iron skillet against the flue of her new Monitor stove, making Charlotte's eyes blink with each slam. His eyes, she noted, remained wide open and hotly fixed on her person as if he would do her bodily harm.

"A fine gentleman you are," she huffed, "behaving this way in the home of the very lady who saved your wretched hide. I should've let them string you up and be done with it."

"Stringing me up would've been a helluva lot better than starving me to death," he yelled. "Would you read to me, Miss Lottie? Like a bird perched on my windowsill?" he mimicked.

"Shut up!"

"Do you like Byron, Mr. Granger?"

"I said, shut up!"

"You've got the disposition of an angel, Miss Lottie," he went on.

"You wretched worm, I'm warning you," Charlotte said, while looking around for something to bring down onto his vile head.

"I'll live in agony until you return," he said, not taking note of the danger that flashed like a beacon in the depths of her blue eyes, announcing the storm that was fast approaching. Charlotte didn't have red hair for nothing.

"I'll just bet he'll lie in agony if it takes you as long to return with his next meal as it's taken you to give me mine."

"I said, shut up!" she shrieked, and grabbed the handle of the pan of oatmeal sitting on the stove and hurled the contents toward him. Great gray-brown globs of goo flew from the pan and settled precariously on his person, some globs remaining where they'd landed—in his hair, splattered against his shirt, sticking to the chest hair curled at his throat—while others began to quiver uncertainly, then descended like an avalanche, leaving a trail of slime as they ran down his forehead, settled in his thick brows, and trailed across his ears, dropping beneath his collar.

The woman with the disposition of an angel gave a horrified gasp.

Walker wiped the oatmeal from his eyes, unable to express the anger he felt. He really couldn't understand what had driven him to provoke her the way he had. What did it matter to him if Charlotte fluttered like a lovesick calf around that oaf in the other room? As soon as Riley showed up, he'd be gone from this godforsaken town without letting his shirttail hit his back.

"You pushed me," she said. "You just kept on and on."

"You are absolutely right," he said, wiping the oatmeal off his face with a towel. "I most certainly did antagonize you. Now, the question is, what are we going to do about it? I provoked you and you threw oatmeal in my face. Do I retaliate and by so doing give you license to come at me again, or do we stop this nonsense here and now, and let me eat my breakfast before I faint from hunger? Because I might as well tell you, I am starving to death. And if you do much more to stand between me and nourishment, I will not be responsible for the consequences."

Charlotte was so stunned, she was incapable of speech for a moment. "Fate has forced us together, and the way I see it we have two choices," he said. "We can either continue this aggravation that seems to exist between us, or we can do our best to avoid each other's company, striving to be civil and adultlike whenever we're forced together."

He watched as she went marching to the table and set his place, slamming his plate down hard.

She was out of breath and obviously embarrassed about losing control as she had, but she wasn't reserved or conscious of her appearance, and her words were not strung together with that strained tightness he was accustomed to. She was perspiring, and her hair was slipping from its knot, but she looked like she was enjoying herself, and Walker felt his heart twist painfully, felt his desire for her shove him just a little closer to the edge. It was all he could do not to push her back on the kitchen table and make love to her next to the cracked plate. It seemed she wasn't the only one out of control, but it was too late for him to do anything about it. He looked at her strangely. "It seems to me, Charlotte, that you're always throwing things at me. I wonder why that is."

"I haven't the faintest idea. Perhaps it has something to do with the way you have of bringing out the red in my hair."

He couldn't help but smile. "There are a few other things I could bring out in you, Charlotte," he said softly, "if you'd just let me."

She watched him, trying to decide if he was as serious as he sounded or if he was only trying to frighten her. Unable to take her eyes from him, she handed him the damp towel she had just picked up.

Holding her gaze, Walker finished cleaning

the mess Charlotte had made of him. He leaned against the kitchen table, his legs crossed in front of him, the expression in his blue eyes dark and unreadable, as he studied her with an intensity that made her uncomfortable. She felt the nerves in her body humming and the muscles along her shoulders and neck bunching in tight little knots. He gave no indication as to how he was taking things, so she didn't know what to expect.

She made the mistake of looking at him. His eyes, deep and brooding, locked with hers. "You know what I think? I think this whole thing is a simple matter of elementary biology. I'm a man and you're a woman and every time we get near each other there's something magnetic that leaps between us, but you refuse to acknowledge how you really feel. You're hiding behind that stiff white collar of yours, trying to deny the female part of you that really wants me to take you in my arms and kiss you senseless. Isn't that right?" He could see that he had really gotten to her this time, and he felt a little sorry for her. He wondered if he should say something, but she clutched her fist tightly against her breast, as if she was having difficulty breathing, then looked away.

Walker pushed away from the table, moving toward her until he was just inches away. Still she kept her face averted. He lifted his hand and stroked the hollow of her cheek with his knuckles. "Tell me what you want," he said, his voice soft and strangely low.

She jerked back her head and turned fully

away from him, her hands gripping the edge of the counter, her back to him. "I don't know what I want," she said. Her voice was subdued and full of uncertainty. "I don't know how to take you. I don't understand the things you do, the way you make me feel so angry—both at you and myself. You make me uncomfortable and self-conscious like I'm standing in church on Sunday morning without a stitch on and I don't know which part of me to cover first. I feel so... so exposed and..."

"And vulnerable," he added gently. "You're like a flower," he said, "all velvety and pink and newly opened, not knowing if you will be admired from afar, or if some busy little bee will come along and steal your nectar, then buzz happily away, leaving you less than you were—or perhaps some uncaring brute will come along and pluck you from your vine and enjoy you for a while, but when you begin to fade and drop your petals, he'll toss you aside."

"You're wrong," she snapped. But he had disturbed her more than she cared to admit. She didn't like the direction things were taking but felt helpless to do anything about it.

"Am I?" His eyes bored into her. "I wonder. There is one way to find out."

Walker was quick—so quick he had her in his arms before she even saw him move. She pulled against his hold on her, but there was more strength in his hands than she had in her entire body. "Let me go."

"Why would I let you go, Charlotte, when

it's taken me so long to get you in my arms?"

He accepted the anger coming at him from those blue eyes of hers before allowing his eyes to drop lower, moving across her flaming cheeks to the soft skin of her neck, and lower, to where the full curves of her breasts rose and fell with each breath.

"Is this the only way you can have a woman," she said, "by force?"

His face was stone hard. With no more regard for her than he would have for a beetle under his foot, he gripped her upper arms as he slammed her against him, his breath, hot and fragrant, teasing the loose tendrils along her neck as he pressed his mouth against her waiting flesh. Then she felt herself turned slightly and drawn more fully against him, his hands doing things along the soft skin of her neck that made her breath catch in her throat.

"Don't," she said with a quiver to her voice as his kisses moved from the softness of her neck to the pounding at her temples, then touching each eye briefly before moving to her mouth.

"Why not?" he whispered into her mouth. "Relax. I'm only going to kiss you." The words seemed to dissolve on the end of his tongue as it moved across her lips, seeking entry. He pressed closer against her, driving her back against the counter with the hardness of his body. Then he paused, as if giving her time to adjust to the alien feel of his body touching her in so many places. Even through the layers of her dress and petticoat, she could feel the most intimate part of his body. He was very long and very hard against her.

"Please," she said in a barely audible whisper.

"Oh, I please, all right," he said as his mouth moved over hers once more.

"No," she said, pushing away from him. "No. Leave me alone." Her voice trailed away to nothing as his face hovered above, his lips soft and plying as they played across hers.

She pushed against him again. "Leave me alone!"

"I don't think I can, Charlotte. You feel too damn good right where you are."

If it were possible, *that* part of him seemed to be getting larger as it pressed against her abdomen. She trembled with fear.

Walker felt the shiver that gripped her, and it seemed to counteract the anger that had seized him earlier but did little to dissipate the white-hot surge of desire that swept over him. Why was he even attracted to her? She was far too prim, too proper, too angry at the world about something—more than likely, at the lack of men in her bed. She had lived the spinster's life too long. But while he was telling himself this, his blood was sluicing in hot waves through his veins, slamming into his brain with such force that he had a flash of doubt about being able to let her go. Why her? Why this woman? What was it about her that burrowed into him like a woodworm?

He glanced down at her face and felt a stab of remorse. This woman had saved his life, and she looked as if she might be having second thoughts about it now. Something about that and the way she held her face in stiff resolve struck him as funny. At first he tried to suppress the sudden flow of humor that bubbled up inside him, but then, thinking that he could use it to extricate them both from a hopeless situation, he made use of it.

"Charlotte," he said softly, "I know there are some men that can live on love, but I'm not one of them. Do you think you could feed me?"

CHAPTER
❧ SIX ❧

A woman is never stronger than when she is armed with her weaknesses....

Walker's eyes narrowed and a thin smile tugged at the corner of his mouth as he watched Charlotte working in the kitchen. Whenever she was trying to ignore him, she wore what Walker thought of as her "separate look."

She was a private person. She hoed the garden and hauled feed and wrung the necks of chickens and wore those plain dresses, while trying to hollow out a little space for her womanliness to exist, crowded into a life of drudgery, sacrifice, and hard work. He felt pity for her then, because being a woman demanded so much more than being a man. He was conscious in a sympathetic way of what it took for her to subdue her wild spirit for the work of survival. And there was admiration there, too, for the responsibility this indomitable woman stoically assumed for nothing more than a life of loneliness and privation. And always tenderness, a part of him that wanted to take her in his arms and tell her that sometimes life's privations were easier to abide when the heart was treated better than the belly. But she wouldn't understand. Not yet.

All sorts of emotions were struggling across Walker's face and he looked quickly away, gazing beyond the tiny kitchen to the world outside and seeing nothing but a vast emptiness on every side. But it was a world and a way of life familiar to Charlotte: every fence post, hay rake, windmill, chicken coop, and flower bed. Not a tree or hill broke the broad sweep of barren prairie that made a thirsty mouth want to turn up toward the sky. The sun baked everything, putting dry cracks in the rich brown soil and sucking the green from the grasses and turning the tops brown. Everywhere he looked, he saw brown. Strong, quiet brown. A wholesome color. The color of the earth, born of the sun's blistering stubbornness and the fiery temperament of the wind. There was something about Charlotte that was strong and quiet and solid, like the color brown. There, in her kitchen, she was like a woman fulfilled, padding around familiar surroundings, touching each object with affection, approaching each task as a labor of love. A little brown wood thrush, simple and plain, with the sun's own stubbornness to see a thing through to the end. But in bed... *Ah, in bed... Sweet Charlotte, would you be all fire?*

He was almost startled by the sight of Charlotte moving past him to the pie safe by the window, the shy aroma of vanilla stirring his senses. It occurred to him that she always carried the scent of vanilla—not the deliberate enticement of expensive French perfume, or even the delicate subtlety of rose or lavender water. No, not for a woman like Charlotte, who lived by the code of genteel poverty.

Charlotte was not destitute, and food was plentiful, but there was just never enough money for life's little luxuries, for things she could not raise or make herself. Learning to make do with essentials required that one live by certain self-imposed standards, and Charlotte had learned long ago how to do without. Although living by her self-imposed standards held no irresistible appeal, it did give her tremendous freedom to exercise her imagination and creative instinct. On one occasion, years ago, she'd dabbed a little vanilla on her wrists. It was a comment from Archer, later that day, that had turned that flash of inspiration into a habit.

"I swear, Charlotte. You smell good as apple pie."

So each morning, when she busied herself in the kitchen. Charlotte took the little brown bottle of vanilla down from its place on the spice rack and dabbed a little on each wrist and behind each ear. From time to time, when she was feeling more frisky than

115

usual, she dabbed a little between her breasts, as she had done this morning.

And Walker could smell it clear across the room—vanilla and warm, damp skin. He could think of little else. It caught his heart. A woman who smelled that good... would she taste as good? He was not a man to be long satisfied with imaginings.

His expression changed as he quit his musings. Charlotte was still standing by the window, putting something—a pie, he guessed—into the pie safe. She looked up and smiled at him, and nearly fell over the kitchen stool.

He laughed. "Have you had much success walking through solid objects?"

"I was just moving it out of the way," she replied rather curtly, then looked quickly away, as if she were suddenly interested in something outside the window.

Walker knew she wasn't really seeing anything. It was one of the things that irritated him—how she seemed never to recognize her own humanness, her own shortcomings, or allowed herself to make a mistake. It was as if she had never been allowed to be a child, but had simply been put here and given nothing but a small space to grow in. And Charlotte had a way of dealing with that lack of nurturing. Over the years she had developed a way of closing herself off and sequestering her thoughts, keeping a part of herself withdrawn and secret. It was this deliberate withholding that tantalized and tormented Walker to the point of insanity.

"Tell me about yourself... about your family."

"My brother, Nehemiah, is my family."

"What about your parents?"

"They're dead."

"I'm sorry. I shouldn't have asked."

"It was a long time ago. It doesn't matter anymore." She lifted the back of her hand to her forehead and brushed away the little curls that lay there.

He was watching her, aware of the exact moment when she closed the doors of her mind against him and entered a world of her own. The hand that had brushed the curls from her forehead now lay against her throat, toying with the button at her collar.

Walker took the small hand fast in both of his and looked down into her face.

"Oh don't, please don't, I'd rather you didn't," she said, trying to withdraw her hand and looking frightened.

"I didn't mean to frighten you." He released her hand, surprised that she didn't bolt from the room. "What are you thinking, Charlotte?"

Her voice was husky when she spoke, and the words were said so softly that he had to stoop down to catch them. "When? Just now?"

He nodded, smiling at her, "Right now."

She smiled back. "Truthfully, I was thinking I'd rather be raking the pigpen than standing here right now."

As if he was pleased by her answer, his smile grew wider. "And before that? Before you discovered that you preferred your feet in slops than having your hand in mine?"

She thought back, seeing her life in retrospect, a stretch of time without the love of a man. She had planned her future to be the same. This man was a step beyond that, something she had not planned to interfere in her life. He was not a necessity like her garden or her livestock. He was a luxury she could not afford. She had touched fleetingly the world of other women, women who had time for flirtation. But she had no time for that. "I was wondering why we don't have some rain. The whole earth seems parched and weary. It's become a test of endurance between the elements and myself. I find I'm beginning to question the sense of it all. Why do I struggle so against something as enduring as the weather? The sun will still be burning constant long after it has bleached my poor old bones white." She turned from the window. "I don't know why I waste my time thinking about it. We've got weeks of sun before the rains come... if they come at all."

"No wind always blows a storm," he said cheerfully. "You'll get your rain and be duly rewarded for your patience."

"The only thing you get for patience is tribulation," she said, turning away from the window.

Walker studied her intently, noticing the way the sun's hot eye seemed to look brazenly upon her, and he was struck by the way her hair absorbed the light. What a mystery the color brown was, somber and discreet like a smile half-hidden, yet as full of energy as a child's laughter when teased by the sun to let its shy nature come forth. A provocative burst of fiery red and subtle gold, her hair had suddenly come alive. *Let me touch you like sunlight, darling. Let me be the one to warm you, to inflame your shy passion.*

This wave of tenderness made him feel just a little sorry for pressing her the way he had. *A woman should always challenge our respect, never move our compassion,* Emerson had written... but then, what the hell did Emerson know? Didn't he also say, *A woman's strength is the unresistible might of weakness?* Walker smiled to himself. Even Emerson must've had his trying moments with a woman.

A woman's strength is the unresistible might of weakness.... It didn't sit too well with him to think that he had pushed a woman to the point where she was uncomfortable around him, or that he had bruised her tender heart with hard words. Those tactics might subdue her and make her comply, but he wanted more from Charlotte. More than just her compliance. But compliance was all he would ever gain by force. By pushing her, he had proven himself the stronger. But like the king who built a throne of thorns, now he had to sit upon it.

There was no point in denying it any longer. He wanted her. From the ruffled eyelet of her petticoat to her collar with its little embroidered flowers at the neck. Charlotte, with her thoughtful brow furrowed with deliberation.

Charlotte, with her slim throat that looked too small to bear the weight of such a heavy coil of hair. Charlotte, in wild pursuit of an obstinate hen, breathless, with the fire of determination in her lovely face. His heart thrummed high in his chest. Her effect on him was not easy to understand, even more difficult to describe. How long had it been since the sharp edge of joy had left his life? Not only joy, but expectation, hope, even satisfaction. When had he felt it last?

He tried to think back, remembering how he felt when he and Riley, as young boys, had stripped off all their clothes and run, breathless and gloriously naked, down the beach; he tried to recall the feeling of awe, bewilderment, and reverence that came over him at his first Communion; he remembered the melting sense of perfect peace after he had his first woman, the staggering jolt of discovering that once would never be enough—all these and more he brought to mind, trying to capture the essence of what he believed dead and incapable of revival, only to find that it all stirred to flight with the slightest breath from a woman who had not the vaguest consciousness of what she had given him, of how much more he wanted.

But Charlotte didn't look like she was even close to giving him what he wanted or, for that matter, giving him much of anything, except a hard time. He had to fight hard against his desire to laugh at the absurdity of it.

Still, a chuckle of amusement slipped out. "You take the cake. I don't think I've ever seen a woman that was as good as you at taking the starch out of a man."

"You've got enough starch for ten men. It's high time somebody relieved you of some of it," Charlotte said, looking like she was primed to go a few more rounds. It was as if she knew what had been going through his mind and was determined to get his mind on something else.

She tried food.

But even as he ate, he couldn't keep his mind off her, or his eyes, either. She was a smart woman. She knew she had been spared, handed a reprieve, and he couldn't hide his amusement as he watched her going after those dishes like her virginity depended on it. In a very short period of time, she had the dishes done, a pan of bread dough rising on the windowsill, and had begun chopping okra, going at it like she had some kind of grudge against that particular vegetable. But he knew it wasn't the okra she was sulking over. He laid down his fork. "Look, if I offended you, I'm sorry."

Her look was suspicious. Apparently he could add distrust to his growing list of sins. "I'm not sure I believe you, Mr. Reed."

"I notice you call your other hired hand by his first name. Why can't you give me the same recognition you give Jam?"

Her blue eyes opened wide enough to catch the light coming through the window, and he saw that her eyes weren't just blue but flecked with gray.

She stared at him, a frown on her face,

then she fixed her eyes on the stove funnel and stood there, pale and motionless. She had had a long, exhausting night of it, and now she was heavy eyed and irritable. Not the best form to be in to match wits with someone like Walker. Hot, tired, and dispirited, she watched him remove the lid from the sugar bowl and add two spoons of it to his coffee. "I never put you in the same category as Jam, but..."

She paused, distracted by the look on Walker's face. He took another sip of coffee and made a sour face that looked like he had just turned wrong side out. Then he grabbed a glass of milk and drank some hastily. When he finished the milk, he looked at her with a dreadful pucker to his mouth.

"What is it?"

"You taste it and tell me."

She took the cup he held toward her and, careful not to place her mouth where his had been, took a big sip, choked, and quickly handed the cup back to him. "Salt," she groaned.

"In the sugar bowl?" he said. "Now, why does that surprise me? God knows it shouldn't."

"Before you get yourself all riled up, I must tell you it wasn't intentional."

"No?" Walker watched the flush slowly stain her cheeks and wondered what she was thinking. "I disturb you, don't I?"

"Yes, you certainly do."

"I wonder why that is. I'm a hard worker. I'm not too ugly, and I'm clean. I always mind my manners and say please and thank you."

She felt like a fool for listening to him, but she didn't say anything. She simply studied him carefully, hoping that she was giving him enough rope to hang himself.

"In fact," he was saying, "I'm a downright handy fellow to have around. See?" He took the sugar bowl from her and dumped the contents into the slop bucket. "There isn't anything I won't do for you, Charlotte."

"I was going to save that salt," she said irritably. "It isn't something we grow around here."

He looked aghast. "What? No salt bushes? And I thought Texas had everything."

She mumbled something under her breath about a fool that thought salt grew on bushes.

"Here, let me fill that sugar bowl with sugar. No! I insist! Let me do it for you." He yanked the canister from her, the lid remaining in her hand, the sugar spraying across the floor.

Charlotte looked irritated, and then downright angry a few moments later. Of course, that was after he'd tried to sweep up the sugar and broken the handle on the broom. Then he tried to show her how the bristled end could still be used for a flyswatter and had swatted a fly, knocking it into the pail of fresh milk. When he'd picked up the pail and headed toward the door, reminding her how much cats liked milk, she'd snarled, "I only have one cat, remember?" Then she'd yanked the pail from him with such force that it spilled.

Get out of my kitchen!" she screamed through clenched teeth.

"See what I mean? Here I always looked at myself as being an all-right kind of man." He returned to his place at the table and, once seated, gave her that infuriating grin. "Even my mama loves me. But you... Whenever I'm around you, Charlotte, I feel there's something wrong with me, that I'm lacking something. And I don't know what it could be."

"You aren't average, Mr. Reed. That's what's wrong with you."

"Average? You want average? You sure don't have very high aspirations if you would settle for average."

"Where you're concerned, I don't have any aspirations at all, nor do I plan on settling for anything. Why can't you stop badgering me? Why can't you just be normal?"

"Average? Normal? Those are interesting words. Almost inspiring. Tell me, what does the *average, normal* male have that I don't?"

"Tact and respect, for a couple of things. Let's face it. You and I are two different kinds of people."

He grinned. "Thank God for that. I'd hate to think I'd found myself attracted to another man."

"See? That's what I'm talking about. A tactful man would have more respect for my gender than to make a tasteless comment like that."

"I respect you. If I didn't, you can bet your bottom dollar I would've gotten more from you than salty coffee." She gave him one of those exasperating looks that she was so good at. He shook his head. "So what would a *tactful* man do? Sit here and look stupid?"

"No. But he wouldn't sit there looking at me with the same hankering expression he has on his face when I serve fried chicken, either."

Or sit here thinking how he wanted to take you in his arms, to awaken your desire with the sole purpose of satisfying it.

"I don't know why I try being reasonable with a man like you. It's pointless."

"Maybe you just haven't tried the right approach. There are times when I can be downright normal." He grinned. "Even average, on occasion."

She cocked a brow at him. "I doubt that."

"It's true, though. If you just played your cards right, Charlotte, you could have me purring like a contented old tomcat and eating out of your hand." He cut his eyes toward her to see if she was listening.

"Tomcats are *never* content." she said. "They're always on the prowl."

He wasn't going to let a little thing like her intellect hinder him. "There's a lot about me you don't know... a lot you could learn."

"I always heard you're never too old to learn something stupid."

He ignored that. "If you tried, you just might find something about me that you liked. What if I told you there was another side of me you hadn't even seen yet? What would you say to that?"

"I'd say I've already seen more sides to you than I care to, and I don't like any of them."

He laughed. "You don't think I'm subtle enough, is that it?"

"You're about as subtle as garlic, Mr. Reed."

She had almost made it through the doorway when a pair of arms came out and captured her. Before she could respond, Walker spun her around and planted a big kiss on her astonished mouth. His eyes were light and teasing, his mouth curved beautifully into a smile. "I'm a happy man this morning, Charlotte, and it's all because of you. Surely you aren't going to begrudge me that."

Before she could answer, he picked her up and whirled her around the kitchen five or six times, laughing in such a childish manner that it was impossible not to laugh with him. He spun her around the room with him until she was laughing so hard that she was crying. Then he put her down. The room was still spinning—so fast that she couldn't catch her breath. She felt exhilarated... like the time her prickly-pear jelly won first place on the Fourth of July. Clutching the back of a chair to keep her balance, she was still breathless and laughing when she heard his laugh-soaked whisper, "Damn, if I'm not feeling almost *normal!*" Then more softly: "You best be on your toes, my girl. We normal men have a way about us."

When the room stopped spinning, she turned around to find the kitchen empty. *Oh, Walker. You're so good at this. No one has your charm and appeal. Is it not enough to conquer? Must you destroy as well?*

It was much later that afternoon when Charlotte decided to take the buckboard into town to see Archer Bradley. She told Walker that she was going to see her brother. She didn't like deceiving him, but neither could she tell him she was going to see the sheriff. He would want to know why. How could she tell him that it was about him? She told him in the barn, when she went for the harness to the buggy.

"Here. Let me harness the mare for you," he said.

She smiled at him without really thinking about it. "Thank you, but I can manage."

"I'm sure you can, but I want to do it."

"I know, and I appreciate it," she said, and catching the look of doubt in his eyes, she smiled wider, then broke into a laugh. "Honest!" One hand came up to her chest and made an X, and she laughed even harder. "Cross my heart!" she said, laughing up at him, her eyes full of teasing, like a child's.

She was laughing and damply flushed from the exertion and heat, her hair was falling down again, and she had forgotten that she had her spectacles on, but he had never seen her so happy and full of life and... yes, beautiful. It was all he could do not to make love to her. Now. Here in the barn. He had to get his mind on something else. What, he did not know.

Seeing the thoughtful look on his face and thinking he didn't understand, Charlotte reached out and placed her hand on his arm. "I've always harnessed the buggy. If I start relying on you, then I'll start enjoying the luxury of having you help me. And I won't always have you here to help."

"No, you won't always have me," he said, his voice strangely hushed. He wanted to take back the words the moment he saw the joyous mirth fade from her eyes. "You're right, of course," he said, turning away and losing himself in the dark shadows of the barn. He wondered if she had any idea just how much effort that had taken.

Charlotte found Archer on the front porch of the jail, his spurs hooked on the railing, his chair tipped back on two legs, and his hat pulled low over his eyes. A fly was making busy little circles around his hand, lighting here and there, and when Archer made no move to shoo him away, Charlotte knew he was asleep. With a shake of her head and a smile, she made her way down to the dry-goods store, where she purchased a modest shirt and breeches for Jamie Granger and a length of white muslin to make herself a new apron.

When she returned to the jail, the sheriff was awake. In fact, he was talking to Nehemiah. Charlotte paused for a moment, her gaze on her brother, wondering why he was scowling at Archer. Apparently they were discussing something that wasn't sitting too well with either of them. When those two locked horns, it was best to stay out of the way. She released a sigh and with a shake of her head continued along the street. Seeing Charlotte, Nemi's face brightened and he threw her a wave before resuming his conversation with Archer.

128

Charlotte waved back and smiled at the only family she had.

Nehemiah. He had been only a boy of fourteen that August day in Kansas when he became a man. It was Nemi who spotted Quantrill's Raiders coming across the wheat field. It was Nemi who helped their mother, Dinah, hide ten-year-old Charlotte in the woodpile and then rode into Lawrence for help. When he returned to tell them that no help would be coming, that Quantrill and his men had nearly destroyed all of Lawrence, it was Nemi who worked for hours with Charlotte to bury their mother. No more than a child himself, it was Nemi who stayed with her throughout the war, working like a man in the fields, not understanding what had happened to his sister, never knowing the horror that Charlotte had seen that day after he rode for help.

But then the war was over and their father returned, crippled and in poor health. Nemi saw the horrible thing their father did the day he returned, saw his sister slip further and further away. When he was seventeen, Nemi left Kansas and went to Texas. When he returned, he found his father dead and Charlotte living alone.

"You're coming to Texas with me," Nemi had said. "I'm making a new life for us, Lottie. I've got a nice spread, a good wife, and a promising future. There's a new life there. Lots of folks, just like us, leaving the scars of the past behind, building something out of the ashes. It's a good place to start over."

He had watched Charlotte, seeing by the dazed look on her face that she didn't absorb what was being said to her. "Don't be afraid, Charlotte. You can live with me and Hannah. You'll like her. She's a good woman."

Over the years Nemi had watched his beautiful sister shrink away from any man who came near her with the intention of getting close to her. She got along fine with older men, and married men, but the younger, unmarried ones she shied away from. More than once Nemi and Hannah had tried to match Charlotte with a suitor, watching her discomfort at being the center of a man's attention even when they were in the room with her.

Now Charlotte shifted the bundle she was carrying to her other hip and returned to the sheriff's office.

"Afternoon, Miss Lottie," Archer said, tipping his hat.

"Afternoon, Archer," Charlotte said.

Nemi nodded in greeting. "Doc said you missed your calling, that you should think about being a nurse."

Charlotte laughed. "If that's meant to give you and Doc free rein to drag every wounded man you come across over to my house, it won't work."

"I'll try to remember that."

"When did you talk to Doc?"

"Yesterday. He's been keeping me posted on your patient's progress."

"Well, he won't anymore because Doc said Jamie was doing so well he wouldn't be back out unless I sent for him."

"That's what I heard. That's why I haven't been back over. Work sure has a way of piling up when I'm on a cattle drive."

"I was just going to ask what you were doing in town this time of day. Hannah will have your hide if you miss supper."

Nemi's face took on a serious cast. "I just got wind of something that doesn't sit too well with me," he said as he watched Charlotte settle herself in the chair Archer had pulled up for her.

"What's that, Nemi?" Charlotte asked.

"One of the Kennedy boys said Archer brought a man to stay at your house."

Charlotte nodded. "You brought a man to my house, too, Nemi, or have you forgotten?"

"A wounded man—not one awaiting trial for murder," he said with a frown that was very much like Charlotte's.

"We don't know he's guilty yet," Archer said. "We're ninety-nine percent sure he's Walker Reed, just like he says he is, otherwise Judge Saunders wouldn't have suggested Miss Lottie keep him."

"What I don't understand is why a decent man like Judge Saunders would send a suspected murderer to stay with a woman living alone. Besides being dangerous, it's plain stupid. What's to keep him from walking off, free as a bird?"

Archer was primed for that answer almost before Nemi had asked the question. "Well, for one thing, Judge Saunders put fifty thousand dollars that belongs to Walker Reed in the bank. A man would be a fool to ride off and leave that kind of money, and Judge Saunders figured Miss Lottie of all people would be safe from Walker. After all, she did save his life."

"Just the same," Nemi said, his eyes narrowing, "I don't like it."

"Well, you may not like it, Nemi," Archer said, "but there sure ain't a damn thing you can do about it."

That comment was one that would cause Nemi to get his stinger up, Charlotte knew, so to keep the peace she tried to smooth things over. "If it'll make you rest any easier, Nemi, Mr. Reed isn't staying in the house. He's staying in that little cubbyhole out in the storeroom, and he's a big help with the chores," she added.

Nemi's frown grew deeper. It was easy to see that he and Charlotte were related. His hair was a shade darker, not the gleaming russet of his sister's but a deep burnished mahogany, but his eyes were identical. "You never complained about not being able to get your chores done before," he said.

"No, but then you never before brought me a dying man to care for, either." Before Nemi could answer her, Charlotte looked at Archer. "What have you found out about Walker Reed?"

"Nothing much. Like he says, he's a rancher from Santa Barbara. Has one brother, a year or so older, who's married."

"Why would he be carrying around such a large sum of money? Do you suppose it's his?" Nemi asked.

"Oh, it's his all right," Archer said. "Apparently the Reeds are well known in California. Seems old Grandpa Reed made a fortune during the gold rush—enough money that the younger generation is hard-pressed to find ways to spend it all."

Charlotte thought of the near poverty they had lived in during the war and the lean years afterward. Even now, fifteen years later, money was scarce as hen's teeth for most people. Life, she guessed, must have been easy for Walker Reed. More than likely he hadn't fought in the war, with California being so far removed.

Noticing the lateness of the day, Charlotte rose to her feet, then stooped to pick up her parcels. She couldn't help but notice that her brother was still scowling. She was wondering what she could say to smooth things over, but Archer didn't give her the chance.

"Where you rushin' off to, Miss Lottie?" he said, standing and reaching for her bundles. "Let me get those for you."

"I can manage, Archer. Nemi looks like he's still got quite a bit of talk stored up inside him, so you might as well stand here and talk until one of you drops from exhaustion." Her eyes traveled from one to the other. Seeing the stubborn way they both stood there, Nemi with his hands rammed in his pockets, Archer squeezing the life from her packages, she realized that this could go on all night. "You're worse than two billy goats that can't decide if they want to butt or back off." She could see that her words weren't helping any. "Well," she said, "I've got to get back. Poor Mr. Granger will be wondering about his supper."

When Charlotte reached for her packages, Archer was jarred into consciousness. "Why don't you let me drive you home? Whatever it is that's eating on Nemi will be here when I get back," he said.

Charlotte threw him a surprised look. "Now, why would you be wanting to drive me home, Archer?"

"Because I might be wanting to ask you to go to Fletcher's barn raising with me," he said, a slow grin spreading across his face.

The color drained from Charlotte's face as she snatched her packages from Archer. "I'm not going to Fletcher's barn raising," she said. "You, of all people, should know that." She turned, crossing the street without once looking back.

Archer stood there scratching his head in confusion as he stared after her. "Now, why'd she say a fool thing like that for?" he asked Nemi. "Why should I know she ain't going to Fletcher's barn raising?"

"Because, buffalo breath, you know Charlotte won't go to socials like that and she won't have a beau."

"Well, why in tarnation would I know a thing like that?"

"You were sweet on her long enough to know that," Nemi said. "And you've been turned down often enough to know better than to ask again." He threw Archer a questioning look. "God a'mighty, Bradley, sometimes I think your pump ain't been primed."

Archer still looked puzzled. "I thought things might be a little different now. She seems friendly enough to me... now. I thought she liked me, thought we were friends."

"She does like you, Archer. And she is your friend. Just don't try to be more than that. I don't understand why she feels the way she does about men, but it's what she wants, and I respect that." Nemi slapped Archer on the back. "Don't look so down in the mouth, Archer," he said, then stepped off the porch. "You just aren't the man to change Charlotte's mind, or you'd have done it by now."

"Do you think there's a man alive who can do that, Nemi? Do you really believe that?"

"Oh, I believe it all right. My sister has a lot of funny ideas about men, but when you get right down to it, she's still a woman."

"I don't know, Nemi. I just don't know if I agree with you. Miss Lottie's a tough nut to crack. I'm not sure there's a man anywhere that can make it across that block of ice she's sitting on," he said.

"Oh, he's around. We just haven't met him yet, but he's around somewhere." Nemi untied his horse, moving to the left side. "I'll be seeing you, Archer," he said, and swung into the saddle.

"Yeah," Archer said, obviously still puzzled by what had happened.

Nemi laughed. "You know, Bradley. You just might've had a chance with Charlotte... if you hadn't been so ugly your folks had to tie a pork chop around your neck to get the dogs to play with you." Nemi kicked the gelding to a trot.

135

As he rode out of town he heard Archer laugh.

"You may be right, Nehemiah Butterworth, but like a steer, I sure can try."

CHAPTER
SEVEN

Charlotte sat morosely on the hard buggy seat and stared at the tracings hitched around the singletree. She had her silent processes going full force, but her face wore an expression that could only be described as inscrutable. Of late, everyone had the irritating habit of misunderstanding everything she said and did, so her feminine shrewdness prompted her to give them as little as possible to grapple with. Blank, emotionless faces were becoming a specialty of hers, particularly when she ruminated on the complications in her life. Nothing was done with diplomacy anymore. Bold as brass, the Triple K boys had ridden into her yard to hang Walker Reed. Brazen as a hussy, Judge Saunders had sent Walker Reed packing out to her place with a court order tucked in his belt. And bold as a burglar, Archer had ridden out to her place with Walker in tow. Even Nemi... to have the cheek to bring that wounded man to her house. And her friend Doc, putting her feet to the fire, making it impossible for her to refuse lodging for Jamie Granger. She couldn't understand why these things were happening to her. But one thing was clear as branch water: She'd had all she was going to take. Someone had overwound the watch. Each little wrong, each insult, each slight and transgression against her stimulated her vocal cords and she began to expound on it. During one lengthy soliloquy that was mostly adverbs and adjectives, Charlotte decided it was because the whole heathen world had a sixes-and-sevens way of doing things.

Life was something Charlotte liked to organize. Over the years she had developed the habit of giving particular periods of her life a title, much as an author would give titles to the chapters of his book. Last week's title had been, "A Rose Between Two Thorns," while the week before that had been, "A Bed with No Pillows." This week's title was causing her some difficulty, however. A ghastly vision of the past week rose in Charlotte's mind— the blessed progress she had made with Jamie Granger's illness, the long sleepless nights, the intense heat, the despicable behavior of men in general. Somewhere between the long sleepless nights and despicable behavior emerged the uncomfortable throb of the strange feelings she felt when she was near Walker Reed. By the time Butterbean broke a sweat, Charlotte had settled the matter of a title for the week: "Milestones and Millstones."

She was so preoccupied with her predicament that she almost missed seeing Jam riding down the road on Rebekah at a drunkard's pace. He waved and Charlotte waved back.

It must be six o'clock, she told herself, because Jam always went home at six o'clock.

Proceeding through the heat of the late afternoon as rapidly as possible, Butterbean moved at a gait that would've put a young horse to shame, Charlotte made up her mind to ignore Walker Reed. When she reached her house and turned down the drive toward the barn, she saw no sign of him. Her disappointment was, she told herself, only because she didn't get the opportunity to ignore him, and there was nothing that irked her more than making up her mind to do something and then not being able to do it. And any fool knew you couldn't ignore someone who wasn't there. There was, she noticed, about a quarter of a cord of wood that had been chopped and neatly stacked by the back door—cut too uniformly and stacked too neatly to be Jam's doing. Apparently Walker had been busy while she was gone.

Charlotte unhitched the mare and led her into the corral, returning to the barn for a measure of oats. When the bucket was full, she closed the lid on the oat bin and turned around, then gasped with surprise. The bucket of oats dropped from her hand, the oval seeds spilling in a golden shower across the packed-humus floor.

"Why are you so jumpy, Charlotte?" Walker said.

"I'm not jumpy. You just startled me."

He laughed. "You're about as jumpy as a cricket on a hot stove."

That comment merely added to the irritation

138

she was already feeling, which was intense enough as it was. She gave him her usual look—the look of a woman who wants you to know that she would rather be anywhere other than standing there with the present company.

Seeing that she was going sullen on him, Walker tried again. "You know, a mule when he sulls will get a move-on if you rook him."

To Charlotte's mind, Walker's comparing her to a sulling mule was the final irritation. No woman in her right mind would allow such a man on her place, much less listen to him make her the object of ridicule, so she didn't say anything. She simply looked at him, one eyebrow raised a little higher than the other, and snorted.

But Walker was unperturbed. "I don't know how you rook a mule here, but back home we poke dry leaves under his tail, get a good grip on the reins, and set the leaves on fire."

By now, Charlotte was so determined to ignore Walker, and so put out because he was making it impossible, that she was looking as cross as a bear that hadn't wintered well.

She reached for the bucket, but Walker was quicker. "I'll feed the mare," he said, expecting her to walk with him and surprised when she turned without a word and stomped outside, leaving him standing there watching after her with an empty bucket in his hand. She was a strange woman, he thought, and refilled the bucket from the oat bin.

After she'd unloaded her packages in the house, Charlotte found Jamie sleeping and hurried to the kitchen to start supper. When she had a pot of vegetable soup simmering on the stove, she went to the garden for fresh tomatoes. It was while she was bending over the tomato vines that she disturbed a wasps' nest attached to the stick used to support the heavy vines. She didn't see the papery nest until she touched it with her hand and felt the stabbing sting of a thousand sharp needles shoot up her arm. Jerking back her hand, she saw that it was covered with wasps. Before she could knock them away, she suffered six or eight stings on her left arm and both hands. Still smarting from the pain of those, she felt another stabbing pain at her throat, and then another, a little lower, at the V of her dress. Soon they were all over her. Leaving her basket of tomatoes where it was, she began slapping frantically, and when that didn't work, she ran to the trough, plunging her hands into the water and splashing it on her face and neck. The water did little to relieve the pain, but at least the wasps were gone. She hurried toward the house, meeting Walker as he came toward her with her basket of tomatoes.

He stopped in front of her. "You left this in the garden," he said.

"I was coming back for them," Charlotte said, trying to keep her voice at a normal tone, despite the pain she was in.

Walker did not move, nor did he say anything. He just watched her, the way she stood before him, small and quiet. The heat had flushed her face and covered it with a damp sheen. Her eyes were bright and staring at him with a dazed sort of look he had not seen before, and felt a slow coiling of desire in his loins. He wanted to touch her, to touch the peachy texture of her cheek, to touch the curls lying soft and damp at her nape.

Charlotte licked her lips against the pain, her eyes dropping to the basket of tomatoes he held. Something pricked at him when she broke their eye contact. He wanted her eyes back on him, wanted to look into the depths of those eyes and see what it was there that made her evade him. He spoke without being conscious that he was doing so.

"The Spaniards, when they introduced tomatoes to Europe from South America, called them love apples. They believed they had aphrodisiac properties." He picked up a tomato and held it away from him, as if studying it intently. "Did you know that, Charlotte? Is that why you were gathering them?" The look in her eyes was wary, yet unusually bright. Her breathing, he could see, had quickened. Her tongue came out again, to moisten her lips.

Walker replaced the tomato and stepped toward her. "You don't have to ply me with love potions, Charlotte," he said in a soft voice. He stared down at her, at the way her white skin gleamed beneath the opening of her dress. Then his eyes saw the red, angry-looking wheal. Then another. And another.

"Have you been in stinging nettles?" he asked. "There's a red—"

When he reached toward her to point at the swollen wheals, Charlotte swallowed a scream.

"Don't touch me," she said, her hands coming up to slap his hand away.

Quickly he caught her wrists, intending only to quiet her alarm, then he saw the wheals on her hands. "My God," he said. "What have you been into?"

"Nothing," she said as she twisted away from him and ran toward the house. For a moment he was tempted to let her go, but the number of wheals he'd seen on her, coupled with the brightness of her eyes and the dampness of her skin, concerned him.

He found her in her bedroom, standing before her dressing table, gasping for breath, her dress unbuttoned to the waist, the collar spread wide. Tiny dots of perspiration glittered on her flushed face. She was holding a small bottle of camphor, trying to remove the lid. Her hands were trembling. He stepped around her, taking the bottle from her shaky hands. "Here, let me."

She looked up quickly, her eyes wide with panic, but she let him take the bottle from her.

"What caused these red marks?" he asked, his hands applying the soothing liquid to her face.

His voice was low and gentle, yet it carried a hint of force. Dazed, she stared at him, indecision thrumming through her brain. The part of her that hurt said, *Let him*, while the female part of her said, *Don't let him put his hands on you*. A wave of dizziness and nausea rolled over her, taking the decision from her.

"Wasps." she said, swaying enough that

142

she had to grip the dressing table for support.

Warm arms closed around her, lifting her from her feet. He set her on the bed, then lit the lantern and brought it close. "If the stingers are in any of these, they'll have to come out. Where are your medical supplies?"

"In the kitchen," she said, in too much pain to watch him leave or even to care about what he was going to do. Her vision was blurred, her head buzzing. She vaguely heard him leave, but she was unaware a few minutes later when he came back into the room.

He picked up her right hand, checking each sting, then rolled up her sleeve. There were nine stings on the arm, stingers in three of them. After he'd removed the stingers, he bathed her arm in cool soda water, then covered the wheals with camphor. He moved to the next arm and did the same thing. There were six wheals on that arm and only one stinger.

He paused for a moment to look at her. Her eyes were closed, but even so, he could tell that she was hurting. His eyes dropped to her fair throat and the wheals marring her tender flesh. Checking, he found no stingers. While applying lotion, he let his gaze drop to her breasts rising and falling with each labored breath. He noticed another red splotch that was barely visible beneath the pink ribbon of her camisole. When his hands touched the ribbon, her eyes flew open, her hands going to his wrists.

"It's all right," he said, maintaining the same gentle but firm tone. "If you can stand to let a wasp bite you there, surely you can stand to let me doctor it."

They stared at each other for a moment. Her hands, gripping his wrists, neither pushed him away nor released him. Finally, after hesitating for a moment longer, she released his hands and turned her head away, her eyes squeezed shut.

Charlotte lay there, her breathing quick and shallow, the blood in her veins rushing to her head like champagne bubbles. She knew why she was so light-headed.

Insect bites had always affected her more fiercely than they did most people—and never in her lifetime had she been stung so many times at once. Still, in spite of her pain, she couldn't help but think that the breathy light-headedness was caused in part by the nearness of the man, the sensation of his rough fingers against her skin, working the ribbons of her chemise that lay between her breasts.

Walker pulled the bodice of her dress farther apart. The thin chemise below did little to hide the swelling of her beautiful breasts. But it was the angry-looking wheals that held his attention. It was difficult to steady his hand, though, especially when he removed the stinger, and the side of his palm pressed against the soft pliancy of her breast. More than once he fought the temptation to slide his palm fully over her breast, but when he saw the pain etched across her face, he wasn't convinced that it was all from the wasp stings.

It was more to remove the temptation to

caress her than to spare her further embarrassment that Walker yanked the bodice of her dress together, a little more roughly than he'd intended. When he finished fastening the last button, he knew her eyes were on him, large and luminous, like those of a frightened animal released from a trap and momentarily paralyzed, not knowing it was free to go.

"You don't like the touch of a man's hands on you, do you?"

"It isn't proper. No woman would—"

"I'm not talking about propriety, Charlotte, I'm talking about a woman's reaction to a man. At first I thought your aloofness to me stemmed from dislike. Then later I decided it was from the natural feminine modesty that arises when a woman finds herself attracted to a man. But I realize I must apologize—I judged you wrongly. It's more than that, isn't it? What you feel is a complete aversion to men. All men. It's not just me, is it?"

Charlotte tried to get up, but he leaned across her, his hands trapping her arms to her sides, his body holding hers immobile on the bed. His eyes held neither a hint of ridicule nor the heat of passion, but a look of genuine concern. She didn't want his concern or his inquiry. What she wanted was to be left alone.

He saw the rimming of tears in her eyes and wondered if he should let things be, but something drove him on, something more than simple curiosity. That he might truly care for her never entered his mind.

"Tell me," he said softly. "Tell me what hap-

pened to you. What made you feel this way?"
When she didn't answer, his voice came back,
stronger: "Who did this to you, Charlotte? Who
made you afraid of a man's touch?"

Thousands of words she wanted to say to
him were jamming her throat, yet all she
managed to say was, "Nothing happened to
me. I just don't like a man pawing me."

"But that's not a normal reaction to a
man's caress, Charlotte. Your revulsion stems
from fear, and I want to know where that
fear comes from. Were you ever—did a man
ever force his attentions on you?"

"You mean like you're doing now?"

Anger flared in his eyes. Controlled anger.
"No, that's not what I mean. I was referring
to rape. Have you been raped?"

"Not yet."

With a mumbled oath he released her arms.
He studied her for a moment, and she saw the
anger melting from him. He didn't say anything for a long time. He just sat there staring at her. Considering. Wondering. Forming
questions, and then answering them. Finally,
he spoke. "We're going to conduct a little exper-
iment."

Her eyes narrowed suspiciously. "If you
think I'm going to lie here while you paw
me—"

Fingers, warm and strangely gentle, came
out to press against her lips, stopping her words.
"I'm not going to paw you, Charlotte. Wherever you got that idea, it's wrong."

"My attitude toward men isn't something
I dreamed up," she said, unable to stop the

tears from spilling over and tumbling down her cheeks.

"What are you talking about?"

"I know what men do to women! I've seen firsthand... what happens when a man gets the look of lust in his eyes."

"You don't know anything about love-making, Charlotte. You couldn't and react the way you do. It's something that's meant to bring pleasure, not revulsion. You've been misinformed, my girl."

"I saw it. I saw it!" she sobbed. "Oh, God, I saw it with my own two eyes." She rolled away from him, drawing her knees up toward her chest, trying to isolate herself in the misery that consumed her.

Walker leaned over her, turned her toward him, and drew her against his chest. When she strained against him, trying to break his hold, he held her more firmly. "The more you struggle, the tighter I'm going to hold you. Relax, Charlotte. Relax. You have nothing to fear from me. But I'm not going to let you suffer this alone."

"I've suffered it alone for years. What makes you think your sudden appearance can change anything?"

"I've already changed something," he said, gently stroking her cheek and wiping away her tears. "You've shared something with me, spent time in my arms, and haven't suffered because of it. Now close your eyes, sweet Charlotte. Close your eyes and stop crying. I won't let you go until you do."

Eyes as blue as bachelor's buttons closed,

but Charlotte told herself that she only did it to escape the uncomfortable scrutiny of his eyes, not from any desire to please him. She lay there, her body tense and stiff, exhausting herself from a constant state of readiness—readiness to bolt the moment he laid a hand on her. And he would. Men were all the same. He would wait until her guard was down, then he would press his case. But she would be ready. Sometime later, however, the alertness of her mind gave way to the weariness of her body and she drifted off to sleep.

She wasn't sure what woke her, but when she opened her eyes and stretched, her hand came in contact with several of Walker's ribs at the same moment as her eyes saw the full length of his body stretched beside her. *Dear God, he's in my bed.* She glanced down to make sure her clothing was undisturbed. With a jolt of indignant surprise, she tried to roll away from him, but he obviously was not asleep, for he pinned her to the bed with his arm, dragging her back to his side. She knew his face was mere inches above hers; she felt his gentle, fragrant breath brushing her cheek. She knew it was coming at that moment, and she braced herself for the rough, kneading caresses of his hands.

Moments passed and nothing happened. In the distance a dog barked, blending with the noise of a trapped fly buzzing against the windowpane. Slowly, she opened her eyes.

"Men are as different in behavior as they are in appearance, Charlotte. You can't blame all men for the mistake of one."

"It wasn't just one man," she said. Her words seemed to cause him pain, and that puzzled her.

"Who were they?" he said, carefully enunciating each word.

"It doesn't matter." She turned her head away to stare at the pattern of bouquets on the wallpaper of her bedroom.

"It matters to me," he said, his hand coming from nowhere to cup her chin with infinite tenderness and turn her face back to his.

She would never be able to explain just why the words came tumbling out—slowly at first, then so rapidly that she was unaware of what she was saying. "The raiders," she said softly. "During the war, in Kansas."

"Quantrill's Raiders?" His words lay somewhere between a question and a statement—tentative, yet possessing a glimmer of understanding.

"Yes," she said in a breathless whisper, feeling the tears seep from her eyes. "The raid of Lawrence—that's where we lived, my mother, Nemi, and I. My father and my two other brothers were fighting somewhere in Georgia."

"How old were you?"

"Ten. Nemi was fourteen."

"Tell me what happened—what you saw that day."

"I can't." Her throat seemed to be filling with tears, leaving her unable to speak in anything but a faint whisper. "I've never told anyone, not even Nemi."

"But you can tell me," he said plainly.

She was so surprised at the calm effect his words had on her that she stopped crying.

"What you saw that day—was it something they did to your mother?"

"Yes."

"Where were you?"

"Nemi saw them coming and ran home, through the cornfield, to tell us. There wasn't much time, so they hid me in the woodpile, stacking the logs around me, then Nemi took the horse and headed for town to get help, but she was dead before he got back."

"Did you see them rape your mother? Is that what happened?"

She froze. She couldn't tell him. She couldn't. But somewhere deep inside, something hard and painful was swelling, and she felt the need to tell someone, to share what had happened that horrible day with another living person. She had carried the secret too long; the burden of it was too heavy. "They didn't rape her," she said in a flat tone. "It was worse. Much worse."

"Worse? Merciful God! How can you do worse than rape?" His tone was still gentle but now revealed the confusion he felt. "In what way?" he asked. "How was it worse, Charlotte? What did they do to your mother?"

"They desecrated her body." She was crying again now, her hands over her face, trying to drive back into the deep shadows of her mind the pictures that ran like blood before her eyes. But the words had a will of their own. Like a volcano they poured forth, hot and painful, impossible to stop. "They tore her clothes off, and when she fought them, they hit her and hit her until she fell. Then they took their belts off and strapped them around her ankles and wrists and tied her to the ground, and then one of the men said she would be sorry she didn't want them between her legs, because when they finished with her she would wish for what they had offered her."

Her sobs were coming in uncontrolled waves, blocking her words. Walker pulled her against him, rolling to his side and taking her with him, her head cradled in the crook of his arm.

"Let it out, Charlotte. Don't keep it inside any longer. Release it. Give it to me." He stroked the back of her head. "Give it to me. Tell me what happened, Charlotte."

"They put sticks inside her—inside—where a man would leave his seed. She screamed and screamed, but they kept doing it until she didn't scream anymore. Then they rode away."

"Dear God!" he said, rocking her against him. "Dear merciful God. What a horror for anyone... much less a child." After a moment he said, "They never saw you—never touched you?"

"No. After they left, I dug my way out. I didn't want anyone to see her like that, so I put her clothes back on her and waited. When Nemi came back, he said Quantrill's men were killing everyone in Lawrence and we wouldn't be getting any help. But we didn't need any help then. We buried her together."

Walker held her for a long time, his hands

stroking her gently. When he spoke, his words were tender and gentle, as he was. "I want to show you something, Charlotte. I want to teach you you don't have to fear all men because of the actions of a few butchers. Trust me." Then, when she didn't respond: "Can you trust me?"

"Yes."

"Good. I'm not going to touch you, but I want you to touch me. No, don't pull away. Put your hand on my face—just my face. Go on."

When she hesitated, Walker took her hand in his and placed her open palm against his jaw, holding it for a fraction of a second, then releasing it. "I'm going to close my eyes, Charlotte, and I want you to close yours as well." He closed his eyes. "Are your eyes closed?"

"Yes."

"Now, pretend you're blind. Using your hands, I want you to tell me what I look like."

"I can't," she said. "This is silly."

"So is throwing oatmeal at a grown man. But you did it, and you can do this. Now describe me, Charlotte. Here, I'll help. Find my nose and tell me about it, but resist the temptation to pinch."

She couldn't hold back a small smile. Slowly her other hand came up to join the one touching his jaw and together they moved to his nose.

"Well?"

"It's not too large—for a man's nose. The

top is slender, but there's a knot just below the eyebrows—like maybe it was broken."

He chuckled. "It was. My brother Riley has a hot temper."

"Your brother broke your nose?"

"Not intentionally, but we're getting off the subject. Are your eyes are still closed?"

"Yes."

"Tell me about my eyes, Charlotte."

He felt her stiffen, but he held his features expressionless, not wanting her to feel his reaction. "Just my eyes, sweetheart. Tell me about them."

It was such a simple request, much like a child would make. She hesitated for only a moment, then felt her way to his brow. "Your brows are thick, almost touching each other. You aren't very old, because I don't feel any wrinkles."

He chuckled again. "That's because I'm lying on my back."

"Do you want me to finish this game or not?" she said, as much to her surprise as his.

Her lips quivered with amusement when she felt his brows rise in astonishment.

"I want to finish. Go on."

"Your lashes are long and curved—thick, too. Your eyes aren't too deeply set. Your forehead is wide and smooth; I think that indicates intelligence. Your face is rather squared, and your chin has a small cleft. In all, I'd say your features were very refined and pure."

A surge of triumph made him want to put his arms around her and kiss that mouth that was doing all that talking. She had done what he had hoped. She had become comfortable enough to venture on to the other areas of his face—all except one.

"What about my mouth? Did you forget that?"

"No, I didn't forget it. I think we've done enough for today."

"Just my mouth, then we'll be finished. Surely you aren't going to let one mouth stand between you and success?"

Tremors rippled across her and she wondered if he could feel it, but he made no move, said no words. A slow throb of heat seemed to pass from his warm lips through her fingers to spread like wildfire through her body. She knew he was holding his breath, and that told her that he wasn't taking her simple exploration lightly. Somehow, the knowledge that her touch was affecting him, too, brought her a sense of pleasure coupled with fascination. Slowly, she allowed her fingertips the freedom they desired. His lips were firm and dry beneath the fleshy pads of her sensitive fingertips.

He allowed her a length of time before he spoke. "Tell me, Charlotte," he said softly. "What does my mouth tell you about me?"

She felt the crease at the outer corners of his mouth and said, "You smile a lot."

He smiled beneath her exploring fingers. "What else?"

"I think you have a good disposition, you're basically happy, and—"

"And what, Charlotte?"

"Sensitive," she said, remembering the feel of his warm breath across the top of her hand.

"My mouth tells you that?"

"Yes."

"How?"

"Your mouth is full and soft, not hard and rigidly held. The lower lip is fuller than the upper, and to me that speaks of sensitivity."

He said nothing else, gave her no further instructions, and after a moment she ventured a peek at him. He was lying perfectly still, his face relaxed and without emotion or expression beneath her hands. Because she had succumbed to his desire for her to touch him, she had expected some emotion to be present—pleasure, self-assurance, supremacy, arrogance, pride—but she saw nothing save a deep pensiveness, as if he too was trying to come to grips with what had just passed between them.

This did not fit the picture she had sketched of him in her mind, and certainly not the picture of men in general she had carried with her since that August day in 1863. Was he right? Was there no need to fear all men because of the actions of a few?

Of course Charlotte knew that not all men were guilty of such heinous crimes as Quantrill's men were. Her fear of men stemmed from her certainty that all men were capable of such crimes. The discussions of neighbor women over the years, at quilting bees, church socials, and the like, had supported that fear. She had never heard even one woman speak about pleasure and happiness between her and her husband. But Charlotte had heard plenty about the insensitivity, cruelty, domination, and possessiveness of their men, not to mention the descriptions of the act of copulation. Men used women for their pleasure, rutting like animals. They were all guilty of it—and yet...

She did not like the direction of her thoughts. She had lived for seventeen of her twenty-seven years convinced of men's inhumanity to women. She did not want to be told different. She did not want to be proven wrong.

She suddenly became aware of his gaze. How long had he been watching her? What had he read in the emotion she was sure her face had shown? With her lower lip quivering, her voice hesitant and unsure, she asked softly, "What do you want me to do now?"

"Whatever you like," he said, watching her intently. "What would you like to do, Charlotte? You have my complete agreement on whatever you choose."

"I want to get up," she said, thinking that was probably not one of her options.

"That too," he said, pushing away from her and rolling to the side of the bed. In an instant he was on his feet and through the doorway.

Abruptly, and without a word, he had granted her wish, but as Charlotte lay listening to the crickets chirp, she was thinking that his absence wasn't really what she wanted.

She saw the indentation where he had lain

on her bedcovers, and she placed her open palm on the center, where the indentation dipped the most. It was still warm and somehow vitally alive with his presence. She rolled over, lying on the place where he had lain, wanting the feel of him pressed against her. But she felt nothing but the wrinkled bedcover.

Curiosity overcame her, and she wondered why he had left so suddenly. She rose from the bed and walked to the window, drawing back the ruffled edge of the curtain. In the last glow of the sunset she searched the yard and outlying buildings for a sign of him, finally locating him at the well.

He was drinking from the dipper tied to the post that supported the small roof over the open well. He was close enough that she could see the streams of water that ran over the sides of the dipper and down his tanned throat to disappear beneath his shirt. Then, with some exclamation she could not hear, he tossed the remaining water away and thrust his hands before him to brace against the crossed support beams, his head dropping low between them. He remained that way for a long moment, then abruptly he straightened. Without warning, his hands fisted, and she watched in awe as he pounded his fists repeatedly against the rough beams and shouted something that sounded a lot like, "Why?"

CHAPTER
❧ EIGHT ❧

The *Farmer's Almanac* predicted rain. The Widow Peabody's bad back predicted rain. The farmers gathered around the pickle barrel down at the general store talked about it. So did the ranchers taking shots of whiskey at the Dust Devil Saloon.

In fact, as befitted its importance, everyone in Two Trees was talking about the weather and how it was acting mighty peculiar—and how that was the cause of the unaccountable things that were happening around town.

It was blamed for Mrs. Mercer's peach tree blooming out of season and for pranksters stealing Flax Johnson's longhandles off the clothesline and putting them on Clem Robinson's billy goat. It made someone drink Floss Dexter's home brew sitting on his back porch and refill the jug with liquid blacking, which caused Floss to give Mr. Dent, the barber, a busted lip when he couldn't get the blacking off Floss's teeth. It was the reason why Maybelline Scott was shocked by her electric corset, and why her husband was shocked as well. The odd weather even caused mild-mannered Mrs. Selby to lose her temper—for the first time in her sixty-year marriage—and to raise a goose egg on Mr. Selby's bald head with a teakettle. And everyone in the whole county knew it was the reason why Carmine Random gave Buster Brewster's ring back.

Yes, the weather was queer, and consequently the townsfolk were acting peculiar.

Even the animals were carrying on and behaving curiously. Twice this week Mrs. Brewer's mama sow had dug her way out of the pigpen, and Stumpy Whittaker's mule turned white overnight. Down at the livery, the horses were off their feed, while over at the Thatchers' place the hens weren't laying.

Yes, everything predicted a change in the weather. But still it did not rain.

On the edge of town, at Charlotte Butterworth's place, the sun was suspended overhead—a glaring molten ball pasted in a cloudless sky, scorching everything below. Intense, throbbing, and without mercy, it beat down on the backs of Walker and Jam as they pushed themselves beyond endurance to rake the last of the cured hay and heap it into rounded stacks. In this kind of heat, cut hay did not take long to cure. And if all the predictions about rain came true, they didn't have very long to get their work finished.

"You can't keep up this pace," Charlotte had shouted at Walker that morning as he and Jam left for the field.

"If we don't, you'll find yourself short of hay this winter. We've already cut and turned. If it isn't stacked before the rain hits, it'll rot. Is that what you want?"

Charlotte had looked at him for a moment and then shaken her head. There wasn't any use in bickering with him about it. If he wanted to kill himself making hay, he would kill himself—with or without her permission. There was stubbornness in him. A streak a mile wide and twice as long, but there was strength, too. Strength and determination and a tenacious spirit. He would never give up. Not when he believed in something or knew he was right. She couldn't begrudge him that. Not when she knew the same was true about herself.

"I'll help you," she'd said then.

"No, you won't. A woman has no business in the fields. That's a man's work. Besides, you've got Granger to see to, chores around here that need tending." Seeing the disappointment on her face and feeling he had spoken too harshly, Walker had added, "You could bring us some lunch so we won't have to lose time coming in and going back out."

She had given him a half-smile. She wouldn't give him a whole smile because he hadn't let her come with him. No, a half-smile was all he'd gotten, and that was only because he had gone out of his way to make her feel that she was included. But no matter how right he was, or how much sense he made, or how much he had gone out of his way, she had still been just a little miffed. So, the half-smile had been a weak one.

Several hours later, Walker paused, leaning against the handle of the rake, and pulled his handkerchief away from his neck to mop the sweat from his face. He pushed back his hat and glanced at his shirt hanging on a fence post. Not five minutes ago when he'd hung it there, it was dripping wet, but now it was bone dry—just like he was. He threw back his head and looked at the sun—a slow-moving devil that made him wonder if it had fused itself to that particular spot overhead.

Jam was working on a row about twenty yards away and was raking a new stack. Walker's eyes, red and tired from a full week of dust and bits of flying chaff, surveyed the field. It would take six men a week to do what he and Jam had done in the same amount of time. He reflected on the past week, trying to pinpoint exactly what it was that had made him so determined to stack all the hay in this pasture in such a short period of time. Part of it was the anticipated rain, but that wasn't the only reason. He glanced across the field. The main reason was coming through the gate right now, a basket swinging from her arm, her red hair reflecting the brilliant sunlight and leaving him feeling as if he'd been staring at the sun too long.

She was no more beautiful than a dozen or so women he could name, poor pitiable creature that she was, yet there was something about her that stirred him, brought forth emotions and responses he hadn't ever felt before. Charlotte was something tangible, something solid and dependable he could reach out and touch, knowing she would be there. Other women he had known always possessed a certain amount of elusiveness, which had intrigued him. Until now. He began to understand it, for to Charlotte, life wasn't a game, something to be toyed with and trailed along like a sash dragging in the dirt. The need to survive, the fierce determination to beat the odds so heavily stacked against a

161

woman supporting herself and living alone—
that was crucial to her. Few women possessed
that. It shocked him to realize suddenly that
his mother was that way. Walker thought back
through the years that the strong hand and
bountiful wisdom of his mother had guided
him. His father had been the image for him to
model himself after, the one to instruct him in
the ways of a man as well as the ways of the
world. His father had given him much, but it
was his mother who had touched his heart. No
other woman had done that. Until now.

He squinted against the sun to bring the shimmering image of Charlotte into sharper focus.
She was real, all right. As real as the dryness
that sucked at his throat, and the dust that
burned his eyes, and the tightness in his chest
whenever he looked at her.

Walker had to fight the lunatic desire to laugh
that came over him suddenly, bewildered
that it should take *this*, of all things, to smite
him with Cupid's sharpest arrow and bring
him swiftly to his knees. He knew the beauty,
the fragility of what he had found, and the
improbability of finding it with anyone else.
But he knew honor, too. Honor. So simple to
say, so difficult to uphold. Honor. That heav-
iest of words. The most binding of bonds.
Honor. A mortgage on the soul. A man always
met his obligations, kept his word, held himself to an ideal of conduct, regardless of the
cost to himself. His father had taught him that.

*"Why must I have honor, Father? It's only a
word."*

"If you toss out such words as honor, integrity,

honesty, and principle, Walker... if you tag them useless, you toss away the qualities they express as well. Remember what your mother read to you the other day from Whittier?"

"Was it about honor?"

"Yes."

"I don't think I remember."

"Yes, you do. We talked about how a man can be alive and yet be dead."

"Oh, I remember that. When you lose honor, you die inside."

" 'When faith is lost, when honor dies, the man is dead.' "

Later, when he had talked of this to his mother, she had stroked his cheek.

"Your father is an honorable man, Walker, and it is a good thing to be. But you must also be true to yourself. Wisdom and virtue are like the two wheels of a cart."

Was he using wisdom here, in dealing with Charlotte? Was it wrong to hide his compassion for her under a hard shell? Was he ruthless in wanting to show her there was more to life than being born crying and dying disappointed? *What are your real motives here, Walker? Careful, my man. Don't involve yourself too much. Don't make yourself such a shelter that you eclipse the sun. Remember what we have here: a few short weeks at best. Don't let your admiration and pity develop into too much affection, for affections are difficult to end. And end, this must.*

Was it pity he felt for her, then? Pity and not compassion? For lack of a better word, he had called it compassion. How else could he explain his overwhelming desire to ease the pain and misery in her mind—an old wound, unhealed and still releasing the poison left there by the brutal actions of a group of men more animal than human?

He watched her make her way toward them, her skirts lifted in one hand, her steps quick and dainty, as she wove her way through the small mounds of hay to bring them their lunch. Even from this distance he could see her discomfort, sense her insecurity. Charlotte could handle a casual friendship with a man, but since that time, over a week ago in her bedroom, she had gone out of her way to avoid any real contact with him. It didn't ride too well with Walker that he was the force that had caused this change in her attitude toward him. He had hoped his actions would put her at ease around him, but in essence the opposite had happened. Perhaps he deserved it. Perhaps she was too old, too set in her ways, too scarred emotionally ever to change, ever to see that all men weren't the same, that some could even be trusted. Trust. It was the one thing Charlotte did not have. It was the one thing Walker wanted to give her.

But he had not succeeded. Had he taken unfair advantage of her? Guilt inched its way into the back of his mind. He tried to erase it by telling himself that she was a pathetic creature and he was only trying to help. But he hadn't helped. Not really. *Let that be a lesson,* he told himself. *Leave Miss Charlotte Butterworth with her wrong feelings and distorted views of mankind. Haul your ass back to California and leave her to her manless existence with a future no brighter than her past.* He could see it now, stretching drearily before her like an abandoned country road that covered a lot of miles but went nowhere.

But Walker wouldn't go back to California. Not until he finished what he had set out to do. He didn't know why, but he felt a sense of commitment. He couldn't go back, yet he wasn't sure how to progress. Somehow he had to gain Charlotte's trust. For some unexplainable reason, that was important to him. And not just because she had saved his life.

As he watched her draw closer, saw the hesitation in her step and felt the uncertainty in her eyes, it occurred to him just what he could do. She had given him back his life. He would do the same for her.

"I hope you've got something wet and cold in that basket of yours," he called as she came near.

Her smile was shy. "Only cool water from the well. That's all Jam will drink when he's working in the fields, so naturally I just assumed... that is..."

"You were right. Water will do fine," he said, mopping his face once more before retying the kerchief around his neck.

He reached for the basket and lifted the checkered cloth to see what was inside, which gave her time to study him. Walker, sweating from the day's labor under the baking sun, was bare chested and brown as a biscuit. She had seen only two men bare chested—her brother and Jamie Granger—but neither of them had that exact symmetry of line and curve, the smooth, harmonious blend of hard muscle. As Walker poked around inside the basket, Charlotte watched the network of muscles across his chest, upper arms, and shoulders. Her stomach felt strange. *It must be the heat,* she told herself, and took the bonnet that was dangling from her arm and placed it on her head, not bothering to tie it under her chin.

She looked at him again. He had moved to one of the raked piles of hay and was placing the basket in a nest he had hollowed out. Tall and slim hipped, he stood with his back to her, the sun a fiery ball blazing down on his naked brown back. Even from this angle, his body spoke of boldness and something she could only call a primitive rawness, something that made her think of how splendid he must look completely unclothed. Like a work of art. Nothing to be ashamed of, but something to be admired. She looked away quickly, hearing his low rumbling laugh.

"Aren't you afraid your skin will burn if you don't wear a shirt?" she asked, hurrying into conversation before he could say anything about catching her looking at his nakedness. "Where's your shirt?" she added, glancing around for it.

"Hanging on the fence post over there," he said, pointing. "And no, I'm not afraid I'll burn without my shirt. I'm used to the sun." His eyes were brilliant and sparked with something that passed across her skin like a caress as he studied her. Then he added, "Would you prefer I wear my shirt?" Before she could answer, he turned away. "I'll be right back."

She watched him lope across the field like a lanky jackrabbit, going to the fence, yanking his shirt from the post, and loping back. By the time he reached her, he was fastening the last button.

"No gentleman would ask a lady to dine with him when he wasn't wearing a shirt," he said. "I apologize if I offended you, Charlotte."

"You haven't offended me." The man was so smooth. He made even a simple apology sound sensual. A quick glance at the crystal clearness of his eyes told her that he wasn't making light of her, nor was he trying to make her uncomfortable. Everything about his manner and speech bespoke sincerity, yet she couldn't have been more aware of him as a man if he had stripped his pants off as well.

He moved to sit on a pile of grass, he had bunched together. "Would you care to join me?"

"I've got my lunch waiting back at the house," she said, sounding a little distracted.

"I would share mine with you."

"No. Please. Go ahead. I really couldn't eat right now. I'm too hot." *And you're too distracting.* "Besides, I need to take Jam his lunch." There was something quite diverting about the way the perspiration dripped from his hair to meander in thin little trickles down the tanned column of his throat and disappear beneath his blue cotton shirt. She rose, taking Jam's lunch in her hand.

"Will you come back after you give Jam his

lunch? I have something I want to ask you."

At first he thought she would refuse, then turning away and heading toward Jam, she said, "I'll be right back."

When she returned, he was looking at her, still sitting where she had left him, his colors vividly alive against the sloping dome of sun-sweetened hay rising behind him. She had to fight the urge to run to him, much as a child would, throwing herself against him, sending them both tumbling into the hay. Her throat was dry, her expression unsure, her confidence flagging. *You're a fool, Charlotte. He isn't for you. A man like this... experienced... beautiful... He could have so many women.*

Walker was surprised to see her return, even more surprised to see that she didn't stop several feet away but walked much closer, stopping a scant few feet from him. He could have reached out and captured those slim ankles that rose above heavy, unflattering shoes. "Would you sit with me while I eat? You've nothing else to do while you wait for us to finish, have you?" He looked up at her, a chicken leg minus one bite gripped firmly in his right hand, his smile wide and strong, his eyes squinting against the ruthless sun, and she wondered at the beauty of him. What would it be like to have this man belong to her? To have him spend the rest of his life looking at her like this... She remembered something she had read to Jamie the other night, still feeling embarrassed because Jamie must have known that the passage struck her deeply and he'd erroneously thought it was because of him. But as she'd read the words of Byron, " 'Tis sweet to know there is an eye will mark/Our coming, and look brighter when we come," she'd been thinking only of Walker Reed.

Charlotte remembered the feel of his face under her fingers and wondered if the rest of him felt the same way. The memory of the proud flare of his nostrils, the texture and surprising softness of his lips, seemed to hang in the back of her consciousness, heavy like an anvil. She wondered what his lips would feel like pressed against her own. She looked at his mouth, wide, firm, and oh, so sensual, and wondered what stories that mouth could tell. Stories about the women it had kissed, the endearments it had whispered, the number of women it had pleasured. With a small gasp of alarm, she realized where her thoughts were leading. She was growing too accustomed, too familiar, too comfortable with this man.

"Is something wrong?" he asked.

"What? Oh, no. No. Nothing is wrong. An ant—there was an ant on my arm, that's all."

He was quiet for a moment, his eyes dark and inscrutable as they watched her. "It's a good thing you noticed it. It would be my guess that any insect bite would affect you the same way as a wasp sting, and we both know what happens when you are stung by wasps."

The gentle reminder of where the two of them had ended up after her episode with the wasps was not lost on her. She remembered. She remembered considerably more than she wished.

169

"Come on," he said gently, his hand extended. "Sit with me."

The lure of that smile, those eyes, the genuine tone of friendship in his voice—they all served to overpower her hesitation. She placed her hand in his and let the strength of his arm balance her as she settled herself on the tufted mound of field grasses he had prepared for her.

Her eyes went wide as his shadow passed over her, but then she noticed that he was only reaching behind her to rearrange the hay to give her back support. *He's got me jumping at shadows.... Does he really want my company?* She folded her hands in her lap and stared down at them in embarrassment.

A long stem of grass came out of nowhere to tickle her nose, invading her consciousness. Around her everything was intense and hot, and so very still and silent. She was so aware of everything around her, acutely in touch with her senses. She felt gauche and foolish, insecure and unsure of herself, and as transparent as glass. She didn't know what to do. *Why don't you try talking? Say something. No, don't talk. If I talk, he won't be able to eat.... True—but if he isn't eating, he'll have time for other things....What other things?...Whatever things he enjoys doing— besides eating and drinking.* Charlotte's heart thumped madly. She had read once that men had three simple but basic drives: the need for water, food, and sex, in that order. The moisture gathered at the back of her throat was swallowed with a loud gulp. She looked at the food. She looked at the water. *What should I do now?* The only advice she could remember ever receiving had been from Nemi: *"Don't talk back. Keep the wood box filled. Don't stake the cow where she'll eat wild onions."* And none of those seemed to apply here. *This is ridiculous. Walker isn't going to do anything out here, in broad daylight. No man is that desperate to steal a lady's virtue.* She looked at him. He was a man who could steal flies from a spider. He could have any woman he wanted. Just for the taking. If she caught his eye.

Now, Charlotte knew she was no raving beauty, but her face wouldn't sour buttermilk, either. And there was definitely something that made Walker aware of her. She began to fidget and to smooth her skirts.

Walker was feeling as keen as a briar, just watching her fuss with her skirts. A slow, knowing smile crossed his face, matching the spark of humor in his eyes. She was so painfully honest. Even with her expressions. His gaze rested at the V of her dress for a moment, then he looked up to her face. "Now, isn't that better than standing?"

The warmth drained from her face like rain sliding off a tin roof. "It would be better if you would release my hand."

He should have kept in mind her revulsion at being touched by a man. Her smiles, her humor, her witty comments were all directed at him because he was a human being, not because he was a man. Instantly, he released her hand. Then, to distract her, he said, "I know most people call you Miss Lottie. Do you mind my calling you Charlotte?"

"No. Why would I object to that?"

"I don't know. Sometimes I get the feeling there are a lot of things that you take exception to around me." Seeing the angry glint in her eyes, he grinned and patted her hand, careful not to prolong contact. "I'm only teasing you, Charlotte. Relax."

She quickly looked away and saw that Jam was up and moving along the rows of cured hay. He was almost out of sight. "Are you almost finished? I've a mountain of ironing waiting in the kitchen."

"I am," he said quietly.

She turned back to look at him. He met her look, his expression one she had not seen before. " 'Miss Lottie,' " he said thoughtfully. "I don't think it really suits you."

Would you rather call me Miss Butterworth?" she asked in a rather caustic tone.

"No. That isn't appropriate either.... There's a part of you that, at times, *is* Miss Lottie—warm, friendly, caring. Sometimes you can even be *Miss* Charlotte—proper, ladylike, dignified." He made a sound deep in his throat like he did when he was amused. "Why, I've even seen a glimpse or two of stuffy ol' Miss Butterworth."

She smiled. "And how do you see stuffy Miss Butterworth?"

He laughed, falling back against the large haystack, and tucked one arm behind his head. The other hand he extended toward her, palm up. "Take my hand, Charlotte."

"No."

"Take my hand in yours and I'll tell you."

Frowning, Charlotte shook her head, but there was nothing in the relaxed way he was

172

lying there that made her afraid of him. Quite the contrary. He looked so good when he was relaxed like that. Laughing. Alive. Open. Harmless. The more she studied the palm opened before her, the more she recognized it for what it was, a symbol of friendship and mutual understanding. He wasn't making fun of her. He wasn't forcing her. He was asking her. Leaving the decision to her.

Finally, after long moments, she placed her hand in his strong, brown one. She fully expected his hand to close over hers, and the moment their flesh touched she felt a scream collecting in the back of her throat. But he did not grip her hand or even hold it tightly. He merely closed the tips of his fingers over hers, ever so lightly, and began to stroke them gently.

"So tell me," she said. "Tell me about Miss Butterworth."

He closed his eyes. "Ah, Miss Butterworth, the spinster—she never wants you to forget that, you know."

"She doesn't have time for nonsense."

He opened one eye. "She's too damn proper."

"She has too much work to do."

He opened the other eye. "Ah, yes, the last place to hide—good old respectable responsibility."

"I don't have time for foolishness."

"Why not? It's perfectly natural, and not against the law. I don't know of anyone that's ever caught the plague from it. And it's one of the few things you can enjoy for free.

There are no laws, man's or God's, that call it forbidden. It's only your mind that does that for you, Charlotte. It's your mind that's afraid to find pleasure in life."

"Pleasure is like an itch. Scratching only makes it itch more."

"No, Charlotte. Pleasure is like stored wine. If you wait too long to taste it, you'll find it's gone sour."

"Well, I think it's too late for me. I feel like I'm the last bottle left on the shelf."

He was grinning now, and he leaned over and kissed her hand lightly, then fell back against the hay. "Ah, 'the daintiest last, to make the end most sweet.' "

She smiled, shaking her head. "It's impossible to be serious around you when you're like this."

"Like what? Reciting Shakespeare, or just being my usual charming self?"

She laughed. "Both. And you're a rascal and a scoundrel for bragging so. I think your mama must have spoiled you terribly."

"She did... still does. It's the secret of my attraction."

She threw a handful of hay at him. "Oh, shut up and tell me about old Miss Butterworth, you spoiled charmer." She hugged herself, laughing.

Perhaps it was the heat of the afternoon, or even the oddity of the weather, that made the moment magical, as if some field fairy had sprinkled them with enchanted pollen and bewitched the moment. She suddenly felt young and silly, and as protected as a rabbit in a fur-lined burrow. So beautiful it was, she was sorry to hear him speak, afraid his words would chase away the golden spell.

He said her name painstakingly, as though it were a new word he was trying to learn, one he wanted to remember. "Charlotte."

Her laughter vanished. She felt vulnerable there, out in the open. She was aware of him and only him: the way the sun seemed to come from inside his hair, a bloom of cheerfulness and ecstatic rays of color, rich and warm; the eyes, bluer than a field of rainwashed bluebonnets, the lashes thick and dark by comparison; but it was his lips, beautifully shaped, soft yet firm, capable and elusive, that warmed her tender heart. But a warning went off in her head. *This man is slicker than a boiled onion, Charlotte. And he's coming after you like a cat goes for clabber.*

"Now, where were we?" There was a puzzled tone to his voice.

"You were going to tell me—"

"About Miss Butterworth, the one that wears spectacles only at home and wears white gloves to town, and puts so much starch in her dresses that they can stand up by themselves. And no one but Miss Butterworth would dare to name a horse Butterbean."

She laughed, unable to help herself. Then she stopped suddenly and looked at him. His gaze was clear and steady. A faint breeze had stirred, drying the sweat on his face, giving him a more somber look. There was something terribly disturbing, a sense of inquisitiveness, that distracted her. It lodged in her stomach like too many green figs.

Desire shimmered clear in her blue eyes. Walker felt his muscles knot. "That," he said ever so gently, "is what I've known all along."

"What?"

"That there's another side to you, a side you keep hidden." He rolled to his side and turned her palm up, tracing the outer perimeter of each finger before moving to her thumb and then to the fine etching of blue veins that crossed her wrist. A moment later he curled his fingers around hers warmly and lifted her hand to his mouth, where he kissed the inside of her wrist.

Charlotte tried to jerk back her hand, but his hold was firm. "Close your eyes, Charlotte. Close your eyes and feel my hand touching yours, feel the touch of my mouth on your wrist, and tell me to release you."

He kissed her wrist again. Softly. And only once. His hold was light enough that she could have pulled her hand away if she had desired, but, for some reason she could not explain, she did not.

"Tell me to release you, Charlotte."

"I can't," she said, trying to reclaim her imprisoned arm.

"Do you want me to release you, or do you want me to tell you about the other woman I've discovered? You can't have it both ways, Charlotte."

He stared at her, at the way her head was thrown back, causing the yellow sunbonnet to fall away from her head and revealing all that glorious ginger-colored hair. Little Miss Muffet, and he the frightful spider. *Ah, sweetheart, if you really knew what I was feeling for you right now, you wouldn't look at me so damned innocently.* He had to fight against taking her in his arms and pulling the pins from her hair and pressing her back against the hay. *This isn't any easier for me than it is for you, darling. Help me to remember it's your mind I'm trying to soothe, not your body.* Her throat was slender and gracefully curved, like a swan's, and just as white. *So very innocent. A little lamb to my wolf. Can I do this? Can I give you what you need by denying what I want?* He felt a rush of warmth and was flooded with a tender feeling for her—another sentiment he could not remember having felt for any other woman, save his mother.

"What is your other name, Charlotte?"

Her eyes opened, blue and confused. "What?"

"Tell me your full name."

"Augusta. Charlotte Augusta Butterworth."

"Ah," he said, his eyes closing as he brought her hand to his mouth for another kiss. "Augusta. Augusta the venerable. The missing woman. Augusta the undeclared one." He opened one eye, studying her intently, then grinned widely. "No. Not Augusta. Gussie." He drew back to look at her as if discovering the hidden personality. "Gussie with the alabaster skin and titian hair—a paradox. A tragicomedy. She walks. She talks. She throws oatmeal. But she has known pain. She suffers still." Stroking the back of her hand with his fingers, he smiled, as if to ease the moment's severity with lightness. "She would like you to think she is all manners and starch, but that's only on the outside. Inside, I'm guessing, is a woman of fire, hidden away and hoarded like a golden coin."

Charlotte had no warning. One moment she was sitting there with her eyes closed, her chin resting in her hand, listening to his words, warm and sleepy in her ear like the lazy drone of a bee. The next thing she knew she was lying back against the fragrant, newly cured hay, Walker Reed's long, hard body aligned perfectly with hers. For the briefest fraction of a second she lay there, her breasts pressed into his chest, her thighs pinned beneath the ridged muscles of his legs, her mind not fully registering that she was supposed to feel revulsion.

Slow awareness began to build at the back of her mind, but still she did not move, waiting instead for him to make his move so that she could classify him, as she did all men. Long seconds passed. The heat was growing uncomfortable, perspiration becoming the bonding agent that held her clothes plastered against her skin. A slow trickle of sweat began at her temple and then curved to drop into her ear.

"I'm not going to do it, you know." His voice was low, vibrating.

"I never thought—"

"Oh, but I think you did. You're wearing your martyr's face, Miss Butterworth—waiting patiently for me to assault you, to use you to my advantage so you can smugly slap my face and say you knew the kind of man I was all along."

"You don't know what you're talking about. I wasn't—" She stopped, squirming beneath him, her eyes searching the horizon in a helpless manner for Jam. Not seeing him, she said, "What must I do to convince you you're wrong? I wasn't—"

"You may be afraid of men, but you're still a woman with a woman's intuition and a woman's wiles."

"None of this is my fault. I never asked you to squash me flatter than a pancake in the middle of a haystack."

"No, you didn't. The fault was mine. You simply lay there, neither willing nor resisting— a temptress. You were baiting me, waiting like a patient spider for me to become hopelessly ensnared, and then, when I made a move toward you, you would slap me in the face with it."

"That's not true!"

"It's true and we both know it," he said. "In a way, I'm pleased that you feel comfortable enough with me to try it. Tempt me if you wish. Bait me if you must. But remember this: I won't ever hurt you, Charlotte. But I am a man. If you approach me as a woman and I respond to you as a man, don't ever use that against me. Don't play games with me, Charlotte. Not now. Not ever."

He watched the slow accumulation of tears that lay like a casket of shimmering jewels in her lovely eyes. Her lips quivered, and he had never felt the urge to kiss a mouth as greatly as he did now. "Do you understand?"

"Yes," she said softly. "I won't play games with you."

Attempting humor he did not feel, he said, "Then give me a kiss." When she looked at him in a shocked way, he laughed. "Kiss me, Gussie." And then, ever so gently: "Please."

"I can't."

"Yes, you can," he said. "A week ago you didn't think you could touch me, either, but you did. This is no different."

"It's a great deal different and you know it."

He grinned. "Ah, Gussie, are you so experienced, then?"

"You know I'm not, but neither am I a fool. I know there's more to kissing than two sets of lips colliding with each other."

His eyes filled with humor, then softened, his tone becoming husky as he leaned over her. "It will only be what you want it to be, Gussie. I asked you to kiss me. How, and for how long, is entirely up to you."

"That's terribly considerate of you."

"Where you're concerned, I try to be considerate. But even my patience can run out. I asked you to kiss me. It's up to you. You'd give water to a dying man, wouldn't you?"

She eyed him suspiciously. "That's a pitiful comparison."

He shrugged. "I know, but it's the best I could do with such short notice. Now, are we going to kiss or spend the rest of the afternoon talking about it?"

"You won't force me?"

He looked hurt that she would ask that. "You should know by now... Oh hell! No, I won't force you."

"You'll let me stop whenever I want to?"

"Dammit, Gussie! I asked for one damn kiss, not the convening of Congress. If you don't hurry up, we're both going to die of heat stroke."

She looked into his face and saw his steady blue eyes. Suddenly he rolled away, resuming his position on his back, once again folding his hands behind his head. "See, I'll even make it easier for you. Harmless as a babe in nappies, I am."

Charlotte was thinking that Walker was about as harmless as a bull at breeding time, but in spite of that fact, she moved closer to him, like a tiny brown wren, nervous and fluttering. "Close your eyes," she said, her face a few inches from his. "I can't do this if you're watching."

She fully expected some teasing jab and was taken by surprise when his eyes blinked once, then closed. Leaning farther toward him, she closed her eyes for a moment, becoming familiar with the smell of him that mingled in a most pleasant way with the scent of cut grass and sweat. As if she had done this a thousand times, her lips found his, one quick touch, no more than the brush of a moth's wing against a pane of glass, then a second time, and when he made no move to grab her, she placed her mouth more fully against his. Confused shocks of reaction shuddered across her body and a tightness crushed her chest.

She felt the heat from his body, the caress of his breath, shallow and fast, against her skin. Soft and warm and dry was the feel of his lips against hers, molding perfectly to her own. Although her heart was pounding painfully in her chest and sending the blood slapping against her ears like floodwaters against a dam, she felt immediate frustration.

She was neither repulsed nor satisfied, and this she found baffling. She let her mind wander through her limited resources, which included kissing, but never having been kissed in a romantic way by a man, she could only draw to mind pictures of Nemi and Hannah. What she could remember of their kisses wasn't much, but she did remember one thing: They didn't stand there with their lips pressed together like two pieces of flypaper coming in contact with each other.

Slowly. Experimentally. Charlotte moved her head, feeling the texture of his lips as they passed beneath hers. With her mouth she felt the ridge of the outer extremity of his lips, the deep cleft where the two halves joined. He was right. This was like touching his face with her fingers, only better.

Charlotte was doing her best, but her best was a pretty poor imitation of the real thing. She knew that one should do something with one's mouth besides letting it stand in readiness like mounted troops waiting for the call to charge. But what? Frustration was eating away at her. Why didn't *he* do something? What was he waiting for? But she knew the answer: force. Walker wouldn't take from her. Not unless she gave.

The knowledge that he was waiting for her went straight to her head. Pressing forward against his body, she whimpered as his hand, warm, gentle, and coaxing, lifted, then curled around the slender nape of her neck. As she felt the slight increase of pressure against her mouth, her lips parted slowly, in awe of the hopeful expectation that bloomed within her. She wanted this kiss. Wanted it with every fiber of her being. Just this once, she wanted to know what it was like, wanted to understand, at last, the mystery of a man's mouth moving with desire against her own. His hand was gently caressing the lower part of her neck, stroking the nape with sure fingers, then spreading delightfully through her hair. Everywhere they touched, she was burning and alive. Coaxed gently, she parted her lips, allowing the curious tip of her tongue to explore more fully the mystery of the lips that parted beneath her own. The moment her tongue slipped between his lips, she felt his reaction by his indrawn breath. Evidently Walker hadn't learned to master his respiration, either.

Heat suffused her, the source of it seeming to lodge in her stomach, spreading like the penetrating rays of a sunburst. Never again could she say she had never been kissed, or deny the slow, sleepy seduction of desire. Desire. She felt it now, and Walker must have felt it too, for his breathing was harder now.

She wanted him.

"Does this make you uncomfortable, Gussie?" he whispered, his tongue edging her earlobe, his breath murmuring a message of its own.

"Yes."

He didn't stop, but continued doing what he was doing so well. "Are you sure?"

"I..." she breathed as his tongue encouraged her, "I think so." Sure, determined strokes parted her lips, and his tongue told her what words dared not. "Walker, are you kissing me now?"

"I'm trying my damnedest, Gussie, if you'd shut your adorable mouth and let me."

She closed her mouth and her eyes, feeling the alien hardness of his thigh against her legs, the firm press of hard desire against her stomach. He buried his face against her neck, kissing her throat with a gentleness that seemed out of step with the sizzling hunger of his body.

Here came the magic again, heavy and golden, a sprinkling of fairy pollen. His fingers stroked her face, his lips tracing the curve of her cheek. "Soft as a baby's breath. I've dreamed of this sweet little mouth of yours kissing me like this, but the dream is nothing like the reality," he said, and gently kissed the tip of her nose. "Easy, sweetheart. I may be kissing you, but you're still in control." His mouth dragged over her lips, back and forth, a gentle exploration that possessed an element of the unbearable. She was dissolving around him, absorbed by the touch of his mouth on hers. Her hand spread against his chest, she felt the warmth of him, the wonder of lean, firm flesh over a heart that thudded in time with the breath that came too rapidly. Breath mingled with breath, his mouth moving more fully against hers now, wider, searching, his tongue touching, encouraging her, while his fingertips curved around her throat in a manner so arousing that the urgency of it sang in her blood. Everywhere he touched her, she felt it like a burn. She felt her hands grip him, digging into his flesh, as if she were afraid of falling away. And Walker responded to that with a swiftness he hadn't planned on. *Oh, lady, sweet, sweet lady... I want you.* His hand came out of nowhere to cup her breast.

She wanted him, but she was afraid.

Suddenly opening her eyes, she pulled away, looking at him in a bewildered manner as her eyes focused. He made no move to touch her, or even to speak for that matter, but merely stared at her for a long, long time, then with a movement so swift that it startled her, he rolled away and sprang to his feet. In one quick move he pulled her up and thrust the basket into her hands.

"Thanks for the lunch."

A reply hovered in the static air between them, but before she could utter it, he turned away and picked up his rake, and with his back to her he began raking the cured hay with sure, swift strokes.

For what seemed to her an eternity, Charlotte stared at him. At last, when he was far down the row, she gave a sigh of frustration and turned toward the house, her basket swinging on her arm. But the old restlessness, the unease, went with her. She tried to rationalize things, to see herself as she really was, to see Walker as he was. Whatever trusting comfort she had felt in his arms was only because he had willed it. But in the end, he had shown her, by one simple act, that she wasn't woman enough to hold his interest. He was obviously accustomed to striking a woman like lightning and then leaving her smoldering, but she wasn't equipped emotionally to handle a love-'em-and-leave-'em attitude. If Walker had told her anything with his cold, cutting words, it was that she wouldn't have to worry about him anymore. Obviously, he did not enjoy kissing beginners. That he would tell her in such a heartless manner was galling and embarrassing. And she was angry at herself for taking so long to recognize it. If she hadn't been so surprised and confused, she would have known immediately. And then she could have whacked him over the head with his stupid rake. The more she walked, the angrier she became.

She was no longer hungry when she reached the house, so she washed her face and hands and made her way to Jamie's room. He was sitting up, his lunch tray balanced on his lap, but his head was tilted to one side, his breathing deep and untroubled, his eyes closed. Charlotte tiptoed across the room and lifted the tray ever so gently, so as not to wake him. Just as she reached the door, he spoke.

"I'm not asleep. I was just catnapping."

She turned around. "How are you feeling?"

"Much better now that I've got something as pretty as you to look at. You seem to heal me much faster than any of that foul-tasting medicine Doc left."

Never having received many compliments, Charlotte didn't know how to take one when she did receive it. Her composure ruffled, she felt the heat of self-consciousness steal to her face.

"I didn't mean to put you on the spot. It's just that I've never had anyone look after me the way you have. You've plain ol' spoiled me, and I probably won't be worth a plug of tobacco by the time you tell me to hit the road."

Charlotte looked aghast. "Why, I would never do that. You're welcome to stay here for as long as necessary."

A slow-spreading grin split Jamie's face, and his eyes took on the twinkle of those of a schoolboy about to dip a girl's pigtail in the inkwell. "You better watch what you say, Miss Lottie. I might just find it necessary to hang around here indefinitely."

Charlotte knew he was teasing, of course, but his words still made her shy—besides, he needed his rest. "I wish I could stay and visit, but that pile of ironing won't do itself."

"I had my heart set on a game of cards. Are you sure you won't reconsider?"

She shook her head with a smile. "I've got ironing spread all over the kitchen. I can't start supper until it's finished and put away."

"You're a stubborn woman, Miss Lottie. Making a poor helpless man spend his afternoons with no one to talk to."

Her voice rich with humor, she said, "Helpless, my little finger! Are you sure you aren't a politician? You could talk a tiger out of his stripes. I do have to finish my ironing, but if you'll take another catnap, I'll hurry. Then we'll see about cards."

"That would be just peachy, Miss Lottie. Just peachy, indeed."

She sailed through the door like a feather on an updraft, Jamie's eyes following her. He thought about all the coarse women he had known down in the valley and how Miss Lottie was like none of them. She was a real lady. As fine a lady as any he'd seen in Kansas City. He imagined what she would look like dressed in the latest fashion, with a hat weighted down with feathers and a saucy little parasol twirling over her shoulder. He carried the thought of that with him as he closed his eyes. A few minutes later he was asleep.

It was almost time to start supper when Charlotte finished her ironing. After putting away the neatly pressed stacks of flatwork, she stood for several minutes at the back door, her hand rubbing the stiffness from her spine while she waited for a cooling breeze. The ironing had taken longer than she'd expected. There really wasn't time for a game of cards, but she had promised. Besides, there couldn't be much harm in delaying dinner for just a little while. There weren't many times she was given the opportunity to play cards.

Hurrying to her room, Charlotte slipped out of her dress and poured a basin full of cool water. After a quick sponge bath, followed by a liberal dusting of her best talcum powder, she slipped into a pale pink-and-white gingham dress with white embroidery along the collar, then hurried to her parlor, where she located the cards in a tin Nemi had given her several years ago. When Nemi had given it to her, it was full of horehound candy. The candy was long since gone, but the tin was still useful, and Charlotte never disposed of anything that was either a gift or useful. Suddenly she felt very young. All work and no play. So much for schedules. So much for supper. So much for spending your life doing what was expected of you. Just once in her life she was going to do something for the pure satisfaction of doing it because she wanted to. Feeling no more than twenty-two, Charlotte skipped lightly down the hall and into Jamie Granger's room.

CHAPTER
❧ NINE ❧

The kind of attention Jamie Granger showed Charlotte over the next two weeks made her feel lighter than one of her soda biscuits, and she made the lightest soda biscuits in all of west Texas. Charlotte tried to avoid Walker Reed, which wasn't as difficult as she had thought it would be. Since that day in the hay field he had made himself scarce as hen's teeth. Of course, that thought made Charlotte's conscience take a few nibbling bites at her. Walker's absence around the house wasn't really all his fault. The new sucker rod for the windmill they had ordered out of St. Louis had finally arrived, and Charlotte had intentionally assigned the job of replacing it to Walker just to keep him out in the pasture. When he arrived at her house each evening for supper, he was too tired to give her much trouble, and besides, she spent very little time in the kitchen with him—her nightly card games with Jamie being the primary reason.

On this particular evening, Walker caught Charlotte in the kitchen before she had time to scamper away for her nightly ritual with Jamie.

As usual, she was toiling over her Monitor stove, pots simmering and lids rattling as thin spirals of steam rose in her face, tugging wisps of hair loose from their moorings to curl in tight abundance about her face. The heat brought more color to her face, and the steam caused the bodice of her dress to cling, forming an outline of her breasts.

That was the sight that greeted Walker when he stepped into the kitchen. He wondered if anyone had ever told her she was lovely, and would be even lovelier if she would smile more often and yank those confining pins from her hair. Watching her fuss over supper caused a powerful need to rise within him, a need to protect her, to bring some life and sparkle into her drab existence, a smile to those perfectly shaped lips. But she had been cauterized at an early age and formed her life around that painful event. There was no place for a man in that numbed domain. He understood it, but he was finding it harder and harder to live with.

"I'm finished, Miss Lottie."

The sound of Jamie's voice grated on Walker's nerves and he stepped farther into the room. "Evening, Gussie."

Charlotte gave him a chastening look. She had given up trying to stop Walker's irritating new preference for calling her Gussie, having resigned herself to chastening looks. "I'll have your supper in just a minute, but I need to get Jamie's tray."

Walker watched her rush from the room. Charlotte might fool herself into thinking she was infatuated with that oaf in the front bedroom, but Walker knew better. She felt safe around Jamie. Safe and flattered by all the idiocy that rolled out of his mouth every time he opened it. And it was just as well. Riley should be here soon and he would have to leave her. She was a tempting little witch, but there was just too much depth to her and his time was limited. He would do what he could in the time he had. He hoped it would be enough. She was beginning to ride pillion in his mind, invading his dreams with the memory of her shy touch, the timid exploration of her lips, soft upon his. That was dangerous. They were worlds apart. But somehow, the thought that he might be waking Charlotte to a new realm of sensuality for a man like Jamie Granger to enjoy sat about as well with him as after-dinner dyspepsia.

His eyes lifted to the doorway when he heard her approach. She entered the room much in the same rushed manner as she had exited, only this time she was carrying a tray. When Walker saw the small crystal vase with a bunch of her prized snapdragons in it, he couldn't quell the irritation that began swelling like gout within him, growing even worse when he glanced at his place set at the table and noted that there wasn't a snapdragon in sight.

"What? No snapdragons for me, Gussie?"

Charlotte set the tray down much harder than she'd intended. "You have two perfectly good legs that are more than capable of carrying you to my front yard, where you may look your leisure at my snapdragon bed. Jamie, on the other hand, has been confined to bed day after day. This is the first day Doc has allowed him to get up. Are you begrudging an injured man a few measly snapdragons?"

She gave him her most severe look, which evidently worked, because he said no more, but turned and took his place at the table. Charlotte thought the sight of a grown man sulking quite unbecoming, so she slopped up his collard greens and ham in a hurry, shoving the plate before him. "I promised I'd help Jamie to the front porch. Do you need anything else before I go?"

"Nothing I can't get for myself."

Charlotte nodded, picked up a pitcher of

tea punch and two glasses, and walked out of the room, leaving Walker with the sound of her swishing skirts ringing in his ears. A few minutes later she returned for the cake.

It was pleasant on the porch in the evening when the blistering sun was nothing but a harmless red ball on the horizon. A cooling breeze always lifted about this time of day, ruffling through the jasmine leaves and stirring the scent of flowers. Charlotte had never spent much time on her front porch rocking and sipping tea punch, but since Jamie's wounds had begun healing and Doc let him out of bed, she wanted it to become a habit.

She considered it her good fortune to have a man of Jamie Granger's caliber convalescing at her home, a man who could talk at length about Byron, Shelley, and Keats, and not only talk but quote them by the hour. She couldn't help but remember when she had asked Walker Reed if he was familiar with Byron, Shelley, and Keats, and he had sarcastically replied, "Don't they make saddles in Wichita?"

Listening to Jamie's praise for her bismarck cake, after he'd eaten four healthy slices, Charlotte found herself smiling more and more, in spite of herself.

"I'd be happy to write the recipe down for you to take with you when you leave."

"The thought of leaving you is as painful as that gunshot wound," said Jamie.

"Painful or not, it's something you must face. I'm sure your ranch won't run itself indefinitely."

Jamie returned his glass to the table next

to his rocking chair and reached for his pipe. "Do you mind if I smoke?"

"Not at all. My father smoked a pipe. I've always loved the smell of one."

Jamie plugged the pipe with tobacco and then lit it with three long draws, exhaling the smoke slowly. Charlotte pushed back in her rocker, closing her eyes and inhaling the faintly cherry-flavored smoke. Jamie's voice startled her.

"You're right, of course. I do need to get back to my ranch. Things will be tight for a while. I had counted on having the money from this last drive to do some expansion, but I guess that'll have to wait awhile."

"Nemi says the cattle boom hasn't got much longer. Do you think he's right?"

"Without a doubt. There'll always be a market for cattle, but the big boom we knew after the war won't ever return. Every year I think that will be my last drive. Before long we'll be shipping our cattle by railway. Too many cities. Too many farmers. Too many fences."

"It'll be sad to see it all go," Charlotte said, watching a solitary lightning bug blink in the distance.

"Yes," Jamie said pensively. "Yes, it will. Kind of like seeing the South die. Painful, but little you can do to stop it."

"Are you from the South?"

"Georgia originally. We were wiped out, lost our land, our homestead. One of my brothers stayed there, but me and my younger brother hung out our 'Gone to Texas' signs and hightailed it." He paused. "What about you? Did you grow up in the South?"

She didn't answer right away. "No. I was born in Virginia, but my family moved to Kansas when I was a baby. I had three brothers. Two were killed in the war. My mother died before the war was over. My father returned home crippled and in poor health. He died soon after his return. Nemi sold our farm and moved us to Texas."

"Why haven't you ever married, Miss Lottie?"

"I never wanted to."

"I see."

No, you don't, Charlotte wanted to scream, but she didn't. Quiet settled, the sound of two rockers creaking, the yelp of a coyote occasionally breaking the stillness. She thought of Walker in the kitchen eating alone and felt a stab of guilt.

"I hear a buggy," Jamie said, his rocker stopping suddenly.

Charlotte's stopped, too, and soon she heard it, the steady clip of a horse, the unmistakable sound of buggy wheels cutting through the thick layer of dust that covered the road. She looked up, seeing the sharp black outline of a buggy, like a silhouette against the blood-red sky. It was Doc Tyree who drew up in front of Charlotte's gate and, tying his mare to one of the pickets, came up the walk.

He left his bag in the buggy, so Charlotte thought this was a social visit. She offered him some of her bismarck cake and tea punch.

"Don't mind if I do," Doc said, eyeing the

cake. "Make that a healthy slice while you're at it." Charlotte smiled. Doc had never eaten anything that wasn't a healthy slice.

While Doc ate, he quizzed Jamie about his wounds, the falling price of cattle, and the weather. "Sounds like you're healing faster than I expected. Far as I'm concerned, you can strike out whenever you feel up to it. No point in hanging around any longer than you have to—except for Miss Lottie's cooking."

"That's why I keep looking for another ache or pain to keep me here a little longer, but now that she's heard it straight from the horse's mouth, I guess I'll have to start making plans to return home."

Doc and Jamie went back to discussing his wounds, how serious they were, how they might affect him in the future, and how lucky he was that Nemi had found him when he did and how much luckier he was that Nemi had had the sense to bring him to Charlotte's house.

"How are you getting on with that other feller that's staying out here—Reed's his name, isn't it?"

"Yes. Walker Reed," Jamie answered. "He seems nice enough, but I have to confess I don't see much of him. He's stopped in a couple of times just to chew the fat, but I suspect Miss Lottie is keeping his nose to the grindstone."

"Smart woman to take advantage of free labor when she can get it. I heard Sheriff Bradley say today that he received another wire from Reed's brother. He was in Phoenix last week. Said he'd send another wire when he reached El Paso. I guess he'll be leaving before long." Doc pushed his glasses back on his nose, "What'll you do, Miss Lottie, when all these visitors of yours pack up and go?"

Be lonesome, she wanted to say, but she didn't. Instead, she rose and began gathering the dishes and glasses, stacking them on the tray. "I'll probably have a lot less laundry and cooking to do and more time to work in my snapdragon beds," she said, stepping into the dark hallway. Bidding Doc good night, she walked back to the kitchen, feeling a twinge of disappointment when she saw that Walker had washed his dishes and slipped quietly away.

Doc and Jamie were still talking, but somehow the magic of the evening had vanished for Charlotte, so she washed the dishes and went to her room and, in the darkness, lit the lamp. Then she removed her clothes, washed her face, slipped her gown over her head, and moved to the window, pulling back the curtain. A faint light glowed in the small window in Walker's room and she wondered what he was doing. She stood there staring at that small yellow square of light, then with a weary sigh she dropped the curtain back into place and turned to her bed.

Sometime in the middle of the night the sound of a horse snorting woke her. Charlotte heard the softly muffled sound of a horse walking not far from her window. After slipping from her bed and searching the nightstand for her spectacles, she moved to the window. A dark figure on horseback approached the barn and rode inside. She had no idea who the man was, but he had no business in her barn. She grabbed her wrapper from the peg behind her door and slid her feet into her slippers, then hurried to the kitchen, where she yanked her Winchester from the shelf and tiptoed outside.

The cool dew-covered grass brushed against her bare legs. By the time she reached the barn, the hem of her gown was heavy with moisture. She stopped for a moment just inside the barn, allowing her eyes to adjust to the darkness, her ears waiting for the slightest sound. Faint noises were coming from the other end, near the last stall. Quietly she picked her way along the corridor, and just as she drew even with the door to Walker Reed's cubbyhole, a hand, warm, strong, and tasting of horses, whipped out of the darkness to close around her mouth. She found herself yanked hard against a body, the fumes of whiskey nearly rendering her unconscious.

Charlotte fought against the intruder, trying to free her mouth. If she could only scream, Walker would hear, but the brute holding her had arms of steel. The next thing she knew, he had wrestled her to Walker's door. Kicking it open, he threw her across the bed, pinning her there with his leg while he lit the lamp.

"What the hell are you doing out here half-dressed at this time of night?" Walker said.

"Walker Reed," she said between gasps

for breath, "you are drunker than Cooter Brown."

"And what if I am, Gussie?"

"Are you crazy? Don't you realize I could've shot you? Why would you want to do a fool thing like going into town and getting drunk? If you need a drink, I've got a bottle Nemi left in the kitchen."

Walker was looking at her strangely, then he released her. Charlotte rolled to the side of the bed and sat on the edge, pulling her wrapper tightly around her. She was suddenly aware—very aware—that she was in Walker's room, on Walker's bed, indecently dressed, and that Walker was a very drunk man.

"Whiskey wasn't the only thing I went to town for, Gussie. Surely you know that."

She looked at him with a curious expression, but then, something about the way his eyes raked over her caused slow recognition to dawn. Realizing what he had obviously found in town struck her like a swift chop to the throat. She was speechless. But then she imagined him with one of the lovely but wicked women who worked at the Dust Devil, kissing her, touching her, and she found her voice.

Springing to her feet, Charlotte said, "I understand perfectly why you went to town, and you were right to do so. There is certainly nothing here that would fill *that* need."

Walker saw the look of disgust and bewilderment on her face and it made him sick inside. He saw her duck her head and walk around him. Without realizing it, his hand shot out, going around the soft, slender upper arm and yanking her against him. She was so close that he could feel the terrified pounding of her heart against his chest, feel the flutter of her quickened breath against his throat. He looked at her then, her glorious hair wild and fragrant around her face, her eyes angry and covered with spectacles.

"Why, Gussie, you're wearing your spectacles. Is that to get a better look at me?"

"You overplumed peacock, I hope I never see you again!" she said, yanking her glasses from her eyes and thrusting them into her pocket. The fumes of whiskey were still making her dizzy, the musky heat rising from his body serving only to make it worse. A wave of light-headedness swept over her and she placed her hand against his chest to steady herself.

"Gussie... ah, Gussie. What's wrong, love?" Walker said, pulling her closer against him and cradling her head against his chest.

"Please don't. I don't feel very well. I want to go inside. I'm going to be sick."

"Sweet Gussie, I adore your love talk."

"Please. I want to go."

"I'm afraid I can't let you do that, Gussie. You were wrong, you know. There is something here that will fill my need, and you damn well know it. Let me make love to you, Gussie. Lie with me. Let me show you how it can be. Let me show you just how beautiful it is between a man and a woman."

For the flash of an instant she felt herself beguiled by his whiskey-soaked words, but then she imagined him saying those same words just a short while ago to some other woman, and she felt the slow curl of revulsion twist in her stomach. "I'd rather lie in slops with a pig than get in your bed," she said. "Let go of me."

Charlotte forced herself to look into his eyes, willing him to see that she knew the truth, knew he was nothing more than a silver-tongued devil who would seduce her and leave her without batting an eye, but when she stared into the deep blue of his eyes, she felt the strangest pull. She wanted to step closer to him instead of move away.

Walker saw the confusion in her eyes and lifted a finger to trace the satiny contour of her cheek. "Gussie girl, don't you know the dangers that can befall a young woman who wanders around in her nightie at night?"

She wanted to say something clever and experienced, but all she could manage was, "No, but I'm sure you do. I'll thank you to restrain yourself and stop the after-hour visits to town—as long as you're staying here." She wasn't even aware of what she'd said, so fascinated was she with Walker's mouth. There was a certain animal allure that stirred something responsive deep within her. The wonder of it made her remember the feel of his mouth beneath hers, and she found herself wishing that he would shut up and kiss her.

He stepped closer, and Charlotte thought her wish was about to come true. "I work here, Charlotte. You do not own me. What I do on my own time is my own business. Now, if you want to hop in that bed with me and give me what I've been going to town for, I'll be glad to stick to this place like glue. Otherwise I'll get drunk and pay visits to the ladies when I damn well please, and I'd advise you to keep your smug little nose out of it, or I just might be tempted to give you a sample of what you're so hotly criticizing."

He stared at her, the vivid blue of his gaze raking the smooth perfection of her lovely face, the proud thrust of her chin, the flush of peachy color across her high cheekbones aroused by his reference to what it would take to keep him from straying. Her look of derision cut through him, though it was not visible on his controlled features.

Charlotte stood straight and quiet, the soft orange glow from the lantern catching like drops of heated amber in her hair, dusting the purity of her features like a priceless overlay, and giving the blue of her eyes a depth and defiance he had never before seen. As his eyes dropped lower, he saw that the glow seemed to penetrate the fine weave of her wrapper, illuminating the porcelain smoothness of her throat, which the wrapper and gown did not cover. The pale oyster color of her bedclothes was illuminated in such a way as to form a golden nimbus that touched her with a degree of angelic wantonness.

Walker's eyes were intense and pleading as he stared at her. Deep in her eyes, he could see the hurt that his words had caused her, although her countenance bespoke only confidence. The muscles along his jaw rippled.

Charlotte felt a sudden tightening in the vicinity of her heart. "Then go, by all means. But remember this. The next time you do go, take your things with you, for you won't be coming back here. Court order or no court order, I'll have no fornicating womanizer hanging around my place." The look she gave him then was so cold and cutting, it knifed into him, her words burning like fire the tender wound left by her hurtful stare. "As you're so good at telling me: It's your decision. I won't *force* you." She turned to go, his hands warm and throbbing on her arms.

"Gussie—don't," he said tenderly. "Not like this. Never like this." His hands moved to her shoulders with infinite tenderness and a thread of underlying strength, then slipped lower to circle the slimness of her waist, his fingers spreading flat against her back to draw her against him. His quickened breath brought the fumes of whiskey to her nostrils, and the stubble along his chin scrapped her temple as he bent his head to brush the sensitive skin of her neck with his lips.

"Stop it!" she said, her breath quick and painful. She pushed against him with a sharp little twist, trying to free herself, but he held her firmly.

"What's the matter? Are you afraid you might enjoy this thing that leaps between us whenever we're together?"

The low vibrations of his voice and the warm lure of his breath against her cheek were threatening to overwhelm her. With the spirit of an experienced woman she tossed back her head to glare at him, her hair spilling over his arms in a fiery fall. "Just because all the women you've known fall into your arms like ripe apples doesn't mean I will do the same. Falling for your obvious seduction is the last thing I'd do, especially now that I know you and understand what motivates you."

"And what might that be, Gussie?"

"Stop calling me Gussie, and stop trying to distract me. I may be inexperienced, but I'm not stupid. I have a mirror and I look in it daily. I know my limitations. I am not a beautiful woman—never have been, never will be. I am neither wealthy nor young. I am a mousy spinster, well past my prime and horribly set in my ways, and the topping on that piece of cake is that I wear spectacles." She pulled her spectacles out of her pocket and positioned them on her nose.

And such a cute little nose, too, Walker thought. Could it be that she really saw herself as mousy? He wanted to take her in his arms and kiss the doubt from her adorable mouth, but he decided to ride this one out, just to see where it would end up. "What do you think is the motivation behind my attraction to you, then?"

"Intrigue and nothing more. Just intrigue. I'm obviously cut from a different bolt of cloth, a different breed of cat, and that engages your interest to a certain degree. But like a child who's fascinated with a ball of yarn, your interest would wane the moment you had me all unraveled."

The smile that lit his eyes soon found its way

204

to his mouth. "Aw, Gussie, I could spend the rest of my life with you and not have you unraveled, but the idea of having half a chance to do it holds a certain appeal for me." He grinner wider. "I can think of nothing I'd like more than to see you unraveled. Shall we start now?"

"You're despicable—"

"But you like it."

Her mouth pinched and quivering, she stood poised before him like a wary animal, cautious but determined. With a slight adjustment of her posture, an elevation of her head, and a straightening of her back, she said in a voice dripping sarcasm, "Why is it that the levelers in the world always want to bring everyone else *down* to their level, instead of elevating themselves *upward*?"

"Don't start giving me one of your fifty-dollar lectures filled with ten-dollar ideas," he said. Then softly, his arms curling around her: "Not now, Gussie. Not now when I can't think of anything but how good you feel in my arms, how much I want you. You feel so damn good, right where you are now," he said in a voice muffled against the soft kisses he was pressing against her throat, and Charlotte Butterworth felt the edges of herself unraveling.

He raised his head and stared at her in a way that made her toes curl. It was impossible to believe that she was standing half-naked this close to a man and not feeling terrified. In fact, terror was far down on the list of things she was feeling.

Never taking his eyes from hers, he lowered his head to cover her mouth with his. His kiss was firm and warm, and the whiskey she'd found so repulsive earlier now made her want to drink from this fountain forever. Although her proper side, dominated by Miss Charlotte, told her to resist him, her sensible side, governed by Miss Lottie, said that she should stand firm and see what he was about, but the longer the kiss lasted, the more Charlotte was conscious of Gussie's voice saying, *Yield*. It must have been because Gussie's voice was the last she heard that Charlotte could no longer prevent the stupor that settled over her by slow degrees, bringing her breathless and limp against him. Again he lifted his head to stare down at her, and she looked back at him, her eyes huge and full of wonder, her lips swollen and moist from his kiss.

She remained that way for a moment, then lowered her gaze. Taking a deep breath, she forced out the words that had lodged in her throat. "Be careful, Walker, that you don't bet more on this game than you're willing to lose. Risking your own emotions to win mine might leave you the beggar with the bowl."

"Your concern touches me, but if that should come to pass, you stand to lose as much as I, sweet Charlotte."

"How do you arrive at that crossroads?"

"If you win the heart I'm gambling with, it's quite likely that in my boundless adoration I would be unable to separate myself from you when the time came and therefore

206

would be forced to remain here as your slave, or—"

"Or what?"

"Take you with me," he said softly, just before he captured her mouth once more. This time his kiss was more adventurous, more exploring, as if his purpose was to see if there was any truth to her words. His expertise mustered every force possible to come against her, and the assault against her pitiful resistance left her crumbling. She was dimly aware of the gradual ebbing of her mistrust of him and the gentle response building within her.

As he sensed her response, his movements became more deliberate, though still gentle. His hand that had been kneading her waist slid up to cup the unfettered softness of her breast, his thumb brushing over the soft covering of fabric that did little to hide her reaction to his touch. His groan came hot and urgent against her throat, his hand that still gripped her waist sliding lower to press her against the hot proof of his desire for her.

That drove through her like the hot probe of truth that it was, leaving her with the terrible hatred of betrayal. Her own body had betrayed her—not only betrayed but done something much worse. For a thin slice of a second she had felt a stab of feeling for him, and not just feeling but something warmer and deeper. She wasn't fool enough to call it love, of course, but it was uncomfortably close enough to cause her both amazement and acute dismay.

A shiver of disgust slapped her like a wet dog's tail. Caught in the instant and feeling complete revulsion for everything that had passed between them, Charlotte could think of nothing but the overwhelming need to get as far away from Walker as possible. Catching him as unaware as her emotions had caught her, she twisted and broke from him.

Wiping the evidence of his kiss from her mouth, she said, "Don't think that you can come to me with the memory of another woman fresh upon your mind and expect the same results. Feed your driving lust if you must, but keep your hands off me."

"Charlotte," he called after her, but she was running across the wet grass. Moments later she slipped through the back door, hurrying down the dark hallway to the safe refuge of her room.

She had no more than removed her wrapper and reached for her damp gown to pull it over her head than she heard his plea come soft and urgent across the room.

"Charlotte, it isn't like you think."

The moon was high, piercing her window with a cold, impersonal slice of light that illuminated his face as he stepped toward her. She should have locked the front door, she thought. *Next time I will.* Ignoring the concern etched on his face, Charlotte clutched her wrapper against her breast and whispered, "Get out of here."

He stepped closer, his hands coming forward to grip her arms. "I won't touch you, Charlotte. Just listen to me. What happened between us—it isn't wrong and it had nothing to do with another woman. Do you understand that?"

"There is nothing to understand," she said, meeting his gaze with defiance.

"There is a chance you could be right, but I prefer to disagree with you. There is one hell of a lot to understand and no better time to start than right now," he said, his blue eyes colorless in the dark. "Charlotte, look at me."

There was an urgency in his tone that she could not deny, and she looked at him. It was a mistake. One moment she was looking at him, the next she was locked in his arms, his kiss saying the things he could not. For a moment she forgot her anger as it evaporated to nothing, as his lips moved in soft exploration over hers, coaxing her mouth into welcome openness. His arms were tight around her, one hand sliding over her back and lower, his palm lifting her into the hard cove of his hips. With a compulsion she didn't understand, she was drawn forward into the welcome warmth and security of his long body, her body seeking him, wanting to know the feel, the secrets of his flesh, the beloved detail of each curve, each hollow, leaving the admonition of her mind behind.

Charlotte leaned away from him, focusing in a slightly besotted manner, as if she had been the one drinking whiskey. Kissing Walker was like swallowing opium. It made her unaware of danger, careless, carefree, and it was addictive. It was also dangerous. And for someone like her, who had never tried opium, to take a dose this large the first time...

She was suddenly afraid. Afraid of what might happen if she did lose her fears, if she did begin to respond to him as most women did. That was a little silly, she knew, for it was obvious to her that she had already done more than respond. She was just afraid to acknowledge it, choosing instead to resist and analyze it to death. But in a passion-weakened moment, it had rushed into her, flooding her reason and overriding all negative thoughts.

But negative thoughts now prevailed and she broke away. "Walker, stop."

He tilted his head slightly. "Is there a valid reason for that, or is it because you don't trust men... or is it because they're oversexed and are after only one thing."

"I just want..." She swallowed audibly, her heart thumping madly as if it were lodged in her throat. Somewhere she found the fortitude to raise her eyes, but only as far as his chin. She didn't trust herself to go any farther. Suddenly he sighed and released her, his hands coming away from her back, but finding her hands and holding them. He didn't say anything, but just stood there looking down at his hands holding hers. Was he aware of how softly he was rubbing them? How slow were the circles made by his thumbs. Some part of her was urging her to pull free. Some other part was inhaling the warmth and gentleness of his touch, the pleasure of his nearness. Somehow, this was different from any way he had ever touched her before. As if in a daze, she stared at their joined hands and knew full well what he was about, and let him be about it.

With infinite slowness he tucked a kiss into her waiting palm, his eyes closing as if he was overcome with what he was doing. Then his head came up and his arms went around her again.

"Oh, dear God, not again."

"Why the hell not?" he murmured, while his lips scorched a path along the curve of her throat.

"Because this is ridiculous. Every time you kiss me we start to fight and—" He stopped her with the explorations of his mouth, while his hands were busy doing a little exploring of their own. "What are you doing? Keep your hands still or—" Once again his mouth got in the way of things.

He was kissing her, whispering things into her mouth. "Don't think about it, Gussie. For once in your life, put those thoughts behind you and don't fight what comes naturally. Don't complicate things. Don't think. Just feel. Feel it, Gussie. Let it come as it was meant to, slow and natural. Give in, Gussie. Give in." She had words to say to him, but they bunched in confusion in her head as he deepened the kiss, making her pulse hum loudly in her ears. With one firm press of his arms, he settled her against him, allowing her to know what lay beyond the thin fabric of her nightgown.

He was long. And hard. And she wasn't frightened.

Everything shut down for her, everything but Walker and what he was doing. Things were happening to her. Changes were taking place, within and without. Apparently her body was as confused as she was. Places that were normally dry were suddenly wet, while places that were normally wet had gone dry as a bone.

And Walker must have known. "Lord, Gussie, let me," he said against her damp skin. "Let me."

"No. Don't. Please."

"Let me hold you, Gussie. Let me hold you and touch you and make you my woman. Do you know what that means, Gussie? Do you know what it means to be a woman? My woman?"

Because she was so in tune with him and so out of touch with herself, she forgot her rigid control, and because it was a natural and honest feeling, she leaned toward him and kissed him, of her own volition. At first, the touch of her lips on his was fainter then the drift of a flower petal on a wind current. Feeling her uncertainty, he furthered the contact until he felt her mouth begin to respond beneath his.

"Ah, Gussie, what have you done to me?" he said, and the words swept them both away, so that they did not notice the faint glow of a lantern that streaked across the floor through the open door of her bedroom.

Hearing the muffled tread of footsteps and whispered voices, Jamie had opened his eyes and listened for a moment until he was sure that someone was in the house. Lighting his bedside lamp, he quietly left his room, going down the hallway with a slow-paced limp. From the sounds, he determined that they were coming from Miss Lottie's bedroom and he headed in that direction.

Whatever Jamie had expected to see, it wasn't what greeted him when his apprehensive eyes followed the thrust of lantern light that brought the two tangled figures into full view.

There was someone in the house, all right, but instead of the expected prowler, this man looked invited—not only invited but terribly welcome. In one brief instant, Jamie saw the rumpled bed, the discarded wrapper and the damp, mud-smeared hem of Charlotte's gown. Not only was she cavorting with a man in her room, but apparently the hussy had been brazen enough to go after him. The thought that he could have been so deceived by her disgusted him. To think he had actually placed her on the same pedestal with his beloved mother.

"Miss Butterworth, what is this all about?"

Charlotte froze.

"This doesn't concern you, Granger," Walker said.

"You could've at least had the decency to shut your door," Jamie hissed.

Charlotte managed to extract herself from the stranglehold Walker had her in. "I know how this must look, Jamie, but it isn't what you think."

Her words did little to placate him, however. "Incredible," he said, "how I was duped by your gentle ways. Do you know that I actually entertained the thought of marriage?" He laughed bitterly. "I would have honored you with my name, but I see you much prefer to be tumbled in the dirt like some—"

"I would advise you to take your accusations along with your person and get out of here," Walker said. "I hate to render a wounded man unconscious, but if you say another word, I'll be forced to do just that."

Charlotte was beside herself. "Jamie, please, just listen—"

"I have nothing more to say to you, Miss Butterworth. I will be leaving in the morning. Good night."

CHAPTER
❧ TEN ❧

Unbeknownst to Charlotte, Jamie Granger left the next morning, just as he'd said he would. In fact, he was walking into Two Trees when she heard the rooster crow and opened her eyes. Fighting a strong desire to roll over and pull the covers over her head, she finally forced herself to get up and dress. She couldn't bring herself even to look at Jamie's door when she left her room and headed for the kitchen to fix breakfast. An hour later, she decided she couldn't put off facing him any longer. Picking up his breakfast tray, she walked to his room.

It was empty.

There was something sad about the way that

room looked, something bittersweet about the memory it stirred. There would be no more lengthy discussions about Byron and Shelley and Keats; no more evenings absorbed in the rich sound of Jamie's baritone reading Elizabeth Barrett Browning; no more discussions about whether or not he had intentionally let her win at a game of cards. Standing there surveying the room, Charlotte realized that it looked exactly the same as it had before Nemi had brought Jamie into her life, but she knew in her heart that the room would never be the same. Not really.

Although Jamie had removed himself from Charlotte's house, he had unknowingly left a great deal of himself behind. Her eyes paused on the vase of wilted snapdragons beside his bed before moving to the bed itself, and she noted with a piercing pain in her heart that Jamie had made his bed, the quilted counterpane drooping to touch the floor at the foot of the bed, the wire springs exposed near the head. There was something poignant about the way that bed was made, something that made her eyes feel all peppery.

"Darn fool man," she said, wiping her eyes and hurrying to the bed to smooth out the lumps and straighten the counterpane. "Can't even make up a bed properly."

It was over.

The weeks of steady, exhausting work, of cooking, washing, tending, and caring for Jamie when he was unable to care for himself. There had been nights when she was so weary of sitting by his bed, of caring and bandaging and feeding, of applying cool cloths to fever-ish skin, or warm blankets to keep chills at bay when the fever was gone. But all that had changed now. The taking care of him was over. Finished. The wounded man was healed. Gone from her life. There would be no one to pick snapdragons for, no reason to open the windows to let in the cool morning breeze, no one who would smile when she fluffed the pillows. No one to notice that she existed and to seem happier for it.

No woman could undergo such a trial as Charlotte had and not find herself changed; and no woman of Charlotte's mien and met-tle could come through it without some pri-vate languishing and hostility toward both Walker and Jamie. She had done all she could, going far beyond her physical and mental limits. As a mirage offers hope to a desert voy-ager, Jamie Granger had offered new and sparkling hope to Charlotte's wizened spirit. How ephemeral, how momentary were those dreams of finding a partner in life... a mate... a husband. And how soon were they absorbed like raindrops falling into the ocean of drab existence.

While Charlotte tidied the room and raised the windows to air the reminders of Jamie Granger from her life, she thought about his reference last evening to marriage. With a stab of regret, she thought that for the first time there had been a man she could see herself spending the rest of her life with. But that was pointless to think of now. She would just go on with her life and try to forget that a man as gentle and considerate as Jamie Granger had ever existed. With one last look around the room, Charlotte turned and walked out the door, closing it firmly behind her.

A few days later, when Walker came into the kitchen for supper, he was ready for a change in Charlotte's mood. "I suppose this waspish atmosphere has something to do with Jamie's departure."

It was the first time either one of them had mentioned Jamie's name since that awful scene in her room the night before Jamie left.

"*If* I am waspish, it may not be over his departure as much as the circumstances that forced it."

"If he was any kind of man, he wouldn't have tucked his tail and slinked out of the house in the middle of the night like some egg-sucking dog. You don't see me doing that."

"No, I certainly don't, but then you didn't catch me in my bedroom in a compromising position with another man, like Jamie did."

"It wasn't a compromising position. And even if it was, that was no reason to jump to conclusions."

"It really doesn't matter now. That ear of corn has been shucked. Let's just leave it. I don't want to discuss Jamie, or the reason he left, if it's all the same to you. Now, do you want some more mashed potatoes or not?"

"What I want is a few kind words. It's damn sure not my fault that Granger took off like a turpentined cat, and while I'm at it, I might add I'm tired of being expected to crawl on my knees before his hallowed shrine. Face the facts. The man left you, Charlotte. Left you without a word. How can you hang on to his memory like some sacred endearment?"

"I don't expect you to understand."

"Good! Because I sure as hell don't." Before he could say anything else, Charlotte ran from the room. A few moments later her door slammed. Walker tried to finish his supper, but it was no use.

How could a man put his thoughts to nourishment with a woman crying her heart out in the next room? It occurred to him then that Jamie had somehow managed to endear himself to Charlotte more by his leaving than he ever could have by staying. With an oath, Walker shoved himself away from the table and went to his room. Sleep was a long time in coming. For Charlotte as well as for Walker.

It was many days later when Charlotte came to grips with Jamie's departure and opened the door to his room, deciding at last to incorporate it once more into part of her home and her daily life.

Days had passed and turned into weeks, and life had begun to distract her once more, and she realized that all her dashed hopes, her nipped buds, were merely that—dashed hopes and nipped buds. Life went on. Soon, crushed dreams lost their rainbow colors and faded like a candle in the sun.

But a new sense of awareness had been born in Charlotte, a discernment that came from ministering to the needs of another. A man. The realization came with a traitorous leap of her heart, a hungering for the close companionship, the intimacy that comes from having someone close, someone who cares. A man.

A man, she had learned, was not all lion; there was a grain of lamb there as well. Jamie had left, roaring like a lion, but Charlotte had experienced something that only comes from the strong giving to the weak. She realized with a sort of happiness that she really wasn't in love with Jamie but had simply succumbed to the power of gentleness. In her youth, when young men had been attracted to her, fear and anxiety hid the possibilities with dark, foreboding wings. Then she had removed herself, trying to spare herself pain by complete detachment, but in so doing she had lost a part of herself. She was like a fruit that is born too late in the season to mature and ripen. Too alive to drop away completely and fall to the ground, she was merely existing.

Charlotte understood now that there was a difference between what was walled within and what was walled without. Her fear of men had protected her from the pain of love. But what would protect her from the pain of loneliness?

Like a visiting angel, Jamie had come into her life, not to be the one she would love, but to prepare the way for another. It was a grand feeling, but a strange one, too. Inside, she felt all quivery and fragile, like an egg just dropped from its shell.

It was in the middle of her prayers late one

night that these feelings and revelations came to her. Outside, it was dark, and she was alone in her house; the breathing and the occasional squeak of springs coming from Jamie's room—sounds she had grown so accustomed to—were now strangely quiet. Yet, she felt his presence, that part of him he had left behind, something as fragrant as the sweetness of spring, and she smiled into her pillow. Jamie had left her something dear—the peace of freedom—and taken, in exchange, the hollow ring of fear.

Charlotte awoke the next morning, her heart cleaned and aired like the front bedroom after Jamie's departure. Silvered threads of anticipation ran in and out of her mind as she went about her chores that morning, but there were times when the old memories returned and robbed her of her newfound optimism. But like a flower following the sun, Charlotte drew strength and confidence from the knowledge that freedom brings with it a kind of pain different from that of imprisonment. No longer would fear hold her back. Hope would push her forward.

She spent the rest of the morning with the laundry on the back porch, taking out her frustrations on the clothes she was scrubbing against her rub board, which did little to the clothes and a whole lot to her knuckles. When the clothes were washed and rinsed and piled in her basket, she put a chicken in a pan to boil for chicken and dumplings. Clapping the lid on the pan, she wondered how much longer she could adhere to this diet of chicken.

Over the past two months, since her supply of salted beef had run out, she had lived on chicken: boiled, hashed, deviled, steamed, boned, roasted, smothered, stewed, fried, fricasseed, and made into pies. It would be November before hog-killing weather arrived and along with it a few months of pork, and then she would become as sick of it as she was of chicken. Even the occasional opening of a jar of collard greens and ham that she had canned last summer couldn't remove the taste of chicken from her palate.

Unable to stand the steamy smell of the chicken, Charlotte picked up the laundry basket and, balancing it against her hip, went outside to the clothesline. Built by Jam and Nemi last year, Charlotte had what had to be the fanciest clothesline in five counties. While most women were still draping their laundry across fences or bushes, Charlotte had three tight lines that ran from two wooden Ts sunk in the ground. What she liked most about the new clothesline were the three lines that enabled her to hang mentionables like sheets, towels, and tablecloths on the two outside lines while reserving the center line for her unmentionables. It just wouldn't do to have a man ride up while her drawers were drooped over the back fence, which is precisely what had happened to her a few years back, before Nemi and Jam had built the clothesline.

Just as she always did, Charlotte filled the two outside lines with clothes before moving to the center line, where she hung her chemises, petticoats, drawers, and the assortment of soft cotton rags she used for five days out of every thirty. Only today it was a little harder to hang things on the center line because the wind was up, whipping the clothes with a loud snap and beating Charlotte as she worked her way down the middle. She had almost reached the end, having only two pair of drawers left in the basket, which she bent over to retrieve. When she straightened up, there stood Walker Reed, bigger than Dallas, his hands on his hips and grinning like a born fool. Just as she felt the color rise from her neck and over her tight white collar, a sudden gust of wind came along, filling the legs of one pair of her drawers with air and whipping them out horizontally, one leg going in front of Walker's face, the other around the back of his neck. Turning toward her with a wide grin on his face, he said, "Gussie, does this mean what I think it means?"

Feeling her dander rising faster than the temperature, Charlotte could only sputter, "Maybe it's just my way of reminding you that you aren't out of the woods yet, Mr. Cocksure. You could still hang."

He laughed. "True, but what a way to go... with Charlotte Butterworth's thighs locked around my neck."

"Those are not my—those are not part of my person, you vile, uncouth brute," she said, her lips trembling with anger and embarrassment. Unable to stop herself, she felt two big tears roll out of her eyes and splash down her cheeks. Humiliated because he had seen her drawers and been crude enough to make mention of the fact, she was now embarrassing herself further by crying. A sob caught in her throat. "You never miss an opportunity, do you? It isn't enough that you repay my kindness by treating me like some saloon floozy and cause the one man in my life that I felt comfortable around to look at me like I was a leper, unable to get away from me fast enough, but now you must rub salt in my wounds by degrading me. What have I done to deserve this? When all I have done is treat you with kindness and save your wretched hide—which, I might add, I regret with every miserable breath I draw. Now, before I go into the house, is there another pound of flesh you would like to extract from me?"

The teasing in his voice was gone. "Would it change anything if I said I was sorry?"

"No, it would not. You can't go through life dealing out misery and expecting to erase the results by saying you're sorry." She started to leave, but stopped. "You know what you are? A blight! A blight to all my hopes. Now leave me alone!"

"Hey," he said, "how did we end up like this? I just wanted to tell you to keep an eye on the sky and get your laundry in quickly if you see or hear anything unusual. I don't like the looks of those clouds building in the distance."

Her eyes flicked toward the heavy, dark mass of clouds banking along the horizon. "It looks like rain," she said. "Even *I* have enough sense to get the clothes off the line before it rains." She turned to pick up her basket.

His hands came from nowhere to grasp her shoulders. "All the same," he said gently, "I want you to keep your eyes peeled. There is something strange about the weather today. It's hotter and stickier than usual—even the animals sense it." His eyes were dark and searching. "You will be careful, won't you?"

"I'll be careful," she said, turning away once more and yanking her basket off the ground.

"Charlotte," he said softly, as if he had something he desperately needed her to understand, but she never so much as looked his way, ducking beneath a white muslin sheet and disappearing.

Nemi came by after lunch, and Charlotte persuaded him to have a bowl of bread pudding, and when he had finished, he talked himself into another one. While he contemplated a third helping, Jam came tripping across the stepping-stones that led up to the back door, where he paused and banged loudly on the screen.

"Come on in, Jam," Charlotte said.

"Afternoon, Miz Charlotte, Mr. Nehemiah."

Charlotte and Nemi both responded, Nemi asking Jam what had brought him to the house in such a hurry.

"Mr. Vandegriff—he done stopped by the field where me'n Rebekah was plowin'. He said tell you they's witching for water down at the Gilkeson place and that you never seen the likes of it and to get yourself over there in a big rush."

Jam thanked Charlotte for the two molasses

cookies she gave him before he left. Charlotte turned to Nemi. "You aren't going, are you? I never had much faith in water witching."

"Me neither, but I might be having a little more faith in it if I were Sam Gilkeson and had dug as many dry wells on my place as he has. I heard he had hired a water witch outa Kansas. Why don't you ride over there with me?"

Charlotte was skeptical, but it wasn't too often that she had the opportunity to go anywhere with Nemi, so she rolled down her sleeves and put on her bonnet while Nemi hitched Butterbean to the buggy.

As they set off down the road, Charlotte was watching the clouds stack themselves higher and higher. Walker had been right—it was unusually hot and humid. He'd been right about the animals, too—even good-natured old Butterbean was showing her worst side. Charlotte swatted at a hornet that buzzed by her bonnet.

"You know, I like Walker Reed," Nemi said, slapping the reins, urging the mare into a canter.

Charlotte looked at him as if she expected to find the reason behind those words written across his forehead. "Nehemiah Butterworth," she exclaimed, "you never cease to amaze me! Whatever brought that on? And when have you been around Walker Reed long enough to know if you like him or not?"

Nemi slapped Butterbean again. She was only into a half-canter, but she responded to the reins and eased herself into a full canter. "I've seen him several times."

"When? Where?"

"He's stopped by my place a few times. Hannah likes him, too. He brought her a mess of snapdragons day before yesterday and she invited him to supper."

"*My* snapdragons?" Charlotte said, choking on her words.

Nemi grinned. "I didn't ask whose snapdragons they were, or where he got them. It isn't polite to quiz a fellow about a gift. Don't you know that, Charlotte?"

Charlotte chose to ignore that one, strictly because her curiosity was getting the best of her, and when her curiosity was getting the best of her, she couldn't contain herself for long. "Just what excuse does Walker Reed use for paying you those visits?"

"Don't reckon he needs one. He's just being neighborly."

"Humph!" Charlotte snorted. "Neighborly—I'd sooner believe dogs had blue eyes."

"Did I ever tell you about the blue-eyed dog I saw in Oklahoma when—"

"No, you didn't, and I don't want to hear about it now. You just tell me what you and Walker discussed."

"You."

"Me?" she repeated. "*Me?*"

Nemi gave her a full stare. "Does that surprise you?"

Charlotte looked away. "Frankly, yes."

"Why?"

"Why would he ride all the way over to your place to talk about me?"

"I guess he wanted the answers to some questions."

Charlotte gave her brother one of those looks that said she didn't have to see a rat to know it was there. "What kind of questions?"

"Just questions, Charlotte. He had a few ideas about some things that would improve your place, but he wasn't too sure how any suggestions coming from him would sit with you. Then we got to talking about the war and such—"

"Was he in the war?"

"He's from California, Charlotte. They didn't take sides, remember?"

"No, they were worse than Yankees."

Nemi gave her a quizzical look. "Now that's a comment that bears some explanation. I didn't think there was anything *worse* than a Yankee in your eyes."

"Well, I've just found something worse. Californians. 'You are neither hot nor cold, therefore I will spew you out of my mouth.' Even the Bible speaks against fence-riding neutrals."

"I don't think the Bible was referring to the War Between the States."

"Apples or oranges," Charlotte said, "it's all the same."

Nemi laughed. "Somewhere, I'm sure, there is some deep, profound female logic nestled in that comment, but I'll be damned if I can find it."

"Never mind that. What else did you tell Walker?"

"He asked about our family," Nemi said, remembering vividly the turn of their conversation:

"We had two other brothers: Jason, killed at Vicksburg; Carlton, killed at Bull Run. Our mother—"

"I heard about your mother."

"From Charlotte, I guess. Did she tell you what happened after Pa came home when the war was over?"

"Just that he was in bad shape. Was there more?"

"Pa was crippled up pretty bad, but that wasn't the worst of it. His mind was messed up. I remember the day he rode toward the house. Charlotte and I were in the cornfield trying to save the crop from cinch bugs when we saw this moth-eaten horse meandering up the road. We didn't recognize him, so we stopped slapping at the cinch bugs with our burlap sacks and watched. He went on down the road a piece, and when he drew even with the fence that surrounded Ma's grave, he stopped. He just sat there for a long time, then he dismounted and walked inside the gate. It looked like he was reading the inscription on the cross Charlotte and I made, then he turned slowly and walked back to his horse and removed something that we thought might be a gun, so we ducked down in the corn so he couldn't see us. After a little bit, we stood up to see if he was still there. That's when we realized it wasn't a gun he had in his hands, but a shovel."

"A shovel?"

"He was digging her up."

"Lord! Was he crazy?"

"If he wasn't before, he was when he saw Ma's grave."

"What happened then?"

"Charlotte lit out screaming and I took off after her. By the time we got there Pa had opened her coffin, but I didn't really see anything because Pa whirled around and hit me with the shovel and knocked me out cold. Poor Charlotte saw it, though. She saw it all. Mr. Van Husen, our neighbor who was coming up the main road, heard Charlotte screaming. He said he'd never seen anything like it. Charlotte was standing there beside Ma's open coffin, screaming and screaming. Mr. Van Husen had to slap her several times to snap her out of it."

"What happened to your father?"

"He was harmless after that. He never said a word. He just sat in the rocker and stared off into space. After a while, I couldn't take it anymore and I begged Charlotte to leave with me, but she wouldn't leave Pa. Then one night I took off. I ended up in Texas working for the Waggoner outfit. That's where I learned my cowboying. I met Hannah and we married. Hannah was real understanding about my going back to see about them. By the time I returned, Pa was dead and Charlotte was running the farm, or what was left of it."

"You have any trouble getting her to come with you?"

"No. There wasn't anything left for her there."

"I guess going through something like that makes you awfully close."

"I'm protective of her, if that's what you mean. I'd kill any son of a bitch that did the least

229

thing to bring her any pain. She's had more than her share. I aim to see that she doesn't have any more."

"Then we agree on one point, at least, because my thoughts are the same as yours."

"Nemi… Nemi! Are you stone deaf?" Charlotte said loudly enough to be heard in Abilene.

"What?"

Louder this time: "I said, *'Are you stone deaf?'* I've been talking to you for the last five minutes and you're just sitting there like a bump on a pickle."

"I was thinking."

"My Lord, Nemi. When you think, you're unconscious. You passed the turn to the Gilkeson place."

"So I did," Nemi said, giving her a nudge in the ribs with his elbow. "So I did."

It was the hottest part of the afternoon when they headed back. The sky was growing darker, the clouds moving in, churning and rolling, thunder rumbling in the distance.

"Damn. If I didn't know better, I'd say it looked like a hail storm abrewing," Nemi said.

"It would almost be worth it, just to cool things off," Charlotte said.

"When we get back, Charlotte, I need to head on home and see about my livestock. I don't feel right about the way those clouds look. I'm going to open the door to the storm cellar for you before I leave. You stick close to the house, and at the first sign of anything unusual, you hightail it into that cellar, you hear?"

"Oh, Nemi, it's only a thunderstorm."

"You heard what I said, Charlotte. At the first sign of anything unusual."

"I heard you, Nemi. I heard you," Charlotte said, but she was already lost in her recollections of the water witching. She still had her doubts about what she'd seen, but she had to admit that the water witch had put on a good show.

When they reached the house, Nemi stopped Jam, who was just unhitching Rebekah from the plow. "Before you leave, Jam, unhitch Butterbean and turn her out in the pasture. Turn out any livestock you've got penned or any you have in the barn. I don't like the looks of those clouds. When you're done, you head on home."

With another warning about the weather, Nemi headed for his house, and Charlotte told Jam about the water witching.

"He used a forked branch of a willow tree. He gripped it in both hands and stooped down, kinda low, and walked back and forth all over the place. After a while he got another stick, exactly like the first one, and held one in each hand. Then he started walking back and forth again. He kept saying that where there was a vein of water running underground, the sticks would point down right away. Of course everyone laughed, but it didn't seem to bother him none."

"He find any water?"

"I never saw any. They'll have to dig a well

to know for sure, but I'm telling you one thing, Jam, I've never seen anything like it. One minute he was walking around with the willow sticks pointing forward, and the next minute the sticks pointed down, and after a couple of steps they dropped completely until they were pointing straight toward the ground. It was a sight to behold."

They talked for a few minutes more, until the thunder grew louder and closer and Charlotte sent Jam home while she hurried into the house to get her basket. By the time she had removed the clothes from two of the lines, the dark, churning clouds had completely covered the sky, blocking the sun, and the wind was blowing harder than she had ever seen.

Half a mile away, Walker was pushing his gelding for all he was worth as they ate up the distance to the house. Leaning low over his mount's neck, the coarse hairs of the horse's mane whipping in his face, he realized what it was that drove him with such desperation to reach Charlotte. Fear for her safety was, of course, the primary reason, but with startling clarity he realized that something might happen to her before she had a chance to really live, before she experienced the beauty of what made her so afraid.

He dismounted before his horse had come to a complete stop, running for his life against the staggering force of the wind—first to the storm cellar, and finding the door flung back, he called out to her, but the cellar was empty. Next he checked the house, coming out the back door in time to see her fighting the wind to retrieve the last of her laundry.

"Charlotte!" he shouted, but the wind drove his words back into his mouth as he struggled toward her.

Looking up, Charlotte saw the rounded underside of a nearby cloud start to bubble and boil, twisting and churning every which way. Before her eyes the twisting began to whirl and whirl, until a crooked funnel began to form, a snakelike coil that dipped down to the ground, skipping across the pasture in an irregular path before it withdrew into the clouds above. Transfixed, she watched the funnel materialize again, like the thirsty trunk of an elephant siphoning everything in sight. Suddenly the funnel took a sharp turn in her direction. Lightning was flashing and now it began to rain, the drops coming down faster and faster, pelting her with bruising intensity before she realized it wasn't rain at all, but hail that was being driven against her with such force.

Within mere seconds, a strange hissing sound seemed to come out of the thunder as the funnel dropped again, becoming a loud roar, louder than any train she had ever heard. Charlotte dropped her basket. The wind was blowing her breath back into her nostrils, her brain telling her to scream, but her body unable to find the air to do so. She started for the house, then remembered the storm cellar. The wind was whipping her skirts between her legs, making it difficult to walk. She stumbled to her knees time and time again. As she fought her way across the yard, her knees were scraped, her hands raw with several deep cuts, but she kept going until she realized that she wasn't making any headway against the fierce winds.

She would not make it.

She knew that with dead certainty now. She looked in the direction of the cellar and realized that the wind was pushing her off course and her strength was fast dissipating. Her skirts were acting like sails, catching the wind and pulling her along. She was being carried like a boat on a river, a human barge in a sea of wind. She was alone. She was going to die. She did not want to die alone.

Just ahead of her was the well. She wondered if she could hold on to the rough-hewn beams that gave support to the roof, and then she wondered if the driving force of the wind would push her over the side and down into a watery grave. It might be weeks before anyone found her. She fought to change her course, but the well was rising before her like a brick wall.

She slammed against it with crippling force. Pain, white hot and stunning, raked along the side of her face, across her breasts and ribs, but her arms, which clutched the thick oaken beam, held fast. The beam was rough, and her hands and arms filled with splinters, her nails broken and her fingers burning. She tried to see how close the funnel was, but her mind was buzzing with the deafening roar, her eyes filling with blowing debris and leaving her blinded.

She buried her face between her arms and clutched the beam for all she was worth. The roar of the twister combined with the stabbing pain in her head and she tried to block out everything. She wasn't sure how long she clung like that before something struck her, driving the wind from her lungs. Something coiled around her waist and she shuddered, thinking it a snake, and screamed.

"Put your arms around me," Walker shouted in her ear, the wind whipping his words about her.

"It's no use. We're going to die."

"Listen to me, Charlotte. There's a chance we can make it if we don't stand here debating. If we're going to die, we might as well die trying. But I don't plan on losing you before I've had a chance to finish what we've started."

His arms tightened about her, pulling her against him, and, following the urging of his body, she released her hold on the beam and locked her arms about his waist, her face finding warm solace in the haven between his arm and chest. Following his lead, she began to walk with him, their bodies bent forward, leaning into the wind. She was on the verge of telling him that it was no use when she stumbled over something and felt herself pushed down the steps of the cellar. Walker was close behind her, his arms still holding her tightly and guiding her. Once they reached the floor below, he released her.

"I've got to close the door. See if you can find the lantern and light it."

The noise was deafening as Walker fought

his way back up the steps and disappeared into the mouth of the opening. He would never be able to close the door in this wind, she thought, but moments later the dark shadow of the door hovered over the opening, then slammed shut as Walker drove the bolt home. Tumbling down the stairs, he was hurled against her, throwing both of them to the dirt floor, where they lay, too exhausted to move.

Outside, the twister roared, wreaking havoc and filling the world above with strange sounds, but below, safe in the earth's small pocket, Walker and Charlotte remained as they had fallen. Within minutes both of them were asleep... in the darkness.

CHAPTER ELEVEN

Gradually the roar dwindled and the thunder rumbled away into the distance. The earth no longer trembled but lay stripped, still and silent, the world above strangely quiet. The lack of air and noise was what brought Charlotte to full consciousness. She opened her eyes.

On a narrow shelf overhead, a tiny lantern put forth a weak light that barely touched the rows of canned goods that lined the tiny cellar. Charlotte stirred, her hand striking a burlap bag of potatoes stacked in one corner. She tried to pull herself up and felt an imme-

diate stab of pain to her head and unbelievable soreness in the rest of her body. With a
weary sigh, she dropped her head back and
closed her eyes, listening to the steady hum
and thump of a horsefly bumping against
the rows of canned goods overhead.

Next to her, Walker too was awake. He
must have lit the lantern, she realized as she
saw him lift his head to look at her. He supported his weight on one elbow. He watched
her from where he lay, watched the occasional flutter of her eyelids, the intermittent
shudder of her body, following with his eyes
the rippling effect as it traveled along the
curve of her back to the slender length of her
legs. Her hair was hopelessly snarled and
tangled, filled with bits of leaves, chaff, and—
he smiled when he saw it—the mashed bloom
of one of her snapdragons.

She felt the heat of his gaze and opened her
eyes. Then, realizing that she was lying with
her back to him, she rolled over and stared
up into the face of the man who had saved her
life, coming close to losing his own in the
process. She frowned. His disregard for his
safety and complete dedication to ensure
hers puzzled her. She bit her lip in deep concentration.

He stared at her for a long time, and she wondered what he was thinking. The ache she felt
seemed permanently settled in her bones,
and she wondered if she would be able to walk.
Her muscles convulsed, then eased into
numbness. When he finally spoke, his voice
was strained. "So you didn't die after all."

She swallowed—a difficult thing to do since she was fighting the urge to cry. She attempted a smile. Walker felt a responding tightness imprison his heart. He touched her face with the back of his hand, then jerked it away.

"No," she said quietly, "I am very much alive, thanks to you."

"My pleasure, I assure you."

Her eyes closed against the harsh sound of his voice. When she opened them, she said, "I owe you my life. I will find some way to repay you."

"The debt was settled before the first cloud gathered. The debt was mine—my life for yours. We begin again. This time on even terms."

There was still so much confusion in her mind—she wasn't ready for his roundabout way of speaking. It was difficult for her, surely he knew that. A sob rose in her throat.

"Don't," he said, and took her in his arms, understanding her fears and answering them in the only way he knew, by offering the comfort of his body.

There was a promise in his warmth cradling her, solace in the infinite care he took to remain impersonal, in spite of the throbbing heat of his body against hers. She could smell the drying odor of sweat, neither pleasant nor unpleasant, but human, and that human quality she sensed in him, coupled with his nearness, left her feeling dizzy in a way she hadn't felt since she was a child and had played crack the whip and went whirling across the yard to fall in a laughing heap with her head spinning.

Walker shifted his weight, bringing her head more fully against his shoulder. Listening to the steady beating of his heart, Charlotte tried to understand this complicated man who went to great lengths to win her trust. The question was, why?

She no longer believed, as she had earlier, that he did it for the sole purpose of taking her virginity—a pitifully poor reward for the trouble he had put himself to. Yet, it didn't seem wholly likely that his actions were born purely from a genuine love and concern for a fellow human being.

She followed his lead and shifted her position, settling against him more comfortably until she felt the hard length of a particular part of his anatomy pressing against her hip. She froze and heard his corresponding chuckle.

Was it possible that she had misjudged him? For so many years she had lived with the idea that men, with very few exceptions, were insensitive, cruel, full of lust, and after their own gratification, regardless of the cost to others. Jamie had offered her friendship and love, but the feel of a man's body against hers was alien, something she still feared. Why, then, was she finding such pleasure in the nearness, the touch of this man? And why was she not repulsed at the thought of that most male part of him growing hard with desire for her?

She incorrectly called it a mere response to having another human being for companionship when just minutes ago they had both come so very close to dying. It was the aftermath of the fear of dying, surely, that gave her such comfort in the nearness of him. Overcome with some unknown emotion, she buried her face in the hollow of his throat, absorbing the masculine smell of him, feeling the heated moisture of his skin bonded to her cheek. The sheer pressure of it swelled in her throat and she could no more stop the tears that slipped down her cheeks to splash on his chest than she could call back the twister that had thrown them together.

"Why are you crying?"

"I'm not."

"Pardon me," he said with a chuckle. "Why are you perspiring so profusely?"

"Don't make fun of me."

"Never that."

Unsure of his meaning, she tried to pull away, but he held her firm.

"Where are you going?" he said, his words ruffling through her hair and teasing the sensitive skin on her neck.

"I don't linger where I'm not wanted."

She saw the surprise in his blue eyes. "Where would you get that idea? Not wanted? Lady, if you only knew—" Then he laughed. "You little tease. You know my desire. You aren't that ignorant."

"I never said I was."

He smiled as he looked at her tightly drawn mouth, the color that had nothing to do with the heat that rose to stain her cheeks. "Let's stop all this silly banter. Kiss me, Gussie."

"See? I knew you would get physical—"

"Shut your mouth and kiss me."

"I can't."

"Yes, you can. I'll help you."

"I was never worried about that."

He laughed, but before the sound left his throat she felt herself pulled more tightly against him. His face was so close that when she tried to speak, tried to tell him that she couldn't, her words came out muffled against his lips, and the sensation of her lips brushing against the softness of his made her forget that she had been about to refuse him. A new sound, gurgling and satisfied, rose in her throat as her arms went around his neck and her mouth molded itself to his.

His lips parted willingly, as if inviting her inside, and she blindly answered him with an invitation of her own. His tongue, soft and sweet flavored, came out to curl gently around hers, coaxing, teasing, until his arms tightened around her, one hand closing warmly over her breast. He heard her indrawn breath, not knowing it was a gasp of pure pleasure and taking it for the opposite.

He stopped suddenly, knowing that his leap into the lead, his desire to touch her, would bring recriminations from her. "I'm sorry. I didn't mean to frighten you."

Disappointed, she couldn't think of anything to say. She only knew that she could not let him move away from her. "Please," she whispered. "Please hold me. Hold me for just a little while longer."

His breathing was ragged, the heat of desire

strong and intense in his eyes as he watched her. Floating somewhere deep within him was the same frustrated ache of longing as she felt, but along with his need was the desire to remove forever the grip of fear that held her. Above all things he wanted to please her, to bring her troubled mind to perfect peace, her untouched body to its complete fulfillment, and to find his own rapture in the process. Riley would be here soon. He didn't have much time.

"What you are asking, Charlotte, is not an easy request to grant. Not because I am unwilling, for the proof of that lies hard between us, but a man's desire for a woman is not something he can turn up and down like the wick of a lantern. Do you understand what I am saying?"

"You are saying no?"

He released a sigh of frustration. "I am saying, sweet Charlotte, that I will try, but beyond that, I can offer no guarantee."

He met her halfway, their lips touching, lightly at first, then by slow degrees increasing the pressure until they were kissing blindly, his arms strong and firm around her, the weight of his body shifting to lie across her. The delicious weight of him pressed her farther against the cellar floor, but Charlotte was oblivious to where she was, being conscious only of the man she was with. His hands kneaded her arms and shoulders before traveling up to thread in the tangled profusion of her hair.

"Are you out of control yet?" she whispered with a sudden stab of fear.

He smiled, the humor obvious in his voice. "You little witch. Is that your objective, then? To see how quickly you can bring me to the brink?"

"No, no," she said, hoping he couldn't hear the thrill of female pride that surged through her at his words.

"Don't be afraid of me, Charlotte. When I feel myself 'getting out of control,' I'll stop." He fanned his fingers to spread her hair more fully around her face. The dim light from the lantern absorbed all the color in her hair except the flaming red, making each strand seem alive and bursting with color.

"That's the way I've imagined you would look," he said as his mouth took possession of hers once more, his tongue, swift and sure, stroking at hers until she welcomed him within. She could have been swimming in cream, so rich was the feeling of luxury that surrounded her. If a mere kiss could bring her this much pleasure, she thought, she was likely to die if he did more.

She felt the shivering response of her skin as his fingers glided along her throat, dropping lower to the neckline of her dress, then pausing gently on the gentle rise of her breast. Her breathing was audible to her ears, coming in short, jerky gasps as he followed the line of buttons on her dress, as if by magic leaving each one open as he passed on to the next, his mouth warm and worshipful as it trailed kisses along the path between. With a soft groan, he pressed his face closer, drawing the unique scent of her into his lungs and tasting the velvet softness of her skin with his inquisitive tongue.

She thought that surely her heart would burst, so intense was the pounding within her chest. It was a strange sensation, to have parts of her body dulled to inactivity, boneless, weightless, and unable to function, while other parts of her were aroused to acute sensitivity, almost to the point of feeling the very hairs on her head growing. Walker's breath, warm and constant, wafted across her throat as he parted the bodice of her gown, slowly pushing it from her shoulders to bare one breast, which he covered with his mouth.

Charlotte was a mass of nerve endings, completely unaware of his hand drawing up the hem of her dress until she felt the fluttering waft of air in contrast to the warm surface of his palm sliding up the smooth surface of her stocking, stopping at the point of her garter.

Ripe with longing, she lay before him like an open book, half-read, the next chapter promising so much more than the preceding one. He was a master at seduction, this man who quelled her fears with soft, cajoling words and buried her embarrassment beneath the sure stroke of his sensitive fingers. He appeared wondrous and half-magical to her, able to be so many places at once—kissing her mouth, her breasts, stroking her legs, kneading the tender flesh of her thighs.

He was a man who knew how to please a woman, and he pleased her. Dear God, he pleased her in so many ways. But one thing pleased her above all others. His manner, his bearing, his confidence, his experience, and yes, even his words—they all spoke of control. With some feminine instinct, some primitive intuition, she knew that as sure as ducks had webbed feet, Walker Reed was not as much in control as he would like to be. The knowledge of that leaped through her like an electric current, leaving her heady with the thought of having some power over this wonderful man. The satisfaction of it aroused her as no soft-spoken words or tender touch could have. It was this one thing, this basic knowledge, that made her turn her face to him like a sunflower following the path of the sun across the sky.

She took his face between her palms and looked at him with such tenderness, such complete honesty, that it ripped through him like an explosion when she said, "Make love to me, Walker."

He had been aroused by many women well versed in the art of erotic stimulation, but he had never, never been aroused to such a fever pitch by such simple words: *Make love to me, Walker.*

Would he ever forget the look in her eyes, soft and luminous with desire, the glowing countenance of that exquisite face, soft as a flower petal? He didn't think so. The memory would remain throughout the days of his life. The memory and the desire.

Squeezing his eyes tightly against the emotions running rampant within him, Walker willed his racing heart to still, then he lifted his head, forcing order into the chaos within his brain.

"Do you know what you're asking?"

Her words were no more easily spoken than his, and for that reason it was a moment before she could collect the things she was feeling and turn them into words. "There are so many things I will never know if you don't show me, if you don't teach me the wonder of it all."

"While that may be true, it provides no answer to my question. Are you sure you want me to make love to you? Speak with your mind, Charlotte, not your body, for if you say yes, there's no way in hell I will turn back. I know you want me now. Question is, will you feel that way when the deed is done?"

"There is no other I would trust to the task—"

"No task," he whispered as his mouth brushed hers, "but infinite pleasure."

His words melted any response lingering on her tongue, and she felt the involuntary rise of her body against his as his hands began to know the secrets of her. The slow, insistent movement of his hands was driving her crazy by degrees. Mindless nearly to the point of idiocy, she felt the muscles of her stomach contract beneath the soft-whispered touch of his fingers as they swept lower.

His hand closed over her, his finger seeking and gaining entry, subtle and lightly penetrating, then stilling the motion, neither pressing forward nor withdrawing but remaining constant, giving her time. Her virginity was expected and even welcomed with fierce male pride, but, dear God, the tightness. She was so small. Forcing his patience to the limit, he gradually began to ease his way forward, gently, until he encountered the tightly stretched membrane. Pressing with slow spiraling movement, he calmed her with gentle words when she flinched against the first burning sensation that came as he gently violated the confirmation of maidenhood, half-breaching the barrier to ease the entry that would soon come, the pain that was to follow.

Holding her against him with one arm, he removed his breeches, then returned to her, his hard-muscled thigh coming between hers.

Suddenly the door above them rattled against its hinges, and the accumulation of dust poured through the cracks like strangling fingers of creeping fog and dropped onto them.

"Charlotte!" Nemi's voice rang out. "Charlotte, are you in there?"

"Nemi," she whispered.

"Nemi," Walker repeated slowly. "He picks the most damnable times to pop up. How can he suddenly appear out of nowhere? It's damn frustrating to court a woman who has a brother with a talent for dropping out of funnel clouds." He dropped his forehead against hers, the frustration of thwarted desire etched across his handsome face.

Charlotte knew what he was feeling, for she felt it, too. There were times when Nemi was too protective, and this was one of them.

Sometimes she wanted to pound his fool head into the ground. "Is that what you were doing, Walker? Courting me?"

"Yes. At least I was doing my damnedest—until that brother of yours appeared out of a cloud to rebuild the walls of Jerusalem." A grim smile replaced the tightly drawn lips. "It seems he was a little early. I didn't have time to breach them."

"No," she said with a smile as she kissed him lightly, "but you sure stormed the cellar."

Nemi's voice rang out again, and Charlotte answered him as Walker rolled away and stood, fastening his clothing. Then he extended his hand to her, drawing her to her feet, kissing her lightly.

"I'll stall a few minutes trying to draw the bolt so you'll have time to straighten your clothes." He turned and started up the steps, then paused and turned toward her. Seeing her thus, her dress open to the waist, her hair down, her lips wet from his kisses, was overpowering.

"What is it?"

"Nothing. I just wanted to remember you like this," he said. She smiled shyly and lowered her head, fumbling with her buttons. Walker jumped off the steps and returned to her, sweeping her into his arms. "It isn't over, Charlotte. Like you once told me, 'You have a postponement, not a full pardon.' "

She nodded, then smiled. She put her clothes in order while Walker fiddled with the bolt, stalling Nemi while he kept assuring him that Charlotte was still in possession of all her limbs. He neglected to say just what she had been doing with those limbs when Nemi had started pounding on the cellar door.

Finally, giving Charlotte a quick glance and seeing that she was as composed as a woman who had just come through a twister could be, he threw the bolt and waited while Nemi pulled the door open.

The strong shaft of sunlight piercing the dark interior of the small cellar was temporarily blinding. While Walker and Charlotte shielded their eyes and made their way up the narrow steps, Nemi couldn't keep from saying, "God, I've unearthed two moles."

Reaching the top, Charlotte placed her hands on her hips and glared at Nemi. "Nehemiah Butterworth, I love you to pieces, but honestly, sometimes you can pick the most damnable moments to rebuild your stupid walls!"

Walker let out a crack of laughter as a puzzled Nemi pushed his hat back on his head and cast a furtive look at the two of them. "*Now* what did I do?"

Charlotte was about to respond to that when she looked over his shoulder to where her barn stood.

Only the barn wasn't there.

CHAPTER
❧ TWELVE ❧

Charlotte was devastated. The damage done by the twister was inconceivably extensive. Everywhere she looked, havoc had been wreaked, yet, miraculously, her house was untouched, and so—she thought thankfully— was her snapdragon bed.

The barn was gone. Completely. Not so much as a splinter remained. The chicken coops were damaged but still standing, and while Charlotte was looking at them she saw the strangest thing. She turned an astonished face toward Nemi and Walker, but it was obvious that they had already seen it, for both of them were convulsed with laughter.

Charlotte glanced back and, unable to contain herself, began laughing as well. There, strutting around the dilapidated chicken yard, was her flock of hens. Naked as the eggs they had hatched from—not a feather on any of them. But the most humorous sight of all was the old red rooster as he flapped his wings from the top rail of the fence and crowed. Naked.

"What happened?" she said, turning to face Walker and Nemi.

"Damned if I know," Nemi said. "I guess the wind plucked them. I've never seen anything like it."

"I've heard of twisters doing strange things," Walker said. "Once, when I was in St. Louis, I heard about a twister that drove straws through solid oak doors."

"I verily believe," Charlotte said, surveying the damage around her, "that it's quite ridiculous for me to think I'll ever find my basket and my laundry."

"Oh, I don't know," Nemi said, giving Walker a wink. "I hear tell there's a pair of women's drawers stuck on the flagpole in front of the post office."

"Funny, Nehemiah," Charlotte said as she picked her way through the debris. Quick and cautious, she entered the house; it was the only thing she could think of to get her away from Walker and Nemi for a little while, bent on humor as the two of them were. It would never do for Nemi to get wind of what had almost happened in the storm cellar. Without giving her brother or Walker a further look, she closed the door behind her, not seeing the burning intensity in Walker's eyes as he watched her.

But Nemi did.

The next morning, Charlotte was up early. It was Sunday, and she was going to be early, as everyone else in Two Trees would be. People in Two Trees always turned out for church early whenever there had been a big happening, and a twister was most certainly classified as a big happening.

After her bath, Charlotte yanked a blue dimity dress from her wardrobe, rubbing her hand over the rough twilled fabric, thinking of a similar texture along a particular section of Walker Reed's jaw. Standing in her petticoat and chemise before the mirror, she looked at herself. She didn't look any different from yesterday, but my, oh my, did she ever feel different.

"I must be in love," she said, holding the blue dimity against her and twirling around the room until she was quite breathless, then she paused, a wave of self-chastisement sweeping over her. "Charlotte Augusta Butterworth, a fool is what you are!"

Responding to the name she had just called herself, Charlotte picked up her brush and yanked the celluloid pins from her hair, throwing her head back and enjoying the feel of her hair cascading down her back. Her hair was still damp from being shampooed, so she stepped to the window, parted the curtains, and hung her head outside, brushing her hair upward so it hung out the window and hid her face.

Walker, too, was up early, so he decided to hitch Butterbean to the buggy that Nehemiah had had a couple of hands drop off for Charlotte's trek to church, since her buggy was wherever the twister had decided to drop it. Butterbean trotted up to where the barn would've been if it hadn't blown away. Walker wasn't surprised to see her, fond of grain as the mare was. Butterbean put in an appearance at the barn each morning and each evening, knowing that a bucket of oats would be waiting. Hitching the mare to the buggy, Walker decided that it was a good thing Nemi had told Jam to turn the livestock loose before the twister struck. They wouldn't have had a chance in that barn.

When the buggy was ready, Walker glanced toward the house, wondering if Charlotte had noticed that he had spent the night in her front bedroom, since his accommodations had blown away with everything else. Sleeping in that little bedroom and knowing only one thin wall separated him from Charlotte had been pure hell, and his face showed just how much sleep it had cost him.

While he was thinking and staring at the house, he suddenly noticed Charlotte's head hanging out her bedroom window, and he stood immobile and watched her brush the unbelievable length of her coppery hair. He had never seen hair with that much life expressed in the color—he had never seen hair quite that color, but he had seen that color before, on a priceless breakfront his grandmother had brought with her from Normandy, the rich patina of the wood, vibrant and glowing with deep, vivid color, exactly the same shade as Charlotte's hair.

There was something terribly sensual about watching a woman brush her hair, even if she was virtually hanging upside down as Charlotte was. He laughed to himself. Any other woman would've arranged herself provocatively on the windowsill, draping her long cascade of hair over one shoulder and trying to see how much havoc she could create. But not sweet Charlotte. There she was, all shiny and squeaky clean, hanging out her window like a possum up a tree. He had never seen her looking more adorable.

But then Charlotte raised her head and

saw him leaning against the buggy, watching her. She was so startled that she forgot where she was and jerked her head up, cracking it on the opened window above her, a sound so loud Walker that heard it and winced.

"Need any help?" he shouted.

"No, you peeping pervert," she shouted, "I do not need any help."

Before Walker could shout his teasing reply, Charlotte slammed the window. Walker turned toward the well to wash up for breakfast, a smile on his face and an airy little melody humming its way into his heart.

Meanwhile, Charlotte had lost some of her exuberance. Down, but not out, she twisted her hair into its customary coil and rammed the hairpins home in much the same manner as she stabbed pickles from her pickle barrel. Next the blue dimity came sailing over her head, then she put on her stockings and her best, Sunday go-to-meeting shoes. On her way out the door she yanked a bottle of vanilla from the cabinet and doused herself with it as if she were going for a second baptism, and, in a way, she was—washing her sins away.

Walker was sitting at the kitchen table drinking a cup of coffee when she came down the hall. He looked up and saw her stiff posture and knew what she was about. As clear as spring water, she was, and he decided not to prod her about her funny little ways. If she wanted to wear vanilla, that was her business. If it made her feel better about what had happened between them, then it was all right with him for her to give him a double dose of stiff-necked propriety for a couple of days—just as long as it didn't last more than a couple of days.

He watched her come into the room, the air between them charged with electricity—and something else. Whatever it was, it was stronger than a skunk's pouch, and he forgot about his decision not to prod her.

He grinned. "You spill your toilet water this morning, Gussie?"

She gave him one of her looks, and that was about it—just one of her looks. Then she pulled her apron from the peg, tied it around her waist, and lost herself in preparing breakfast.

Inwardly, Walker cursed himself. His stupid blunder and his insensitivity to her mood had obviously made her feel foolish. He studied her. The dress was one he hadn't seen before, and, come to think of it, he had never known her to wash her hair on Sunday morning. It occurred to him that she had taken extra care, even to the point of too much vanilla, just for his benefit, and like a lovely petal beneath his boot, he had crushed it. He wondered what he could do to make it up to her, then he hit upon an idea.

"I don't suppose you have any of Nemi's clothes around here, do you?"

She stopped slicing bacon and looked at him. "I do, but why would they be of interest to you?"

"I thought I might shave and go to church with you, but I'd have to have some clean clothes. Mine are probably hanging on the flag-pole at the post office along with yours."

"Oh, my stars!" she said, her hand flying to her mouth. "The barn! I completely forgot. Your clothes—your bed—everything." She paused. "Where did you sleep last night? I feel terrible that I just rushed off to bed, never thinking about you."

He told her where he'd slept, and it surprised him when she offered him the use of the room until his brother came or the barn was rebuilt, whichever came first. Before he could thank her, he noticed the way her face flushed as if she was suddenly embarrassed, then she lowered her eyes and began placing the bacon in the skillet.

"It shouldn't be too much longer before I'm out of your hair. I would've thought that Riley would've sent that wire from El Paso by now. Maybe after church I'll mosey on over to Archer's office and see if he's heard anything."

Something he said must have registered with her, because she suddenly jerked, pulling her hand back from the skillet quickly.

"What's the matter?"

"Nothing. I just burned my hand," she said, turning away and reaching for the butter crock to spread some on her hand.

Walker was up and beside her in an instant. "Here," he said, "let me see."

She should have refused, but for some strange reason she did not. He stepped in front of her and held out his hand, into which she placed her burned one. They stood there for a moment, looking down at her small white hand lying like a wounded dove in his darker, larger one. His other hand came out to push her fingers back, and he saw the inch-wide burn, the blister already forming across her palm.

He raised her hand to his mouth and gently placed soft kisses along her injured skin. "Don't you have any ointment?"

"Butter will do."

She kept her hand relaxed in his hand as he scooped a dollop of butter from the crock and dropped it into her palm, massaging it into her skin.

"Charlotte," he said softly. "Where are Nemi's clothes?"

"In the back bedroom," she said equally as softly, her eyes never leaving the textured stubble on his cheek. "But why are you going to church today? You never have before."

His arms came around her and he pulled her against him, kissing her shiny, scrubbed forehead. "Because, sweet Charlotte, before you weren't my girl."

Charlotte had heard that prospect was often better than possession, but she found not one word of truth in that. The prospect of having Walker take her to church filled her with awe, and the possession of it was something she would treasure for a lifetime.

She changed into her least-serviceable dress, a blue sprigged muslin, and redid her hair—it wasn't the same plain knot as usual, but a braided coil that sat imperially on top of her head. When she walked outside to where Walker waited in the buggy, he jumped down lightly. He reached out to help her into the buggy and paused, looking her over in a heated manner that made her ache inside. "Being my girl agrees with you, Gussie."

Charlotte smiled and offered her hand to let him support her as she stepped up into the buggy, but before she knew what had happened, Walker had clasped her around the waist and, after swinging her around two or three times, swept her into his arms and carried her into the buggy, depositing her on the seat before climbing in beside her. Before collecting the tracings, he picked up her gloved hand and turned it over, placing a kiss just above her glove at her wrist. "Charlotte, my girl, you look beautiful."

And she felt beautiful.

The churchyard was filled with people by the time they arrived, and Charlotte found most of the community curiously pleased to see her with a man. Well, most of the community, but not all of it. As whispers preceded them, friends and neighbors stopped to greet them, inquiring about the weather and asking after Charlotte's well-being and how she had fared with the tornado. Being with Walker like this was so natural to Charlotte that she didn't stop to think about it for a long time. Then suddenly she understood Nemi's closeness to Hannah and had a brief glimpse of what it would be like to have a mate for life. She saw Walker in the fields—their fields—working, and returning to her each evening, the weariness in his face easing at the sight of her.

She saw him laughing and tumbling on the floor with their children, and frowning in concentration as he tried to pin on a diaper.

She imagined the solid warmth of him beside her in bed each night, the familiar passion that flared between them, and the comfort she felt in knowing it would always be like this with them.

She felt his strength and goodness and the loving support he gave her, like something alive and growing within her. And when he left, it would all go, all that warmth and strength would go with him. But she wouldn't think about that. Not now. For now, she would enjoy each treasured moment, knowing that after he was gone, there would be time enough for mourning.

When they entered the church, a few people who had not seen them outside turned and looked. And Prissy, Mary Alice, and May kept on looking. All during the service, they were sneaking sidelong glances at her whenever Charlotte looked their way. She had acknowledged them with a smile and a nod, only to have them give her a hard, hateful stare and turn quickly away. After that, she didn't bother.

After church they mingled for a while, then Charlotte, seeing Nemi and Hannah leaving, left Walker talking to Archer for a minute and called after them.

After she had talked with Nemi and Hannah and walked them to their gig, Charlotte was weaving her way through gigs and buggies to where Walker and Archer were still talking. Passing behind one gig, its folding top up and hiding its three occupants from view, she heard familiar voices.

"The hussy has her nerve," Mary Alice was saying, "flaunting her lover in church like that. In front of God and everybody."

"Do you think he really is her lover?" Prissy asked.

"Do birds fly? Of course he is. Didn't you see the changed look in her? She was dressed for a man today. And she has that satisfied look, like a cat with a full belly."

"Well, it's a good thing they came to church, then, if *that's* what they've been about," May said.

"Sometimes," Mary Alice said, "you can be so utterly stupid, May. If you think they looked like two repentant sinners, I have a gold mine in my backyard I'd like to sell you."

"But why would he pick *her* of all people?" Prissy said.

"He probably didn't. That's the closest Charlotte Butterworth has ever come to a real man. She simply couldn't resist," Mary Alice said.

"Could you?" asked May.

"I wouldn't want to," Mary Alice replied.

"Oh, never mind all that," Prissy snapped. "What do you think he's like? I mean, judging from the change in Charlotte, he must be pretty good at it."

"You can tell that by looking at him," Mary Alice said.

Charlotte, who was almost on the verge of

tears, suddenly understood what was happening. They weren't maligning her out of hatred or even dislike. It was simply out of jealousy. She had something, or they thought she had something, that they all wanted. Walker Reed. Something sensual and arousing about him had stirred their female curiosity. Walker, besides being breathtakingly handsome, was from California, and that was removed enough from the parched plains of west Texas to mark him as different. That and the fact that he was just a little bit different. Nothing blatant, but a subtle difference in his speech, his manners, the way he dressed and combed his hair and wore his hat. Just enough to make him a little exotic and wickedly forbidden and oh, so desirable. He was the center of all their whispered imaginings, the essence of what they wished for, the reality of what they could not have. So they bickered and snickered behind her back, angry and jealous, thinking that she knew the answers to what they could only speculate about.

With a sudden uplifting of her heart, she turned and walked away.

Archer had moved off to talk to old Mr. Gillingwater, but Walker was still there, right where she'd left him, his eyes on her as she came toward him. "How were Hannah and Nemi?"

"Fine. They're going to stop over as soon as Nemi finishes fencing and Hannah gets her beets pickled."

For a moment Walker looked like he was going to say something about Hannah's pickled beets, but he changed his mind. Charlotte was of half a mind to tell him about a few other pickles she'd encountered that were pining for him, but decided to let the matter drop. After all, it was a glorious sunny Sunday, and she had the best-looking man in six counties on her arm. And hadn't the good reverend quoted just this morning, straight from Proverbs, "He that is of a merry heart hath a continual feast."

With a merry heart, Charlotte walked to the buggy with Walker.

Monday morning came right after Sunday night, just as it always did, and, just as she always was, Charlotte was up with the rooster.

Nemi dropped by late that afternoon and talked to Walker while Hannah and Charlotte made tea punch, carrying it along with some anise cookies to the front porch.

The afternoon heat was still with them, and Hannah was keeping time with her fan, synchronizing it with the squeak of her rocker. Another hour would bring the blessed relief that always came after sundown.

Hannah watched a scissortail in Charlotte's elm tree. "Do you know just how fortunate you are that your trees didn't get carried off in that twister? A barn you can replace, but trees—well, you're mighty lucky."

"Is that what Nemi and Walker are discussing—replacing the barn?"

"I believe so. Nemi said we could spare you a few hands before fall calving, and since our place wasn't touched, he decided now was the best time to start. It's a good thing you've got Walker here to take charge. I don't think Jam could find his way out of a pair of pajamas, and those cowhands are good only if someone tells them what to do. But on their own they don't know come here from sic 'em," Hannah said.

"I only hope Walker is here long enough to see the job through," Charlotte replied.

From the side of the house came the loud squeal of a cat, followed by the sound of masculine laughter. A moment later Walker and Nemi rounded the corner. Charlotte set her glass of tea on the tray and looked up to see her yellow tabby tearing up dirt clods to get out of their way. Realizing what had happened, Charlotte and Hannah laughed.

"Which one of you brutes stepped on Mildred's tail?"

Nemi gave Walker a jab in the rib with his elbow. "It was Walker. You ought to be able to tell that by just looking at his feet. They lay a track wider than the Southern Pacific."

"It was an accident, Gussie, so don't you go throwing that pitcher of tea at me," Walker said with a laugh.

Charlotte had been so intently studying that magnificent body of his, she hadn't caught what he'd said, but when everyone burst into laughter, she knew she'd been found out. She felt the heat of her guilt rising like a red flag to cover her face.

Seeing her discomfort, Walker took the steps in two strides and fell into the porch swing next to her, giving it a quick shove and sending them back, the chains above giving a rather ominous creak.

He looked up. Her eyes followed. "I hope this thing will hold both of us," Walker said, his hand going to his pocket. He pulled out a harmonica and, bringing it to his lips, began playing. After three songs, Nemi was in the mood and sprang to his feet.

"Charlotte, do you still have that old Jew's harp that belonged to Pa?"

"While you track down the harp, I'll go get more tea," Hannah said.

Lord. Charlotte hadn't thought about that old thing in a decade, but she knew exactly where it was. "It's in a leather pouch behind the Winchester shells," she answered, her head still resting on the back of the porch swing, her eyes still closed as she listened to the haunting melody Walker was playing.

"Where are the Winchester shells?" Nemi called from the front hall.

Charlotte opened her eyes to see Walker watching her. As she started to rise to get the harp herself, Walker's hand came out to stop her. "Just tell him where it is. He can find it."

"It won't take me a minute to get it," she said.

But Walker pushed her back. "In a minute I won't be in the mood," he said.

She gave him a puzzled look. "In the mood for what?"

"In the mood to kiss you."

"Charlotte! Where are the shells?" Nemi's voice boomed.

"Behind the soda crackers in the pantry," Charlotte's voice boomed back before Walker silenced her in a most delicious way.

Hannah and Nemi returned together, and while Hannah poured another round of tea, Nemi began to twang on the Jew's harp, catching his lip on the first two tries. By the second glass of tea he was better, and Walker joined him with the harmonica. On the fourth song, Walker dropped the harmonica back into his pocket and leaped from the porch swing, taking Charlotte with him.

"What on earth!" she exclaimed as he whirled her around.

"Dance with me. I'm feeling like a young boy again."

"An old fool is more like it," she said, which set Hannah to laughing, until Nemi told her to hush or he'd start laughing, too, and the dancing music would be all over.

"I don't know how to dance," Charlotte shouted, but Walker paid her no mind, or so she thought. But Walker, as he spun her around the porch, was thinking about a lonely little girl stuck on a Kansas plain with nobody to love her, nobody to tell her how beautiful or how special she was, nobody to teach her dances. There were so many things she had either been denied or had denied herself, so many things he wanted to show her—if only he had time.

Like all good things, the dance with Walker had to come to an end. The hour was growing late. Hannah and Nemi had to be getting home. Walker offered to help Nemi hitch the team to the wagon while Hannah helped Charlotte carry the tea and cookies back to the kitchen.

Charlotte found Nemi's quick acceptance of Walker puzzling. Nemi was a typical Texas rancher: slow to speak, slow to form an opinion, slow to make or break friendships. His family and Charlotte had always come first with him. Never before had Charlotte seen him as warm and open with another man as he had been with Walker. Hannah noticed it, too.

"It's a shame Walker will be leaving," she said. "I've never seen Nemi like he was tonight—frisky as a calf in tall corn."

Charlotte studied Hannah but couldn't bring herself to say anything. A large woman, Hannah was as soft and gentle as they came. Three years older than Nemi, she was already getting gray streaks in her brown hair, but in her golden eyes the light of youth was still dancing.

"He's a hard man to keep your eyes off of, isn't he?" she said after a long silence that threatened to grow even longer, so lost in her thoughts was Charlotte.

"Who is?" Charlotte said rather absently.

"Walker Reed. He's quite a sight to look at. Why, I bet he passes through towns like the circus, with every eye on him—"

"And a few juggling acts between the sideshows," Charlotte added.

"Do you believe he's guilty?"

"No, of course not. I never did."

"Would it change anything if you found out he was guilty?"

"Either way, he will be leaving. What's there to change?"

"Feelings, Charlotte. I'm talking about feelings."

"Do you think Nemi would change the way he felt about Walker if he found out he wasn't who he said he was?" Charlotte countered.

"No."

"Neither do I."

Charlotte rinsed the crumbs from the platter and handed it to Hannah to dry.

"Do you know much about his family?" Hannah asked, taking the platter.

"Not really. He has one brother, Riley. He had a younger sister, but she was killed four years ago when a horse threw her. Both his parents are still living, quite richly, if the account Archer got from the sheriff in Santa Barbara is correct."

"How rich?"

Charlotte laughed. "I didn't ask, but the wire said that Walker's grandfather made a mint during the gold rush. Their ranch is, according to Archer, one of the largest in the state."

"Hmmm."

Charlotte cast Hannah a speculative glance. "Hmmm, what?"

Hannah laughed. "Hmmm, handsome, virile as a randy buck, rich. He's quite a catch."

"I'm not fishing."

"Why don't you just cast your line a time or two and see what happens?"

"Hannah, I don't even know how to bait the hook, let alone cast the line."

Charlotte was standing in front of the pantry, putting away the tin of tea, and Hannah was wiping the table, when Nemi and Walker came into the kitchen, the heavy *tromp, tromp, tromp* of their boots announcing their arrival. Charlotte turned, a smile on her face and a greeting on her lips, when she saw Archer Bradley trailing in behind them.

"Lord," Hannah said, "this is like old home week around here. Hello, Archer."

"Hannah, Miss Lottie," Archer said, eyeing the room.

"The cookies are in the cookie jar, Archer," Charlotte said.

"Thanks."

While Archer fished out a fistful of cookies, Hannah handed him a plate and Charlotte poured him a glass of tea.

"What brings you out to this neck of the woods this time of night?" Charlotte asked.

Archer spoke between bites. "I was just telling Walker and Nemi, that damn—er, darn fool Jethro Cubbs that the county hired to be my deputy ain't worth the lead it would take to shoot him."

Charlotte looked at Walker, his shoulder propped against the cupboard, his hands hooked through his belt loops, and smiled at him. He smiled back at her, his eyes alive with mischief, and, displaying some of that mischief, he winked at her, which left her completely flustered. "Why, Archer," she said quickly, "only last week you were singing Jethro's praises to the sky. What happened to cool your heels?"

"The telegram, that's what."

Charlotte's eyes flashed back to Walker, the smile draining from her face as she noticed the twinkling light go out of his eyes.

"What telegram?" Walker said.

"The one from your brother, Riley. It came over a week ago and I gave it to that half-wit to bring out here," Archer said.

"We never received a telegram," Walker said; then, looking at Charlotte, he added, "Did we, Charlotte?"

Before Charlotte could answer, Archer answered for her. "Of course you didn't," he said. "That's what I've been trying to tell you. I've got the telegram right here in my shirt pocket. I found it tonight when I cleaned off my desk—laying right where I put it when I told Jethro to bring it to your place." He shoved the last bite of cookie into his mouth and fished around in his pocket for the telegram. Walker shoved away from the cupboard, his hands coming away from his belt loops as he reached for the telegram.

Leaving El Paso tomorrow. Stop. Making good time. Stop. Two more weeks should put me there. Stop. Don't get yourself into any more trouble. Stop. Until I get there. Stop.

Riley

Nemi looked at Hannah. Hannah looked at Walker. Walker looked at Charlotte, and Charlotte, unable to meet his gaze, looked away.

"What's everybody looking at?" Archer said, pushing himself away from the table.

269

"Just each other, Archer," Hannah said, taking his plate and glass.

"Well, I'd best be shovin' off. Sorry about the delay, folks. Good night."

"I guess we'd best be heading on home ourselves," Nemi said, giving Charlotte a hug and then shaking hands with Walker. "See you two tomorrow. Come on, honey. We've got a long ride ahead of us."

Hannah put her plump arms around Charlotte and whispered, "You can stand there looking pale as a ghost and watch that man ride out of your life, or you can do something to keep him here." She turned and walked to the back door. "Coming, Nemi?"

When they had gone, Charlotte remained where she was, trying to absorb the fact that Walker's brother could turn up any day and knowing full well what it meant when he did. She wasn't ready for that. She hadn't had time to adjust to the new and tender feelings that were emerging like tiny green plants and struggling against tremendous odds. How was this affecting Walker? She was afraid to look at his face, afraid of the elation she would see there, elation over the fact that he would soon be leaving here—leaving her.

When she could stand the suspense no longer, Charlotte lifted her eyes to gaze at him. He was still standing by the table, the telegram in his hand. But that wasn't what struck her with such unexpected strength and surprise. No. What struck her with knee-weakening intensity was the look of regret etched across his beloved face, the message of apology his eyes were sending her.

If my love can hold you, she thought, *you won't be able to turn from me,* but even as the thought flashed through her mind, the sound of it rang hollow in her heart. She was inexperienced in these things, these matters of the heart. She had neither the expertise nor the wiles to hold a man like Walker. She had been right when she told Hannah she had no bait. She wasn't even sure she had a hook.

"Well," she said, wringing her hands, "I guess it's time for bed, so I'll say good night."

Walker saw the stab of questioning vulnerability and doubt, and it came to him swiftly that he had cast himself in a role he could neither quit nor play to the finish. If he had not taken steps to win her confidence, her trust, he would not have run the risk of winning her heart as well, and he knew that Charlotte's heart was involved. No woman looked at a man like she did unless her heart was involved—deeply so.

He had done many things to her that he regretted, but at least, thank God, he hadn't taken her in the storm cellar. He had been wrong to think he could love her and leave her a better person because of it. No. He wouldn't love her. And he would leave.

"Good night," he answered with a soft note of sadness to his voice, and watched her walk to her room, like a woman to the guillotine, and gently close the door.

"Damn," he said, ramming his fist into the wall. "Damn. Damn. Damn."

CHAPTER
❧ THIRTEEN ❧

Walker rode into Two Trees early the next morning to send a telegram he had spent a good part of the night composing. He'd thought he would feel better after he sent it, but he didn't.

He stopped by Sheriff Bradley's office and after leaving there rode quickly back to Charlotte's, wanting to see her, not knowing what he would say when he did.

The horse ambled along the road, his ear twitching against a persistent fly that kept lighting there. Walker passed a family with a wagonload of children squirming and fighting while the parents paid them no mind. All the children had blond hair and fat rosy cheeks—all except one little girl who sat shyly in the corner. Her hair absorbed the sun like a newly minted penny. Beautiful hair. All rich and warm like the finest Kentucky bourbon. Just like Gussie's.

Gussie. Hell! What have I done?

A rabbit ran across the road. To his right, a cluster of thirsty cattle were bunched around a tank fed by a solitary windmill, the water it pumped down to a thin trickle.

Mr. Jamie Granger, Uvalde, Texas.

Walker stood in the saddle to ease a cramp in his left leg. He crossed a dry gulch. The gelding shied from a roadrunner that darted from a mesquite bush. He saw the roof of Charlotte's house in the distance. Charlotte.

Make love to me, Walker.

The house was closer now. He saw the front porch shaded by the two big elms, the three windows on the east side of the house. He wondered what Charlotte was doing now.

Charlotte's hair, her small birdlike hands and blue eyes. Her body beneath mine. My mouth on her breast. Why did I send that letter to Granger when I want her for myself?

The sun was higher in the sky, burning off the last of the morning cool. The gelding had slowed to an easy walk, his head bobbing up and down, keeping pace with each step. Walker was close enough to the house to hear the sparrows chattering in the elms. They sounded like the women's talk coming from Charlotte's Thursday sewing circle. A snake doctor landed on his hand. He brushed it away.

I did what I thought was right.

A terrible longing came over him. His face was covered with sweat. His throat was dry, too parched even to chew a stick he'd cut from a mesquite. He tossed the stick away. The gelding got some life into him, knowing they were close to home. Walker eased back on the reins, slowing him a bit. The gelding tossed his head and sidestepped. Walker saw Charlotte moving around on the front porch.

I'm giving her back what I took away. She won't forgive me when she finds out. And she will find out. Just as soon as Jamie Granger shows up on her doorstep.

Walker rode to the front gate. He swung down from the gelding. The collar and the back of his shirt were dark with sweat. He tied the reins to one of the pickets in the fence. The gelding immediately lowered his head and began chomping grass. Walker looked at Charlotte. She had been watering her flower boxes, but when she saw him she stopped. The terrible longing he'd felt earlier turned to reproachful grief.

The softness between her legs. Her kittenish sounds. The feel of her breath against my neck. Her hair loose and curling over her naked breasts. Lord! I could be happy here. With this woman. What have I done? She won't forgive me. I won't forgive myself.

She stood still, the watering can in her hand. She looked at him. The thing between them leaped, sizzling and crackling like a static charge, leaving a trail of heat that seemed to connect them, one to the other. Yet she felt something else coming from him, rising like the steam from a kettle, something distancing. Something that sliced across the distance that separated them, cutting like a knife. Severing.

"Charlotte?"

Not Gussie. Not Miss Lottie. Charlotte. She felt light-headed. The current between them had been broken, the two ends flopping like two halves of a dying snake. The light and heat from it was blinding. She closed her eyes against it.

"Charlotte? Is something wrong?"

That's what I want to ask you, Walker. She opened her eyes. He was closer now. Close enough to touch. He was looking at her. Strangely. A hot tingling went through her as if one of the ends of that snake had suddenly

274

whipped out and touched her. It went through her like a thunderbolt. She saw it in his eyes. *Dear God! He is leaving me. It's too late. He wants to tell me. He doesn't know how.*

A great weight was pressing down on her. *How can I love you when I hate you so much?* She stood and watched him for a little longer. The silence vibrated between them like a plucked string. A cold chill crept up her spine. She stood before him, hesitant and indecisive, half of her wanting to confront him, half not wanting to hear what she knew he would say. She stared into his eyes, waiting for some sign, but there was a strangeness there, a remoteness she had never seen before, as if he saw but didn't really see. Like a sleepwalker. He seemed a stranger to her now; the white-hot flame that existed between them only moments before had gone out. Now they were separated by a distance that was both cold and dark. Feeling the coolness of his stare seeping into her bones, she turned and hurried into the house, the screen door banging behind her.

Charlotte saw him that afternoon as she carried a bucket of slops to the hogs. He was working on the barn. He looked up from his hammering as she walked past. She wanted to look up, to see him, to see his face, those eyes that had watched her so warmly in the past, that mouth that had taught her a whole new way of communicating. But she was a stubborn woman. She kept her eyes on the path before her, never looking in his direction.

She felt his eyes boring into her back. Her pace quickened, the dry dust beneath her heavy boots rising up to settle thickly around the hem of her dress. The hog pens were just ahead. The old sow greeted her with a grunt and Charlotte responded with a few kind words. More grunts. A squeal. The sow rooted her snout in the damp earth, then heaved herself up; her squirming piglets, disengaged from their warm supply of milk, began squealing. One determined little piglet was apparently connected better than the others. He hung on, his mama dragging him along with her until the suction was broken and he, too, fell off. Charlotte tossed the slops over the fence and turned her back.

Meanwhile, Walker smashed his thumb and dropped the hammer. Climbing down to retrieve it, he was cursing himself for a damned fool. She was avoiding him and he was letting it get to him like some lovesick schoolboy. Reaching the top of the ladder, he drove in another nail, pounding it furiously.

Charlotte walked by him again. He was pounding the hammer like a madman. His shirt was wet with sweat. His arms beneath his rolled-up sleeves glistened. As she watched him, a tremor traveled up her spine. He clenched his jaw as he hammered.

"What are you trying to do, drive that nail through the board?"

Walker stopped hammering, but he didn't turn around to look at her.

"It's rather pointless, isn't it? Kinda like beating a dead horse?"

He laid the hammer on a crossbeam, then turned to face her. With one finger he pushed back his hat and with his sleeve wiped the sweat from his face. The skin on his forehead was lighter than the rest of his face. "The way I see it, it isn't any worse than asking a man to make love to you and then getting your stinger up when he tries," he said. "Or are you avoiding me because I didn't get to finish what I started?"

"I'm not avoiding you."

"The hell you aren't!"

He wasn't going to allow her to do this to him. He wasn't going to let her make him feel bad about what had happened in the storm cellar. The fault was hers more than his. She'd been asking for it all along. He had seen it in the way she looked at him, her blue eyes full of hidden thoughts; it was in the way she walked, the way her body worked together like a well-oiled machine, just made for loving; the affirmation of it was in the things she had shared with him, things she had never told another living soul. Not even Nemi, whom she loved.

Does that mean she loves me as well?

But the fault was still hers. It was her fault for being a woman—a strange woman—aloof and reserved, giving the impression that she'd rather be alone than have a man around. The fault was hers, for telling him things she had no right to tell him if she didn't want him to care. The fault was hers, for saving his life. But the whole time Walker was telling himself that the fault was hers, he knew, deep inside himself, that it was as much his fault as hers. Something they shared. Like a warm, wet kiss.

He noticed that she was just standing there, staring at him like she'd never laid eyes on him before. He searched his mind for something to say, but no words came to mind.

"You're leaving, aren't you?"

"What?"

"I said you're leaving. That's what this is all about, isn't it?"

"I don't know what you're talking about. Hell! I don't think *you* know what you're talking about."

"I'm talking about the way you've been acting toward me ever since the twister. It's been worse since you went to town this morning. I know you're leaving."

"You've known I was leaving since the day I came here. I never said I'd be here forever."

She looked hurt.

"Crap!" He started down the ladder. When he reached the bottom, he saw that she was still standing there. Still looking hurt, but waiting—as if to hear the words that would make everything all right between them. He took a step toward her.

Suddenly she began to laugh. "No, you never said you'd be here forever. I knew you would leave. I can accept that."

"Then what in the hell is eating at you?"

"I never thought you'd leave like this."

"Like what? Lord a'mighty! I'm not even gone yet and you're riding my ass about it."

Charlotte felt drained, as if someone had slit both her wrists and she stood there watching her blood soak into the ground. "When were you going to tell me? How was I supposed to find out? When I found your bed empty and your horse and gear gone? Is that the way you planned it? To sneak out during the night like Jamie did?"

Walker didn't say anything. He looked embarrassed. He shifted his weight to the other foot. "That's not what I planned," he said. "You know I could never do that to you."

She had turned her head away from him, staring off toward the windmill. From the side, he saw the moisture in her eyes, but she did not cry. He didn't think words were appropriate right now, so he just kept looking at her, willing her to look at him.

But Charlotte wouldn't look at him. She couldn't. Not now. For if she turned and looked at him, if she met his gaze, if she let him look into her eyes, he would see something there. Something she couldn't share with him yesterday. Something she herself hadn't known until this moment. Something she would keep from him now.

She loved him.

Gussie. If he calls me Gussie, I'll know.

"Charlotte," he said in a quiet voice.

The bucket she was holding dropped from her hand. Walker stared at it for a long time after she had gone. Then with a string of oaths he picked it up and hurled it as far as he could. The bucket sailed over the fence and hit the ground with a thump. Then it rolled out of sight.

He worked until suppertime, when the other hands quit, then he continued to work until the light began to fade, stopping only long enough to light a lantern. It was dark when he saw Charlotte come out of the house and cross the yard. She paused at the back gate, calling him in to supper.

When he entered the kitchen, the first thing he saw was the copper bathtub in the middle of the kitchen, filled with steaming water. His eyes lingered on the tub for a moment, then he looked at her.

"I figured you'd like a bath and a chance to clean up before supper."

"Why, Charlotte?"

"No reason, except I know how hard you've been working, trying to get the barn finished before you leave, how much you've been pushing yourself. It's my way of saying I've noticed and I appreciate it."

She left the room while he bathed, returning when he called her to pour a bucket of water over his head to rinse the soap from his hair. After she left again, he dressed, then called to tell her he was decent. When she came back into the kitchen, she made him sit down at the table while she shaved him. When she finished, she cleared away the mess, then made him promise to stay where he was while she ran into the other room. A few minutes later she came skipping into the kitchen, holding something behind her. He thought she had never looked more like a little girl, or more adorable.

He smiled at her. "What are you hiding, Charlotte?"

"I have a surprise for you," she said, handing him two large packages wrapped in brown paper.

He stared at the packages. He stared at her. Speechless he stared some more, then finally he said, "What's in there?"

She laughed. "You'll have to open them to find out. It wouldn't be a surprise if I told you."

He unwrapped the packages. Stunned, he went back to staring again. First at the complete set of clothing in his hands, then at her. "Where did you get these?" he said at last.

"I made the shirts," she said proudly. "The pants and socks I bought in town."

"But why? Why would you do this for me?"

"I can't have you going back to California wearing those ragged clothes you're wearing now, and since all your clothes blew away with my barn, I thought it only fair—"

"You didn't have to do this, Charlotte."

She looked crestfallen. "Don't you like them?"

He felt self-conscious. "Of course I do. It's just—well, it's just that I'm shocked. I've never had anyone that wasn't a member of my family do something like this for me. I don't know what to say."

" 'Thank you' would do nicely," she said.

He reached for her. "Sweet, sweet Charlotte, I thank you from the bottom of my heart, but if I'm going to be perfectly honest, I have to say I've been thinking of a different way to thank you."

She speculated silently on those words. "And how would that be?"

"Come here," he said, "and I'll show you."

"No, you don't," she said, slapping his hands away when he made a move toward her. Then she pushed him toward the door. "You go back there and try on your new clothes while I get dinner on the table. Tonight I've fixed all your favorites. It's sort of—I just thought we'd make this a special night, a kind of celebration before your brother gets here—a going-away present from me to you."

Charlotte would have been thrilled to see the way Walker stood in front of the mirror holding the clothes. He didn't hold them in front of himself to see how they would look on him, nor did he try to put them on. No, he just stood there, the two shirts she had made for him in his hand, his thumb moving back and forth over the fine English cotton, unable to believe that she had gone to so much trouble for him. He might have stood there all night if he hadn't heard Charlotte call him with a warning that the steaks were getting cold.

He dressed quickly and hurried to the kitchen.

Charlotte's face was as clear as her conscience—hiding her sentiments about things was not something she did with any finesse. She was too loving, too genuine, too open to stoop to subterfuge. When she was happy, it showed on her face. When she was unhappy, that showed, too. So it was no wonder that her grief over the fact that Walker would soon be leaving showed on her face. But she made an attempt to disguise it under a smile and a nervous little shot of vivacity when she saw him, having no way of knowing he had been standing there for some time, watching her.

So completely was she involved in her thoughts that when Walker entered the kitchen with a complimentary remark on his lips about his fine new suit of clothes, she didn't hear him. But then, the complimentary remark was never spoken. Instead, he braced his arms in the doorway, watching her reflection in the spotless pane of glass in front of her.

Exhaustion and some lowness of spirit had stolen her sparkle, taking with it the animation that contributed so much to her beauty, and it reminded him of the first time he had seen her, when, about to hang by the neck until dead, he had looked up to see a plain-looking woman with a pinched expression pointing a Winchester at his captors. Memories of the past few months with her came flooding into his consciousness, memories of the way she gradually began to reveal herself to him in oh, so many little ways, opening with painstaking care like the slow-blooming Christmas cactus that blooms only during the season of joy. He wondered if it was something he had done, some callous word he had spoken, some little thoughtfulness he had overlooked, some rebuff unconsciously given, that had brought on this weariness, this sadness to her face. His talks with Nemi and with Charlotte herself had made him fully aware of what she had been through before he'd tried to get himself hanged in her front yard, and knowing that, he now understood just how terrified she must have been to step between him and death as she had done, just what it had taken for her to confront a group of men with murder in their eyes. There was something haunting about her tonight, like the melody of a sad song heard only once but never forgotten. That quality, that remote sadness in her, had always touched him, but now it did more than just touch him. It was as if someone had planted the seed of some strange and exotic plant within him, and suddenly it had sprung to life, spiraling and coiling its leafy tendrils to every remote corner of his body. Seeing her as she appeared to him now was like looking at a holy place, and he was overcome with the urge to throw himself prostrate at her feet.

She was washing something in the dishpan, but she stopped, turning her head slightly, and stared off into space. A dim, glowing lantern at the end of the cabinet threw a golden color onto her face. Her eyes he could not see, but he knew well enough the deep cornflower blue of them against the brilliant splash of her russet hair. No diamonds draped themselves across her bosom, no precious gems twinkled in her ears. There was nothing about her appearance that bespoke a lady of quality, but oh, she was that, and more. Her unadorned dress, one she had made herself, was in essence like her: sturdy, well put together, made of simple lines that contrasted with yet complemented the rich color. The strings of her pristine apron were tied in such a perfect little bow, and his only thought was of crossing the room swiftly and pulling the strings.

She let out a long sigh, something akin to pain touching, but not lingering, on her face. Then she raised her hand to push back a fine coil of hair that had escaped confinement, and she saw him. She smiled beautifully, innocently seductive, but there was something wrong. It was too perfect, too well executed, too hastily brought to the surface, trying too hard to disguise, and because of that he felt the white-hot flame of desire begin to smolder in his loins.

Walker had learned at an early age to control both his emotions and his features. About the only time any degree of feeling was visible was when he meant to expose them or when, on those very rare occasions, his emotions were swept beyond control or conscious thought. Because of this, when Charlotte looked at him, she saw a man who was studying her with deep thought. Looking at him, his eyes brooding, brought back memories of the old terror of men, reminding her that even at his worst this man had always shown more concern for her than for himself. Her smile faded; moisture pooled in her throat; her pulse, quiet until now, began to escalate. It broke her heart to look at him as he was now, wearing the shirt she had sewn, pouring all the love she could find in her heart into each stitch—but there he stood, magnificently propped in the doorway, his arms extended and braced against the jamb. Lantern light teased the contours of his body, illuminating the slim hips, the long-muscled thighs. Her breath was trapped somewhere between an inhale and an exhale. The sound of his voice made her want to cry.

"Sweet Charlotte, what has stolen your sparkle?"

Their eyes locked across the table that groaned under the weight of all the foods he had ever mentioned liking, but she said nothing in response to his question, giving him a little shake of her head instead.

He pushed away from the door, crossing the kitchen and coming around the table, his steps smooth, his pace unhurried as he came to stand before her, his eyes still intent on hers. His hand, as if by its own accord, lifted slowly to her cheek, where, with the back of his knuckles, he defined the contours of it.

"Hey," he said softly, "I thought this was supposed to be a celebration." Her mind poured forth a hundred retorts, but her lips were silent. The wide-eyed apprehension he saw told him that she was troubled, and it pained him to think that she could not, or would not, share it with him. But even the fact that she took such great pains to hide something from him brought him a degree of pleasure. She would not go to such lengths for no reason. The thought that he might have done something during his short stay to endear himself to her was pleasing beyond explanation. When he had mentioned that fact to Nemi last evening, Nemi had given him a rather puzzled look and said, "Those words have a rather perverse ring to them. It's beyond my decision-making capabilities at the moment as to whether I should do all I can to ensure your staying or move to expedite your leaving."

Walker's hand dropped to cup her chin and lift her gaze to his. "If I had it in my power to give you something to make you happy before I leave, Charlotte, what would it be?"

She searched his face as if looking for some element of truth. Apparently satisfied, she stepped toward him, her head coming to rest against his chest, her arms going around his waist to lock behind him. "A night in your bed with you teaching—" Tears came into her eyes and splashed onto her cheeks. "I want just one night, Walker. One night to remember. One night to be held and loved to carry me through all the nights when I won't be."

"Don't, Charlotte. Don't do this to yourself. You don't know what you're saying. Let's sit down and have the dinner you fixed. We'll forget this ever happened, pretend you never spoke those words—"

"I don't want to forget. My life has been nothing but forgetting and pretending." She was crying openly now. "Please, Walker. Give me something beautiful I won't forget, something too wonderful to be pretend."

"I can't, Charlotte. I can't do that to you. It's not my right."

"It *is* your right." she cried desperately. "You're the one who took the time to show me how wrong I've been to blame all men for the wrongs of a few. You're the one who stirred this dead heart of mine, adding new life. It was your mouth that said the things I wanted to hear, your lips that stirred my desire. It was your understanding, your patience, your caring, Walker—not Jamie, not Nemi, not anyone—only you. You've given me a thirst for knowledge, Walker. It's like I just learned to read, and now you want to take away the book. Don't you see? If you don't, no one will. You're my only hope, the only one I trust."

He knew what she was saying. It was the same thing he had been thinking ever since the day she'd fired that Winchester of hers and saved his life. So now—now when she wanted the very thing he had been working toward— why was he suddenly feeling like a heel? He was wrong. He had made a mistake. He shouldn't have brought her this far, because he couldn't, for the life of him, take it any further. He thought about Nemi and the talk they'd had last evening:

"I don't want her hurt, Walker. God knows she's suffered enough. If your intentions aren't honorable, then get the hell outa Two Trees. I like you as well or better than I've ever liked any man—but you hurt her, and so help me God, I'll hunt you down and shoot you like a mangy coyote."

"I don't intend to hurt her, Nemi. I care about her. In my own way, I care as much as you do."

"Then why don't you stay here? Make a life for yourself here. I'm no fool, Reed. I know you care—and not in the brotherly sense. I've got eyes, man. I see the hungry way you follow her every move, and I know you didn't spend your time in the storm cellar counting peach preserves. When Charlotte came out of that shelter, she had the look

of a woman with a little bit of sexual knowledge and a great big thirst for more. You give in to that thirst of hers and you'll have to make it right by her. I'll see that you do. If it ain't marriage you've got in mind, then don't plow in that field."

"I can't marry her."

"Then leave her the hell alone."

"I'm not sure I can do that either."

"Make love to me, Walker. Just once. Just one night."

He whirled away from her, his fists coming down with swift violence against the table, so hard that the dishes rattled and a spoon clattered to the floor. "Goddammit! Don't you do this to me! I admire you, Charlotte. You're a fine lady. How do you think I would feel slaking my lust on you and riding off into the sunset? You're not some two-bit whore I can take and forget! I can't do that to you. I won't!"

"Walker—"

"No, dammit! Don't you go all soft and mewling on me. You're using me, Charlotte, and it hurts. I'm not as callous and uncaring as you think."

He was right. He knew it. She knew it. But it didn't help. She had taken a gamble and lost. She was a desperate woman. But she'd learned that desperation could be humbling. Admitting defeat could be, too. "I understand," she said quietly, turning away.

"Hellfire!" he shouted, grabbing her arm. "No, you don't understand. You don't understand at all."

"No. I do. Really."

"What do you understand, Charlotte? Tell me."

"That you don't want me."

Oh, hell, he thought. *Lord a'mercy, Gussie. Don't you see? Can't you understand I'm doing this for you? I don't want to hurt you. I care. I care more than you know.* He sighed. He should've left town after he'd sent that damn telegram to Jamie. Why had he hesitated? What had made him think he could casually make love to her and walk away? It wasn't as easy in reality as it had been in the dark corners of his mind. "It's not that I don't want you, Gussie. I do—"

"Then why—"

"I do, but I won't. I can't. I can't ride away tomorrow knowing what I've done, wondering if you'll wake up hating me for what happened."

"But I'll hate you more if you don't."

He saw her body tremble as she tried to hold back her tears, and he wanted to touch her, but he knew what touching her now would do to him. "Don't," he said in a choked whisper. "Please don't."

She brought her hands up to her face and wiped away the tears. "All right," she said. Then, taking a deep breath: "All right."

At that moment she was so beautiful that it was painful, so painful he couldn't stay away from her, and he took a step toward her, then another, and another, until he was once again standing before her.

He saw the tension and shame etched on

her face, the uncertainty in her demeanor. A breeze ruffled the curtains at the window; the sparrows were noisy in the elm trees. But inside the small frame house—inside, where they stood so close to each other, yet so very far apart—there was only silence. Walker watched the light slowly fade from her eyes, and he damned himself for not writing that telegram to Jamie Granger sooner, damned himself for delaying his departure one more day. He thought about telling her about the telegram to Jamie, about how he had explained everything, but he knew it would hurt her, make her hate him more than she already did.

If she had fought him, cursed him, even thrown things at him, he could've resisted, but she did none of those things. She merely stood before him, her head bowed in defeat. How could he do this to her? Gussie. Miss Lottie. Charlotte. Old Miss Butterworth. Soft as goose down, gentle as the lingering fragrance of a rose, as lovely and enduring as her beloved snapdragons. She had gone against everything she believed in to step onto her porch late that evening and fire the shot that saved his life. And how had he repaid her? By throwing her feminine pride to the ground and using it for the footpath to walk out of her life. She wasn't asking for much, nothing more than he had given to a hundred women, a thousand different times, yet it was more, and he knew it.

She sniffed, giving her eyes one last wipe, and turned away, going to the pie safe and opening the door, but even then he did not go after her. But when she opened the pie safe and removed the rhubarb pie and turned, there was something about that gesture, something about her remembering an offhanded remark he had once made about how no one had ever made a rhubarb pie just for him—that was his undoing.

Years later, when he thought back on it, he would wonder at the strange workings of the mind, and how he was able to resist her pleading, the smell of vanilla that drifted from her, even the throbbing pain building in his groin, but went loose as a runaway horse when she stood before him with that pie in her hands.

There ought to be a place to lock up a man who loses it over a damn rhubarb pie.

CHAPTER
🌿 FOURTEEN 🌿

One minute he was standing there looking at her, the next he was saying her name... "Gussie," a sound like the breath of life coming from deep in his throat. He closed the distance between them, taking the pie from her hands and placing it on the table, then sweeping her into his arms. "Sweet little Charlotte, don't hate me for this. Don't look back on this moment with regret. Don't make me hate myself any more than I do right now for what I'm about to do."

He would have said more, but she rose on tiptoe, her arms going around his neck to lock at the base of his skull, noticing the drowsy look in his eyes just before she pulled his face close to hers. "I won't," she said softly, and kissed him.

The moment her lips touched his, her pulse leaped ahead, throwing her entire body into acute awareness. The tortured yearning for him in her heart spread throughout her, and she swallowed painfully as his talented fingers slipped upward to stroke with unbelievable lightness the stricture there.

"Kiss me, Gussie," he whispered, drawing her face closer, the words breathless against her mouth.

A desperate craving to move inside him coursed through her veins as she brought her lips to his. Suddenly modest, she was immediately aware that only a minute ago she had thrown herself at him without pride, begging him to make love to her. The thought of her brazen behavior caused her to hesitate, her response to his inquiring kiss to flag. Sensing her mood, Walker looked at her questioningly, but the look soon changed to one of disbelief and then, coming as swiftly as his indrawn breath, to a smoldering coal of desire when she brought her hands up to release the strings of her apron, letting it fall to the floor, then moving to undo the buttons down the front of her dress.

He did not wait to see what she would do next, but swept her into his arms and carried her swiftly down the hall to her room, shoving the door open with his shoulder. Within a few short minutes she was standing by the bed, her dress gone, soon followed by her petticoat, leaving her standing before him in her camisole and drawers. His eyes locked on hers. He caught the end of the pink satin ribbon that was threaded through the eyelet that edged her camisole, pulling it slowly until the knot gave and the edges fell away, exposing the petal softness of the gently sloped valley between her breasts. Using only the tip of his finger, Walker traced the fine edge of her camisole from the pink satin ribbon to her waist, then back up again, this time going up the other side. When he returned to the pink ribbon, he lifted his other hand and, taking a ribbon in each hand, gently spread the sides apart.

The soft moonlight spilling into the room bathed the milky paleness of her skin, touching her breasts with a faint sprinkling of silverdust. His words, though barely audible, were spoken with indrawn breath. " *The fortune of us who are Moon's men.'* "

"Moon's men?" she whispered.

"Minions of the moon, thieves and highwaymen who rob by night," he answered, taking her lips with his own and kissing her deeply.

The soft moonlight shimmered like fairy drops on her hair, giving her cheekbones the luster of a pearl, the triangular hollows below hidden in shadow. The twin peaks of her breasts stood proudly before him, gleaming silver in the light. "You are beautiful," he said, wanting to go on, wanting to tell her just how exquisite she was, just how there was nothing beneath that spinsterish dress of hers that bespoke an old maid. She was a woman as sultry and warm as a late August evening. His eyes cast about the dark room, lingering on the bed. He looked back at her, standing before him all strawberry cheeked and slim, and watched the soft undulations of her chemise as it slid from her body. Sanity, or what little of it remained, vanished, and his heart, held so rigidly in check, cracked like an acorn.

"Lord, Gussie."

She met his kiss, her slender arms winding themselves around his neck. Coaxing her with his tongue and hands, she responded, timidly at first, then slowly overcoming her initial shyness, imitating his actions, then growing bolder and inventing a few of her own that seemed to please him.

Her hands, trembling with desire and uncertainty, loosened the buttons of his shirt, then pushed it aside to expose his sun-bronzed chest. Shy fingers explored the surface, where there was such a contrast between his soft skin and the taut muscles beneath. Overcome with emotion and the pure joy of touching him like this, she pressed the side of her cheek against him, nuzzling, awed by the wonder of it all. Her fingers trailed across the fleeced curves of his chest, interspersed with kisses that were neither expert nor very well placed.

"Gussie," he whispered thickly. His hands came up to plunge into the wilds of her hair, then drifted lower, to her nape, his thumbs caressing her ears with maddening slowness. Her breath caught in her throat.

"Show me what to do," she whispered.

"You're doing pretty good on your own," he groaned in thick tones.

She threw back her head with a little laugh, triumphant, yet feeling a little uncertain. "I'm just relying on instinct and—" She stopped suddenly, her eyes closing as if she were trying to hold back the words that pounded at the back of her throat with each throb of her heart.

"And what?" he said, his fingers wreaking all manner of havoc on her nervous system as they continued to massage her ears.

Unbelievably blue eyes opened, looking up at him through a thick mist of adoration. He watched in utter fascination as the lips that had so inexpertly kissed him parted and an expression settled on her face, an expression he could only call— Good God! She spoke the words at the exact moment he read their full meaning on her sweet, adoring face.

"Love... I love you, Walker."

And I, you. But it can't be, little love. God help us both. It can never be. He closed his eyes against the knife-sharp pain of her words, drawing her close against him, pressing her head against his chest, absorbing the aftermath of shock that her words had caused. "Sweet little love... What you feel is desire, the gratitude of your first awakening. Don't confuse it with love. Like a newly hatched gosling, you want to attach yourself to the first living thing you see, but it's wrong. It wouldn't work. I'm not your kind, Charlotte. My world is so removed from all this... from you. There's

another life waiting for me in California...
responsibilities... obligations." He wrapped
his arms more tightly around her. "God help
me," he said. "I want to stay here with you,
but I can't. I can't be trusted. I'll only hurt
you. Don't you see that?"

"I know all that and I don't care."

"But you will tomorrow. Think, Charlotte.
Think about what you're doing. You don't need
this in your life." *You lying hypocrite. She was
made for it, and you know it.*

"You call this a life?" Her words were
choked and full of emotion. With a twist in
his gut, he regretted being the one to show
her how shallow and dull her life really was.
But Charlotte was so lost in the delight of him,
the wonder of his body, the astonished awakening of her own sensuality, that his words were
as lost on her as a word of caution to a wave
crashing on a rock-lined coast. For Charlotte it was the wonder of first breath, first kiss,
first love, all compressed and magnified a million times. What she felt was love, vulnerable
and defenseless with the pain of it, not a
superficial emotion. She could not love and
be wise, nor did she wish to. She knew only
that something wild and wonderful rose and
blossomed within her each time she looked
at him, like the tears that rose in her eyes to
splash onto her breasts. Oh yes, this was
love, her heart had told her so in many ways,
and the wounds of it left her feeling hopeless
and a little pathetic.

She was as still as a wax figure in a store window, the moonlight playing tricks in her hair

and bringing it to life, all heat and fire and soft seduction. He wanted to wind his hands in it roughly and drag her to bed, bruising her mouth with the strength of his feeling for her. And he knew then that there would be no peace of mind for him until he fed his desire and took her to bed. But he knew that the pleasure of making love to her would last only a moment, the pain of parting a lifetime. He loved her. There was no language that could tell her, for the secret of it was beyond the limits of expression.

His hand came up to touch her lower lip, softly rubbing back and forth, feeling the gentle swell of desire growing beneath the pad of his thumb and the quickening of his own body. Her breasts against his chest were aching and the muscles of her stomach were taut. She was drawn nearer, harder against him, drinking in the breathy heat of him released in a ragged sigh of resignation.

"Are you sure this is what you want?"

Charlotte looked up, seeing his beloved features all shadows and light. She lifted her hand, drawing her fingers along the line of buttons on his shirt, up and over his collar to the strong curve of his neck. She traced the line of his rugged jaw and his cheek, finding the subtle traces of stubble—a gut-wrenching reminder that he was a man. All man. All the man she would ever want. She sighed and closed her eyes, as if to prolong the moment and the exquisite feeling of having him there like that.

She lifted her eyes to his, searching the

shadowed depth of his, her own eyes wide as she tried to say something, but her voice failed her, and the only thing she heard herself say was, "Yes—make love to me. Show me how it is with you...."

"God help us both," he said. "I cannot deny you. Honor be damned. I'll pay the price tomorrow." Suddenly she was locked in his hard embrace, his mouth making her dissolve by slow degrees. His kiss, exquisitely gentle, sent a tremor rippling along her nerves to settle in the deepest privacy of her body. Something unknown within her seemed to take her over, guiding, leading, controlling as her arms encircled him, one going inside his shirt to press flat against his back, the other twisting into the soft texture of his hair.

Once again she found herself lifted in his arms, being carried to her bed. His fingers, so nimble and quick, found the rest of the hooks and buttons of her clothing, making soft snapping sounds as he tugged at them. A small shudder of panic filled her, but she refused it and sent it on its way. This was Walker, whom she loved and trusted to do the deed. She desired the task to be done by no other. At last, she was completely naked, kissed by the moon's cool fingers, her senses reeling with the strain of desire and anxiety. She knew only that she wanted him desperately, with a wild, incoherent need to feel his bare skin against her and to drown in the pleasure of it.

"Dear God, I must be dreaming... or dead. You are beautiful... a dying man's dream of

the hereafter, and damn near too much for me."
His eyes, hot with desire, looked her over
slowly. "You *are* beautiful, Gussie. What you
do to me is beautiful."

She laughed. "What I *want* you to do to me
is beautiful."

"Yes," he said. "That it is. And it will be.
I promise."

She lay there in perfect peace as he began
to undress before her. Shirt and belt, boots
and pants, his clothing fell away from his
body.

The moonlight turned his skin to phos-
phor bronze, as luminous as the metals of the
earth from which it was formed. He was
Adam, God's first man, made perfect. Her pleasure at seeing him thus could not have been
greater.

For a moment he was naked, silent, and
hardly breathing, as if in a trance. Then he
turned to look at her, his breathing suddenly
rapid and deep, his eyes caressing like a warm
palm, giving her time to know him as well.
Inside, he felt the same desperate ache of
longing as he saw in her eyes. And he knew
then that she was his, that she belonged to him,
yes, had even been created for him, for this
purpose. He came to her then, turning toward
the bed, his knee bearing the weight of his body
as he covered her with his nakedness.

Heat. Heat everywhere. The heat of his
mouth filled her and the heat of his body
took away the coolness of the night. The
touch of his hands was gentle, the muscles of
his body hard and contracted as he held him-

self in restraint. Then he shifted his weight, supporting himself with his elbow as he brought his other hand to spread across the width of her abdomen, spanning her hips with ease. His fingers were long and tapered, the fingers of an artist or a musician, but the rough calluses said it was the hand of a man who did hard labor. He said not a word as he studied her body, his eyes coming to rest at last on her face, amazed at her composure, assured of the rightness of it. Still holding her with his gaze, he lowered his head to take her nipple in his mouth, circling it with the warmth of his tongue before drawing it into his mouth. When it was hard and contracted, he moved to give the same attention to its twin.

Rich and warm as fire, her hair spread across the pillow, and Walker told her it was beautiful, "As beautiful as spun copper," he said, before bringing it over her shoulders so that the long, shimmering strands covered her breasts. Then, with infinite slowness, and using only his mouth, he separated the silky strands and drew the straining peaks into his mouth, first one, and then the other.

He trailed kisses across her throat, pausing at the hollow where her pulse beat like a trapped wild bird's. Across the curve of her jaw, his mouth explored, while his hand caressed her belly, his fingers spread and moving lower. Invaded by magic, and filled with mounting pressure, she felt the first stirring of a frantic need and sought the warmth of his mouth with her own. With a groan, he kissed her, and she was lost in the incredible sweetness of his mouth. He had never kissed her quite like this before, nor had she ever felt so filled with heated joy, or dreamed it could be possible to feel so. Never would she have dreamed that a man could do so much with his hands and mouth. Never would she have believed that she could lie completely naked with a man who was naked as well, and feel no shame, no embarrassment. And never would she have believed that a man like Walker, with an almost wicked sexual maleness, would be so gentle and take such pains to bring her pleasure. An overpowering need raced hotly in her veins. She felt like she'd had too much to drink and lay in an inebriated state, unable to function mentally or make her body respond. For now, her body was a thing apart, something separate from her, with a mind of its own.

Thoroughly kissed, and glowing with love, she lay with half-closed eyes, wondering what he would do next. She was taken by surprise when he paused, then rolled off of her and drew her against him, as if to gain control of himself. "What's wrong?" she asked.

"I don't want to hurt you, Charlotte. A woman's first time—it needs to be slow. But it's hard. I want you, and sometimes when a man wants a woman badly—it's hard to convince his body to take it easy."

She could understand that. She was having trouble enough bringing her own body under control. "I don't—"

"Shhh," he said, softly stroking her firm breasts. "We've got all night, Charlotte."

302

Walker felt her frustration in the dissatisfied little sigh that escaped her, and he chuckled against the tumble of curls spilling over his shoulder. Yet, he remembered the other time he had almost taken her, in the storm cellar, remembered how small, how tight she was, how firmly the warm softness of her closed over his seeking finger. He could not remember having had a virgin before, but he most certainly knew that he had never experienced a woman as finely made and delicate and small. Knowing that his own size ran in the opposite direction, he was worried that he would hurt her in more ways than just breaking the thin membrane of her virginity. This was the only experience he would have with her. The pressure to make it as perfect for her as he could was eating at him. God help him if it didn't go well and he left her more scarred, more afraid of men than she'd been before. Yet, in spite of all that, and in spite of the fact that he'd hinted at it, he couldn't bring himself to remind her that this was their only night together.

He rolled to his side, his lips, firm and moist, trailing kisses along the slender length of her throat. "I'm going to make love to you. I'm going to touch you in ways no one has ever touched you, do things with your body you never dreamed could happen. If I frighten you, or make you uncomfortable, or if you want me to stop, just tell me."

"And if you do none of those things? What should I say then? What should I say, Walker, if I like it?"

"Oh, love," he said deep in his throat, "you will tell me that with your body, with the soft little pleasure sounds you make." He kissed her again, speaking into her mouth. "I'm as nervous as you."

I doubt that, she thought as he lowered his head and kissed the swelling softness of her breasts, learning with his hands and tongue the supple firmness, the taste of rose petals. His hand drifted lower. Years of modesty made her draw her legs together, but he stroked the smooth length of her hip and thigh. "No, love. Don't." Gently nipping at her neck, he said, "Relax."

The ruffled lace that edged her pillow framed her face and supported the satiny coils of russet curls that spread beneath her, and the faint aroma of spring flowers and starch and woman drifted over him like a warm blanket. The slow, sure stroke of his hand on her hip faded and his fingers spread with infinite slowness across her flat belly, measuring the distance between her pelvic bones with the spread of one hand. *So tiny,* he thought.

For Charlotte, the slow torture of his fingertips, light on her sensitive skin, was like being seated at a banquet and told not to eat. She squirmed with frustration, feeling the hard, rigid length of him hot against her hip. A sudden flood of thick fluids warmed with desire came into her with a dull, throbbing ache. She moaned, wanting something, unsure of what it was.

But Walker knew.

His fingers abandoned the soft cushion of

her belly to drop lower, to the soft bed between her legs. His hand rested there, while her breath jammed in her throat.

When he made no move to touch her further, she wondered why. Had he changed his mind? Sensing her panic, he whispered against her ear, "Ease up, love. I'm just giving you time—"

"I don't want time, Walker. I've had a lifetime of that."

He smiled against her glossy curls. "What is it you want, Charlotte? Tell me."

"I want you to hurry."

He smiled against her neck, biting her softly. Then, whispering his desire, he turned her toward him, his hands going around her to cup her bottom and pull her closer. Desire for her leaped within him like kerosene tossed into an open flame. With heated tenderness he sought her fragrant softness. The cool, satiny shafts of her hair against his parched lips were intoxicating, the floral sweetness of her recent bath mingling like a rose and brier with the earthy scent of woman, sending his raging desire spinning out of control. He kissed her just enough to keep them both at that fever pitch, then with agonizing slowness he slid his other hand up to grasp hers, drawing it down to where his own desire lay huge and hard. Then his mouth closed over hers with near violence, his tongue matching with perfect rhythm the thrust of his hips, while his hand dropped low over her stomach, searching, and finding a place of infinite pleasure to her.

He continued to move gently against her, driving her nearly to insanity with the light kneading motion of his hand. In a state of anxious impatience she lifted her hips as his finger, lubricated with the love fluids his talented hands had coaxed from her, slipped into her.

Mindless with wanting him, she opened her eyes at the moment he positioned himself above her, feeling the probing point of his manhood. His eyes, filled with a dreamy haze, gazed down at her as he began to ease into her with burning heat. Pain, white hot and searing, shot through her. "No!" she shouted, her fists pounding against him. "No! Stop it. It hurts!"

She tried to roll away from him, but his arms snaked around her, pinning her beneath him. "Oh no you don't," he said through gritted teeth. "You aren't going to do this. You aren't going to pull away from me now and wither with all your wrong notions of lovemaking."

"I've changed my mind," she said breathlessly.

"Forget it," he said, just as breathlessly. "I finish what I start, and, lady... you were started... most deliciously so." Then his voice softened, and the hardness in his eyes melted as his mouth lowered to hers.

Walker would have kissed her all night if necessary, but Charlotte responded to the soft plying of his mouth with a low, strangled sound as she moved against him. That was all it took. "I can't wait any longer, Gussie. It has to be now. I've waited too long... wanted you too much...."

Hot and powerful and alive, he entered her, and she was lost. She vaguely realized that there was some connection between his burning entry and the membrane of her virginity, but it was a burden she was relieved of now. Never again would she not know the way of it. She was amazed and surprised at the reaction of her body. She had never felt any sensations as strong and intense as the ones that swept through her now. She loved everything he was doing to her, loved everything about him, from the taste of whiskey in his mouth to the salty smell of his skin. The need to be with him like this, to get closer to him, was akin to desperation.

Feeling her response, Walker gradually eased himself deeper and deeper, establishing a sweet and faithful rhythm against her. His whole body trembled with restraint as he kissed her mouth, her face, her throat, touching her everywhere, leaving her breathless. His passion was out of control now, his hands urgent, almost rough, his whispered words ragged and telling her what she did to him, how much pleasure he found in her, how perfect she was. But soon his words were incoherent, and soon after that, her mind was, too. Then suddenly the whole world seemed to hover above her in vivid and beautiful colors, then descended on her with trembling vibrations, spilling over her like rose-scented oil, warm and fragrant, bursting into flame.

Gooseflesh rippled across her; a smothered cry was torn in breathless wonder from her throat. "I love you, Walker. I love you."

"I know, love. I know," he said against the damp curls plastered against her temples, his mouth touching hers with an apology for the words he could not say.

Charlotte had not meant to tell him again, having heard no such declaration from him, but the words would not remain hidden. She was bursting with joy and love and she wanted to climb to the highest roof and shout it to the world. What was it about him that turned all her resolve to jelly and filled her with such intense feelings? She had no answer. She knew only that his kisses drove her wild and the touch of his hands on her left her feeling a desperate need. She looked at him and felt the old, familiar tightness invade her heart. He would be leaving soon. He'd made no mention of staying. The distress of it was more than she could bear. To have had him with her like this, and then to have it all taken away. It was a cruel twist of fate, and fate had dealt harshly enough with her in the past.

He held her close to him, stroking her damp skin, telling her how lovely she was. Hammered by the intensity of her release and her newborn feelings for him, she buried her face against his neck and cried, which was the only way she could release all that she was feeling. And as she cried, she poured out all her anger at the thought of him leaving. She wouldn't let it spoil this night. She would have a hundred other nights when he wasn't there to mourn his leaving. But tonight—tonight he was all hers. And she intended to take advantage of every moment.

Walker held her close, stroking her back, his senses acutely alive to the feel of her naked body against is. When she quieted, he continued to stroke her, learning every inch of her lovely body so languorously stretched against him. Feeling the slow rekindling of desire for her, Walker eased away from her, afraid he would frighten her if he made love to her again. As he began to move, Charlotte opened her eyes and looked at him and what he saw there surprised him. Dear God, it couldn't be desire—not after the intensity of what they had just shared. He rubbed his eyes and looked at her again.

"Are you leaving?" she asked softly.

"No. I just thought you didn't look too comfortable all tangled up with me."

"I like being tangled up with you," she said, a hint of mischief in her voice.

"Aren't you sleepy?"

"No. Are you?"

"No." He paused, looking at her, drinking in the ravished-angel beauty of her, the well-loved glow to her skin, the well-kissed pout to her rosy mouth. A shudder passed over him. "The night is yours, then. What would you like to do now?"

She opened her mouth to tell him, but when her eyes locked with his intense gaze, she felt a tinge of embarrassment and tucked her head into the space between her pillow and Walker's shoulder.

He just stared at the back of her curl-tossed head, unable to absorb what had transpired. Had she meant what he thought she meant? What he hoped above all hope that she meant? Dear God, did she want him again? A thrill of delight sluiced through his veins and a deep rumbling chuckle of pure joy shook him. Then, realizing fully what had just happened, he drew her against the throbbing hardness of him and kissed her senseless. "We can do that, too," he said with a healthy laugh.

CHAPTER
FIFTEEN

When the first rosy fingers of dawn crept through the curtains, Charlotte opened her eyes and stretched. Then she groaned. Last night she had romped like a kitten in clover. This morning she was creaking like an old rocking chair. Lovemaking might have made her body sing last night, but it was making her hum this morning. *I'm too old for this,* she thought, rolling onto her side and wondering if she had the strength to sit up.

"Good morning," said a cheerful, gravelly voice from somewhere behind her. Before she could see if her voice was working any better than her body, a warm hand slid over the curve of her hip, drawing her back and pressing her flat on her back.

Charlotte looked up to see Walker, tousled hair and all, leaning over her with a wide, satisfied grin. "You weren't thinking of leaving, were you?" he said, dragging his whiskers back and forth across her belly.

"Stop that," she said, sucking in her breath at the thrill of pleasure that washed over her. "It tickles—"

"Your fancy, I hope," Walker cut in, the scraping of his whiskers subsiding and soft kisses taking over.

Charlotte wilted like one of her snapdragons left too long in the sun.

"The best thing for sore muscles is to use them again," Walker said, continuing to kiss her belly, his tan hands gently kneading her waist. "The soreness will be gone soon."

Just like you will, Charlotte thought, the reminder filling her with sadness. Walker felt her body go limp, and when he looked at her, he saw the laughter in her eyes slowly fade to a deep sadness. He knew her as well as the back of his hand, knew the *Thou shalt nots* that were running in reckless confusion through her mind.

He stretched out beside her, drawing the sheet up over them both, and held her close, mulling over his thoughts and wondering what to say. The somber expression on her face told him that this was no joking matter and any attempt at humor would fall as flat as one of the pancakes. He cocked one brow and studied her for a minute. She didn't look responsive to any attempts at lovemaking, but this fierce male pride told him that he could bring her around soon enough, but even the thought of that brought a hint of self-chastisement. He wondered if her guilt was as great as his own. He considered telling her how worthless and guilty he felt, so as to ease the way for her to place the blame on him, but somehow he couldn't see Charlotte choosing that route of escape. No. She would be more for self-immolation. Knowing that Charlotte wasn't one to be tricked, beguiled, coddled, or persuaded, Walker decided to be honest. To put them both in the right frame of mind, he leaned forward and kissed her. It wasn't a kiss of gratitude or even of passion, but simply a gentle, warming recognition. This surprised Charlotte. She was prepared for his frontal attack, or at least his bushwacking her with a passionate embrace and hot, demanding kisses. This kiss was the most threatening of all, because of the gentleness of it, the understanding that came with it. His sensitivity, his unbelievable insight and understanding, his concern—they all made it so much harder to come to grips with the fact that lay before her as cold and hard as his Colt revolver.

He would leave soon.

"Gussie," he said, his breath warm and generous on her breast, "this isn't something you experienced alone. It was a mutual sharing, an act of will on both our parts. The fact that I'm a man, or even more experienced, doesn't make me any more self-confident than you. I have the same niggling feelings of guilt, the same fears that I didn't please you, the same horror that somehow you think less of me. The coming of morning always seems to shed new light on something that seemed so perfectly right in the darkness."

He kissed her forehead.

His kindness. His gentleness. His understanding. They all made it too difficult, too painful to accept the brutal reality that nothing had changed between them. What had happened last night between the damp sheets had served no purpose, except to heap both of them with more guilt.

For over an hour she had lain beside him in the predawn shadows and prepared herself for that moment. She had anticipated his mood, one of several she had braced herself for: humor, regret, avoidance, nonchalance. But he had shown none of those, and his warmhearted consideration had served only to deepen the gaping wound left by his imminent departure. The need to hold him for just a little while longer was so overpowering that she buried her head in the warm cove of his neck.

"Oh, Walker—"

The heavy tread of booted feet and then the blows on the door as it burst open interrupted her words, and Charlotte, clutching the sheet against her bare breasts, sprang upright and stared into the scowling face of a very handsome stranger.

"Riley, what the hell?" Walker said, leaping from the bed and thrusting his long legs into his breeches. "What are you doing here now?" The anger in his voice was low and threatening.

"You better thank your lucky stars I'm here

now. A few minutes later and you'd be buzzard bait." He glanced at Charlotte. "If this charming lady is Charlotte Butterworth, then you better make yourself scarce, because she has a brother that's madder than a treed coon and he's about ten minutes behind me."

Walker was buttoning his shirt. "What are you talking about?"

"I'm talking about having breakfast with the sheriff this morning when Nehemiah Butterworth came in and joined us. I'm talking about when he found out who I am and that I'd seen you yesterday. He shot out of there like somebody had powdered his behind with buckshot. I had to ride like hell to get here before he did."

Charlotte stared at Walker, then at his brother, Riley. Her confused gaze came to rest on Walker's angrily clenched jaw, then on his tightly balled fists. She saw his outrage but did not know the cause of it. Nemi wasn't a hothead, and there was no way he could've known about last night. So what had set him off?

She didn't have long to wait for the answer.

She'd barely had time to splash cold water on her face, twist her hair into a coil, throw on a clean dress, and hurry to the kitchen when Nemi burst through the back door as if he'd been fired from a cannon.

Charlotte was heating water for coffee. Riley and Walker were seated at the table. Nemi stopped just inside the door, his gaze going from one to the other, then stopping on Walker.

"You son of a bitch! I warned you."

"Nemi! What on earth's wrong with you?"

It was going to be another scorcher. Already the sun was warming the kitchen, and outside not a leaf stirred. Charlotte couldn't help wringing her hands as she waited for Nemi's cold, hard stare to leave Walker Reed and nail her.

"He used you, Charlotte. No—spare me, please. Don't try to deny what went on here last night. I wasn't born yesterday, and neither am I a fool."

Walker shoved his chair away from the table and stood. "I don't think we need to drag Charlotte through this. We can go outside to settle things."

"You should've thought about that yesterday."

"Nemi," Charlotte interrupted. "Nothing happened that I didn't want to happen. You can't blame Walker. The fault lies with me."

Nemi laughed, a deep, cynical laugh that Charlotte had never heard before. "Oh, no, sweet sister. You can't accept the blame— not unless he told you."

Startled, Charlotte turned to Walker. Without taking her eyes from him, she said slowly, "Told me what?"

"That his brother was in town yesterday morning. That Archer Bradley released him to leave right then, but oh, no, Walker Reed had left some loose ends out here. He had one stone that was left unturned."

The screen door opened and Archer Bradley stepped into the kitchen, looking sheepishly

315

from Charlotte to Walker to Riley and then to Nemi and back to Walker. "I'm sorry, Walker. I didn't realize my flapping tongue would cause a ruckus like this."

"You came back out here yesterday with one sole purpose in mind, Reed. You wanted to use my sister to your own advantage before you left. Why her, of all women? Damn you! Why her?"

Nemi's words rang through Charlotte's head. She glanced at Archer, whose face flamed red as he looked away. *Oh, God! What have I done? I have shamed myself before my brother and my friends.*

"It isn't like you think," Walker said.

"No? Then enlighten me," Nemi said harshly. "Tell me how this seduction was different from all the others. Tell me how you will justify this to your fiancée when you get back to California."

Charlotte stared at Walker, a look of disbelief on her face. *Fiancée?* It couldn't be true. Not after... But then, why hadn't he told her that Riley was in town waiting for him? Had she misjudged him so much? Had he really ridden back out here with the sole intent of ensuring her fall from virtue? Had seduction been his only motive? Her look was pleading, begging him to deny the accusing words.

Walker stood mute.

The coffee began to boil, the hissing steam escaping through the tiny spout of the pot, the mad thumps of the coffee perking and splashing against the lid, filling the room with its pungent aroma. Walker, hooking his thumbs in his belt loops, turned and looked directly at Charlotte. "I never meant to hurt you. You know that."

The guilt in his tone stunned her. Nemi cursed and punched the table, startling Charlotte out of her daze.

Riley looked from Walker to Charlotte, his eyes, large and full of apology, lingering on her pale face, the defeated slope to her shoulders. But he also remembered the magnificence he'd seen earlier: the white, softly rounded shoulders; the generous swell of breasts beneath the sheet she'd clutched so tightly; the flowing mane of rich, amber hair, sprinkled with cinnamon; the unbelievable eyes. Riley looked at his brother, a gleam of understanding in his eyes as he shook his head, knowing full well what had prompted Walker to the action he had taken. But Walker saw no humor in the situation and he deepened his scowl.

"Why did you come back out here, Walker?" Charlotte asked, locating her voice at last. "You could have left the moment Archer released you. There was no need for you to ride back out here, to spend another"—the word when she spoke it was strained—"night."

She could see the pain, the regret that lingered in Walker's eyes, yet he did not say the words that would have spared her. "I came back to see you one last time, Charlotte."

"For the purpose my brother stated?"

Walker stared at her. A cricket chirred. A fly buzzed. The clock in the hall chimed the half hour. But he remained silent.

He would have given anything to spare her this. Her words cut through him like a knife. "It is done, then. There is nothing more holding you here. I want you gone."

Walker looked only at her. *He knew all along,* she thought, aware of his penetrating stare and not caring. She lifted her eyes to his, seeing him wince at her cold, hard features, the death of all emotion in her eyes. She felt as empty as a dried locust shell and as worthless. He couldn't have wanted her very much, if he'd thought that only one night would slake his need. It wasn't a very flattering thought, but it was true. When you play with snakes, you shouldn't be surprised when you get bitten. The pain is not lessened by knowledge.

"You heard her, Reed," Nemi said. "Get out. You aren't welcome here anymore."

"I'm not leaving until I have a chance to talk to her."

"No—" Nemi said.

"Let him have a few minutes, Nemi," Archer interrupted. "What can it hurt?"

Charlotte stared at Archer. Even her old friend was coming to Walker's defense. Apparently, she had fallen not only from grace but from all friendships as well.

"What can he say that he hasn't already said? More lies?" Nemi responded.

"I never lied to her," Walker said hotly.

Charlotte leveled a stare at him. "You never told me the truth, either."

Walker watched Charlotte. He felt the tug of his emotions—remorse for hurting her and wanting to explain, hurting because she didn't understand, didn't trust him to the point where explanations were not necessary. Even then, while torn between the desire to go to her and anger at her lack of understanding, he was distracted by the sight of her, the pale, colorless face, the pout of rosy lips that had been well kissed, the contrast between her pride and the humiliation forced on her. His hands retained the feel of her body moving beneath him, the texture of her skin, the soft fullness of her breasts, while the essence of her lingered in his mouth, and the memory of what they had shared seared like a brand in his mind.

He continued to watch her, feeling the stirring of admiration for her pride while sensing intensely the widening gulf between them. He felt an unfamiliar tightness in his chest. It was as if he were woven entirely of yarn and one tiny length of it was connected to her; every time she took a step away, some part of him unraveled. Could she not see that? Surely she didn't believe that he could casually ignore what had been between them—yet, he knew his leaving reinforced that impression. There was little consolation in the fact that he had taken great pains to show her that he shared the responsibility for her loss of innocence.

The harshness of Nemi's voice cut through the warm air of the kitchen. "The fat in the fire has all been fried. I see no reason to prolong this discussion or Charlotte's discomfort." Turning to Walker, he said, "I believe it was your intention to leave with your brother for California this morning. That gives you about two hours to make your deadline."

Charlotte's eyes sought Walker's and she felt a peculiar sense of despair when they found him. She stared at him, her eyes wide with the pain of apprehension. He was so handsome, speaking with swift phrases and confident gestures, strangely savage, tender in such a familiar way. How could she bear to let him go?

But she had to. *He belongs to another woman.* All the color drained from her face at the thought. He had come into her life like the twister, a wild, unrestrained fury, consuming with a vital force of energy, knowing that it was never meant to last. *He has another woman....* He had ripped parts of her away while leaving other parts intact. Wild, temporary insanity that it had been, he had left her with more than he had taken. No other man had cared enough even to try. Only Walker. *And he has another woman.*

Truly, he was a moon man, a highwayman, a thief by night, and he had given as well as taken. By his perseverance, his gentle unrelenting pursuit, he had taught her to trust, shown her that he, as well as other men, were only human, the same as she—some good, some bad, but not all of them one or the other. But she found it hard to forget that all the while he'd been doing so many things for her, he had another woman waiting for him in California.

320

He is going to be married. She would carry the knowledge of that within her for the rest of her life, and perhaps, in time, she would grow to trust another man enough to allow him close to her. *No wonder he couldn't tell me he loved me; he's in love with someone else.* Still, even those thoughts did not completely remove the love she felt in her heart. But the betrayal, the hurt she felt, made her angry enough to push back the more tender emotion. At least for a little while.

Walker's eyes narrowed at Nemi, his fists clenched at his sides. Mindful of the tightening of the muscles in her stomach, Charlotte prayed that the two men she loved so dearly would not resort to physical violence.

Archer Bradley evidently had the same fears, because he quickly stepped between the two men. His words were directed at Riley, who stood next to Walker with a helpless look on his face. "I'll ride back into town with the two of you. There's quite a large sum of money being held in the bank, money I'm sure Walker would like to have before he leaves here. If we leave now, we can make the withdrawal before Martin Weisner closes the bank for lunch."

Riley looked relieved. "I'm ready right now—"

"But I'm not," Walker said sharply. "I requested a moment with Charlotte. I'm not leaving until I get it."

All eyes were on Nemi—all eyes except Walker's, whose gaze was fixed on Charlotte.

"Five minutes," Nemi said harshly. "I'll be waiting outside."

As fast as it had filled, the kitchen emptied, leaving Charlotte wringing the corner of her apron and staring at the floor.

"Look at me," Walker said.

She knew there were too many things written on her face and visible in her eyes, which made her reluctant to look at him. It took an inordinate amount of self-control just to lift her head, an unbelievable amount of restraint not to throw herself into his arms when her eyes locked with his.

He was standing before her much as she had seen him stand a hundred times before, yet today there was something different. If Charlotte had to choose only one word to describe him, it would be *shattered*.

"I never wanted to hurt you."

"I know that."

Her words were flat and emotionless, leaving an ache in his chest, more painful than any he had ever known. He hadn't much time. He knew that nothing he might say would penetrate the barrier she had placed around herself and that it was pointless to try. There was no way to breach the wall, save spending more time with her, but that was the one thing he did not have.

He looked at her, his gaze steady. "I haven't much time, but I want you to know I'm leaving information with Archer on how to contact me. If you should—"

"I won't have any reasons to contact you."

"Dammit! Will you listen to me? There are

certain things... complications that could rise out of what happened last night."

Charlotte knew exactly what he was talking about. But his matter-of-fact reference to the possibility that she could be pregnant removed all hope. In her mind, he had heaped the final degradation onto her, delivered the final blow that separated her from him forever. He couldn't have hurt her more if he had tried to pay her for last night. With a thickening lump in her throat and the burning sting of tears in her eyes, she knew he would leave—and not only leave, but in all likelihood never give her a second thought.

He went on talking, but her mind was flooded with the thought that Walker was now part of her past and the question of what she would do if she did find herself with child. She knew one thing: Never, even faced with starvation, would she let him know. She would let the people of Two Trees brand scarlet *A*s all over her forehead before she would accept one red cent from him.

To Walker, Charlotte's thoughts were as clear as branch water. "I knew this would happen," he said. "I knew you would blame yourself and hate me. I tried to tell you that last night. But what's done is done. We can't change that. I have to leave. You've known that all along."

"Of course I knew it," she said. "I just didn't know why."

"What do you mean?"

"Even dried-up old maids have scruples. Had I known you were betrothed to another, I would never—" She turned away from him, suddenly unable to go on.

"Charlotte," he said, stepping toward her.

"Please," she said softly, "don't take that tone of pity with me. Save me some remnant of pride. I thank you for your concern, but if I should find myself in the family way, I will turn to my family for help. You needn't worry. Now, if you'll excuse me, I'm way behind on my chores."

"Dammit! I'm not worried. What the hell do you expect? What do you want from me?" he shouted. "You aren't going to saddle me with the guilt of your possibly being pregnant and carrying the burden of it alone. If you don't have a lick of sense, at least Nemi and Archer do. You're a beautiful and sensuous woman. You have a lot to offer a man. Don't make the mistake of withdrawing from the world. What we shared didn't *ruin* you. You aren't a fallen woman. You're acting like a child. Grow up. I'm a man. You're a woman. There was something between us that neither one of us could deny. We both wanted what happened last night. We both enjoyed it. Face up to the fact that it was something we did together. I'm not going to let you paint me black. I'm not the villain in all this."

"Good," she said. "You just keep telling yourself that, all the way out of town."

"Okay, okay. Do what you have to do. Make yourself a martyr. Be miserable. I can't—"

He never finished his sentence, because at that moment a voice boomed from the back porch, "Your five minutes are up, Reed."

324

Nemi let the screen door bang behind him as he stepped into the kitchen and crossed his arms over his chest. With a nod in the direction of the door, he said, "Your brother has your horse saddled and Archer is waiting." Turning to Charlotte, he said, "You've got three cows out there that are mighty uncomfortable. If you don't intend to milk them, I'll find Jam."

"I'll do it," Charlotte said.

Walker angrily jerked his hat off the hook by the back door, slamming it on his head. "Goodbye, Charlotte. Nehemiah."

The harsh sound of his farewell quivered deep within her, like an arrow shot into solid wood, the shaft vibrating with a dull throb. The words had all been said. There was nothing left. He walked through the door and out of her life.

Charlotte stood at the door, watching Walker cross the yard and say something to Riley before he mounted his horse. As he turned, he saw her, and brought his hand to his hat, and then with a nod he whirled the gelding and dug in his spurs. The horse leaped ahead, the other three men following close behind. A cloud of dust rose as the wild bunch rode out of her yard.

When the dust had settled, Charlotte couldn't help thinking that Walker Reed had ridden out of her life in much the same manner as he had entered it.

Stepping outside, she looked at the three milk cows standing along the fence near the partially constructed barn and thought that the barn wasn't the only thing Walker had left unfinished.

She picked up a milk pail and crossed the yard; at that moment there wasn't anything she wanted to do less than milk three cows.

The day went on, much as any other day. The sun climbed higher in the sky, and everything drooped from the heat of it. Routinely, Charlotte went through her chores, one by one, until they were all finished. Then, as it always did, the sun went down, the stars came out, and a cooling breeze stirred.

After a cold supper, she pulled out her copper tub and tried to soak the sadness from her bones, but when the bath was finished and the last of the bathwater had been sloshed out the back door, all she felt was clean.

Wearing her wrapper, she stood in the kitchen and looked around. There was nothing else to be done. She had put it off as long as she could. Picking up the lamp, she carried it down the hall and into her bedroom. Seeing her bed neatly made, she was glad that she'd changed the bed linens earlier in the day, but as she pulled back the covers and settled in, she realized that it was going to take more than clean sheets to erase the memory of Walker from her bed.

Charlotte turned out the lamp and lay in the dark room, her hands folded behind her head, watching the curtains at the window lift with each breeze that stirred, then fall, silently waiting for the next one. The evening sounds began to creep into her consciousness—the crickets, the clip of a horse grazing around the house, the howl of coyotes in the distance. Slowly, Charlotte let the assurance of the familiar soothe her, and she relaxed. The curtains fluttered again; a pinch of fall was in the air, laced with the heavy sweetness of the honeysuckle bush outside her window. From her bed she could see the Big Dipper and the pale silvering of moonlight on the grass. The moon was coming up. Soon her room would be bathed in shadows. She thought of Walker and wondered whether he was sleeping in a warm bed somewhere or lying in an open field, staring at the same stars. The memory of him rose like a fever within her. For the first time in her life, Charlotte felt that lonely stab of emptiness, that pain of a woman sleeping alone.

She thought about her night with him and counted herself lucky. Fate could have dropped a man in her yard who was bumbling and inept. In Walker, she had found the perfect lover. Never in her wildest imaginings had she visualized the magic that came with the union of a man and a woman. She felt just a little guilty for letting him leave as he had, thinking that she hated him and was sorry for what had happened. Neither of which was true, but she had allowed the pain of his leaving to rob her of the pleasure of being held in his strong arms and kissed one last time by that beautiful mouth that would haunt her for the rest of her life. She had let her pride color her feelings and understanding.

Perhaps he was right. Perhaps she had acted like a child. If he only knew, if she could only tell him that now—but it was too late. She wanted to tell him that she understood, that she was feeling no longer a child but very much a woman. A tear spilled across her cheek and wandered aimlessly, and as the smell of honeysuckle wafted over her once more, she rolled onto her side and closed her eyes. Here, in her bed, where she had made love with him, she felt Walker's presence. It wasn't a feeling she understood, or one she could explain, but it brought her comfort, and soon she slept.

Her sluggish mind awoke to a scraping sound nearby. Charlotte opened her eyes, looking with breathtaking alarm toward the window. A man's hunched shadow was climbing over the sill, a black mass blocking the silvery shaft of moonlight. With a sudden jerk, a thump, and a corresponding grunt, the man thrust one leg into the room, secured his footing, then drew his other leg in behind him.

A scream formed in her throat. As if sensing this, the man crossed the distance to her bed quickly and clamped a hand over her mouth. Before she could respond, she was caught in his arms as he turned with her and fell across the bed. She felt the biting stab of the butt of his gun striking her hipbone, and a biting stab of something else as his hard length came against her. She grew rigid and tried to push away.

"It's all right," Walker whispered. "It's all right, sweetheart."

Charlotte felt disoriented. Desire and anger warred within her, one telling her to open her arms to him, the other encouraging her to use them to push him away—one hotheaded thought even going so far as to suggest that she yank the pistol from his belt and beat him over the head with it. However, she did none of those things.

Walker lay motionless against her, holding her head against his shoulder, her face pressed against his neck. "Let me go. And *you* can get out of here—*now!*" she said, her voice trying to convey the anger she felt while at the same time she was overrun with the bubbling of joy inside her.

"Charlotte, please..."

"Don't sneak in my window like some sidewinder and think you're going to curl up in my bed. That pleasure belongs to your *other* woman. To the one you love."

"Charlotte, let me explain."

"There's nothing to explain. Even my childish mind can understand something as simple as falling in love and wishing to be married. I was simply a diversion, something temporary you took advantage of. You could have at least been honest with me. Why rob me of the pleasure of feeling like a harlot if I'm going to play the role of one? Who knows? I might enjoy dressing the part. Tell me, Walker, what does a harlot wear? Black satin, I would think. And red—on the lips of course... and feathers, I'm sure—in my hair... and maybe a mole on my cheek and one on my—"

He shook her. "Dammit. Shut up! You're no harlot and I've never treated you like one. Get that through your thick head."

"No, you didn't treat me like one. You just *used* me like one. And perhaps someone as gullible and blind and stupid as I was deserved it," she said, anger and love combining to make her words sizzle.

"Charlotte... please. We don't have much time."

"Oh? And why don't we? Because everyone will be up and about in a few hours, and they might see you here?"

"That's not what I meant."

"Oh, but I think it is. That's why you came sneaking through my window. Because you didn't want anyone to know." Humiliation and anger empowered Charlotte with enough strength to shove Walker hard, and, caught off guard, he fell to the floor. While he was cursing under his breath, she rolled to the other side of the bed and sprang to her feet. Her anger was full-blown rage now, fortified with the pleasure of having shoved him from her bed. She turned on her heel and walked toward the door.

"Charlotte! Come back here!" Walker commanded. "We aren't through with this yet. Not by a long shot."

"Oh, yes we are," she said. "And you can go straight to hell." Her hands clenched into fists, she whirled around with such emphasis that her shimmering mass of coppery hair came cascading over her shoulder to drape across her breasts. Then she shouted, "You don't even pay me the respect of coming to my front door. Even the girls at Belle's Place are treated with more respect than I am."

By this point, Walker had decided that climbing through Charlotte's bedroom window like a thief in the night wasn't such a good idea.

"Don't talk like that, dammit. I didn't come back here for that."

"What did you come back for?"

Calmly he said, "You know why I came back. I shouldn't have to spell it out for you."

Charlotte felt sick. Surely he didn't mean what she thought he meant. Not even Walker could be that cruel. Her heart twisted painfully. Her feelings seemed to drain away, leaving her devoid of love or hate. It just didn't matter. She felt empty inside. Lifting her chin and looking at him as if she hardly knew him, as if he were a stranger, she said, "No. You don't have to spell it out for me. It's pretty obvious, isn't it? You came back for one more tumble with your harlot... one more chance to rub my face in the dirt... one last stab at humiliating me."

"Damn you, stop putting words in my mouth. That's not why I came back and you damn well know it!"

"No? Then you tell me, Walker. I'd like to know. Why did you come back?"

"Because I love you, dammit!"

Seeing the color drain from her face and the shocked expression there, Walker realized that he had spoken the truth. The words had shocked him as much as her. He hadn't meant to say them. He didn't want her to know, for the emotion was too new to him to share. It would serve only to complicate things, and God knew they were complicated enough as they were. But it was true. Heaven help them both—he did love her. And he couldn't leave without seeing her again. He took advantage of her dazed state and stepped toward her, staring into her lovely blue eyes and pale face, wondering why it was this particular face that melted his heart, why he felt such a driving compulsion to have her at any cost—any, except the one he could not bear, the breaking of her beautiful spirit. She had called herself an old spinster and thought herself undesirable, but she had tied him in more knots and cost him more sleepless nights than the most celebrated beauties on three continents. And judging from the way things were going right now, his troubles weren't over.

Charlotte stood there looking at him, feeling as if she'd been struck dumb. He loved her. He hadn't left her. Walker. Here. In her room. But then she asked herself, *What else could he say? Why didn't he tell me before?* And the biggest question of all: *What does he stand to gain by telling me now? One more night in my bed.* Rage, red hot and getting hotter by the minute, swept through her.

Thinking that Charlotte was satisfied, but surprised, Walker caught her by the arms and hauled her firmly against him, only to find that she was anything but satisfied. If anything, his declaration had only angered her further.

"I know it will surprise you to learn there is one woman in the world who doesn't find you irresistible." She pulled away from him, but he let her go only as far as his arms would reach.

"Charlotte, don't be like this. What do you want me to do?"

"Drop dead."

His chuckle was soft. "Besides that."

"Try leaving."

"Come on, Gussie..."

"Don't call me that. I don't want you to call me that ever!"

"Well, I'm as sorry as can be to hear that and even sorrier to have to disappoint you, sweetheart, but that's one request I'll never grant. Now come here, Gussie, and kiss me." This time Walker hauled her against him more firmly, aligning their bodies perfectly.

"What's the matter with you?" she shouted, panic edging her voice. "Have you lost your fool mind? You're engaged to another woman, for heaven's sake. Don't you have any scruples?"

"Not around you." He began to lower his head.

"Stop this nonsense right now, or I'll scream."

This time his chuckle was long and strong. "Now that would take some screaming, to rouse anyone from way out here. You forget, sweetheart, I *know* just how far it is to the nearest neighbor. Come on, yell your head off. You know I love to hear you make sounds when I'm loving you." His arms went around her back, trapping her against him, her arms pinned helplessly to her sides.

"I don't want to kiss you... not ever!"

"Well, I'm as sorry as hell to disappoint you, but that's all I've been thinking about all day," he said in a husky tone, "and I most assuredly intend to kiss you, and keep on kissing you until you melt like a gumdrop left too long in the sun."

"You don't have long enough for that!" she cried, trying to turn her head away, dying with shame at the bitter reminder of how she had melted in his arms the last time he'd kissed her. "That was before... when I was naïve enough to trust you. I'm wiser now."

"How much wiser, Charlotte?" He smiled, bringing his head close enough to speak against her mouth. "Are you wise enough to trust yourself in my arms?"

Walker decided that the only way to shut Charlotte up and get what he wanted at the same time was to kiss her. And kiss her he did. Before she could answer, his mouth captured hers with a kiss that was angry and brutal, but promising. Behind the anger and hostility was a soft tenderness that tempted her to yield, promising that the kiss would change, if she would only give in and kiss him back.

But Charlotte hadn't been called stubborn for nothing. She clamped her lips together tighter and pushed against him for all she was worth. He loosened his grip, allowing her to pull back, but only so far before his grip tightened once more.

"I'm no gumdrop," she said.

He grinned. "You're just one of those hybrid varieties that I haven't experimented with before. A little more resistant." He lifted a hand to caress the smooth skin beneath her ear. "Everything has its melting point, Gussie. Even you."

"You're barking up the wrong tree. I don't melt, or boil, or turn to steam."

"But I do, Gus... every time you kiss me."

That one admission did more to unravel her than all the force he could muster. Stunned by his frank admission, she stared into the steel-blue eyes that were looking at her with such pleading. His quick change of strategy had left her confused and unsure of how to proceed. Before she could regroup, he was drawing her against his long, hard body.

"Wait. I—"

He silenced her objection with a kiss that was both wild and hungry. Caught and kissed senseless before she could recapture her anger, her body was the first to turn traitor, losing its stiffness and molding itself perfectly against his. Whatever objections she was contemplating were in such contradiction to the mad, unruly pounding of her heart that her cautioning mind had no chance. It had always been known that in matters of love, the heart has much influence over understanding, and Charlotte's heart wanted this kiss with every throbbing pulse of overheated blood it pumped through her body. She didn't protest the hand that stroked her throat and then moved lower to cup her breast. Knowing that she should push his hand away, but unable to do it, she felt his other hand spread across the small of her back, forcing her closer to him, and, as if in perfect accord, she slid her hands up along the front of his shirt and over his shoulders to twine in the soft hair at his neck. Walker's groan, the tightening of his hold, and his thumb moving back and forth across her nipple told her what he wanted. And it was what she wanted, too. Everywhere she touched him was taut skin, firm, strong muscle, and fully aroused male. She kissed him back with all the feeling she possessed, made even stronger by the underlying knowledge that this might be the last time, and for whatever time they had she would pretend, if only for a little while, that he was completely hers.

He tugged her gown over her head, and before she was fully aware that he was no longer next to her, he was back. Naked. He led her to the bed, taking her in his arms once again. She felt the caress of night air and the heated throb of him pressing against her belly. He leaned over her, threading his hands through her hair, and lowered his mouth to her throat, nuzzling her with soft words and softer kisses.

"That's better," he said, drawing her closer to him and finding her most cooperative. "Ah, little Gussie," he said faintly, "what have you done to me?"

A strange frailty overcame her, her body growing weak, her muscles falling limp. Her anger was gone. The hurt was still there, though, not so much because he had left her or would do so again, but hurt born of female pride. Pride that came from the knowledge that she lacked what it took to hold him. Whatever they had shared, however beautiful it had been, it wasn't enough to keep him there, and that fact stung like a nettle.

The one redeeming factor in it all was that it had not been as easy for him to leave as she had imagined. His original intention might have been to show her she could trust a man, that not all men would do her harm, but in the process he had made himself vulnerable. In tearing down her defenses, he had left his own unguarded. Whatever it was that he felt for her, it was more than simple lust. No man who looked and moved like Walker Reed had to resort to climbing through the bedroom windows of old-maid ladies. His coming back said he cared.

And that gave her a little hope.

She was not foolish enough to believe it would be a permanent thing. What drew him to California was still there. But perhaps... if what they had was strong enough, the bond they had formed would hold. She wouldn't think about anything—not yesterday, not tomorrow. There was only now. Only this man with his hand warm on her hip.

Walker's hand continued to caress the softness of her hip as his mouth joined hers again. There was not the fierce urgency in this kiss that there had been with the other ones. Feeling her response, he moved his body against her, showing her the depth of his need, soliciting her response.

As naturally as breathing, Charlotte answered him with her body. Her hands, having a will of their own, began to explore the angles and hard planes and curves of his body: the smooth back, the gently bulging hardness of his upper arms, the dark, furred contours of his chest. She knew the heat of his body, the wonderful smell of his skin, the gentle prodding of his desire. There would never be another man such as this one in her life, one who would lead her with infinite patience through the shadowed fears of her mind, coaxing and teaching, giving her back her life as surely as she had given his back to him.

He had returned to her. The reason was unimportant. She could be waspish and bitter and drive him away with her memory as galling as wormwood in his mouth. Or she could come to him with open honesty and sweetness, loving him as she was sure no other woman could, imprinting her image onto his heart and mind like the gentle stirring of a cherished memory. Better that he should forget her smile than remember her hatred. She would see that he would not lose the tender memory of her. He might not find her a lot of things, but there was one thing he would find: She would not be easy to forget.

When he broke the kiss, he drew back, watching her face, welcoming the smile he saw there. "Why are you here?" she asked.

"Seeing if I can improve upon a memory."

Her heart hammered wildly in her chest. Too many beloved thoughts and terms of endearment crowded at the back of her throat to be spoken. "And have you found the answer?"

Walker smiled. "No, but I'm working on it." His look suddenly turned pensive. "How, I wonder, can you improve upon something put to music. You are like a melody that keeps repeating itself in the back of my mind, Charlotte. I've forgotten the words, but the notes still linger."

"Walker, are you drunk?"

Throwing back his head, he laughed, a rich, full-bodied sound. "Only with thoughts of you, sweetness."

"What did you hope to gain by coming back here?"

"A soft breast to pillow my head, an understanding heart, proof that my mind had not played a diabolical trick on me."

"A trick?"

His arms tightened around her, and he buried his face in the fragrant cloud of hair at her shoulder. "A memory, sweet Charlotte. For a moment I held a firefly trapped in my hand, but when I looked again, the light had gone out. Glow for me, Charlotte. Give me a memory, not as brilliant as hope, but just as beautiful."

"I don't understand."

"Nor do I," he said softly. "Nor do I."

He kissed her with such longing that she felt tears collecting in the back of her throat. Her arms wound around him and she drew him against her with a fierce urgency. She felt the need to become a part of him, to crawl inside his head and know his thoughts, to dwell in his heart and feel the rhythm of life, to be swept along with the rapid current of his blood to every part of his body. She couldn't get close enough, or press against him hard enough, or touch him in enough places. Mindless with desire, she wanted only to give of herself, with no restraint, no regret. She wanted to breathe life into him and give him infinite pleasure, to be his source of joy.

Her hand went searching, and, finding him, she answered his soft moan with one of her own. She pressed against him more intently, feeling the swell of savage desire as his body responded swiftly. Like a mist-shrouded dream, she swept over him. "Oh, Gussie," he groaned.

And then he entered her.

Her mind spun away as her body enveloped him, a sensation of dissolving. *Oh, dearest God,* she thought. *So this is love. Welcome.*

She felt tears of joy on her cheeks as pleasure rippled through her, coming hard and fast, in succession, one after the other, like the purging of a wave. When she could bear no more, more came. Again. And again. Until she thought she would die from it, and still his movement became more driven, more intense.

She cried out. He whispered her name in a way that made her open her eyes, catching his intent gaze on her as he carried her with him over the edge. The rapture on his face, the exultant look in his eyes—there was something wholly intimate about it, like seeing into his soul.

For the last time she clung to him, feeling the pounding of his heart against her breasts, the ragged flutter of his breath on her throat. For now, he was hers. Sweetly. Perfectly. Bonded to her by more than the thin film of moisture that held them.

He kissed her softly. "I came for a memory," he said, kissing her again, "but I leave with a dream. You've put strange thoughts into my head. Shall I ignore them or allow myself to become a drifter searching for a restless and airy dream?"

"What kind of thoughts?"

If you only knew how you have snagged yourself on my heart, little love. My going will leave a raveled trail of yarn from here to California, but my heart, Gussie, will remain here with you; one heart on a raveled piece of yarn for you to remember me by. He gave her a puzzled look. "It's not important. Kiss me again, Gussie, before the sun comes up and the memory of you is gone."

Sadness swelled in her heart. "It isn't me that will be gone, I fear... but you," she said.

" 'Like snow upon the desert's dusty face, lighting a little hour or two—is gone.' "When she would have spoken again, he placed his fingers on her lips. "Close your eyes, sweet Charlotte, and let me hold you while you sleep."

CHAPTER
❧ SIXTEEN ❧

He was gone.

She knew it even before she opened her eyes and saw the empty space beside her. She looked around the room. Everything looked the same, yet her mind was fuzzy, and she wondered if she had dreamed Walker's visit. Perhaps she had. There was no reason for him to return. No explanation for the fact that he might have.

Dragging herself out of bed, Charlotte washed her face and was about to dress when she noticed a ray of early-morning sun glinting off something on her dressing table. Moving closer, she saw a tiny golden heart strung on a piece of string. When she picked it up, the heart twirled, first one way, then the other, catching the sunlight in a dazzling way. It was lovely. But why was it suspended from an ordinary piece of string? On closer examination she saw that it wasn't string exactly, but a piece of yarn, obviously unraveled from something. *How odd,* she thought, knowing that the tiny heart had to have been left by Walker. She smiled at the thought, clasping the tiny golden heart closer to her own and closing her eyes. When she opened her eyes to look at the heart again, her gaze went instead to the yarn. Why the piece of yarn? Unable to solve the mystery of it, she moved to the small mirror over her washbasin and tied the tiny heart around her neck. If Walker wanted to give her a heart on a piece of yarn, there must be a reason for it. There hadn't been enough gifts in her life for Charlotte to ruin the specialness of Walker's gift with questions. She tucked the heart beneath her collar, out of sight.

As she went about her chores that morning, Charlotte kept reminding herself that Walker had taught her to trust him, and just because he had walked out of her life was no reason to stop trusting. She would treasure his memory, and tuck it away on her bookshelf, between Byron and Keats, like a book well loved, but too well remembered to need reading again. Now that he was gone, she had to get on with her life. Somehow, the promise of that wasn't as thrilling as it had been at one time.

Nemi and Hannah came for dinner and she fed them fried chicken, biscuits, black-eyed peas, and a slice of her Robert E. Lee cake. Nemi ate three helpings, but Hannah and Charlotte blamed their loss of appetite on the heat.

Soon after Walker's departure, Nemi and Hannah began coming to Charlotte's on a regular basis, their Sunday visits becoming a habit, and by the time cooler weather came, the three of them were laughing and joking as if Walker Reed had never set foot on the place. Charlotte prided herself on the way she had bounced back, but no one knew the long nights she spent locked in the painful throes of memories that haunted her relentlessly.

Hog-killing time came with the cool weather, and with the help of Hannah, Nemi, and Jam, Charlotte butchered the hog she had fattened all summer, relieved to have something besides chicken or the occasional piece of beef Nemi brought her. Fall calving and fall plowing were over, and the new barn was finished and filled to the rafters with hay, the grain bins overflowing with corn and oats. For the past week Charlotte and Jam had been busy harvesting the fall pumpkins and winter squashes, Jam and Rebekah hauling them in from the fields and Charlotte keeping the pots on her Monitor stove simmering with the fruits of their labors. The kitchen was filled with shiny Mason jars of assorted squash and pumpkin mixtures. When she finished the canning, it took three days just to move all the jars into the storm cellar.

Once the canning was done, things slowed to a snail's pace, giving Charlotte more time to finish the quilt she had stretched on a frame in the front bedroom. All in all, things were pretty quiet.

Then one Sunday in November when Nemi and Hannah were having dinner with her and they were all gathered around the table, Charlotte passing Nemi a prime piece of pork, Hannah talking with her mouth full of mashed potatoes, there came a knock on the front door. Charlotte's first thought was that it was Archer, but then Archer never came to the front door.

"Who do you suppose that can be?" she said to Hannah.

"I haven't the foggiest," Hannah said, looking at Nemi.

"Why don't you answer the door and find out," Nemi suggested.

Charlotte answered the door, but she wasn't prepared for what she found there.

"Hello, Miss Lottie."

"Jamie Granger," she said in a tone of breathless surprise, which was no wonder, since she was both breathless and surprised. In fact, she couldn't have been more surprised to see him if he had suddenly dropped out of a cloud right into her lap.

She couldn't think of anything to say, so she just stood there, one hand on the screen door, the other over her surprised mouth, as she stared at the huge man standing on her front porch. If she had given it much thought, Charlotte would have noticed that Jamie was scrubbed, shaved, perfumed, and starched, standing much stiffer than the near-wilted bunch of flowers he held in his hand.

"Fall chrysanthemums," he stammered. "For you." He thrust the flowers toward her, and Charlotte took them.

"Jamie Granger," she said again, as if repeating his name enough would make him seem more real. "Whatever are you doing in Two Trees?"

"I came to see you. May I come in, or is this a bad time?" Realizing his forwardness, Jamie suddenly blushed, and Charlotte found a blush on a man as huge as Jamie Granger quite charming.

"Why, of course you can come in. Honestly, I don't know where I left my manners." She held the screen door open. "Come on into the kitchen," she said, walking ahead of him. "Nehemiah and Hannah are here. We were just having dinner. Have you eaten?"

"I ate in town, before I came out. I'll join you for a cup of coffee, though."

Conversation resumed, Nemi plying Jamie with questions, which Jamie answered good-naturedly. When the meal was over, Hannah and Charlotte cleared the table while the men went to the barn.

"He isn't fooling me any," Hannah said. "I know what Nemi does when he goes to the barn. I'll bet you a yard of my new bobbin lace that he's already found a hiding place for a jug of whiskey. Mark my word, when those two return, you won't be able to pass a candle within five feet of them without both of them going up in flames."

Charlotte laughed. "At least they're out of our hair for a while." She stopped scraping the plate she was holding and stared absently into the pail of slops. "What do you suppose made Jamie Granger come back to Two Trees?"

"You, I imagine," Hannah said, taking the plate from Charlotte's hand and giving it a quick dip in the dishpan.

"Oh, I doubt that," Charlotte said. "He was so mad the day he left he was spitting nails. No. There has to be something else that brought him here." She paused, seeing that Hannah's attention was focused on something outside the kitchen window. Moving closer and peering over Hannah's shoulder, she saw Jamie and Nemi emerge from the barn and walk a few feet to the wagon bed, and then, leaning against it, Nemi rolled a smoke, offering his makings to Jamie.

"I wonder what they're talking about," Hannah said. "Whatever it is, I've never seen Nemi so intense."

Going up on her toes to see around Hannah's ample frame, Charlotte studied her brother's serious face. "Neither have I," she said. "Something isn't sitting right with him, and I don't think it's my cooking."

Charlotte was right. Something wasn't sitting too well with Nemi, and it wasn't her cooking. It was the matter-of-fact answer to the question he had just asked Jamie: "What brings you back to Two Trees?"

"Charlotte."

Nemi's brows went up. "Charlotte?" He looked at Jamie for a minute, then pulled a match out of his pocket and struck it along the rough-planked side of the wagon. The match burst into flame. Cupping his hand around it, Nemi brought the flame against his cigarette and inhaled. After two or three drags he handed his cigarette to Jamie so that he could borrow a light.

Even after both cigarettes had been lit, Nemi didn't say anything for a long time. He rested his forearms against the planked sides of the wagon, staring into the empty wagon bed, taking an occasional drag from his cigarette. Jamie, standing no more than a foot away, did the same. In the house, Charlotte and Hannah were beside themselves with curiosity, wondering just what it was in the bottom of that wagon bed that made the two men stare at it so.

"They're plotting something," Hannah assured Charlotte. "That's Nemi's plotting look if I ever saw it."

"I don't think so," Charlotte said. She glanced at the two men again—just as Nemi spoke—dying to know what he was saying.

"From what I heard Charlotte say, you were in a mighty big hurry to get out of here when you left. I can't imagine why you would want to come back now."

"I came back to ask her to marry me."

"Why?"

Jamie looked surprised. "What do you mean, why?"

Nemi gave him a direct look. "Why do you want to marry Charlotte? Why now? And what makes you think you have a chance with her after the way you left?"

Jamie pondered that for a minute. "I want to marry her because she's the kind of woman I need on my ranch. Solid. Dependable. Hardworking. Not given to airs on false impressions of her own value or beauty. She's an honest woman. She would make any man a good wife."

"You haven't mentioned the one obvious reason," Nemi said. "What about love—or doesn't that enter into it at all?"

"Of course it does. That will come later. Charlotte and I have a lot in common, share the same interests. Given time, that will grow into love."

"And if it doesn't?"

"We will still have a good marriage. I'll continue to be a good husband, and I am sure she'll be a good wife."

"What made you realize Charlotte's assets after you left? Why didn't you mention these things to her while you were here?"

Jamie looked guilty. "Because... Dammit,

man! I didn't think I had a chance with her. Not with Walker Reed lurking about. I saw the way he looked at her, heard the way they argued. They were like two magnets, attracted one minute, repelling each other the next. Then some things happened, some things I didn't understand. I thought Charlotte had given herself to Walker, and if that was her choice, I had to live with it. So I left."

"What changed your mind? What made you come back?"

Jamie took one last drag from his cigarette and sighed. Then he dropped the butt to the ground, grinding it into the dirt with his foot. "I would rather you not tell Charlotte what I'm about to tell you." He looked at Nemi for agreement.

"I can't make any promises until I hear what you have to say, but I can tell you this: I won't tell Charlotte anything that would cause her more grief, or anything I think would be best kept from her."

"Fair enough," Jamie said, then he pulled a piece of folded paper from his jacket and handed it to Nemi. "I received this telegram from Walker Reed, telling me he was leaving—"

"And reminding you what you owed my sister," Nemi finished.

"Yes, to some degree, but that isn't why I came back. I came for the reasons I've already stated. After I had time to think, I knew Charlotte wasn't the kind of woman to give herself to a man without marriage—"

"That's no longer true," Nemi said, catching Jamie's stare. "I'm telling you this only

349

because I think you need to know before you talk to Charlotte. If that's something you can't live with, you can get the hell outa here right now. I don't want you to build her hopes up, then walk out on her a second time."

"I didn't walk out on her. I thought that was what she wanted. But regardless, it doesn't make any difference. Not to me."

"Are you sure? A minute ago you were spouting virtue, hailing her merits as a true and loyal wife. Now that you know you won't be the first, that there is even the possibility—remote, but possible—that she's carrying another man's child, you say it doesn't make any difference." Nemi paused. "I am slow-talking, Mr. Granger, not slow-witted. You don't strike me as the kind of man that would take too kindly to raising another man's child and fostering it as your own."

"It wouldn't matter."

"What if it was a boy? Your legal heir?"

"It still wouldn't matter," Jamie said. "Charlotte isn't the only one with ghosts in her closet. If we marry, she comes to me no longer a virgin and possibly carrying another man's child. I, too, would be coming into this marriage not as I should be." He looked directly at Nemi. "I cannot sire children, nor can I have relations with a woman—not in the normal way. I was wounded in the war, wounded in the worst of all possible places. By rights, I should have died, but instead I recovered, although not completely. My reproductive organs were destroyed."

"Good God! You've got your grit, offering

a woman—any woman—marriage. What kind of life would that be?"

"I don't think that would matter to Charlotte. She has already stated her preference for remaining a spinster. If there is such a thing as a married spinster, I guess that's what she would be. She would never want for anything. I would be good to her, a good companion for her. I honestly don't think she would miss the... miss the other."

"Maybe she wouldn't... before. But things are different now. She's in love—felt a man's hands on her, experienced the delights of the flesh. To deny herself that would be like trying to swim up a waterfall."

"There is nothing wrong with my hands."

"That's a mighty poor substitute. She deserves more than that. I want you to bid her goodbye and get on your horse and ride out of here the same way you came in. She need never know why you came or what we discussed. Your secret is safe with me."

"I can't do that. I came to ask Charlotte to be my wife, to court her, if necessary, and I intend to do just that."

"You hurt her and I'll kill you," Nemi said flatly.

"Look. I don't want to have words with you. Hell, man, you may be my brother-in-law soon. I'll tell you what I think is fair. I want to stay, to court Charlotte, to ask her to marry me, but I promise you I'll tell her the truth about me before we wed. It will be her decision. If she can live with it, why can't you?"

"It's her decision, then," Nemi said, turning away from the wagon and walking toward the house. When Jamie approached his side, all Nemi said was, "You just remember what I said. You hurt her and I'll kill you."

CHAPTER
SEVENTEEN

Wearing a suit of midbrown faille, a darker brown jacket of camel's hair trimmed with passementerie, and a chocolate velvet hat with ruched silk under brim, Charlotte tucked her Bible under one arm and pulled her tan woolen gloves on as she hurried out of her room and into the parlor, where Jamie was waiting to take her to church, just as he had done for the last three Sundays.

"I hope we won't be late," she said, giving him a hasty smile. "I had the devil's own time finding my other glove."

The wind was icy and full of moisture, the kind that penetrates, made even colder by the sun's hiding behind pearl-gray clouds. As Jamie put up the top of the buggy, the cold wind chilled Charlotte's face, and she burrowed beneath the lap robe, scooting far to her side to allow as much room as possible for Jamie.

She stole a look at him. He was like a big brown bear, the rugged tan on his cheeks responding to the cold bite of wind with the faintest touch of red. She looked at his nose, red and rather large, like the end of a thermometer. She laughed into her gloves, hoping to muffle the sound.

As if sensing the lightness of her mood and wanting to take advantage of it, he transferred the reins into his right hand and hugged her against him with his left. Charlotte enjoyed the warm comfort for a few minutes before propriety overruled comfort and she pulled away. Jamie went on talking, just as he had been talking for the past month, telling her about his life in south Texas, his dreams for the future of his ranch. Once, when he mentioned the war, he laughed uproariously when Charlotte referred to it as "the late unpleasantness."

Charlotte, too, was enjoying herself, good moods being contagious. Although she still loved Walker Reed, it was easy to be comfortable around this gentle giant of a man who went out of his way to cheer her, to entertain her, and, yes, to court her, for she knew that was what he was doing.

She snuggled deeper under the lap robe, trying to block the cold bite of the wind. He was such a dear, filling her head with so many compliments that suddenly she was swamped with guilt. It was obvious by his speech that he considered her the epitome of a lady, and Charlotte knew that that included the two big *V*s: Virtue and Virginity. Neither of which she possessed. It was at moments like this that she felt a sense of utter hopelessness. There was no way she could backtrack and regain what she had lost. What she had given to Walker Reed was as gone as her old barn. Wishing it hadn't happened wouldn't change her circumstances—not that her wishes ever turned in that direction. No, she would never be sorry about what had happened between herself and Walker. It was just that she had used her heart to pump blood for twenty-seven years, and then suddenly she had discovered a new use for it.

Charlotte's heart gave a little throb of recognition. Her hand came up to her throat, searching for the tiny heart Walker had given her. Perhaps Walker understood.

Noting the pensive look in her eyes, Jamie patted her gloved hand. "It's a proud man I am to be escorting a lady such as you to church. Why, did you know that if I weren't such a gentle-man, I'd take a wrong turn at the crossroads and head south with you?"

"South? Whatever for?"

"To run away with you." His eyes bright-ened. "Surely you know how easy it would be to keep on going and just take you right on home with me."

Although she knew he was teasing, there was a strange sound of urgency in his voice and a committed look in his eyes. She laughed ner-vously. "Why, we'd be two frozen lumps before we went twenty miles."

"Are you cold?" he asked, pulling the lap robe more securely around her and tucking it in. "I don't want you catching a chill and getting sick on me." His tone was absentminded and the expression in his eyes thoughtful.

She smiled at his tenderhearted concern.

Without thinking, she linked her arm with his and leaned her head against his shoulder. In a way, she felt responsible for his feelings toward her, but more realistically, she felt the heaviness of shame because she could not return those feelings. She loved him as a friend. There could never be more.

Jamie dropped the reins and Charlotte found herself crushed in his strong arms. Her head pounded with indecision and a feeling of helplessness. "Jamie," she said gently, "I can offer you nothing but friendship." His arms tightened around her and he looked down at her through tormented eyes. His suffering hurt as if it were her own. "I'm so sorry," she whispered, "so very sorry."

"I don't want your pity!" he said harshly. Then his mouth came down on hers in a kiss that was very much the kiss of a man, almost brutal in its intensity. Yet, there was something missing.

It was a beguiling, masterful kiss. But there was no naked urgency in it, no rising excitement, no quickening of breath. Nothing. It was as if they were two actors on a stage, going through all the motions of an inflamed kiss but feeling nothing inside. With her body she felt the difference; with her mind she made the distinction. It wasn't because his kiss did not stir her to passion as Walker's had, but because it did not stir him.

He continued to kiss her, her mind groping clumsily to differentiate between what she knew of a man's passion and Jamie's performance. His mouth on hers bore no resemblance to the onslaught of masculine passion she would expect from a man in love. This kiss, this mouth moving against hers… it was wrong.

As suddenly as he had swept her into his arms, he released her. He did not look at her, but took up the reins, slapping the mare on the back. The buggy started with a lurch, Charlotte grabbing the seat with one hand, her hat with the other. She caught her balance and secured her hat, then watched him quietly, assessing her riddled thoughts. She had just been kissed by a man, yet she would have felt no different if Pansy the goat had suddenly licked her face. Curiously, she felt a twinge of culpability, not so much for the act of being kissed itself, but a feeling that she had, by acquiescence, been a party to some unpardonable sin, something abnormal. Over and over she tried to convince herself that the lack of emotion had all been hers, that because of her love for Walker, she was the one who was passionless. But no, that was not true. There was something more. She would not accept the blame.

Wrapped up in her own concerns, Charlotte was not aware of Jamie until he interrupted her thoughts with his shaky words. "I'm sorry. I know I've offended you."

"No," she said, shaking her head. "You haven't offended me. It's—"

"No," he insisted, "don't say anything. It was my fault. I should've waited, given you more time. I don't want to ruin things between us."

"Jamie, please. You didn't offend me. You're

my friend. It would take more than a kiss to ruin a friendship."

"Friend?" he said, puzzled. And then he looked hurt as he understood what she meant. "I don't want to be just your friend. Surely you know that there is more to my coming all this way to see you... my courting you. How can you not know my intentions?" He looked at her sharply. "Charlotte, I want you to be—"

"Please," she said. "Don't say anything right now. There are too many things I need to consider, too many things you don't know about me, things..." She glanced up, seeing the church steeple rising up in the distance. "We're almost there. Let's finish this discussion later."

They arrived at church and Charlotte threaded her arm through the crook of Jamie's and walked into the small, one-room building. No one stared anymore. Everyone was used to seeing them together now; in fact, Charlotte had heard from Hannah, who was social chairman for the Thursday sewing circle, that it was rumored they would be married before spring thaw. All Charlotte could think of was that if it had been Walker Reed escorting her instead of Jamie, she would've thawed a long time ago. But there was no point in thinking about Walker Reed. Spilt milk stayed spilt.

The sermon was a long one, about heathen nations and salvation. After the sermon the collection basket went around. Charlotte noticed little Miranda Jacoby put in a buffalo nickel and take out three shiny pennies. Then her brother Michael put in three not-so-shiny pennies and took out Miranda's nickel. It took Charlotte a few seconds to realize that they had broken even.

December came, cold and windy. Charlotte busied herself with Christmas preparations and making her gifts. Soon the wedding-ring quilt for Hannah was finished and the carved cherry pipe and tobacco she had ordered for Nemi arrived. The only thing she had left to do was the afghan she was knitting for Jamie to use on quiet winter evenings as he sat before a comfortable fire and read. Just as he had done last Sunday evening in her parlor, when he'd invited her to the Christmas dance.

Things had gone smoothly between them since that morning when Jamie had kissed her on the way to church. In fact, their relationship was right back where it had been before the kiss, and Jamie had never mentioned the incident again. Nor had he tried to repeat it. Although he remained silent about his purpose for staying in Two Trees, Charlotte took his continued presence to mean that he was still courting her. And if he was courting her, he must have marriage in mind. But Jamie had never taken any steps to clarify his intentions.

All their conversations centered around their mutual love and respect for literature and music, sometimes reminding them of something funny, and they would branch off into an account of a childhood story. Jamie would talk about his Scottish ancestors; he would entertain her with tales of his two years at West

Point—before the war had broken out and he'd joined the Confederacy. He told Charlotte about his life as a young lieutenant, some of the accounts so funny that she would laugh, and others so serious that she found herself moved by his words. She was beginning to understand the depth and dimension of him, the gentleness and goodness, but the more she understood him, the more she realized that she did not really know him. Regardless of the things he shared with her, how much of himself he revealed, there was always some hidden part of him, some secret he did not disclose.

He mentioned only once that he had been injured critically toward the end of the war.

"How fortunate you were to live through something so dreadful," she said, hoping he would enlighten her more.

"I'm not so sure," he said quietly, "that the circumstances of my survival could be realistically called living."

Before she could question him further, he changed the subject, just as he did every time she tried to bring it up again.

Soon the day of the dance arrived, and Charlotte didn't have time to think about the vague and troubled musings of her mind. She was up early to start her baking for the biggest social event of the year, discovering right off the bat that somehow the lid on her molasses tin had come off when some pesky rodent had gotten into her larder and knocked it over. Molasses was everywhere, except in the tin where it belonged. There was no way to make gingersnaps without molasses, so Charlotte made an unscheduled trip to the general store in Two Trees.

It was a cold drive on one of those frozen, dreary mornings, the kind Jam called "too cold to snow." As she hurried along, she watched the dark gray clouds overhead, observing that they seemed to be broiling and churning as if they were angry. But soon she saw the rooftops of Two Trees just ahead, and she noticed that she didn't have to urge Butterbean into a faster trot.

Apparently Charlotte wasn't the only person up early to brave the freezing weather. When she rode down Main Street, she saw that it was jammed with wagons, buggies, carts, and horses. Every cowboy for forty miles must've ridden into town for the dance, and as she passed the Wayfarers' Hotel she did not miss the No Vacancy sign posted on the front door. Even Old Miss Epperson's boarding-house was full to the gills, and no one ever stayed at Old Miss Epperson's unless they were desperate.

Pulling Butterbean to a stop in front of Lester Schmidt's mercantile and general store, Charlotte pulled her brown wool coat tighter around her, throwing the tails of her knitted scarf back over her shoulder, and climbed gingerly from the buggy. As she tied Butterbean to the hitching post, she glanced across the street at the jail in time to see Archer and a stranger go inside. There was something about the man with Archer that made her stare at the closed door. She stood there, the wind whipping the tails of her scarf back over her shoulder, unwinding it. She caught it just before it blew away, but not before the tightly twisted bun at her nape loosened and her russet hair went flying. Just as her hairpins did.

After collecting her hairpins and tucking her hair and scarf in place, Charlotte glanced back at the jail. The stranger was standing at the window looking across the street. She wondered why it was that a stranger staring out a window could make her feel so uncomfortable. Perhaps it was because she had the feeling that he was staring at her. She saw that he had removed his hat, but the man's face was difficult to see behind the wavy panes of glass. Archer walked up beside him, and she noticed that the stranger was tall and slender by comparison. He ran his fingers through his hair, and for a moment that gesture reminded her of Walker. Butterbean snorted then, and Charlotte turned toward her. When she looked back at the window, the man was gone. Without another thought, Charlotte turned and hurried across the wooden walk and into the warm interior of Lester's store.

Lester came around the counter when he looked up and saw her enter, the bell on the door tinkling merrily as it announced her arrival. "Miss Lottie! What brings you to town this morning? Why, I thought you'd be out at your place getting all gussied up for tonight's big shindig."

"I will be, Lester, just as soon as I get a tin of molasses and finish my gingersnaps. While you're at it, throw in a couple of traps. I think I had a visitor in my larder last night. Molasses all over the place."

"Mice?"

"More likely rats," she said. "Mice couldn't knock over something as heavy as that molasses tin."

A few minutes later, her tin of molasses in hand, Charlotte left the mercantile and climbed into the buggy. As she guided Butterbean into a wide, sweeping turn, pointing her toward home, something made her steal one last look at the sheriff's office.

The man was back at the window.

If the sight of him staring in her direction was unsettling, the close resemblance he bore to Walker Reed was even more so.

"I must be deranged," she said to herself. "Lately everyone I see is starting to look like Walker."

The two shoppers just entering the general store must have thought her deranged too, for they paused to stare at her for a moment, wondering why it was that Miss Lottie was sitting in front of Lester's in freezing weather talking to herself.

Walker stood at the window, waiting for Archer to finish giving instructions to his deputy so that they could go to lunch. He watched Charlotte come out of the mercantile across the street and head out of town. He wondered if she'd recognized him when she looked his way, but her face was so damn hard to read when she held it in that pinched manner she seemed to favor.

The jail was full to overflowing, so Archer was taking longer with his rounds than usual. Walker began having second thoughts about his decision to come back to Two Trees. Riley was probably right—he should've headed for California instead of going on to St. Louis. Or he should've had enough sense go straight back to Santa Barbara when he left St. Louis.

That was what he'd intended to do all along, but something had gone haywire, and when he'd turned away from the ticket window and looked at the ticket in his hand, it was for Abilene, Texas, instead of Santa Barbara, California.

Walker had been anything but pleased to hear that Jamie Granger was back and taking Charlotte under his wing, even though he had sent the telegram to recall Jamie in the first place. He had regretted that decision the moment the telegram began humming through the wires. It didn't sit well with him to see Jamie around town, knowing the reason he was there, or to hear his name mentioned in the same breath with Charlotte's, knowing that he had turned her over to someone else and walked out of her life. He hadn't had a moment's peace since then. One thing he knew for certain: Despite Archer's urging, he couldn't go to the dance tonight.

He could not bear to see Charlotte in another man's arms.

Walker didn't know what to do. He was in a dilemma unlike any he had ever confronted, and for the first time since he could remember, he didn't have anyone to talk it over with. He had always been able to talk things over with Riley, but Riley was gone, and he couldn't see himself telling Archer how much Charlotte's memory ate at him.

He had done his best to erase her from his mind, but no amount of liquor or fast women had been able to achieve that. He could not escape her even when he was asleep, or passed out, dead drunk. She haunted him.

She was not even the sort of woman he was normally attracted to, yet he had never felt such desire. Not even his betrothed, whom he had thought he loved above everything, affected him like this. He had lost his appetite, increased his fondness for liquor, lost weight—and a good portion of his mind along with it. He had thought that coming back would help, that just seeing her again would show him just how plain and ordinary she was and convince him that memory always paints a prettier picture than reality. But it hadn't worked. His heart had swelled in his throat when he saw her ride into town. He'd stood quietly watching her climb from the buggy and secure the mare, his breath leaving his body with a gasp when the wind whipped her scarf away from her head, tossing her hairpins and freeing all that glorious ginger-colored hair. He remembered the cool, silky texture of it, the exact fragrance, the sensual way it curled around his hand when he held it.

No. He had been wrong to come back. It hadn't helped. If anything, it had made matters worse. He should ride back to Abilene. Now. Tonight. He should catch the first train out of there, but he was unable to do that now—now that he had seen her again.

He had to see her just once more. He had to touch her, to hold her in his arms one last time.

And then, perhaps, he could let her go forever.

CHAPTER
❧ EIGHTEEN ❧

The whole world seemed strange and silent as Charlotte made her way home with her tin of molasses. The wind, blowing furiously, made only a soft, mournful noise as it swept across the treeless plain. A sound of loneliness and abandonment. A hollow, empty sound. She turned up the collar of her brown coat and pulled her wool scarf over her nose and mouth. Even poor Butterbean looked lonesome trotting in front of the buggy all alone. Overhead, the sky looked dreary. A hawk was flying solo. One prickly tumbleweed bounced across the road on an endless journey. Everywhere Charlotte looked, the world seemed lonesome, winter browned, and barren.

The pain in her chest grew more intense, the memory of Walker more painful, and she thought of happier times, until the old stabbing longing for love and familiarity crept back into her heart. She was not over him as she had supposed, and as she watched the rhythmical movement of Butterbean's haunches, she wondered if she ever would get over Walker Reed. She guessed not, for loving him was like having malaria: It never truly went away, it just flared up now and then.

Anxious to get home, Charlotte quickened Butterbean's pace, telling herself not to allow the dreary winter weather to overcome her. If she could just keep herself on track, her gloomy spirits, like winter's bareness, would soon be bursting with color. She passed a frozen field and then a broken-down fencerow before she saw the roof of her house in the distance.

Then she heard it, faint and in the distance, but growing louder, overriding the mournful tune of the wind. The pounding sound of a horse coming rapidly behind her was at first very low and far away, then became louder and more intense until it sounded right behind her. Before she could react, the rider passed her on the left side, cutting in front of Butterbean so sharply that the little mare whinnied and reared before a strong arm grabbed the side of her bridle and a voice spoke with calming effect.

"Whoa, now! Easy, girl, easy."

Walker.

The word was such a breathless whisper, Charlotte was not even sure she had said it aloud.

"Hello, Charlotte."

Her heart fell to her feet. The sound of his voice seemed to swirl around her in repetition like the wind: *Hello, Charlotte... Hello, Charlotte... Hello, Charlotte...*

He rode alongside the buggy and dismounted, tucking the gelding's reins into the back waistband of his pants, his hand coming around to pull the brim of his hat more securely against the wind.

"That was you in town," she managed to say, feeling utterly stupid for staring so.

"You noticed."

Oh, Walker. How could I not? He was so beautiful—more than she remembered. Her hand lifted slightly, so strong was the urge to reach out and stroke the rugged line of that beloved jaw, but she came to her senses in time, and her hand fell back against her cold skirt.

"Why are you here? I thought you were in California. Why are you back?" Her voice came in chattering little spurts, but she couldn't tell if it was from the cold or from Walker's presence.

"I never went to California. Riley did. I've been in St. Louis."

"Why?"

He grinned. "Business. I was on my way back when I decided to stop by and see you. Aren't you glad to see me?"

That was the last thing Charlotte had expected him to say. A habit of long standing made her guard her emotions as well as her words. She tensed at his leading question. Of course she was glad to see him—delirious, in fact—but she couldn't tell him that. She repeated her question.

"Why are you here, Walker?"

Without answering, he yanked his reins from where they were tucked into his pants, looped them over the wheel, and leaped into the seat beside her. "You're freezing," he said, jerking his gloves off with his teeth and placing his bare hands on each side of her face and holding them there, allowing the warmth to penetrate her frozen cheeks.

Her hands came up immediately to yank them away. "Don't touch me, Walker. Don't put your hands on me."

Walker continued to hold her hands, his thumbs rubbing the tops of them with sure, strong strokes that unnerved her so. "I don't think I can do that," he said softly.

"You don't belong here. I'm putting the pieces of my life back together. Jamie... Jamie has been courting me. Your presence will only cause trouble."

He looked hurt, then he scowled, his ragged brows coming together as he spoke. "I didn't come back to cause trouble."

"Why did you come back, then?"

"I came to see how you were doing."

"I'm doing fine."

"You aren't pregnant, are you?"

Her heart pounded, her expression one of pure astonishment. Then she slapped him. Hard. Once. But it was enough. She drew back for a second swing but he caught her wrist. Immobilized as she was, she just sat there staring at him.

"Charlotte! Damn you, I asked you if you were pregnant!" he said again, louder this time.

"Get away from me." She reached for the buggy whip with her other hand, but he caught that one as well, holding both wrists firmly in his warm palms.

"I'm not leaving until you answer my question."

"My condition is none of your affair. Now get down."

"Like hell I will…. And your condition is my business. If you're pregnant, it's my child."

"Are you sure?"

His eyes bored into hers. "Yes, damn you, I'm sure." He shook her hard. "Answer me, dammit." He shook her again, until her teeth clattered together. "Are you?"

"No!" she screamed. "No. No. No." Tears were frozen on her cheeks and she angrily tried to wipe them away.

"I'm sorry," he said, trying to put his arm around her shoulder and draw her against him, but she would have none of it and slapped his hands away. "You need to get out of this freezing wind," he said. "We can't talk out here. Why—"

"We can't talk here or anywhere else!" she screamed. "I never want to see you again. Can't you understand that?"

"I think you're lying, Gussie. I think—"

"Don't call me Gussie, damn you! Don't make me remember. It's taken too long to get over you. I don't want to go back. I can't. Don't do this to me anymore."

Catching him unaware, she shoved with such force that he flipped forward, balancing precariously, then lost his balance completely and fell from the buggy. By the time he had righted himself, she had snatched the buggy whip and brought it down on Butterbean's back. The startled mare leaped ahead just as Walker yanked his reins from the wheel. He stood on the road for a long time, staring ahead where the buggy had disappeared from sight.

Charlotte put the buggy away, let herself into the house, and immediately set about finishing her gingersnaps. She wasn't going to allow Walker to fill her thoughts. While the cookies were baking she began heating water for her bath. Then she removed the cookies and placed them on the table to cool while she dragged the huge copper tub into the kitchen.

She stepped into the steaming tub, leaned back, and closed her eyes. She had been soaking for only a few minutes when the back door flew open. Charlotte opened her eyes to see Walker standing in the doorway, a surprised look on his face.

"Get out!" she screamed. "Can't you see I'm bathing?" Before she thought better of it, she snatched her only bar of honeysuckle soap and hurled it at him. She learned one more thing about Walker Reed.

He was a good catcher.

A wide grin broke across his face and he turned to close the door. Moving to her Monitor stove, he opened the door and threw two more pieces of split wood inside. "We're going to have to warm things up a bit for our bath. It's much too cold in here. You might catch your death of cold."

"Our... *our* bath?" she sputtered. "Listen here, you overstuffed piece of confidence. This kitchen was perfectly warm until you stood there gaping like a treed possum and let half the north wind in here."

He ignored that and began milling around the kitchen. Then he spied the cookies. "Gingersnaps," he said, taking a handful.

"Stop eating my gingersnaps," she yelled. "Those are for tonight. Get out of my house!"

His smile was charming. Just as he was. "Make me."

She almost fell for that one, rising in the tub, noticing just in time that he had moved her towel out of reach. She fell back, outraged, splashing water over the sides of the tub.

"Well, well," he teased, looking at the water pooled around the tub, "and here I thought you were such a tidy little thing."

"Listen, if you think I'm going to be a party to fornication here in the middle of my kitchen, you've got another think coming."

He had the nerve to look aghast, then he laughed, a deep, rumbling sort of laugh. "Why, Gussie! How could you think such a thing? Fornication never entered my mind," he said. Then he added softly, "At least not in the kitchen."

She glared at him, crossing her arms over her breasts, which were bobbing nicely near the top of the water. "What are you doing in here, then?"

Seeing her naked skin shimmering in the

water, Walker was having a difficult time keeping his mind on his reason for coming to see Charlotte. If he had learned anything during his time away from her, it was that he had made a mistake—a big mistake—in sending that telegram to Jamie. He wasn't sure how he was going to handle everything, but he was sure that he couldn't let Charlotte go. He would take her to the dance. And tonight he would tell her, and send Jamie Granger packing once and for all.

Walker looked at Charlotte and cringed at the furious expression on her face. His brow furrowed in contemplation. He hadn't anticipated her reacting so violently to his coming back. To be honest, he hadn't really thought about how she would react at all. He had naturally assumed that she would be just as glad to see him as he was to see her. Seeing her hostile expression and hearing her caustic words, he realized that he'd been wrong.

"I asked you a question, in case you've forgotten. What are you doing here?"

"I came to help you get ready for the dance."

She looked aghast. *Help me get ready...* Are you out of your mind? I don't want *your* help. I don't need *any* help. I've been bathing and dressing myself for twenty... for several years."

She started to say something else, but Walker said, "Shh, Charlotte. You talk too much. Did anyone ever tell you that?"

"Yes," she said. "Several times." His smile

was so infectious, she couldn't help but smile a little herself.

He stood watching her, his hip braced against the cabinet. "You're beautiful when you smile."

The smile faded. "Walker..."

"We'd better hurry. Your water will get cold. Where were you when I came in?"

She gave him a puzzled look. "Right here in the tub, you moron." She wondered if he had been drinking.

He smiled. "No, I mean where were you with your bath." She still looked puzzled. "Gussie, I want to know what you had washed and what you hadn't when I came in."

"I had just washed my face and arms and—*What do you mean, what had I washed?*"

"Now, now. Don't get in a stew." He picked up the bar of soap she had thrown at him and went toward her.

"What are you going to do with my soap?"

"I ought to make you eat it." He chuckled, remembering something she had said. "Since when does your vocabulary contain a word like *fornication*? But in answer to your question, I'm going to wash you with it."

She was so flustered by what was happening, she just sat there in a tub of rapidly cooling water, staring stupidly as he approached her and went down on one knee next to her. Without any conscious thought of what was happening, only knowing that this was Walker and anything between them was right, she watched him roll up his sleeves and then plunge his arms into the water, fishing around for her cloth. When he located it, he soaped it well. "Turn around," he said.

"Go to the devil," she replied, shoving his hands away with such force that the soapy rag he was holding squashed against his face.

"You little hellcat!" he shouted, wiping the soapy water from his face with his sleeve. Without giving him a chance to say anything more, Charlotte leaped from the tub and, knowing she didn't have time to go for the towel, grabbed a fresh tablecloth she had ironed earlier and laid across the back of the kitchen chair. Running down the hall for all she was worth, the tablecloth wrapped around her, she darted into her bedroom and slammed the door against Walker's foot just as he came up behind her.

"Get out of my house and out of my life or so help me God, you'll be sorrier than you already are!" She grabbed a vase of peacock feathers and drew her arm back, ready to let it fly if he took one more step, but he just stood inside the doorway, his shirtfront drenched with soapy water, his thumbs hooked in his belt loops, looking his fill.

His face took on a look of deep thought as several extraordinary facts became clear all at once. The sweet, docile woman who had saved his life all those months ago had changed. Gone was the slim, spinsterish woman with a bun and softly spoken words, and standing in her place was a half-naked creature of exotic beauty with a wild mane of sizzling red hair and a stubborn streak of hot-blooded rebellion a mile long. And she

374

was spitting imprecations at him faster than he could count. She was exquisite, gorgeous, and he wanted her more now than he had at any point since he had met her. Here, he realized, was a woman worth fighting for, even if she was the one he had to fight.

Calmly he said, "Put down the vase, Charlotte."

"Over your head, you mean!"

"Throwing that vase at me won't solve the problem, and tomorrow you'll be angry at yourself for breaking it."

"What will solve the problem, Walker? Tell me."

"I think you know the answer to that."

"How can I? I don't even know what the problem is."

"It's quite simple. I came back to see you, and you don't want me here."

"So leave."

He took a step toward her and Charlotte drew her arm back farther. "I'm warning you. I'll smash this over your fool head if you take another step."

She could not believe the glint of laughter in his eyes, the laughter pulling at the corners of his mouth. That alone would have made her throw the vase, even if he hadn't taken another step. Like a catapult her arm went back a little farther and the vase went sailing through the air. Walker ducked and the vase shattered on the wall behind him, a couple of peacock feathers balancing on his shoulder, bits of china in his hair.

"Now *that's* something to laugh at," she said,

turning to look for something else to throw, just in case he decided to advance another step.

Walker stared at her lovely face and had to curb a pinch of admiration for her courage—fool-headed courage, but admirable. "I suppose I should at least be happy I can make you smile," he said.

"You can't *make* me do anything."

The humor drained from his face. "That's where you're wrong, Charlotte. I *can* and I *will*."

Seeing the determined look in his eyes and the resigned set to his mouth, Charlotte reached for the nearest thing, which turned out to be a small music box. As Walker rushed her, she hurled it, terrified that she had hurt him when she heard him grunt as it glanced off his head. But it didn't slow him down any. Darting away from him, she threw a hatbox, which he deflected with his arm. Next came a hairbrush, a box of hair ribbons, a tortoiseshell comb, a bird figurine, and a book of sonnets. Out of ammunition, she began to back away from him. "Stay away from me."

"Charlotte, you have wrecked everything in this room, including me."

"Then it was worth it," she said, out of breath and taking one more step back, coming up against the wall.

"Do you know what I'm going to do to you when I catch you? And catch you I will."

She, of course, was afraid to ask. She was also afraid that he was right. He would catch her. Charlotte swallowed and shook her head, knowing that if he put his hands on her in anger or any other way, she would still want him. Out of breath, she was panting, the tablecloth riding deliciously low on her breasts, her hair spiraling around her face, giving her the look of a woman who has just been made love to—thoroughly.

Walker felt his body leap in response to the sight before him. He wanted her. And he would catch her. Only he wasn't too sure just what he would do with her when he did. With secret amusement he noted her inner struggles. One by one, he was whittling down her defenses, and he knew it would not be long before he had her in his arms. But he would have to match her fiery temperament and rebellious spirit in order to do so. Charlotte wasn't the same woman he had taken to bed months ago. She would no longer respond to the gentleman paying court. The hot-blooded woman before him would be tamed only by coolheaded, authoritative treatment.

They stared wordlessly at each other, and Walker knew he'd better think of something to say fast or Charlotte would hit him with another round of her temper. "Come back to the kitchen. I brought something for you."

"I don't want it."

"Dammit, Charlotte. Will you stop being so stubborn? You can either walk to the kitchen or I'll carry you. If you aren't in there by the time I return, I'll come after you." He turned and walked out the door.

A few minutes later he entered the kitchen, a package under his arm. Charlotte was wearing her wrapper now, standing by the stove, her arms folded around her waist, a sullen look on her face. Walker held the package toward her, but she didn't budge. He ripped the paper off the package and unfolded a dress of shimmering green silk. Shaking the dress out, he draped it over the back of a chair. "I bought this for you in St. Louis."

"Thank you, but I think you should give it to your fiancée."

"If I'd wanted to give it to her, I would have. I bought the dress for you." Walker saw that Charlotte was going to stand her ground, so he said, "Put the dress on. I'll put my horse in the barn and then I'll come see how you look in it." He left the room.

When he returned, she was still standing by the stove, and the dress was still where he'd left it. Watching him approach with wide, wary eyes. Charlotte saw the intense anger in his face, the flexing of the muscles in his jaw. She was afraid that she had pushed him too far. He stopped a few feet from her and yanked the dress off the back of the chair and threw it in her face. "I said, put the dress on."

"And I said no." With that, she turned and dropped the dress into her cold bathwater, watching the water soak into the lovely shimmering fabric.

"Pick it up and put it on."

"Drop dead."

"Charlotte, I'm warning you."

Her eyes spitting sparks of intense blue, she said hotly, "And I'm warning you. Get out of my house, damn you. Get out!" She yanked the sodden dress from the water and flung it at him. "And take your dress with you. I don't want it or you."

"Why?" he asked. "Why are you being like this?"

"I have my reasons, and you're a complete blockhead if you don't know what they are."

He shook his head. "I don't understand. All I know is that I love you. It seems to me that should count for something."

Her eyes sparkled with gathering tears. "It's too late for declarations of love. It's too late for anything between us."

"It will never be too late for us." He took her in his arms. His mouth was hungry on hers, and the feel of her barely clad body against him was his undoing. With a sense of urgency, he parted her lips and filled her mouth, demanding a response as wild and hungry as the one that shook him. For one crazy, wonderful moment, Charlotte gave in to him, nearly dying in the pleasurable pain of being crushed in those strong arms and kissed by that wonderful mouth.

Walker broke the kiss, knowing that if he didn't he would take her before she was ready, right there in the kitchen. When he looked down into her face, his breath caught in his throat as he realized that those were tears and not water sliding beneath her long, wet lashes.

"Charlotte?" he whispered, his body trembling from the emotions still raging through him. Still holding her, he dropped to the floor and, bracing himself on his elbow, stroked the side of her face gently, his thumb wiping away the tears, feeling a stab of pain twisting inside him when another tear quickly replaced the one he'd removed.

"Charlotte, love. Look at me. Tell me what's wrong." When she opened her eyes, they were swimming with tears, her lashes spiked with their moisture.

"Did I hurt you?"

"Every time you make love to me like this you hurt me," she said, her tears now unleashed. Walker watched her, unable to bear her pain or the sight of her crying. He gathered her into his arms, holding her trembling body close to his as she wept.

She cried for a long time, releasing all the pain that had been locked inside her for a lifetime. She cried for her mother and father and for her two lost brothers. She cried for herself and for Nemi and for the childhood and family they'd been denied. She cried for her loneliness, and for the wonderful gift Walker had given her, and also hating him for it, because he intended to take it away. And all the while, Walker held her, stroking her, pushing her wet hair away from her face and kissing her gently, consoling her with his body and his soft-spoken words, not really aware of what he was saying.

When her tears were spent, Charlotte felt weak and exhausted. A shudder rippled through her as she breathed deeply, knowing that there was nothing ahead for her but emptiness and a long, lonely future. She couldn't marry Jamie—even if he asked her—when she felt like this about Walker. But as consciousness of her situation returned, so did consciousness of the way she and Walker were lying together on the floor, his hand stroking her naked hip, her wrapper parted and leaving her bare breasts and belly pressed against him. His hand on her hip had been stroking her impersonally, but the moment she became conscious of it, it seemed to burn like a brand across her naked skin. She lay still, wondering if she had what it took to shove his hand away when he was being so gentle and loving.

He might have gone on rubbing her hip impersonally forever, if Charlotte hadn't looked at him. But she did. And when she looked into his face, wanting to tell him so many things about the way she felt, she nearly gasped at the expression in his eyes as he stared so intently into hers.

Walker was thinking how lovely she was, her skin heated to a soft pink hue, her eyes shimmering and huge like a lost child's, the spiky lashes, the swollen, rose-kissed mouth still wet from his kiss. His eyes moved lower, to the perfect breasts bared between the damp panels of her wrapper, and he knew he would end up making love to her on the kitchen floor after all.

He pulled her against him, all soft, warm, and drowsily exhausted woman, no fight left in her. His hands at her waist moved to push the remaining fabric of her wrapper from her body, exposing the long line of her shapely thighs. His gaze rested at the juncture of those thighs, then lifted to her face. Her eyes were open and she was watching him. With a soft groan, he pulled her against him, his mouth hot and hungry on hers. He moved over her then, one leg going between her thighs, his mouth moving to her breast, his other hand sliding down her hip, touching her where she was warm and wet.

He was kissing the soft skin of her stomach now, whispering against her skin, leaving her quivering, his kisses like molten lava flowing down, his hands drawing her legs up and pressing them apart. He was on his knees between her legs now and she was completely exposed to him. When she realized this, she tried to close her legs, but he held her, and said softly, "No, sweetheart. Don't. Let me look at you. Let me see your face while I touch you here."

He touched her there, again and again, softly and gently, driving her to insanity with the slowness of it. She twisted against his hands, her hips straining upward, but still he stroked her with the same maddening slowness. When she thought she could stand it no longer, his fingers eased inside her, touching her slowly, then faster, in rhythm with her now. She cried out once, twice, and then Walker was unbuckling his belt and removing his pants. He was back before her ripples of pleasure had subsided, his narrow hips between her legs, coming into her with a single, swift thrust. He held his body motionless over her, his hands coming up to tangle in her hair, holding her face as he lowered his head and kissed her.

Then he began to move within her, fast and

deliberately, taking her with a gentle sort of violence. "You belong to me, Gussie." *You belong to me as no other woman could, as no other woman ever will. I'll be back. Wait for me. I don't know how or even when, but I'll be back. I'll come back for you, and if my love is strong enough to hold you, you'll be here waiting for me.*

"You belong to me, Gussie." Charlotte had heard that arrogant declaration. *"You belong to me, Gussie."* Oh, she knew Walker had come back to see her, and to take her to bed, and that meant he hadn't been able to forget her as easily as he had thought. But there was still no doubt in her mind that he would leave for California and she would be left behind. The only way to salvage her pride and save face was to do it to Walker before he did it to her. That he intended to claim her as his at the dance tonight was as plain as the nose on his face. But she would turn the tables on him. She vowed to herself that she would show him how it felt to be made love to by someone who had another waiting on the wings. He had confessed that he loved her and claimed that she belonged to him. He was sure of himself now, sure that he had mastered her. *Well, let him think it.* And then, when he least suspected it, when he thought he had her all wrapped up, she would slap him in the face with rejection as he had done to her. Just when Walker thought he had her in the palm of his hand, she would toss him aside and make her preference known. Before the evening was over, not a soul in Two Trees would miss seeing her put him in his place.

Lifting his body from hers, Walker stood, then helped Charlotte to rise. She looked around the kitchen, groaning at the mess. In less than three hours, Jamie would be coming for her. She had to get rid of Walker, heat her bathwater again, and try to restore her house to some kind of order before Jamie arrived.

Walker left, and Charlotte put a kettle of water on to heat. Then she added more wood to the fire and cleaned the kitchen, before restoring some order to her bedroom, grimacing at the damage she had done in there. She was amazed at herself. She had never in her twenty-seven years known that she had such a temper. It had taken a man like Walker Reed to bring that out. She remembered painfully that it had taken Walker to bring out a lot of other things in her, too.

For the second time that day, Charlotte was in her warm kitchen, relaxing in the copper tub, when the back door flew open. She opened her eyes and sprang upright to see, for the second time that day, Walker standing in the doorway.

"Not again," she groaned.

He noticed that she had cleaned the kitchen. She had also twisted her hair on top of her head. But everything else was the same. He grinned and closed the door. "I told you I was going to help you get ready, and I am." He crossed the room and stood beside the tub, just as he had done earlier. Then he rolled up his sleeves, dropped to one knee, and picked up the soap and cloth.

As if it were something she did all the time, she just sat there, with him at her back, luxuriating in the feel of the cloth making strong circling motions across her skin. With a sigh, her head dropped forward, her chin resting on her chest, as Walker brought the soapy cloth up to her neck and massaged it gently.

"Relax," he said gently. "You're too tense. That's it. Much better."

His hand was warm and the feel of his skin against hers was comforting and strangely secure. She was floating somewhere outside herself when he said, "Now give me your leg."

Seeing that she wasn't about to cooperate, Walker plunged his hand into the water and lifted one creamy, slender leg. The moment his palm touched her calf, an electrical charge slammed throughout her body and her breath caught in her throat. She looked into his vivid, steel-blue eyes.

"Now give me your other leg."

She did, knowing that he had a good view of her in the water. When she looked innocently at him, his expression was tight with desire, his eyes hot and devouring.

She watched the rhythmic motion of his muscular arm, thinking it wasn't like Walker to play the part of a ladies' maid. His voice, when he began speaking, was husky and suggestive. "When I finish with you, Charlotte, there won't be a man within a hundred miles of here that wouldn't give a year's ration of whiskey to dance one dance with you."

He dropped her leg, and before she could

say anything, he reached up and over her head to pull the pins from her hair. Its ruby length uncoiled like a snake and slipped into the water, just before he poured a pitcher of water over her head.

She was sputtering like mad, but he was talking again, and, not wanting to miss what he was saying, she stopped to listen as he began washing her hair. The feel of his fingers massaging her scalp sent her sloshing back against the tub, the angry words she'd wanted to say dissipating and her eyes closing. Slowly she sank into the water, limp and mindless as a dishrag.

"Hey! Not too far or you'll wash out all the soap. That's better. Hold it right there while I get some clean water to rinse you." He crossed the room and was back quickly, carrying another pitcher of warm water. "Now lean forward. Good. Close your eyes. There! All done."

She heard him walking again and opened her eyes. He was standing before her with her towel opened wide between his hands. "Stand up."

She started to rise, but she came to her senses quickly, dropping back into the water.

"Now what's the matter?"

"I'm naked!"

He threw back his head with a shout of laughter. "That's generally the way it is with a bath. You were naked on the kitchen floor with me not long ago, so why the sudden modesty?" Seeing that his words weren't doing much to soften her, he said, "You can stand up now. My eyes are closed."

She stood, looking at him. "You lied," she said as he wrapped the towel around her. "Your eyes were open."

He grinned, wrapping another towel around her head. "I didn't lie, Gussie. I just opened them sooner than you thought prudent."

Walker scooped her into his arms and carried her to a chair he had pulled before the stove. He sat down, still holding her, then shifted her to rest comfortably on his lap. Keeping her there, he began to dry her hair, using the towel and the heat radiating from the stove. When it was almost dry, he carried her to the bedroom and dropped her onto the bed. She watched him walk to her dressing table and pick up her hairbrush, returning to the bed and sitting beside her.

"Turn around."

Her eyes closed at the luxurious feeling of Walker dragging the brush with long sweeping strokes through her hair. "Is that the dress you're wearing?" he asked, nodding in the direction of an amber wool dress draped across the chest at the foot of her bed.

"Yes."

"It's a good color for you. Not as pretty as green silk, but pretty," he said, noticing her frown at the mention of the green silk. Then he was pulling her to her feet. "Now let's do your hair."

"Do my hair? You?" she said with a raised brow.

He laughed. "I'm not too proficient at that. You fix it and I'll watch."

She shrugged and moved to the mirror,

thinking he wasn't going to be in such a good mood when he found out that he had made her beautiful for Jamie Granger. She cringed inwardly, thinking about his reaction when she was all dressed and casually mentioned that she couldn't go to the dance with him because Jamie was picking her up. Brush in hand, she began to brush out her hair.

When she was finished, her hair was braided and neatly wound across the top of her head in a style that was much more flattering than the severe bun she usually wore.

Watching her study herself, Walker noticed the way the lamplight caressed her skin like heated oil, highlighting the hollow in her throat where the tiny golden heart lay. He remembered the night he gave it to her:

"If you only knew how you've snagged yourself upon my heart, little love. My going will leave a raveled trail of yarn from here to California, but my heart, Gussie, will remain here with you; one heart on a raveled piece of yarn for you to remember me by."

He lifted his hand slowly until it touched the side of her face, just above her ear, and began to tug the finer, silkier hairs loose. His eyes were riveted on her face, his hand moving from the side of the nape and around to the other side. When he finished, her face was framed in a halo of soft, wispy curls.

"That," he said softly, "is what a man likes to see. Not a stiff hairdo, but one that looks as if her lover had just run his fingers through her hair." He stared down at her beautiful face and said, "You're too pale, Charlotte. You need color in your cheeks, color that would be there if the man in your life took you in his arms and told you he wanted you, just like this."

He drew her against him, his hands tilting her head back, then dropping to her waist and around her, drawing her more fully against him. "I want you, Charlotte."

She felt the heated flush rise to her face. Walker was making it awfully difficult to remember that she was doing this to show him he couldn't walk on her feelings. His face came closer, so close that the words skimmed across the surface of her skin when he spoke. "That's better. Just a little more color, Charlotte." His lips brushed against hers. "Let's try it again. I want you, Charlotte."

His mouth closed over hers and she went limp in his arms. A groan came from deep within him as if he were in pain. Her hands, which were pressed flat against his chest, rose of their own volition and curled around his neck as Charlotte Augusta Butterworth kissed Walker Reed for all she was worth.

He swung her up into his arms and carried her to the bed, following her down. But Charlotte, remembering who was in charge here, rolled across the bed and stood on the other side, her breathing fast as she clutched the towel against her. "I need to get dressed, Walker. I don't have time for that right now."

His brows snapped together as a flash of anger replaced the desire that had been on his face moments before.

"When will you marry?" she asked.

The calm reason in her tone made him

uneasy, and he tried not to show his surprise at the question. "Why do you bring that up at a time like this?"

"Is there a better time?"

"I would think so, yes. Normally a woman doesn't ask a man who has just crawled from her bed about another woman."

Her eyes flashed deep blue and intense with anger. "Normally a man who is betrothed does not *crawl* into bed with another woman."

"I don't think you brought the matter up because you were interested in my plans. I think you're trying to use it against me, Charlotte."

"In what way?"

"To cloud my thinking. To ply me with guilt."

"Do you love her?"

"I did."

"You did? Does that mean you no longer do?" She noticed that Walker looked calm enough on the outside, but she knew him well enough now to see the seething anger that was building within him.

"Dammit! It means what I said. I did love her. I loved her when I courted her. I loved her when I asked her to marry me. I loved her when I left her to come out here."

"And now?"

"Don't push me, Charlotte!"

"I'm not pushing you. I just don't understand why you came back."

"Don't you?"

"No, damn you, I don't." She wrapped the towel more tightly around her and pulled her dress from the top of the chest. She picked up her underthings and shoes and marched from the room, pausing just outside the door. "I would like a few minutes of privacy to dress—*alone*, if you don't mind."

When she returned, Walker was standing at the window, his back to her. Hearing her enter, he turned around. "I know a lot of things don't make sense to you right now—"

"No, they don't. And neither do you."

"I'm asking you to trust me, Charlotte."

"I trusted you before, remember?"

"Then trust me now."

His words slammed into her with the force of a speeding bullet, bringing the repercussion of shimmering tears to her eyes. This wasn't going the way she had planned. She took a moment to compose herself, telling herself that she was only doing what he would do to her, only she was doing it first. "Under one condition."

His gaze was dark as he studied her face. "And what is that?"

She lifted her arms, her hands going around her neck and untying the golden heart. "Take back your heart," she said, presenting it to him in her open palm.

He looked shattered. "Would that I could, sweet Charlotte. Would that I could."

There was a clatter in the front yard, the sound of a buggy turning into her drive. "Jamie," she whispered, her hands flying to her face. She hadn't meant for Walker to find out like this. She'd intended to tell him before Jamie arrived. When she gathered the courage to look at him, it was like staring down the barrel of a shotgun. Walker was looking at her hard, with those blue eyes of his, leaving not one speck of doubt in her mind that he was furious.

"It would appear that I'm not the only one who likes to spring surprises around here. Tell me, sweet Charlotte, just *when* were you planning on telling me that Jamie was coming for you?"

"I... I was going to tell you earlier, but..."

"I see," he said harshly. "And *what* were you going to tell me? That you were busy playing up to the advances of one man while you had another waiting? That two birds in the hand are worth—"

"Don't stand there lecturing me, you master at deception." she shouted. "If I've learned anything from you, it's how to be deceitful."

"It would appear that you've learned your lesson well. You amaze me, Charlotte. I expected a certain amount of loyalty and trust from you. I see I was mistaken. I don't know how I could have misjudged you so."

"That sounds a lot like the things I've been thinking about you. At least you *knew* about Jamie. You knew he was in town. I told you he had been courting me. It shouldn't come as a surprise that he would take me to the dance. What did you think I was going to do? Sit here on my tuffet and pine for you?"

"I expected more ladylike behavior from you than that."

"*Ladylike!*" Charlotte exploded. "For your information, the only time I behave in an *unladylike* manner is when I'm around you. Jamie treats me like a lady. You're the one who doesn't."

"You aren't going with him."

"Oh, yes I am," she said hotly, "and you aren't in a position to stop me. You happen to be engaged to another woman. You don't have any rights as far as I'm concerned. If you want to boss a woman around, you better point your nose toward California. You haven't slipped a ring through *my* nose... or put one on my finger."

"No, but I would have."

"*You would have!*" she screamed. "What are you? A Mormon? There are laws against men like you. You would have!" She snorted. "I'll just bet you would have. Just *how* many women are you engaged to?" She was looking at him with complete distrust, as if she'd had a lot of experience with men and knew that they couldn't be trusted.

Walker stared at the hotheaded woman in the amber wool dress, her stormy blue eyes shooting daggers at him, and remembered another time when she'd been completely trusting and inexperienced: "*I know there's more to kissing than two sets of lips colliding with each other.*"

His anger drained away and was replaced with a sickening clench in his gut at the thought of her being in another man's arms. But he couldn't blame her for that. He had handed her to Jamie, lock, stock, and barrel. If there were any butts to be kicked, he would have to start with his own.

Charlotte saw the softening of his features, and that caused her to distrust him more. Just what was he up to now? But by this time her hostility was subsiding, and her conscience reminded her that she hadn't exactly been straightforward and honest either. He might have deserved what he'd gotten, but she couldn't help thinking that she hadn't received much pleasure from being the one to see that he got it.

She was on the verge of suggesting that they smoke the peace pipe when they heard knocking at the front door. With panicked alarm, Charlotte glanced at Walker.

"Don't worry, sweetheart. He won't find me here. I've more finesse than that." Then he offered her a lazy, heart-wrenching smile and lifted a hand to her hair. "Don't touch your hair. It's just the way a man would like it." He gently touched the tumble of curls around her face.

And then he was gone.

CHAPTER
NINETEEN

Even the most puritanical people in Two Trees loved dances, and the Christmas ball was the grandest spectacle of the year. Of course there wasn't a palatial ballroom blazing with gaslight chandeliers or a parquet floor for dancing. There were no gilded decorations of bayberry leaves, or ropes of pine garland, or silken streamers of green and red swaying above elegantly clad ladies and gentlemen as they marched the grand promenade. There was only a small country schoolhouse, with the desks and benches removed, the blackboard erased, and the pine floor swept clean. The simple decorations were a small Christmas tree lit with candles and rope chains, made by the schoolchildren, that crisscrossed the room, and a bunch of mistletoe tied with a red taffeta ribbon nailed over the doorway. The guests, dressed in their Sunday go-to-meetin' best, arrived early, children in tow, as well as a few old-maid aunts, crotchety old grandmas, spry, bent-kneed grandpas, married folk, sweethearts, and lots of bachelors—since they outnumbered the women ten to one.

As soon as everyone had arrived, a collection plate was passed to pay the fiddler who had come all the way from Fort Worth. While the women displayed their home-baked wares on a long, cloth-covered table, the men gathered around the punchbowl, into which at least five or six flasks were emptied and the contents stirred. By the time the fiddler drew his bow, signaling the men to choose their partners, the men, having fortified themselves with several glasses of punch, were ready to tackle the sternest, most prune faced of matrons.

Soon the dust was rising from the cracks in the plank floor as the grand march was followed by endless rounds of the polka, the Virginia reel, the waltz, the schottische, and the galop, which raised the most dust of all.

Already too warm from several dances,

Charlotte stood beside Jamie, sipping a cup of punch. A headache was forming and she closed her eyes, her dark lashes stark against her pale skin. The music stopped and Old Man Bannister pushed his son Willy to the front as he shouted, "Git yore pardners for the quadrille. Willy is gonna call."

Charlotte opened one eye a tiny slit. Willy was such a dopey cowboy, dressed to the hilt with chaps, spurs, a big bandanna, and a hat big enough to shade half the county. One thing Willy was not was shy. He began to shout the call, and the floor coughed up another layer of dust. "Swing the other gal, swing her sweet: paw dirt, doggies, stomp your feet." Then came: "Ladies in the center, gents 'round 'em run, swing her rope, cowboy, and get yo' one!" And finally: "Swing an' march—first couple lead, clear 'round the school an' then stampede."

By the time the stampede was over, Charlotte's head was throbbing. She wondered if Walker would come to the dance. No. He would not come. He had said his goodbye. He was gone. On his way to California, to his betrothed. Soon he would marry and settle down to a life of ranching and raising a family, too content and busy ever to think about her.

Charlotte's plight was rather pathetic. How could she possibly consider marriage to another man when she couldn't go more than five minutes without her thoughts returning to Walker? How could she lie beside another man night after night for the rest of her life, listening to him breathe and wishing that it were

396

Walker lying there beside her? How could she bear to let another man touch her intimately after Walker had burned the image of his face into her mind and the touch of his hands onto her body? She liked Jamie, of course, and she enjoyed his company. But was that enough to sustain a marriage?

A loud burst of silliness drew her attention across the room, where Prissy, Mary Alice, and May were talking to Emma Harper and a bunch of the Triple K boys. Prissy, wearing a new dress of rose-colored merino, was the center of attention, standing in a circle of admirers as if she were holding court. Prissy's idea of a good time was to have a group of admirers who would fetch and carry for her, preferably in public, amid incessant, vivacious chatter, laughter, and biting gossip, all enhanced by fluttering hand movements, periodic batting of the eyes, subtle whispers, arch looks, and flirtatious glances. But all Charlotte could see was commonplace behavior, and nothing she wanted to be a part of.

Charlotte groaned, seeing the group breaking up and coming toward her like a flotilla of brightly painted butterflies.

"Why, Charlotte, I do declare this is the first dance I think I've ever seen you at. Are you having a good time?" Mary Alice said with a tone that was about as close to tragic as Mary Alice could come.

"I'm having a wonderful time, thank you."

"I would've thought you'd be dancing with Walker Reed," said Prissy.

"Mr. Reed isn't here," Charlotte replied,

noting that Prissy had called Walker by his first name.

Prissy had the audacity to look shocked. Then her expression was one that Charlotte could only call sly. "Didn't you know he was back in town? Why, I think it's terrible of him not to let you know. Especially after *all* you've done for him." As if for emphasis, Prissy, who had been pulling on her black jet bracelet, let go and it popped back against her arm with a snap.

By now Charlotte's headache was full blown, and she was wishing mightily that this grand inquisition by the local order of zealots were over. "I knew he was back in town, but I came to the party with Mr. Granger."

Prissy's eyes drifted toward the punchbowl, where Jamie was standing with a group of men. "Oh, then I suppose that means..." Whatever she was going to say died on her lips. "*Who* is that?"

Charlotte looked with the rest of them toward the door, where a well-dressed young man of rather slim proportions entered with Mrs. Pruitt and her grandson, Georgie Glass.

"I don't know," said May and Mary Alice in unison.

"That's Georgie's cousin from Wisconsin or some cold place like that. He's here to spend Christmas with his grandmother," Emma explained.

Prissy smoothed her skirts, fluffing the bow at her wrist. "I wonder why he's never been here before?"

"He has, when he was younger. His papa is Hershel Pruitt, old Mrs. Pruitt's youngest son. I think his last wife just died a few months back. And I hear he's already engaged again. This will be the fourth marriage for him, according to my mama."

"Really? Four times?" exclaimed Prissy.

"Mama said he would've been married even more than that, if his wives had been more accommodating and died off quicker," Emma said, suddenly swelling with importance now that Prissy was paying so much attention to her.

"What else did your mama say, Emma?" Prissy asked.

"That she heard Mr. Pruitt was seen in the company of the next Mrs. Pruitt before the last Mrs. Pruitt even died. She said there were men like that... they couldn't seem to settle with just one woman."

"Hmmmm," said Prissy, letting go of the band on her black jet bracelet again.

All that talk about faithless men was making Charlotte think of one such person she knew—one she'd just as soon not think about. She did her best to smile graciously and excuse herself as Prissy announced that they should all "extend a cordial hand of welcome to poor Georgie's cousin."

Watching the parade move away, Charlotte was thinking that in a way she was glad Walker wouldn't be coming. She couldn't bear to see him holding someone like Prissy or Mary Alice in his arms, swinging her around the floor. She preferred the goodbye they had said to one done here, under the watchful eye of the whole community. It was still unclear to her just why he'd returned, but she was glad that he had, for now she had one more golden moment to hang on a chain of memories, a moment of passionate kisses and whispered endearments that would bind her to him forever. Yes, she was glad he would not come.

But he did.

Just as Charlotte found herself alone, Pearlene Carter passed by and said, "Well, bless my bones! Isn't that the fellow that almost got himself hanged from your tree, Charlotte?"

Charlotte followed the direction of Pearlene's gaze, a shock racing through her as Walker stepped into the room and paused, speaking to a group of men, accepting a cup of punch. He was a daunting figure of a man, far more noticeable than any of the other men around him—more in command, more confident, more dashing, impeccably dressed in a suit. She had never seen him in a suit. It was not that he was any taller or any more handsome than the men surrounding him, but there was something powerful and terribly romantic about him—and something almost dangerous—that set every female heart to pounding. Charlotte's own heart began to pound when she noticed the polite way he smiled at something someone said while his eyes scanned the crowd, as if looking for someone. He was searching, Charlotte knew without a doubt, for her.

Panicked, she wasn't sure what to do, when Archer walked by and lifted her punch cup from her hand, replacing it with the one in his hand. "Here," he said lightly, "try mine. It's fortified with a little backbone... something you're going to need."

Charlotte downed the contents just as Hannah came to her side. "Nemi says not to worry about a thing. Walker is too much of a gentleman to start any trouble here. He said for you to just continue being the lady that you are and all will be well."

"Is that *all* he said?" Charlotte asked in a pleading tone, hoping for something a little more meaningful than that.

"No," Hannah said woefully. "He said that just to be on the safe side, you might try praying."

With a terrified gulp, Charlotte scanned the room, looking for a way out or a place to hide. Neither seemed readily available. Slowly, Walker lifted his gaze from the man he was talking to and let his eyes drift around the room, passing over her so quickly that Charlotte heard herself sigh with relief. But then his eyes made another quick sweep, leveling on her like the needle on a compass. For a full minute he simply stared at her, pinning her to the wall with the probe of his eyes, leaving her not one crumb of doubt that he would make his way toward her in the very near future.

"You better make that a quick prayer," Hannah whispered. "Would you rather I left?"

"No!" Charlotte said, her hand coming out to grip Hannah's forearm. "Stay with me."

Hannah patted her hand. "You may be worried for nothing. He may not even try to seek you out or speak to you."

Charlotte would believe *that* when hens grew teeth. Quickly, she looked back at Walker, or to where Walker had been standing, but he was no longer there. Her heart leaped in her chest. "Look around the room, Hannah. Tell me if you see him anywhere."

Hannah scanned the room. "No, I don't see—" Her expression froze. "Oh, my Lord!"

"What is it?"

"He's coming this way. I think I should be going, Charlotte. Nemi warned me to keep my helpful hands out of things."

"Hannah..." But Hannah had already turned and was making her way through the crowd. Nearby, little Howie Porter made a face at her and stuck out his tongue. Without thinking about it, Charlotte stuck hers out at him. Howie began tugging on his mother's skirts.

Charlotte felt her pulse throbbing and a tingling sensation along her nerves that grew until her entire body seemed to be humming. She located Jamie, engrossed in conversation with Nemi.

The next dance started and Charlotte felt herself go weak in the knees with relief when Mary Alice pulled Walker onto the dance floor. Knowing that her face was perspiring and her head was spinning, Charlotte moved to the window. She opened it a crack to let in some fresh air and drive away the threat of nausea. She rested her arm on the windowsill and drank in several deep breaths, reasoning with her uneasiness. There was nothing to be afraid of. Walker was as good as gone from her affections as he soon would be from her life. Tonight she would show him just how little she cared. But the unease was still there.

"A brown little sparrow transformed into a bird of plumage, shy and about to disappear. Were you thinking of climbing out the window, sweet Charlotte?"

She turned to see Walker standing beside her. "Why did you come here?" she whispered, her teeth clenched in anger. "Get away from me! Are you trying to embarrass me?"

"Never. I come in the spirit of Christmas, bearing gifts." He leaned closer, and she saw a twinkle in his eye. "Come outside with me."

She was tempted. Dear God, she was tempted. Just having him so close was a drain on her common sense. Charlotte remembered that the good reverend had preached on temptation just last Sunday. He had said that all are tempted, and there isn't anyone who can't be swayed. And she knew that was the gospel. It was just a matter of putting the right *swayee* with the right *swayer*. And looking at Walker, she felt that she had met her match this time. If this man wasn't the right *swayer*, she'd eat her feather duster. There he stood before her with a face that took her breath away and a body she would never grow tired of admiring, with its pure lines, narrow hips, lean waist, and long, lanky legs. Yes, she was more than tempted to go with him. But a wise man doesn't make a goat his gardener. She had a good idea of what kind of gift he was bearing—the same one he had given her that afternoon. That he would demean her so by showing his face publicly and expecting her to sneak outside for a tryst was humiliating. "I know what you're asking, what gift you wish to bestow."

Annoyance shadowed his face, but then he noticed the pain in her averted gaze. "Do you? I wonder. In your reasonable little mind do you perceive that I would present you with a bauble like this?" He leaned forward to tie the golden heart around her neck.

"Don't," she said, slapping his hand away and mortified to see the curious people all around them craning their necks.

To her horrified shame, he paused and lifted his hand to her chin, tilting her face up to his. "In spite of what you say, I am going to put the heart back where it belongs. I will, however, give you three choices as to how we go about it. You can smile at me like I'm doing something with your full permission, or I will create the biggest disturbance you've ever seen, tying you to the chair if necessary to put this around your neck."

Her face was pale, fright gripping her features. "You said there were three choices."

"You can come outside with me right now and we'll discuss it."

Her eyes flared, but she allowed him to replace the heart, only because she knew that to refuse would mean a scene or going outside with him, which was worse.

"Are you finished?" she asked.

"Not with you."

"What else could you possibly want with me?"

He had the audacity to look amused at that question. He was also wise enough not to answer it.

Her voice trembled with anger. "I know you came back to dress me like a circus pony, to humiliate me in front of the whole community like some monarch relinquishing his mistress. I would never have thought you capable of this—"

"And I'm not. Rest assured, sweet Charlotte, that I have a purpose for being at this dance tonight. I have no intention of relinquishing anything. My sole purpose is to secure and retain what I hold dear."

She turned her head away, afraid she would cry. She knew what he held dear. Why must he flaunt it before her?

"Charlotte," he said softly, his hand cupping her chin to tilt her face toward him, "I fear you have sealed yourself away from me. Come outside with me now." For a brief moment she was mesmerized by his deep blue eyes. "Sweetheart, we can clear all this up if you'd just let me speak to you in private—"

More necks were craning in their direction.

"Don't you 'sweetheart' me, you overripe seducer. I may have let the bird fly over my head, but I *don't* have to let it nest in my hair!"

Walker, charming devil that he was, with more brass than a military band, had the gall to laugh. "Charlotte, you always amaze me with your analysis. Just how did you manage to get us so far off? *Birds* nesting in your hair?" He laughed again. *Sweetheart, if you only knew the restraint I'm employing. You are so adorably confused... and confusing.*

"I was speaking figuratively."

"I see. Well, figuratively speaking, my dear Charlotte, the man who wants the rose must respect the thorn."

"And sometimes it is better to say what you think than to write a dissertation," she said. "Why don't you just tell me, in *plain* English, what you're about?"

Walker threw back his head with a shout of laughter. Then, leaning close enough to kiss her, he said, his voice dropping to a husky pitch, "Ah, Charlotte. I will never grow tired of you."

"No," she said softly, a look of pain crossing her face, "I don't suppose you will have the chance."

He never had the opportunity to respond to that. "Walker," Archer Bradley whispered, "I'm glad you're here. I thought you'd shoved off this afternoon. I need you to come over to the office with me for a minute."

"I had a change of plans." Walker looked frustrated. "Look, can't this wait until later? I'm in the middle of—"

"No, it can't wait. A telegram came for you this afternoon. It's from California. Sol at the telegraph office wouldn't say what was in it, but he did say it was bad news. You better come now."

"All right." The anger he was feeling carried to his voice. "Charlotte, wait... don't... I'll be back as soon as I can. Promise me you'll wait. This conversation isn't finished."

"I'm not going anywhere," she answered. But as far as she was concerned their conversation was finished before it ever started.

Walker nodded at her, then turned, following Archer through the crowd, leaving Charlotte standing by the partially open window.

Just as had happened the first time Walker had left her, it was Jamie who came to her, offering a cup of punch to ease the pain left by Walker's abrupt departure. "Don't drink it so fast," he said. "I don't want you too tipsy to answer the question I'm about to ask you."

Her smile was hesitant, her face drawn and tired. "You've been very considerate of me, Jamie, but I don't feel like answering any questions right now."

He saw her staring at the door Walker had just disappeared through. "It's better this way. He had to go back sometime. You knew that. Now isn't the time to think about what has happened. I'm here now. I want to take care of you, Charlotte."

"There was a time—" Her voice broke and she looked at him with tears in her eyes. "I'm not what you think I am, Jamie. I don't deserve your kindness."

"Let me be the judge of that."

"You don't understand. I—"

He silenced her with his finger to her lips. "I know what you're trying to tell me. It doesn't matter, Charlotte. Do you hear me? It does not matter. I want you to marry me. I think it would be best if we made arrangements to have the wedding soon—just in case. I've already talked to Nehemiah. If there's to be a child, it will be raised as mine." He slipped his arms around her tiny waist, drawing her against him, kissing the top of her head. "Let me make the announcement now, Charlotte. Tonight."

She looked into his eyes and saw the gentleness of a deer in their brown depths. He was a simple man, calm, easygoing. There would be no passion, no fire, but no heartbreak either. She could do worse. Much, much worse. And what better way to drive her point home to Walker, to show him that he wasn't the only one with a marriage in his future? *Thou shalt give life for life, Eye for eye, tooth for tooth, hand for hand, foot for foot. Burning for burning, wound for wound, stripe for stripe.*

But somehow the decision didn't bring the joy she had expected. She couldn't bring herself to speak for fear of crying, so she nodded. She had her retribution. But as Jamie hugged her, she couldn't keep the despair from her heart, or the words of woe from vibrating throughout her consciousness: *Whatsoever a man soweth, that shall he also reap.*

"You have made me very happy, Charlotte. You won't regret this. I promise you that." He grabbed her hand, pulling her arm through his as he led her through the crowd and up to the teacher's platform where the fiddler stood, about to start another song.

"Friends, if I may interrupt your celebrating for a moment, I would like to give you all cause for another celebration to be held in a few weeks' time. Miss Charlotte Butterworth has agreed to become my wife."

Charlotte saw all the color drain from Hannah's face, the frozen expression on Nemi's, but her eyes did not linger on their expressions for long because there was another expression that caught her attention, and that broke her heart.

It was the expression on the face of the blue-eyed man who had just returned to the dance.

The news of Charlotte's engagement slapped Walker in the face as he entered the room, and he stopped suddenly. For a moment he looked completely helpless, as if his heart had been ripped out and he was not yet aware that it was gone. He quickly gained control, moving first to Nemi and Hannah, then turning toward Jamie and Charlotte. He shook Jamie's hand, offering his congratulations as warmly as he could.

Outside, it had begun to snow. There would be a white Christmas, so rare in these parts. Indoors, people crowded to the windows, the children shrieking and begging to go outside and watch. But Charlotte was unaware of all that. There was only one person in the room who mattered to her. And as he spoke, his words were polite and congratulatory, and directed to Jamie, but the icy point of his flaming blue gaze was on her. For the briefest instant Charlotte had the shuddering feeling that she had done something terribly, terribly wrong.

CHAPTER
❧ TWENTY ❧

Nehemiah Butterworth drew rein by Charlotte's back gate, leaving the saddle before his gelding had come to a complete stop. A few angry strides brought him to her kitchen door, which he proceeded to open without knocking.

Her spectacles perched on the end of her nose, Charlotte was just putting a pan of hominy bread in the oven when he slammed the back door. She let go of the oven door and it slammed with a loud, metallic snap. She whirled, her hand across her breast, a look of terror on her face.

"Nehemiah P. Butterworth, haven't you ever heard of knocking? You scared me out of ten years' growth, not to mention what I probably did to my oven door."

Nemi snorted and tossed his hat onto the kitchen table. "Don't try to change the subject, Charlotte."

"What subject? You just got here, Nemi. We haven't even said hello yet. How can we have a subject?"

"We're fixing to," he shouted.

"Fixing to," she repeated. "That's your middle name." She clamped her hands on her hips and tapped her foot with irritation. "All right. Hurry up and bring up the subject so I can change it."

"You made a big mistake. You know that, don't you?"

Her color paled. "About what?"

410

Nemi, who had just sat down, sprang to his feet. "Dammit!" he said, walking toward her, his finger wagging with each word. "Don't you start trying to act stupid. You know well enough what I'm talking about—you and Walker Reed."

"You were right. I'm changing the subject. Did you know Petunia is due to calf in three weeks?"

"I don't give a damn about Petunia." He paused. "I want to know why you agreed to marry Granger without consulting me first." He looked around. "Where is he, by the way?"

"Gone."

"Gone? Where?"

"Back to south Texas."

"Why?"

"He said there were a lot of things he needed to get ready. He'll be back the first part of February."

"Is that when you've planned the wedding?"

"Yes."

Nemi shook his head. "You got any coffee?"

"On the stove."

He grinned. "Don't I get served?"

"Gentlemen I serve. Ogres serve themselves."

He laughed outright, went over to where she stood by the cupboard, and hugged her. "Okay. Okay. Sweet sister, might I trouble you for a cup of coffee?"

Now Charlotte laughed. "You always know how to work me, Nemi."

He looked serious. "I care about you, Charlotte. Besides Hannah and the kids, you're all the family I've got. I know you think you did the right thing by agreeing to marry Jamie, but there are some things you need to know about him... things I don't think he's told you."

"I'm sure he will, when the time comes."

"Some things need to be said *before* the engagement is announced, not after."

Charlotte watched him return to the table. She followed him with two cups of coffee, taking the chair opposite him. "What kind of things, Nemi?"

"Are you in love with Walker?"

She sighed. "I thought we were discussing my marriage to Jamie. Talk about changing the subject. You're worse than I am."

"Just answer the question, Charlotte. Are you?"

"What difference does it make?"

"Charlotte!"

"Yes. But it doesn't change anything. I'm still going to marry Jamie."

"Why?"

"Because... because he'll make a good husband. He cares about me. He'll be a good provider; he'll treat me kindly and fairly and be a good father to our children."

"Children," he said softly. "Is that important to you?"

Her look was incredulous. "Nemi, you know how procreation is one of the primary—"

"Don't start expounding on Baptist theology.

Just answer my question: Is having children a primary reason for marriage as far as you're concerned?"

She didn't answer right away. "I suppose it is, yes. But not the only reason."

"What other reasons do you have? Do you see yourself sharing the warmth and loving of an intimate relationship with a man?"

Her face flushed scarlet, then she laughed. "I thought that was necessary in order to have the other."

"What other?"

"The children."

Nemi laughed. "Your point, madam." His look turned serious again. "Charlotte, would you marry a man if he couldn't give you children, if you knew there would never be a time when he could take you to bed as a wife, if he couldn't make love to you as Walker did?"

Charlotte sprang to her feet, knocking the coffee over and sending it sloshing over the side of the table and onto the floor. "I don't care if you are my brother. You're taking liberties that—"

"I'm not taking any liberties, dammit! I'm trying to talk some sense into that thick head of yours. I'm trying to tell you that by marrying Jamie Granger you'll be sentencing yourself to a life infinitely worse than remaining an—"

"Old maid?"

"If that's the word you choose to use, yes." His gaze, which had been hard up to now, softened. "Charlotte, Jamie Granger cannot have children."

"I've never met a man yet that could. I thought that was the woman's job." Her eyes were bright with humor, but Nemi wasn't about to be humored.

"Listen to me, dammit! This is no joking matter. Jamie was wounded in the war. He cannot function in the way that's necessary to father children. Do you understand what I'm saying? He could never make love to you... not ever. Is that what you want? A life with a man who will spend his evenings reading Browning instead of making love?"

Charlotte clamped her hands over her ears. "Stop it! I don't want to hear any more. You're lying. I know you are. You don't want me to marry Jamie, and I don't know why."

Nemi looked hurt. Shoving away his coffee, he stood and followed her to the counter, where she waited, peering outside, looking at nothing. "You're right, of course. I don't want you to marry him. But you're wrong when you say you don't know why. The man cannot sire children. I want more than that for you." He turned, picked up his hat, and walked to the door.

"I would think," he said, opening the door, "that you would want more than that for yourself."

Charlotte gripped the edge of the cabinet until her knuckles were white. He was right. She did want more than that for herself. The problem was, what she really wanted was Walker Reed. And now he was as lost to her as Jamie was about to be.

When the hominy bread was done, she

removed it from the stove and put it away in the bread box. She wasn't hungry anymore. She poured another cup of coffee and returned to the table, cleaning up the mess she'd made from the last cup. With a sigh, she collapsed into the chair. She had just had what was probably the shortest engagement on record. And there was no doubt that her engagement was broken. She would send Jamie a telegram tomorrow. Because, in spite of what she had said to Nemi, she knew he would not lie to her.

Yes. A telegram was the only way. To confront Jamie personally would be too embarrassing for both of them. Perhaps she could spare him the discomfort of knowing she knew about his injury. Maybe it would be better just to say that she had changed her mind. After all, in essence that is what she had done.

She thought about Walker and wondered where he was. According to Archer, the telegram he'd received was from Walker's brother, Riley. There had been an explosion in a hotel where Walker's parents were attending a political function and his father had been killed instantly. Walker's mother was not expected to live.

Overwhelmed with a tender sadness for Walker, Charlotte found herself wishing that she had known earlier. How hard it must have been for him to congratulate her and Jamie when his heart was breaking. No wonder he'd looked so shocked when he came back to the schoolhouse and heard her announcement. How difficult for him to act like nothing had happened, and how she regretted not knowing and being unable to comfort him. It hurt her to think how Walker must have been hurting. That she'd been unable to say anything to him about it before he left was especially painful to her. She was sorry and sad for him, for she knew how close his family was, and how dear Walker's mother was to him. She found herself praying that his mother would be spared, and if that wasn't God's will, then at least for her to live long enough for Walker to reach her.

Walker, she knew, had left the dance immediately, riding all night to reach Abilene so he could catch the first westbound train. She tried to shake off the lethargy that gripped her. Thinking about him seemed to drain the life from her. With a sigh, she heaved herself up from the table and locked the door. The best way to get over heartbreak was to have a good cry and then stop thinking about it.

But she discovered that heartbreak wasn't so easy to get over, and how there was something almost sublime about suffering. Pain—how it clung to her. There was no way to disguise it. No way to cover it up. Tears would not melt it. Crying did not help.

Charlotte had never reasoned so much in her life. Nor could she remember having felt so terribly low. Why couldn't she cry and have done with it? She had just lost a dear friend in Jamie, who could have been at least a lifelong companion. And Walker... losing him had cost so much more. At times the pain was so great that she felt she would perish from it. Surely the worst part of all was remembering happier times.

All around her, everything was quiet. The house had grown dark now, but she didn't bother to light a lamp. What was there to see? The same old worn furniture. The empty rooms. And everywhere the memories. She sat in the dark at the kitchen table for a long time, not really realizing that she was listening for the sound of Walker in her house. She remembered the way his feet sounded as he came across the back porch with a load of firewood, the bright ring of his laughter, the husky tones of his voice when heated by passion. How very strange that his absence caused her to remember so vividly the things she'd hardly noticed when he was there. How very, very sad that something so perfect and beautiful was now only a remembrance dear. Her time with Walker was like a song put to music. But the memory of him was only a shadow of reality, a flower that blooms, then fades away. From somewhere in the back of her mind crept a verse from Shelley: *Music, when soft voices die, Vibrates in the memory; Odours, when sweet violets sicken, Live within the sense they quicken.* And then Charlotte laid her head on the table and found that she could cry.

CHAPTER
❧ TWENTY-ONE ❧

Elizabeth Claiborne Reed died two months after her son Walker reached her bedside, but not before he had a chance to tell her about Charlotte.

"Marry her," Elizabeth said, her small hand coming out from under the sheet to touch the side of Walker's face. "You are so like your father... always listening to your conscience instead of your heart. You were never in love with Clarissa. I told you that. You were in love with everything she stood for. She's like a fine Thoroughbred—beautiful to look at, with an impressive family background, but not much else to offer. Thoroughbreds run, Walker. They don't do much else. They don't pull wagons, or plows, or even fancy carriages. They aren't much good for pleasure riding because they're either too high-strung or too valuable to risk. So what do you do? Put them in a fancy paddock and look at them. That's the kind of woman Clarissa is, and I don't think that's what you want. She's a lovely woman, but she isn't right for you. Remember, a broken engagement is more surmountable than a broken heart."

"But what about my word? My honor?"

"Honor is like a straight line, and often can be the shortest distance between two points. But you cannot drive straight over a twisting road, Walker. And the mind is incapable of playing the part of the heart for any length of time.... Let your heart guide you in the mat-

418

ters of love, for the heart is half prophet. Honor is a virtue. But above honor, you must be true to yourself. That is wisdom."

Virtue and wisdom. Walker remembered a similar conversation he'd had with his mother when he was just a boy—a time when she told him, *"Wisdom and virtue are like the two wheels of a cart."*

The day of the funeral, Walker stood next to Riley and Gwen, Riley's wife. His gaze was on the gravestones, but his thoughts were on the beautiful woman standing to his left, her slender arm looped through his, a lace-trimmed hanky pressed to her nose. His mother was right.

Clarissa wasn't what he wanted.

He turned to look at her. No woman could rival her classic beauty. She was a flawless blue-white diamond set in platinum. As he looked at her now, she seemed untouchable, unreachable, as if it were her natural right to be so. Against the black beaver trim of her hat and coat, her skin looked smooth and cool, and it seemed strange that he'd ever thought himself in love with her. How could he ever have thought she was a perfect match for him? But he didn't want to hurt her.

The sun came out from behind a cloud, striking Walker in the face with a piercing beam of light. Sunblindness, or some strange affliction, struck him, for out of the center of the brilliant sunspot emerged a dazzling chrysalis that slowly opened to reveal a *champlevé*—a butterfly of exquisite design. The wings slowly unfolded, and Walker could not believe his eyes. His senses stirred. Slow awareness began to infiltrate his consciousness.

"Charlotte?" he whispered, for surely it was she. His ears began to buzz, and his vision blurred as the butterfly spread her magnificent wings, tossing her head, allowing the black chrysalis to fall away from her like a cloak, revealing a pagan queen enveloped in a cloud of ruby hair.

Walker looked around to see if everyone else was as shocked as he, but apparently no one else could see her. His eyes fell on Clarissa, who, sensing his stare, turned to look at him with an expression of polite concern. But quickly her face took on a look of pure arctic chill. His lips tightened, his eyes leaving the icy beauty standing beside him to seek the radiating heat that surrounded Charlotte.

"Why are you here?" he asked. Or had he just imagined it? Before he could decide, Charlotte threw back her head with a deep, throaty laugh that filled him with warmth.

"I've come for you, of course," she said, her arms opening wide as she spun away from him. He was seeing her as he had never seen her before. How had he never noticed her exquisite beauty? How had he never noticed the skin that was as golden as a sun-ripened peach, or the richness of her russet hair, or the captivating blue eyes shaded beneath smoky lids? Her mouth he had always found lovely, but how had he failed to notice the full pout to her lip, the teasing lift at the corner that promised laughter. She was like a new copper penny, rich and vibrant, full of promise and magic. She held the promise of things he thought he'd lost, things he'd never hoped to recapture— the feel of warm sand between his toes, the touch of a butterfly on his finger, the cool, pebbled texture of the skin of a frog clutched in a child's chubby fingers. She was the incarnation of all the things that were good in his life, things he had lost somewhere along the way.

And then she was gone.

"Walker?" It was Clarissa's voice. "Are you all right?"

"What?" he said in a dazed manner. Charlotte was gone, but he was still dazzled by what he had seen.

Someone was shaking him. "Walker, for heaven's sake! What is wrong with you?"

He turned in the direction of the voice, seeing the fair hair, the unsmiling face, the eyes that burned brilliantly with anger.

Suddenly Clarissa whirled and walked away. Then he noticed that the funeral was over and he was left standing by his mother's grave. Alone.

When he reached the carriage, Clarissa was seated, the fur throw across her lap. "You behaved abominably," she snapped, "and at your mother's funeral. How could you make such a fool of me? Everyone was staring at you."

His lips tightened to a thin white line. "I've just buried my mother, Clarissa. I don't really give a damn what anyone thinks. My grief is my own and not a matter for public discussion."

"What are you talking about? Are you ill?" Clarissa tossed her lovely head, her eyes looking quickly around to see if anyone was watching. Her eyes returned to Walker. "I don't know you anymore. Since you've returned, you're a different man. At first I thought it was your father's death and your mother's condition, but I see that isn't the case."

Walker escorted her home in silence. When they pulled up in front of her house, she turned to him. "I think, under the circumstances, it would be best to postpone our engagement. Acting as you have been lately, I'm not all that sure I want to marry you." Clarissa fully expected Walker to play into her hand, as he had done a thousand times before when she'd threatened him like that.

He felt tired, and he looked tired. He didn't know where to start reclaiming his life that had suddenly gotten away from him. He looked at Clarissa. He had loved her once, or at least he'd thought he did. It wasn't her fault that his life was slipping through his fingers.

"You are right, of course. I haven't been at all what I should have been over the last few days. I haven't been fair with you, Clarissa. I haven't been honest. I, too, think the engagement should be called off."

Clarissa blinked in shock, making her eyes fill with tears. "I'm sorry I was so short with you. I know you've been under a terrible strain. I was a selfish, spoiled child to behave the way I did." She looped her arm through his, her voice changing to a soft purr. "We shouldn't delay our wedding. Don't be angry

422

with me, darling. I'll make it up to you. I promise."

"There isn't anything to make up. The fault isn't yours. It's mine." He took her hands in his. "It hurts me to tell you this, but I can't deceive you any longer. I don't love you—at least not like I should. We've known each other for so long, since we were children. Everyone expected us to marry. I guess we just assumed we would. Of course I care about you. That's why I don't want to hurt you. But marrying you when I don't feel anything... I just don't love you that way. I don't know any other way to say it without it sounding so cruel. I never meant to hurt you, but my heart isn't mine to command."

A chill descended on her. Her teeth began to chatter. Fear gripped her. "You don't love me? You've met someone else? Walker, what are you saying?"

"I'm saying our engagement is off. Permanently. You are released from your commitment to me as I wish to be released."

"But why?"

"For all the reasons I've already spoken of."

"Tell me again, Walker. I'm so shocked. I'm not sure I even know what you said. Why can't we marry... if not right now, at least later?"

"Because I don't feel about you the way a man should feel about the woman he marries. Time won't change that. If anything, in time we would grow to hate each other. I don't want to be your enemy. I care for you, Clarissa. We've been friends for a long time. Our families have been friends even longer. But I can't marry you on the basis of friendship."

"Are you trying to tell me you've met someone else?"

"Yes."

Tears welled again in her lovely eyes, and Walker felt a twist of pain. It ate at him to hurt her like this. But he knew that it would be even more cruel to marry her when he felt this way about another woman. "I'm sorry, Clarissa. Sorrier than I know how to say."

"Well," she said, twisting her handkerchief, "I don't know what to say either. We've planned this for so long. Since I was twelve or thirteen, I've known I would marry you someday. It's so terribly sudden." She laughed softly. "But then, where's the point in dragging something like this out? It would only hurt more in the end." She turned to him, laying her gloved hand on his sleeve. "I, too, am sorry. I care for you, Walker. I always have. I fear I always will. But I release you. And as much as I'm able, I wish you happiness." She lifted her hand to the side of his face. "Will you kiss me once more... just for old times' sake?"

Walker kissed her, tenderly and without passion. When it was over, Clarissa knew without a doubt that she had already lost him, and that in releasing him from his pledge, she had done the right thing.

The next day Walker left the ranch early, riding into Santa Barbara. His first stop was the telegraph office.

"I want to send a telegram to Two Trees, Texas."

Charlie Fletcher pulled a large book from the shelf behind him. "I'll have to look that one up, Mr. Reed. Ain't that the place you were when you sent the telegram to your brother and he wired you back?"

"Yes, so I know it's got a telegraph office."

"All right. Just scratch out your message right here. Don't forget to say who it's going to."

"Nehemiah Butterworth," Walker said, taking the pen and hastily writing out: *Need your help. Made mistake in leaving. Stop wedding. Am returning as soon as possible. Will explain then.*

He shoved the message toward Charlie. "Here's five dollars to see it goes out right away, and another five to see the answer is delivered to the ranch as soon as it arrives. Understand?"

"Sure thing, Mr. Reed."

Two days later, Walker was just sitting down at the dinner table with Riley and Gwen when the maid excused herself to answer the front door. A moment later she returned with an envelope, which she handed to Walker.

"A young man delivered this. Said it was urgent."

"And so it is." Walker's words were sharp and clipped, but Riley saw the nervous trembling of his fingers as he took the envelope. Riley glanced at Gwen, who shook her head to silence him.

Walker tossed his napkin onto his plate and, taking the telegram, hurried to his study, where he ripped open the envelope, pulling out the small yellow paper with the answer he had been waiting for: *Engagement broken months ago. Your presence here not wanted or welcomed. Stay where you are. Charlotte no longer lives here. Nehemiah Butterworth.*

Walker uttered an oath, then wadded the paper into a tight ball and hurled it across the room. Riley tapped on the door, then walked into the room just in time to catch the thunderous expression on his brother's face.

"I take it the reply was not the one you expected?"

Walker turned to him. "Not only was it unexpected, but unclear as well."

"What did it say?"

Walker nodded in the direction of the crumpled piece of paper on the floor. "Read it for yourself. Maybe you can make more sense out of it than I did."

Riley read the telegram. "It seems to me the lady decided she didn't want either one of you, and from the tone of the words I would say her brother intends to see things stay that way."

"That makes two of us." Walker felt as flat and empty as his voice sounded. There was an odd hint of passive resignation in his tone as he said, "Tell Carmelita to remove my plate. I'm not hungry." He walked to the door and opened it, then he walked from the room, closing the door quietly behind him.

CHAPTER
TWENTY-TWO

By the end of July, Walker was forced to admit that he had made a mistake. He wasn't getting over Charlotte as he'd thought he would; instead, the memory of her ate at him like acid, becoming stronger, riding in the back of his mind until he was beginning to feel possessed by it. Time, he discovered, did not heal all wounds. It only poured more salt into them.

He felt bad about the way he had treated her. Perhaps it was fitting that she could exact a little revenge in the form of his being unable to forget her. And he needed to forget her, for the longing he still felt for her was beginning to consume him. He couldn't sleep. He couldn't eat. He had lost weight. His disposition was such that only Riley attempted to talk to him anymore.

Evidently, Charlotte had had no trouble getting over him. And it was quite obvious that she didn't want to lay eyes on him ever again. Why else would she have moved away from Two Trees? She had outguessed him on that one, because it was the only thing that prevented him from seeing her. Over and over he told himself that he was going to have to learn to live without her—sooner or later. And that didn't sit too well with him. He wanted to see her, wanted to hear her say that there could never be anything between them. Only he couldn't. He didn't know where she was.

"So find her, then," Riley finally said in exasperation, for Walker was driving him crazy. He had never seen his brother like this. He'd never expected to. Walker was always so independent. Riley would never have guessed that a woman, good-looking, copper-headed wench though she was, could drive Walker to behave as he was. Riley's brows were knitted in an angry expression as he looked at Walker and wondered what in the name of hell he could do to shake him out of this slump.

"I wouldn't know where to start looking."

"I can't believe that you, of all people, would let a thing like that stand in your way. You used to be much more trailblazing than that. What the hell happened to you? If I didn't know better, I would swear I was talking to a girl."

"Careful, brother. You don't have permanent immunity. You just might find yourself flattened yet."

"At least it would be some kind of reaction from you. The first I've seen in months." Riley saw that he wasn't getting through. He was succeeding only in making Walker angry. "Look, I'm not trying to be hard on you. Your well-being is important to me. If you love that woman, find her, for God's sake. Before you drive us all insane!"

"She doesn't want to be found."

"Bull!"

A memory nagged at Walker. Charlotte was a proud woman and he had hurt her by leaving, and his sending Jamie as a replacement obviously hadn't endeared him to her either. But, find her?

"You know Dan Oldham who works for Wells Fargo?" Riley asked.

"What about him?"

"He used to work for Pinkerton's."

"So?"

"So why not talk to him. Maybe you could hire him to find her."

"That's a long shot."

"A long shot is better than no shot. And it may be the only shot you get."

The next morning Walker rode into town and stopped at the Wells Fargo Bank.

A week later, Dan had located Charlotte.

"I feel a little guilty accepting payment for this. It was something you could've done," Dan said.

"What do you mean?" Walker replied.

"All I did was send a wire to the sheriff in Two Trees, inquiring about the whereabouts of one Charlotte Augusta Butterworth."

"And?"

"And the answer is here in this telegram." Dan pushed the yellow paper across the desk to Walker, who read it slowly: *Miss Butterworth resides in Two Trees, about two miles outside of town.*

So it had all been a lie, fabricated to keep him away. He read the telegram once more before he tossed it back onto the desk. Charlotte was where he had left her, obviously angry over his leaving and refusing to see him.

The one thing that puzzled him was Nemi's attitude. Walker could understand Nemi's hostility when he discovered what had occurred between himself and Charlotte, and even his anger when he'd left her to another man. But why would Nemi lie when Walker wired him telling him that he realized his mistake and wanted to come back to Texas? Something wasn't right. He kept adding two and two and coming up with the wrong numbers.

Walker was angry when he left the Wells Fargo Bank. He was furious by the time he reached the ranch. Riley was just coming out of the barn when he rode up.

"I can tell by that sour expression on your face that you found out something that doesn't sit too well with you. You been to see Dan?"

"Yes," Walker said hotly as he swung down out of the saddle.

"And?"

"And she's living in Two Trees, right where she's always lived."

Riley grinned. "Seems she got the best of you on that one. Damn, if I'm not liking that flame-haired filly more every day. You know, she's just what you've been needing." Seeing his brother's hot glare, Riley laughed, but after that he took a more serious tone. "What are you going to do now?"

"Not a damn thing. If Miss Butterworth wants her freedom that bad, she can have it."

Riley grinned again. A big, wide grin that obviously irritated Walker, who said, "What in the hell are you grinning at?"

"You. I can't believe my wild and fierce brother is backing down from a hundred-pound woman."

"Don't forget, she's got red hair."

"Does that make a difference?"

"You're damn right it does. I think that woman's blood is half jalapeño pepper."

"Why should that matter? I always thought you were a fighter."

"I am."

"So why aren't you fighting?"

"Charlotte wears glasses."

Riley looked at his brother, vexed at his reasoning. Lately, he just didn't understand him at all. It seemed that Walker hadn't had his traces hooked up right since he'd left Texas. He was wound up tighter than a watch. And all over a little filly who wasn't easy to break to halter. If it weren't so serious it would be funny as hell. "Charlotte wears glasses?" Riley said, and then louder, "Charlotte wears glasses?"

"She does."

"What the hell has that got to do with your fighting back?"

"I don't fight people who wear glasses."

Riley threw back his head and laughed. He was still laughing when he reached the house and went inside. Walker just stood there, holding the reins of his horse, listening to his brother's laughter. A few minutes later he heard the musical chime of Gwen's laughter joining her husband's. Suddenly the absurdity of it all struck him and Walker began to laugh. Beat him at his own game, would she? He smiled to himself and pulled the saddle from the gelding's back. She should've stuck to something she knew more about.

He never could resist a challenge.

Walker tied together the few loose ends he needed to attend to before catching the train to Texas. He wondered how she would feel about moving to California. What if she refused? He smiled. He would just have to learn to live in Texas. God forbid, but he would, if that's what it took.

As the train rattled and clattered across Arizona, New Mexico, and finally Texas, Walker found himself thinking about his meeting with Charlotte. What would her reaction be? He wasn't foolish enough to think she would hurl herself into his arms. No, more than likely she would be shy and reserved until he could assure her of his reason for returning. Even if she was reluctant or shy, Walker was firmly convinced that there would be a lot more than just Charlotte's resolve melting once he had her in his arms.

CHAPTER
❦ TWENTY-THREE ❦

Charlotte was exhausted, but she couldn't quit now. Fifteen quarts of summer squash were lined up across her kitchen table, but she still had two more pots simmering on the stove that needed to be canned before she could quit. She eyed the gleaming jars she had just washed and stacked on the cabinet—thirty-five in all. She wondered if that would be enough.

She lifted the lid on the simmering squash, forgetting to remove her spectacles. A wave of steam rose, fogging the lenses. Using the corner of her apron, she cleaned her fogged glasses and put them back on, clamping the lid on the squash immediately afterward. Another five minutes or so and it would be ready.

She welcomed the short break, heading for the back door and standing behind the screen. She gazed at the honeysuckle bush that ran along the back fence. Not a leaf stirred. No wonder the kitchen was so hot. And it was only ten o'clock. Her back ached, and without really thinking, she placed her hands at the back of her waist and kneaded the stiffness. The summer's intense heat was taking its toll on her. Her feet were swollen. Her hands, too, for that matter. Her appetite had disappeared weeks ago. Lately, she'd been unable to sleep. The strain was beginning to show on her face.

She opened the door and stood on the porch. It was so hot that even the cicadas were quiet. In the pasture, she saw a few cows crowded around the meager shade offered by a scrawny mesquite bush. In the corral, Butterbean was sleeping—standing on three legs, her broad back turned to the sun. Over by the well, Jam had just drawn a bucket of water, pouring it over his bare head before slapping his hat back on. On the far side of the barn, tumbleweeds were piled three deep, evidence of the sandstorm that had raged for three days before finally blowing itself out during the night. Charlotte studied the dried tumbleweeds, remembering how the children in town made a game out of being chased by the wiry balls as they bounced across the prairie. Children could make the most of even the bleakest situation.

Children. Charlotte turned and went back into the kitchen, the screen door slamming after her.

Grabbing the wooden spoon, she began to stir the squash, her mind jammed with recriminations. If only she hadn't succumbed to Walker's kindness. If only she had married Jamie when he first asked. If only she hadn't spent that last night with Walker. If only she could forget him. If only she had let him hang. She gripped the spoon harder, feeling the surge of anger all the way to her fingertips. "Damn you, Walker Reed," she said, glancing around the kitchen and seeing so many things that brought back memories. He had been gone almost eight months now. Why did she still feel his presence so strongly?

The memory of him was everywhere she looked. Glancing at the table, she recalled the sight of his long legs thrust outward from his chair as he watched her move about the kitchen. And the way he looked with his shirt removed, the muscles of his strong brown back moving smoothly as he leaned over the basin to wash for supper. Even his cup, hanging on a peg near the door, seemed to hold his image, for she could almost see the way his beautiful hands curled around its penetrating warmth on a cold winter morning.

She slammed down the spoon, feeling the heated silence in the house as acutely as the emptiness that filled her. Was this all there would ever be? Pain and loneliness? Emptiness and depression? Would his memory never fade and grow less poignant? In a fit of anger she tore the golden heart from its resting place around her neck and hurled it across the room. "Damn you! Damn you! Damn you! I wish I'd never laid eyes on you."

Then she crossed the room, dropping to her knees in an awkward, clumsy way, and began groping for the tiny heart. When she found it, she clutched it to her breast and cried.

Light-headed with misery and pain, she pulled herself to her feet. She felt a hardening inside her that she had never known before. She had one purpose now, and that was to reach the point where she could drive him from her heart as easily as he had pushed her from his.

The fragile hope that she had so diligently held on to all these months faded, leaving her feeling broken and barren.

So involved in her inner turmoil was she that Charlotte did not hear anyone approach until Hannah said, "I'm glad that's the last of your canning, because I'm going to need a little of your time."

Charlotte turned to see her sister-in-law

stomp angrily into the kitchen. "You look like you're hauling a few words for someone around with you."

"I've got more than just a few words to say."

"Are you angry at me or someone else?" Charlotte asked.

"Have you ever known me to ride twenty miles in a buckboard in the middle of the hottest day on record to tell you I was angry with someone else?"

"No."

"Well then, I must be angry at you—wouldn't you say?"

"I suppose I would, but I don't know why."

"In a pig's eye, you don't!"

Charlotte eyed Hannah, who was looking stronger than new rope. She hadn't seen her this worked up since she got religion. Something was amiss all right, and it had something to do with her, but Charlotte was just too tired to care. She felt lower than a gopher hole, and there wasn't much anyone could say to change that. "It seems to be a talent I've acquired lately, grossly offending those I love without being aware of what I've done."

Hannah's voice softened. "I'm sorry. I didn't mean to come at you like that. I'm just hotter than a biscuit from bouncing around in that buckboard in all this heat. Sometimes I can be so dumb... always shooting my big mouth off. God knows you've had enough to be upset about lately without my adding my two cents' worth. No, now don't you start looking too relieved. I'm still mad enough to fry a snowball." Hannah paused, looking straight at Charlotte, her hands on her hips. "Charlotte... how could you?"

Charlotte looked confused. "How could I what? Hannah, will you try to make sense? What are you talking about?"

Hannah jammed her hand into her pocket and extracted a yellow paper. "This!" she said, sticking it in Charlotte's face.

Even with her spectacles on, the paper was just too close for Charlotte to read it. Taking the paper from Hannah's tightly clenched fingers, she held it at arm's length, recognizing it immediately. It was the telegram that Walker had sent to Nemi several months ago, urging him to stop the wedding. "Oh, that," she said lamely.

"*Oh, that!*" Hannah mimicked. "What I want to know is why you are still here in this house driving yourself crazy with the memory of the best-looking man that ever walked the face of the earth when you could have the original? Charlotte, that man is *prime!*"

"He may be prime, but he's as difficult to live with as any other man. Believe me, Walker can be trying. He isn't without his faults."

"Okay. So that makes him a little less god-like and more mortal. What's the harm in that?"

"You didn't know about the telegram before now?"

Hannah looked at her in silence for a long moment, then she shook her head. "Do you honestly think I would have waited this long to fry your bacon if I did?"

Charlotte screwed the lid onto the last jar

437

and wearily dragged herself to the parlor, where she sat down. Hannah was right behind her. "I don't want to talk about Walker or the telegram," she said flatly.

"No, I wouldn't either if I had made such a fool of myself," Hannah sighed. "Charlotte, how can you expect me to believe such a pure lie? I've seen the way you've mourned his absence like a death. This is Hannah you're talking to, not that husband of mine that appears to be as foolish as you are. I swear, it must run in the family."

"He should have thrown that telegram away," Charlotte said.

"He should have had his head examined for sending the answer he sent. Stay away, indeed. The man has every right to be here and you know it."

"Nemi was only doing what I wanted."

"Was he now? Well, tell me this: Are you happy with what you've got? A shrinking hull of pride, when you could have a man who loves you warming your bed each night."

"He doesn't love me."

"You didn't give him time. He must love you....Why else would he want to come back?"

"If he really cared he would've come, regardless of what Nemi said in the telegram."

"You've been reading too many pirate stories. Walker is a reasonable man, not Attila the Hun. Surely you aren't holding it against him for not coming when Nemi told him not to? And not only that, but that you had moved and didn't want to see him."

Charlotte stared at Hannah. "How can

you say that? Hannah, he left me twice. The only thing he wanted was a night in bed. Then he had the audacity to turn me over to someone else like a discarded mistress. Never once did he mention the fact that he was betrothed. And you think I should welcome him back just because he sends a measly telegram that says stop the wedding? I can't keep putting my life on the back burner like that. I have other responsibilities. You know that." A swirling mass of confusion descended on her like a dust devil. Disbelief. Shame. Misery. Despair. But most of all, acute loneliness. It was just too much. She bent her head, and for the second time that day she cried.

"Oh, goodness! I've done it again! Let my big mouth get me into trouble. Honey, don't cry. I didn't mean to upset you at a time like this. Why don't you tell me to shut my big fat mouth? What goes on between you and Walker is none of my business."

But that only made Charlotte cry harder. "But don't you see? That's the whole problem. That's why I'm so miserable."

"What is?"

"Because there isn't *anything* going on between me and Walker, and I don't know what to do about it."

Hannah smiled, patting Charlotte's head. "Well, it's not hopeless."

"Oh, yes it is," Charlotte wailed.

"No, it's not. Now you go wash your face and take a nap. Then, tomorrow morning you can get up and take the first step necessary in getting Walker Reed back."

"But I don't know what to do."

"You know how to send a telegram, don't you?"

Up came Charlotte's head. Hannah had just performed a miracle that ranked right up there with the parting of the Red Sea as far as Charlotte was concerned. A telegram! A smile of pure, joyous relief flashed across her face. "Do you think he will come?"

"He'll come. Question is, what will you do when you see him standing at your front door?"

"I'll throw myself in his arms and never let go. I'll cover his face with so many kisses he'll have to fight for air. I'll tell him I love him until his head spins."

Hannah rose to her feet. "You just remember what you're supposed to do when he gets here. Don't let the misunderstandings between you cloud your judgment."

"I won't, I promise. When Walker comes, he'll be so surprised."

Hannah laughed. "Oh, I think he'll be surprised, all right."

CHAPTER
❧ TWENTY-FOUR ❧

Charlotte went to bed early. She just hadn't been herself since she'd sent the telegram to Walker two weeks ago and received the reply that he was away from the ranch for an extended period of time. She was certain that he'd decided to go ahead with his marriage. She berated herself for her foolishness. She shouldn't have waited so long to contact him. But that didn't matter now. It was too late. He was away for an extended period of time. Bridal trips took an extended period of time. Charlotte cried herself to sleep.

A cool front, strangely uncommon at that time of year, had lowered the temperature, and a lonesome, howling wind was rattling the shingles, driving the elm branches against the front windows. In the distance, a hungry pack of coyotes was howling. And closer, near the house, a gate was banging. There were so many noises outside that Charlotte couldn't sleep soundly. She had just drifted back to sleep when a loud noise pulled her back. Opening her eyes, she listened. There it was again. Knocking. Someone was knocking at her back door.

It must be Nemi, she decided. No one else would come out there at that time of night and knock at her back door. She wondered if Hannah or one of the kids was sick. Pulling her wrapper off the chest at the foot of her bed, Charlotte lit the bedside lamp and trudged wearily to the kitchen. The pounding came again, just before she opened the door.

"Hello, Charlotte."

Walker. His beautiful voice came out of the night before she could even see him, standing at the side of the porch, hidden in the darkness. Only the faint glow of the lamp behind her allowed her to see that there was a human form there. Walker. Standing there, bold as brass, his legs spread wide, his thumbs hooked in his belt, the same way she had seen him a hundred times before. But this time it was so different.

"What are you doing here?" she asked, her teeth chattering from the unseasonably cool wind blowing through the doorway.

"I came to see you," he said as casually as if he'd just seen her yesterday.

"Why?" she asked, holding the front of her wrapper against her.

"I have a lot of things to explain to you, Charlotte, but this isn't the place to do it. May I come in?" He stepped closer.

Walker. She could see him better now, and she allowed her eyes the luxury of traveling over his face, much as a mother would do to her newborn, checking to be sure that every cherished feature was perfect. His face was pale beneath the bronze skin, the hollows beneath his high cheekbones oddly sunken. She could not see his eyes, but the long, thick lashes she remembered well. Her fingers wanted to trace the outline of his mouth, knowing intimately the firm sensual curves, the soft texture that could become so hard when fired by the heat of passion.

"Charlotte, will you let me in?"

She looked at him curiously. She still didn't know why he had come, and she probably wouldn't until she let him in. Better judgment told her not to let him inside, not with her half-dressed as she was. And she knew that she shouldn't reveal any tender feelings until she understood his reason for coming. The last few times she had seen him he was merely passing through. Was this time any different?

"You might as well let me come in. I'm not leaving here until you do. I'll camp on your doorstep for a week if that's what it takes."

She made a move to shut the door, but Walker blocked it with his foot, pushing the door open and taking Charlotte's arm to push her in ahead of him. Just inside the door, she whirled, her temper primed. "Don't think you can come in here and push me around, Walker Reed. Whatever you have to say to me can wait until tomorrow."

But he wasn't listening. He was still standing in the doorway, the wind coming around him on both sides, chilling Charlotte and driving her wrapper flat against her body, between her legs. In her anger, she had forgotten to clutch the front of her wrapper; the soft flowing folds no longer concealed her body.

Suddenly, all the breath rushed from Walker's lungs. His stomach muscles tightened in recognition. "Holy Moses!" he said, unable to take his eyes off her rounded belly. Dumbfounded and unable to think of anything else to say at the moment, he repeated those words over and over.

Her mouth tightened to a thin white line. She crossed her arms over her stomach as if trying to hide it. "You've already said that. If you're through cursing, you can leave."

"What do you mean, leave? You're pregnant!"

"Well, thank you very much. All this time I've been thinking it was something I ate. Now that you've set the matter straight, you can get out of my house."

He closed the door, thinking he had never heard her sound so cynical, but he knew that that was to be expected. He had hurt her, more than he had known. It killed him to think of her here all these months, going through the agony of knowing she was pregnant... alone. He thought about what he had denied himself. The joy of sharing that discovery with her. The pleasure of being with her, to see the day-to-day changes in her body. And when he thought how stubborn he'd been... how close he'd come to letting things go between them... Dear God! It scared the hell out of him. He looked at Charlotte. He had never loved her more. She could be angry all she wanted. He owed her that much. But he would make it up to her, if it took the rest of his life to do it. She would marry him. And he would break his back to see that she never regretted it. He moved closer, stepping in front of her, blocking her way. His hands came out to grip her shoulders. The narrow gleam of light in his eyes was hard and determined. "Don't be such a stubborn little fool. That's my baby you're carrying."

"Is it?"

That caught him off guard. He had meant to surprise her with his return, but as it turned out, he was the one surprised. He'd been traveling without sleep for days. He was exhausted. But not too exhausted to see what lay behind the anger in her beautiful blue eyes. She was hurt. She would probably make his life hell for the next few days. But when it was done, Charlotte would be his. Her eyes told him that.

With intensified effort, Walker stared into her questioning blue eyes—the blue eyes that had haunted his dreams and made his life miserable for so many months.

His look was unguarded, making it easy for her to see his regret, his pain.

He didn't even hear what she was saying, so happy was he to see her. He let his eyes roam over her beautiful face; then, when he had assured himself that every beloved feature was just as he remembered it, he let his eyes drop lower, from her face to her throat, to the full breasts that had known the touch of his hand, and lower still, to her belly, where his baby lay. The effect of it nearly brought him to his knees.

He groaned, closing his eyes for a moment, then he opened them and gave her a tiny shake. "You know damn well it's my child. Admit it," he said. "Admit that's my baby."

"All right. It's your baby," she said wearily. "I'd admit it was Jam's baby to get rid of you." And with every word she uttered, Charlotte was cursing her flapping tongue. Why couldn't she shut up? Nemi always told her, *"If you want to be seen, stand up. If you want to be heard, speak up. If you want to be appreciated, shut up." Shut up, Charlotte,* she told herself. But it wasn't any use. Something in her refused to give. What pressed her to be so belligerent was beyond her. She probably never would learn. But she had committed herself. It was too late to back down now. But it hurt. Loving Walker was like having an itch in her heart that she couldn't scratch. With a lofty thrust to her chin, she clamped her hands on her hips, giving him a full view of her roundness, as if hoping he would be repulsed by what he saw.

But Walker was anything but repulsed. He simply stood there, looking at her, trying to overcome the shock he'd just received and the joy that washed across him because of it. His senses began to return and he looked at her—really looked at her, standing before him in radiant, pregnant defiance. No, he had never loved her more, nor had he ever feared her more. He had to weigh everything he said. He ran the risk of losing not only Charlotte but his child as well. She had him over a double barrel.

"Why didn't you tell me, Charlotte?" His voice was unbelievably soft, his eyes pleading.

"Why should I? So you could come running back and take my child away?"

"I wouldn't take the child and leave you. You know that."

"Do I? I seem to remember that you left me before. Twice, to be exact. How was I supposed to know this time would be different?"

"I would've married you. I told you that."

"That's not a very flattering reason. Like a prized cow, my value increases along with ability to produce offspring."

"I'm talking about the night of the dance, when you announced your engagement to Jamie. Don't you remember, Charlotte? Why do you think I bought you that dress? And showed you the way a man in love with you would like your hair. Did you think I was talking about Jamie?" He saw by the horrified expression on her face that that was exactly what she'd thought. "Dear God, Charlotte! What kind of man do you think I am? Do you honestly believe I'd sink that low? To spend time with you like that and then send you packing into another man's arms? I was doing those things for me. Can't you see that?"

She was beginning to. She remembered what she had said to Walker when he asked her to trust him:

"I trusted you before."

"Then trust me now."

With despair she remembered saying, *"You haven't slipped a ring through my nose... or put one on my finger."*

"No, but I would have."

And then later, at the dance: *"I have no intention of relinquishing anything. My sole purpose is to secure and retain what I hold dear."* But the most painful part of all was the memory of his face when he walked back into the schoolhouse. Scalding pain began in her heart and spiraled upward to her awareness. "But why didn't you just tell me?"

"Because I know how your proper little mind works, Charlotte. You wouldn't in a

447

million years have considered marrying me until I was released from my pledge to another. And you know it."

Walker saw that his words were having some effect on her. He didn't want to overdo it, though. What he wanted to do right now was something he'd wanted to do for a long time. But it was too soon for that. Right now Charlotte needed his love and understanding. She was a woman who had been ignored by her man long enough. She needed a whole lot of attention.

"It hurts me to think you've had to go through this all alone—that I wasn't here with you." A look of heartsick disbelief crossed his face. "I could have missed the birth of my child," he said, more to himself than to her. "I would've never forgiven myself."

"You still might miss it. Nothing has been settled. This is my house and legally this is my baby. You have no right to be here."

"I was stupid enough to leave you before. I'm not going to be that stupid again. Ever. I want you, Charlotte. I want our baby."

"Well, that's too bad."

"Whatever you say," he growled. "But I'm not leaving." He pulled her against him, gently but firmly. He was thrilled by the shock of her hard belly against him. Hungry and demanding, his mouth covered hers, stopping the flow of angry words. When he had kissed her into sweet confusion, he pulled his mouth from hers, his words coming urgent and hot into her ear.

"Love, I'm sorrier than I can tell you for

what's happened between us, but don't throw our future away. Give me a chance. Let me make it up to you. Marry me." He pulled back to gaze at her stomach, then grinned. "Judging from the look of things, it better be quick."

She shoved away from him with the strength of ten women. "We don't have to do anything, quick or otherwise. I have no intention of marrying you."

Walker was so angry that he wanted to strangle her with her own pink satin ribbon. She was the most beautifully stubborn woman he had ever seen. Stubborn and unreasonable. But then he reminded himself that she was pregnant. And it was his fault. Guilt consumed him.

"Darling, I know you're angry, and you have every right to be, but that doesn't change the fact that we have a child that is dangerously close to being born a bastard. Is that what you want?"

"I'd rather have a child that is a bastard than be married to one."

She saw how her words hurt him, but she wasn't about to go soft. She continued to watch him watching her, wondering why they were both standing there staring at each other when what they both wanted was to be in each other's arms. She didn't move into his arms, of course, but she did continue to stare—at every inch of him, every beloved inch of hard, flowing muscle that somehow had knitted itself arousingly into a shapely romp of angles and curves and sensuously slender masculinity. His blue shirt hugged his wide, tightly held shoulders. Everything below looked so utterly relaxed that she wanted to scream. She let her eyes wander across the snug, faded jeans and scuffed cowboy boots. Magnificent though his body was, it was his face that demanded her attention. How had she ever thought him handsome? He was so much more than that. Beautiful, really. Beautiful in a purely male way, like the archangel Gabriel or the statue of David. Her breath caught when her eyes rested on his erotic mouth, evoking memories of how many times that mouth had fanned the hot coals of desire into flaming passion. But it was his eyes, so brilliantly blue and filled with such yearning, that caused a flush of embarrassment. Behind that face of an angel lurked devilish thoughts. She pulled her gaze away.

The man had endeared himself to her, impregnated her, and left her. He had caused her untold suffering and misery. He was the father of her unborn child, and she loved him above life itself.

Charlotte stood mutely before him, listening to the sound of her fluttering heart laced with the confused thoughts floating through her mind. She did not notice the slight uplift of Walker's mouth or the almost liquid softness in his eyes as, gently, he pressed his lips to hers, showing her all the gently searching eroticism she had so desperately missed. When she tried to speak, he put his fingers over her lips and, finding the moisture there, drew it across her lips with aching slowness before he kissed her again. Mindless with the nearness of him, she did not feel his slender fingers as they toyed with the wisps of hair at the side of her face, until they began to outline the spirals of her sensitive earlobes. While her mind was absorbing the pleasure of that, he began to rotate her head gently from side to side, dragging his lips across hers until she wanted to crawl inside him.

Everywhere he touched her left her burning with fever. Her skin was hot beneath his knowing fingertips. Stroke after stroke brought her to the brink of shuddering pleasure, so acute that a small whimper was not identified as her own. She was falling under his spell again, calling to mind the powerful feelings he stirred in her. His arms went around her, his palms opening flat against her back, his mouth seeking and finding hers once more. His hands slipped lower, cupping her buttocks, then coming around to touch her growing belly.

Embarrassment flamed and she pushed away from him. "No," he whispered hoarsely. "Let me touch you. Let me feel my child. Please."

Even if she had wanted to deny him, she couldn't have found the strength. The side of her face lay pressed against the heat of his neck as his hands touched her with gentleness she would have thought a man incapable of. She felt the pounding of his chest as his head dropped before her, his knees bending as he came to rest his cheek against her belly. Her hands, as if of their own volition, threaded through the silky strands of his hair at the same moment as tears began to trail silently down her cheeks.

"Charlotte, I love you."

Damp spots appeared on the bodice of her nightdress, as one tear after another splashed there. *I love you, too,* she heard her mind say, *but I can't seem to make myself do anything about it.* Perhaps he was right—they needed to talk.

"No, love, don't say anything," he said, rising to his feet, his hand coming up to brush away her tears. "I was wrong trying to rush you. You need time." He grinned. "Just don't take too long." He couldn't stop thinking about the way he had left her, and he wondered if he would live long enough to lay to rest the memory of that most stupid of blunders. His words, when he spoke, were as gentle as hers had been harsh. "I can only promise to love you so completely that in time you will find it in your heart to forget, if not forgive."

"Words!" she snapped. "And lies. You're good at that."

"Sweetheart, I'd sooner cut out my tongue than ever lie to you. If I ever do, you've my permission to cut it out for me."

Before she could utter the nasty remark that hovered on her lips, his eyes began to glow, and the corners of his mouth lifted to suggest a smile. "Darling, don't you recognize an apology when you hear one?"

She wondered if he had any idea just what those eyes and that smile were doing to her. Evidently he did not, because she was sure that if he did, he would take her, standing up, swollen stomach and all.

"Apologies are cheap." It was a rather hollow, immature remark, but before she allowed herself to feel shame, she convinced herself that it was what he deserved. Afraid that he would see just what effect his words were having on her, she said the first thing that came to mind: "Just what do you hope to gain by all this... this flowery eloquence?"

"What do I hope to gain, sweet Charlotte? Nothing more than eternity with you. I want to hold your hand and tell you how much I love you when you're suffering to see our children born—not just this child, but all the ones that follow. I want to comfort you when you cry, as you surely will, when the last one leaves home. I want to go to work each morning seeing the look of contentment in your eyes, remembering the soft pleasure sounds you made when I put it there. I want to sit with you in the evenings, pretending to read while I watch you bent over your sewing."

He studied her face, wanting to sink his fingers into her rosy curls, remembering the times when he had. His voice was a barely audible murmur as he said, "Kiss me." And more softly still: "Please."

Suddenly she was in his arms, his kiss dissolving her will. She couldn't remember if she had gone to him or if it was the other way around. All she knew was that Walker kissed her until she thought she would surely die from it, and then, when the world began to spin like a leaf in a downspout, he stopped. His breathing was shallow and irregular as his forehead came to rest softly against hers.

"You don't play fair," she whispered.

"Oh, love, if you only knew the restraint I'm exercising right now, you would not accuse me so unjustly."

She pulled away. "Restraint? You?"

His vibrant eyes came to rest on her mouth, then dropped lower, past the fairness of her throat to her full breasts. His face looked tired and strained, his eyes pleading with an almost naked urgency. "For over a week I've pushed myself to get here, thinking I would surely lose my sanity if I didn't hold you and make love to you soon."

"Really? Just how long has it been?"

"What?"

"Since you've made love to a woman."

"You know the answer to that as well as I."

"And how would I know that? The last time I saw you, you were heading back to the arms of your betrothed."

"I broke my engagement," he said with a husky voice that sent a shiver through her.

"And?"

He had the audacity to smile. "And I didn't sleep with her. Not once. There has been no one since you. There never will be."

"Who broke the engagement?"

"It was my decision." He paused as if thinking about something. "No, actually there was nothing to decide. Not since the afternoon before the dance." The naked anguish in his eyes reminded Charlotte of how much she loved him.

She shook her head. "Don't try to confuse me." His eyes held her captive, making it difficult for her to sort fact from fiction. He was so good at this—giving her looks that wilted her resolve flatter than yesterday's lettuce.

One fact glared more brightly than all the others: Walker was here—no longer engaged.

As she stood there mulling over that fact, Walker tipped her head back and softly kissed the rosy bud that was her mouth. Then he smiled.

"Sleep on that. I'll see you tomorrow."

She stood there, her feathers ruffled because he could dismiss her so casually, grinning like a baboon as he did. With a scowl, she crossed her arms over her rounded belly and watched him walk away.

Not once did he look back. He didn't look as if he was suffering as much as he claimed to be. He had asked her to marry him and she had refused. He couldn't care too much—giving up as easily as he had. Just when she was close to accepting his offer, he didn't offer again.

But he was back the next morning, before breakfast, and Charlotte, after spending a restless night, knowing that Walker was nearby, decided she had held off long enough. Stubbornness to this degree would never get her what she wanted, which was Walker. So when he knocked on the door, she surprised him by acting pleased to see him.

"Have you had breakfast?"

"I was hoping you'd offer to fix it for me."

"I'm offering."

Walker sat at the table while Charlotte cooked his breakfast, as she had done so many times before, and it was like it was before Walker had left, and both of them, conscious of this fragile peace between them, were afraid to mention the thing that most needed mentioning: marriage.

The fragile peace was interrupted by the sound of a horse coming rapidly into the yard. A few minutes later, Nemi burst through the back door, looking like a swarm of hornets was after him.

"Nemi, what are you doing over here this time of morning, looking like a piece of chewed twine?"

Nemi ignored Charlotte. "You want to step outside a minute, Reed? We've got something that's needed clearing up for some time now."

Walker nodded and stood, following Nemi outside. When Charlotte started to follow them, Nemi said, "This is between Walker and me. It doesn't concern you, Charlotte. You'd best stay inside."

She paused for a moment. But as soon as the back door slammed, she decided that anything that concerned Walker *did* concern her. By the time she opened the door, Walker and Nemi were no longer in sight. After searching around the yard, she headed to the barn. Then she heard it. *Oh, dear Lord! They're fighting.* Now she'd never get Walker to propose again. She broke into a run. They were really going at it by the time she reached them, and all her screaming and pleading was in vain. They just went on slugging and punching each other until they were both a bloody mess.

Seeing that they were going to fight until one of them won, and knowing that they were too well matched for that, she was afraid it would go on until they killed each other. Whirling, Charlotte ran back to the house.

A few minutes later, the sound of a shot rang through the air. When the second shot sounded, Walker and Nemi stopped, Nemi collapsed in a breathless heap against the woodpile, Walker, in similar ruin, leaning against the fence. Charlotte stood before them, her Winchester in her hands. "I don't think I've ever seen a better matched pair of fools in my life," she said, her voice trembling, tears pouring down her face. "What were you trying to do? Kill each other?"

Walker was moved by her tears, her obvious distress, and that worried him. "Charlotte, don't cry."

She looked at Walker. "You pigheaded lout—don't cry, indeed!... What do you expect me to do when I come outside to find you killing my brother? You know how much Nemi means to me. How could you do this?"

Nemi, swelling with confidence, looked at Walker. "You better get your horse and get out of here."

"And you, Nehemiah Butterworth, taking it upon yourself to beat the father of my child into a pulp!"

"I came as soon as I heard, Charlotte. I mean to protect you from him this time. Better than I did last time."

"Oh, you do, do you? And what if I don't want to be protected? Did it ever occur to you that I might *want* Walker here?"

Nemi looked confused. "Why would you want that?"

"Because I love him, you ninny!"

At that moment, Hannah came running around the barn, a double-barreled shotgun in her hands.

"You're too late to stop the fight, Hannah, but you can take this fool brother of mine home and soak his head in a bucket. And see if you can talk some sense into him while you're at it."

"Charlotte," Nemi said, but Hannah whacked him with his hat, which she had just picked up. "Shut up, Nehemiah. You've made a big enough mess of things as it is. Always sticking your nose in when it isn't needed and minding your own business when you shouldn't be."

Nemi looked at her with a puzzled expression, as if he didn't know what to think. "Hannah, why'd you hit me on the head?"

"Because it was the only place you aren't bleeding and this is your good hat. Now get yourself over to your horse, you fool. We're going home."

Nemi tried to stand. He made it on the third try, and Hannah stomped off ahead of him. "Aren't you going to help me walk?" he called after her.

"I wouldn't give you all the hay you could eat," Hannah said over her shoulder.

Nemi limped after her, saying weakly,

"Hannah, I don't think I'm up to a horseback ride just yet."

"You should've thought about that before you started fighting like an old bull moose."

"But, Hannah..."

She stopped and turned to look at him. "You never did have a lick of sense when it came to women."

"Hell, woman! What man does?"

Charlotte turned to Walker, who was still leaning against the fence, looking as though he'd been run over by a milk wagon. "Come on into the house and I'll see about getting you cleaned up."

Two days later, Walker was still stiff and sore but able to make his way, slowly, from his bed. He had never hurt in so many places in his life. There wasn't a place on his body that didn't hurt, except the soles of his feet. Even breathing hurt, thanks to three cracked ribs. The only thing that made it bearable was hearing Doc describe Nemi's condition, which included a few busted ribs as well.

Walker had had plenty of time to think over the last couple of days. Charlotte had admitted to Nemi that she loved him, and he was still dazed from that confession. And she did love him. He was convinced after the way she had taken care of him.

Just then, Charlotte came into the room, and Walker groaned as if he were in great pain, enjoying Charlotte's pampering. But she was onto him, and he saw that she was trying hard to keep a straight face.

But she just couldn't do it. She began to

smile, then as she reached the side of his bed, she began to laugh. Sitting next to him on the bed, she leaned over to give him a quick kiss and put her arms around his neck. "Jam just brought me a note from Nemi."

Walker groaned. "I hope he's not coming for a visit anytime soon."

"I don't think he'll be up to that for a while." She held the letter against her cheek, a naughty twinkle in her eye. "He did say he hoped you learned your lesson."

Walker wrapped his arms around her, pulling her across him, trying to kiss her with his bruised mouth until she began to laugh, and he said, "What a cursed fate, to have you in my arms after all these months and to not be able to kiss you. For what he's denying me, I hope Nemi is in a great deal of pain."

He had to give up on the kissing, so he rolled Charlotte to his side, resting his head against her breasts. "What else did Nemi say?"

"He said you had until he was on his feet to make an honest woman of me or he'd show you the end of his fist."

Walker groaned, then kissed her cheek lightly. "I would have thought that brother of yours would have learned *his* lesson. I'm going to marry you, Charlotte, because I love you more than I ever thought possible. Not because of any prodding by your brother." His hand came up to caress the side of her face. "Will you marry me, Charlotte?" He grinned. "Soon?"

"Yes, you crazy man, and it can't be too soon for me." Her hand covered his, pressing it more firmly against her cheek. "Did I tell you that I'm glad to know you aren't afraid of my overprotective brother?"

"Never that. Nememiah should've known he couldn't win."

"Why?"

"He overlooked one important fact about me when he picked a fight. There was no way he could ever have whipped me."

"How do you know that?"

"Because without you, Charlotte, I was a man who had nothing to lose... nothing."

She was silent for a moment, then softly, gently, she kissed him. "I love you, Walker Reed." She kissed him again, whispering, "And now, my love, you have everything to live for."

"I know."

She smiled, snuggling closer to him, her hand absently trailing in the hair on his chest. Walker laid his hand gently on the softly rounded mound of her stomach. "I bet the day I shot the hat off Spooner Kennedy's head, you never thought you'd be lying in bed with me like this," she said.

Walker laughed. "I beg to disagree with you, sweetheart, but that's probably the first thing that crossed my mind."

"And what was the second?"

"How I was going to accomplish it."

She laughed. "Well, I'm glad you were able to, in spite of all the stumbling blocks I put in your way."

Walker grinned. "That's one of the things I've always prided myself on."

"What?"

"How I've always been able to rise to the occasion."

Was there ever a naughtier twinkle in a pair of laughing blue eyes?

Walker didn't think so.

Behind the neat clapboard house, a sparse little garden, with everything neat and orderly, was set to brave the day's intense heat, while inside, Charlotte forgot all about the vinegar pie baking in the oven of her Monitor stove. The sun, reaching over the horizon to peek through the only lace curtains in the county, shimmered on a mass of tangled rosy curls spread across the wide chest of a man. And in front of the house, an old black man was coming down the road, riding on his old mule, Rebekah, and over by the henhouse, the rooster saw the promise of a new day climbing in the eastern sky, and flapped his wings and gave a mighty crow.

❦ EPILOGUE ❦

Walker was standing in the kitchen stirring a pot of oatmeal, his two-day-old son cradled against his chest. At the kitchen table, six-year-old Samantha was teaching four-year-old Philip and two-year-old Margaret the words to "Silent Night."

"Round John Virgin, Mother, and child…"

"Samantha," Walker said, "it's *'round yon Virgin.* I've told you that three times already."

"But *that* doesn't make any sense. What's a *round yon virgin?*"

"I'll explain it to you later," he said. "Why are you singing Christmas songs anyway? It's almost the Fourth of July. Why don't you sing 'Yankee Doodle'?" The baby began to cry. "Now we've made little Jonathan cry. If we don't be quiet, we're going to wake your mother."

"She's already awake," Samantha said.

"How do you know that?" Walker asked, turning to give his eldest a stern look.

"Because *I* woke her."

Walker let out a sigh of exasperation, thrusting out his hip to better balance the baby. "Sam, I thought I explained how your mother needs rest after having a baby."

"You said she needed *food and rest,* Papa."

"Yes, I did. But that doesn't explain why you woke her."

"Well, I had to wake her to see if she was ready for some food."

Walker stared at Samantha. She had done it again, turned everything around until he

463

had to stop and think, in order to figure out just where he'd lost out. He couldn't help smiling at the mutinous blue eyes that stared back at him. "Well, what did your mother say?"

"She said she didn't want any oatmeal."

"Oatmeal!" shouted Philip, climbing down from his chair and bounding toward the back door. "I *hate* oatmeal." He opened the door and jumped down the back steps, the door slamming behind him.

Walker gave Samantha a reproving look. "Now see what you've done? Now you'll have to find Philip and talk him into coming back."

Walker watched Samantha run after her brother. As soon as she was out of the door, Margaret, sitting in the high chair, began to cry. Hearing that, Jonathan, who had just quieted, began to cry again. Walker was wondering how Charlotte managed all this, when Samantha and Philip came back into the kitchen. As Philip took his seat, Walker said, "Sam, you put these bowls on the table after I fill them. And give Margaret hers first. Maybe she'll stop crying."

"Are you giving baby Jon some too? He's crying," Philip said.

"No, Jon's too little. If Margaret stops, Jon probably will," Walker replied, thinking that calm would envelop the kitchen as soon as the children were eating. But when Samantha put the bowl of oatmeal before Philip, he shoved it away. "I told you, I *hate* oatmeal!"

"Well, you have to eat it anyway," Samantha said.

"But you said I could have ham and eggs," Philip wailed.

"Sam, did you tell Philip that?"

"Yes."

"But why?"

"Because he wouldn't come back in if I said he had to eat *oatmeal*!"

"I *hate* oatmeal!" Philip wailed again, shoving the bowl farther away.

"Oh, hush up, Philip!" Samantha said, shoving the oatmeal back, only to have it shoved back at her. "Okay, crybaby," she said, and with that Samantha dumped the oatmeal into Philip's lap. Philip began to wail in earnest now. Walker stared dumbstruck at his daughter.

"What do you think you're doing?" he demanded, crossing the room with a furious gait.

Samantha stood, looking petrified, but not too petrified to answer, "I was making him change his tune."

"Just why in the name of heaven would you think dumping a bowl of oatmeal all over someone would make him do that?"

"Because Mama said it would," Samantha said with a quaver.

"Has your mother thrown oatmeal at you?" Walker stared at the little fire-haired imp standing before him, wondering how any human being could be so exasperating. "Well, has she?"

"No, but she told Aunt Hannah that she threw some at you and it made you change your tune. She said some more things, too, but I forgot."

"Oh," said Walker.

Samantha began to cry. "I'm sorry I made you mad, Papa."

Walker coughed, shifting Jonathan to his other hip so that he could hug his daughter. Pulling her against his side, he patted her shoulder. "Well, don't cry, my little fire ant." But Samantha only cried harder. "Sammie, my girl, a little oatmeal never hurt anyone."

"It hurt me! I *hate* oatmeal!" sobbed Philip, taking angry swipes at the gooey mess.

A bubbling laugh came from behind them, and one by one, the four crying children began to quiet, three of them, along with their father, turning their eyes to Charlotte, standing in the doorway.

The first ray of sunshine slanted through the window and fell graciously onto the amber curls of his wife, and Walker, hearing her laughter fade and watching her look turn pensive, said softly, "I've really bungled taking care of things, haven't I? Is that what you're thinking, my love?"

Looking at Walker with tears brimming in her eyes, she said, "No, I was thinking how beautiful you all are."

Years later, long after her grandchildren were grown and married, the subtle fragrance of oatmeal lingering in the air would recall to Charlotte a sunny summer morning when her children were no more than babies, and Walker, bathed in the rosy hues of sunrise, had looked at her with such love and commitment that she had known then she would never again whisper, "If my love could hold you"— for indeed, it would for all time.